The
*L*EGACY

JILL ROWAN

snowbooks

Proudly Published by Snowbooks in 2011

Copyright © 2011 Jill Rowan
Jill Rowan asserts the moral right to
be identified as the author of this work.
All rights reserved.

Snowbooks Ltd.
email: info@snowbooks.com
www.snowbooks.com

British Library Cataloguing in Publication Data
A catalogue record for this book is available from the British
Library.

ISBN 978-1-907777-55-4

For my dad, Walter, who is not here to see this book published,
but who lived long enough to complain about his name being used!

&

For James Woodforde (1740-1803), whose serendipitous diary
had languished unread on my bookshelves for over thirty years
before I had the idea for this book, but who now feels like
someone I once knew.

CHAPTER ONE

Yeah, yeah, yeah. Listen to them.

'...so last night I didn't eat anything because I'd had such a big salad at lunchtime, but Bob still insisted on pigging out on pizza. Disgusting. I was glad to get out of the house for a run.'

'I know what you mean. I just had a couple of carrots – detoxing, you know – and got in a good half-hour on the cross-trainer before my usual twenty lengths in the pool.'

I'm in this café on the outskirts of London, listening – or trying not to listen – to two women at the next table talking about food, weight and diets. I hunch up and stir idly at my tea, trying to ignore them, but their voices oscillate in my direction.

'You know Debbie in Sales? She's lost five stone since she went to Weight Watchers.'

'Yeah? Well I can't believe how much weight Linda Simmons has lost since she went on that cabbage-a-day diet.'

'You don't have the details on that, do you? I'd like to try it.'

Yeah, these women are slim. Skinny as sticks, in fact. Whereas, of course, *I* am fat, or as they like to say these days, obese. I prefer the word *corpulent*; it oozes off the tongue like a great big dollop of cream. Not that I *like* being corpulent, although I refuse to entertain the flab-guilt we're being forced into these days. You wouldn't catch me prostrating myself at the feet of some self-righteous TV super-skinny, listening agog as she tells me how disgusting my poo smells. Mind you, size twenty isn't dramatic enough to get you on telly, but it's quite sufficient to encourage people to look down their noses at you.

I nibble at my slice of toast and try to think happy thoughts, because today I have loftier concerns. At long last I'm walking out of my humdrum existence and into a new life. Or at least that's what I hope I'm walking into, although there is a smidgeon of doubt in my mind.

The car's outside, packed up with all the stuff I can be bothered to take, which isn't much. Forty-two years of life packed into one little Metro. My friends think I'm an idiot to give everything up on the promise of a house I've never even seen. They've accused me of running away, as if there's something wrong with wanting to get away from city life, a job I've tired of, a cramped and noisy flat, and from people constantly carping on about my weight. Apart from anything else, life in an isolated, run down shack shouldn't hold too many carpers.

Not that I'm certain it's a shack.

I trawl into my bag, and for what seems like the thousandth time, I pull out the picture sent by Jones, Jones and Wynne-Jones, solicitors. It's so dark and fuzzy that the house is barely visible. It's a kind of grey blob among a swathe of trees. Oddly, the trees are in perfect focus.

The women are still at it.

'...I don't see how anyone can get by without a workout every day.'

'I know. It's terrible the way some people don't take care of themselves.'

The last remark was made with just the tiniest of glances in my direction.

I pretend I haven't heard, but a little imp inside me is hatching a naughty idea. It can be my parting shot at London.

I drain the last dregs of my tea, straighten my back, lift my head and walk towards the stick-skinnies. They look up with some consternation as I reach their table. I bend down towards them, put an expression of great concern on my face and shake my head sadly.

'You poor things,' I say, my voice oozing fake sincerity. 'It must be a nightmare having no flesh on your bones, and *so* uncomfortable when the toilet seats dig into those bony bottoms. Have you ever tried Complan?'

Their twin expressions of surprised amazement follow me as I turn sharply and exit the café. I jump into my clapped-out Metro, giggling like a schoolgirl. So it was childish, but it was fun. I start up the car with a huge sense of relief at escaping London for good. After five years here, it's never felt like home. Not that anywhere has, really – not since I was a kid. Maybe that's the real reason I'm taking such a risk on the grey blob.

I'm just approaching Watford when my mobile rings. It's my sister, Ellide.

'Hey Fally, where are you? Shouldn't you be here by now?' Her high-pitched voice screeches down the line at me. Elli always screeches, especially when she's on the phone.

Fally is short for Fallady. My dad gave us all weird names. I think he was too much into *Lord of the Rings* or something – we all sound like we'd be better off living in Middle-earth.

'I'm nearly there,' I tell Elli.

'Okay, I'll get the kettle on. Can't wait to see you.'

That's the odd thing about our family. The four of us are scattered all over the country now, probably because none of us ever felt we had a base other than Summerdale, the children's home where we grew up, but we're still very close. I'm the only one who never married. My brother Jex lives in Carlisle with his wife and three children, but my sister Desmoran got divorced last year and is living with her new man in Harrogate.

The old Metro chunters into the drive of Elli's superlatively suburban, three-bedroom house. The lace curtain moves, and then she dashes out of the door and gives me a hug, even though I'm rather allergic to hugs. I return her hug stiffly, and she draws back, biting her lip, looking me over.

'Not regretting it yet? Still sure it's the right thing to do?' she asks anxiously, peering at me through her trendy, square glasses, her hair dyed glossy black and straightened into neat obedience around her heart-shaped face. Elli looks pretty good for her age. Her two children have recently left home, so she's suffering from empty-nest syndrome. She makes up for it by mothering the rest of us, especially me – maybe because I've stayed single, which seems so unnatural to my family-orientated sister.

She urges me into the kitchen for the promised cup of coffee, and there's Simon, her balding and unassuming husband, sitting at the table reading the paper. He doesn't get up to hug me. He never forgets I don't like it.

I've always got on well with Simon, and we chat companionably for a while about the cottage and sip at our coffee. I show them the picture. Simon glances up at me in surprise. 'I know you said the photo wasn't clear, but I didn't realize you could barely see the cottage. For all you know that could be an empty space – no house there at all.'

'Don't be daft; there must be a cottage if the solicitors say there is,' Elli says. 'They couldn't lie about a thing like that – could they Fally?'

I shrug. 'They've made a point of telling me there's a proper house there, several times. And Miss Gilbertine was living in it until a few months ago.'

'I'm glad she didn't die there. That would be too spooky, don't you think?' Elli says.

'It looks spooky to me anyway,' Simon adds. 'All those wild-looking trees around. Seems to be a long way from anywhere.'

He's giving me an intent look, as though he knows why I'm going, so I just say, 'Ideal for me then.'

He nods slowly, his eyes back on the picture, but says no more.

'I still can't get over her leaving it to you,' Elli says. 'She must have been very fond of you.' She bites her lip. 'You were so young when we were sent to Summerdale.'

I was five when our parents died in a car crash, and Elli twelve. The home closed down when I was fifteen; Dessy was two years younger. After ten years in Miss Gilbertine's care, we were thrust into the fostering system, separated from everything and everyone we knew. It was a nightmare time for Dessy and me.

Miss Gilbertine had retired to the Welsh borders, but I clung on to my only real mother figure and wrote to her every week. She always wrote back. The home had been her life; she'd put everything into it. Looking back, I realize she was probably glad to hear from any of her former charges.

It was her encouragement that kept me going through the turbulent years between Summerdale and Oxford, when at times it looked as though I'd go completely off the rails. I certainly wouldn't have tried to get into Oxford if it hadn't been for her. Our letters became less frequent in the final few years, but we were still in touch every two or three months. I should have gone to see her as I'd always meant to.

'What are you going to do with yourself once you get there?' Simon asks, frowning down at the photo again. 'Have you really thought this through?'

I shake my head and grin. 'No idea, and don't really care. I'm just going to take things as they come. With my savings and the five thousand Miss Gilbertine left me, I won't have to worry about money for a while.'

Simon frowns, and Elli looks anxious. 'I don't know, Fally,' she says. 'It's all a bit reckless.'

I look from one to the other with a small smile on my lips. As far as I'm concerned, it's time to be reckless. All I've done for years is mess around with computers. Okay, so I loved it when I started as a systems administrator, but now it's become a daily grind.

The sun's creeping around the edges of pallid clouds by the time I wave goodbye to Elli and Simon. As I drive off, they recede in the rear view mirror, standing on their suburban drive, quite happy in a life that seems utterly dull: Elli the traditional housewife and mother, Simon the conventional breadwinner with a managerial job. Things like that mystify me. When I try to understand them, they slip away like quicksilver.

It's almost five when I arrive in Tref-ddirgel. It's a small, pretty riverside town amid farmland and wooded hills, but there's not much time to admire it as I dive into the solicitors to pick up the keys. The receptionist gives me a good look up and down before showing me into an office that smells of dusty old books. The two dusty old solicitors within also take their time checking me over.

'Miss… ah… Galbraith. Yes. I have the keys here for you,' says the younger of the two, who looks about seventy. He opens a wooden box and lifts out a bunch of gigantic, ancient keys, which he hands to me solemnly, his eyes never leaving my face. 'I hope that Felin Gyfriniaeth is everything you expect it to be.'

'Me too,' I murmur. 'I mean, like I've said on the phone, your photo doesn't really show much. More like a blur. I'm just assuming there's a house there.'

The two solicitors exchange significant glances. 'Yes, yes, there's a house there all right,' says the older one. 'A perfectly fine house.'

'And everything's in order – I mean, there's nothing I need to worry about, like a leaky roof or holes in the floorboards?'

'Certainly not,' says the older Jones. 'It's been very well maintained.'

'And the phone and electricity *are* on, aren't they?'

There's a tiny pause before the younger Jones says, 'As we advised you in our correspondence and on the telephone, Miss Galbraith, we've ensured that everything is ready for your arrival.'

'Can you explain about the two-year clause?' I ask, although I've already asked them on the phone, or tried to. This peculiar clause says that I must live in the house for two years before it becomes properly, legally mine.

'I'm afraid Miss Gilbertine's reasons weren't given,' says younger Jones.

'But –'

'Mustn't dally, Miss Galbraith,' booms the older Jones, interrupting my half-formed question. 'You'll be needing to move your things into the house while it's still light. Now here's a map showing the route. You shouldn't have too much trouble finding it.' He attempts to chivvy me out of the office, fluttering the map at me.

'It's a couple of miles outside Tref-ddirgel isn't it?' I persist.

'That's right, yes. Five miles. It's actually in England, just over the border in Shropshire. Nice and cosy in its own little valley. Used to be part of Wales of course, back before Henry VIII. Off you go now. We'll be here if you need us for anything.'

They almost push me out of the door, and I stumble back on to the small main street. The keys in my hand feel oddly warm. As I put them into my jacket pocket – they only just fit – I spot a couple of women standing nearby staring at me openly, heads nodding in agreement.

There's a small supermarket just a door away. I ignore the women and enter but find myself under further scrutiny from the girl at the till and the only other customer, a man in his sixties. He at least has the decency to look away when I stare back, but the checkout girl carries on shamelessly, right up until I take my small pile of goods to her.

'Candles,' she says abruptly.

I jump. 'What?'

'You're going to need candles. Miss Gilbertine might have left some, but you need to be on the safe side.'

'You know who I am? I mean, what do you mean about candles? The solicitors said Felin Gyfriniaeth definitely has electricity.'

The girl smiles tightly. 'It's obvious who you are. We saw you go into Jones and Jones. Everyone knows Miss Gilbertine left the house to an old friend. Yeah, the house is on the mains, but you'll be needing candles.' She stares at me implacably until

I pick up a packet. 'Better take a couple of packets at least. Tomorrow's Sunday. Shop's shut.'

I buy three packets and a box of matches, and she seems mollified. The man is still giving me surreptitious looks from the other side of the shop.

'You still haven't explained why I need candles,' I say.

She hands me my change with a shrug. 'You'll find out.'

I sense her eyes scorching my back as I leave. The two women are still there gawking, as though they were waiting for me to reappear. I begin to imagine there are people watching from every window, and when I get into the car it feels like a welcome oasis of normality. I slam my foot on the accelerator, and the Metro, protesting, jumps and stutters because in my momentary panic I forgot to change gear. Exit Fallady, looking a complete pillock.

It's a relief to escape on to the winding road that leads up into the hills. Was there anything normal about Tref-ddirgel? Am I about to encounter a bunch of albinos playing banjos and spitting, like in the film Deliverance? I shiver as the car moves into the countryside. Could this be the biggest mistake of my life? Even bigger than moving to London or turning down Andy's proposal? When it comes to making what the pop-psychologists call 'bad choices', I'm a natural.

CHAPTER TWO

After a few miles, the road begins to dip down, and the fields, sheep farms and copses eventually give way to woods. I pass a 'Welcome to Shropshire' sign just a few seconds before a faded, wooden signpost appears at the side of the road. It actually says 'elin frini th'. I turn with a bit of a squeal into what I assume is the driveway of the house. It isn't. The tiny dirt road winds on through the woods for a further couple of miles, the only indication of civilization the telegraph poles marching in the same direction. I'm starting to sweat at my own folly. This house is ridiculously isolated. Okay, so I knew that already, but imagining it through rose coloured specs in London and confronting the solid reality are two very different things.

The road finally crosses a bridge over a stream, and I draw to a halt as the house comes into view. I just sit there staring, so enthralled that I forget to turn off the car engine. The grey blob certainly didn't do the house justice. It's an old watermill, built of stone and with a slate roof. There are five windows on the front and a disused waterwheel on one side. Behind it, a stream cascades down a rocky outcrop in a series of small waterfalls and into a mill pool. Around the house, stream and pool is what must once have been a beautiful garden but is now overgrown and unkempt. There really are roses around the door, but they're in serious need of attention. A forest of rhododendrons in glorious trumpeting bloom clusters beside the stream. The early evening sun slants through the trees, and the house stands out like a light in the darkness. It sounds fanciful, but that's how it feels.

The keys in my pocket are emitting enough heat for me to feel through the folds of fabric. I reach in and touch them: they're hand hot. Must just be my body heat, I tell myself, trying desperately to cling on to normality. After all, the house looks normal. It's there, it's real and it's distinctly not a run-down shack. This isn't the enchanted wood. I hope. I read far too much Enid Blyton as a kid, but right now I need to get a grip.

I have to push aside the trailing ends of overgrown roses to get at the front door, and the keys seem to vibrate as I insert the biggest one into the lock. Agitated, I push the door gingerly and look in around the edge as it creaks open.

Nothing happens. Really. No elves or goblins jump out; no witches fly out on their broomsticks. The only thing that does emerge is a musty smell. Miss Gilbertine had been ill and in hospital for months before she died. The house hasn't been lived in for almost a year.

I pad in over the worn and faded matting of the hall. Doors on either side lead into fair sized rooms. The first had obviously been used as a living room and the second as a study. Both are full of antique furniture and each has a large fireplace as its centrepiece. There's a piano in the living room, and in the study I eye the shelves full of old hardback books with a flutter of excitement. One oddity is the oil lamps and candles set on every surface in both rooms. Slightly anxious, I flick the light switch on the study wall. Nothing. I suppress the urge to panic; the electricity would have been turned off for safety, wouldn't it? I'll need to find the fuse box.

I move down the hall to the last two rooms. One is a dining room and has a window overlooking the waterfalls and a large, antique, polished (though now rather dusty) table, which actually sports a couple of candelabra. The second room is a cavernous kitchen with old style cupboards and dressers full of crockery, a wood-burning range, a scrubbed kitchen table and a large pantry through a door on one side. Thankfully a washing machine and a fridge provide a more modern touch, although neither looks less than twenty years old. Another door in the kitchen leads to the cellar, where I'm guessing the fuse box might be. The stairs disappear into darkness, and with no electricity I need some light, but I didn't bring a torch with me – how often do you really need a torch in London? It looks like I'm going to need a candle after all.

I head back out to the car and unload. I throw my bags and suitcases into the living room for the time being, grab the box of matches I bought at the village shop and light one of the half-used candles that are scattered all over the place.

To my relief, the cellar staircase is actually quite short, and there is an old fuse box at the bottom, draped in cobwebs. I flick the stiff switch to ON. Nothing happens, as I'd forgotten to turn on the light switch before descending the stairs.

I lift up the candle and look around. It's quite a large cellar and there are a lot of bottles of wine on racks. I pull out one of the dusty bottles of red and go back to the kitchen, glad to be in full daylight again. A flick of the switch and the bulb in the middle of the ceiling bursts into light. I blow out the candle and study the wine bottle. It's old. I waste a couple of minutes wondering how old wine can be and still be okay before deciding fifty years is probably all right. Miss Gilbertine had only been living here for around twenty-five years. Who lived here before her, and how had she come by the house? Did she buy it, or was it left to her?

I leave the tempting wine bottle behind and climb the uncarpeted stairs. Four doors open off a wide landing. The first is a bathroom, with a large, old-fashioned, claw-footed bathtub and brass taps, an old-style toilet with a high cistern and a chain and a standard white washbasin. Next to it is the master bedroom. A wrought-iron double bed sits on the polished wood floor, and a small rag-rug by the bed provides a touch of comfort. There's a dressing table, a large wooden chest of drawers and a matching wardrobe. I lean out of the casement window and admire the view to the mill pond and beyond. The second bedroom's pretty similar but a bit smaller, also sporting a wrought-iron double bed, and the third bedroom is just big enough for the single bed and chest of drawers it contains. It's as though I've stepped into the 1950s. Miss Gilbertine never seemed particularly hard up, so why did she never get the furnishings updated?

Apart from the washing machine, fridge and electric kettle in the kitchen, there's very little modern equipment in the house. No central heating, no microwave, no toaster, no TV, no DVD player, not even any electric heaters. Instead there's the piano and a radio out of the 60s in the living room, and even more surprisingly an ancient wind-up record player in the study, beside which is piled a large collection of 78rpm records. It might have been a mistake to sell so many of my worldly goods, such as my hi-fi, before leaving London. My CD collection is going to be gathering dust. At least I brought my laptop, and there's a phone line here, so I won't be completely cut off.

I check the phone – another relic with a dial – and, as promised by the solicitors, there's a normal dial tone. I call Elli's number and am oddly relieved to hear it ringing.

'So what's the house like?' she asks eagerly.

'It's great. A bit old fashioned, but bigger than I expected. It's in an amazing spot.' I go on to tell her about it being a watermill, but don't mention all the oddities that have conspired to make me uneasy.

'Mmmm… well, it sounds good, but very lonely,' my sister says in a slightly worried tone.

'I'll be fine,' I say, trying to seem determined and sounding a little feeble even to myself.

After we've rung off, I go out of the back door in the kitchen and find myself facing a long, low outbuilding that looks the same age as the house. It unlocks with one of the plethora of keys. Inside there's a large woodpile, and next to that a huge boiler. The other half of the room is taken up with a sort of sluice area comprising a stone sink with a mangle by its side and drying racks set into the wall. I give the mangle a turn – the rollers move easily. It's obviously in full working order. Why keep all this antique equipment? I've only ever seen a mangle in history books. It's like being in a museum.

Further down the garden, there's an ordinary wooden garden shed, full of gardening equipment of various kinds, but nothing modern like a lawn mower or a strimmer. Did Miss Gilbertine do all the gardening herself?

I take some logs back to the house with me and attempt to start a fire in the living room. Even though it's May, I'm feeling slightly chilled; a fire might create an aura of cosiness to warm the edges of my disquiet.

While the logs smoulder but refuse to catch, I check inside the airing cupboard in the bathroom and am relieved to discover a normal immersion heater. I switch it on with a contented smile. Maybe there's nothing to worry about after all.

Twilight is deepening to darkness by the time I've unpacked all my things, stashed the food and provisions in the fridge and pantry and made up my bed in the master bedroom. The fire's finally burning nicely, and I'm eating sardine sandwiches and sipping fifty-year-old claret while listening to the radio. I feel oddly naughty about the wine. I'm sure it must be quite valuable, being that old. It's hard to think of it as mine, since even the house isn't really mine. Not yet anyway.

CHAPTER THREE

Surprisingly, I don't wake in the night to lots of creaks and groans, rattling of chains and white shapes bumbling about, but instead open my eyes to dazzling sunshine bursting through the open window, a pheasant croaking loudly outside and someone whistling. Whistling?

I jump out of bed and peer through the window. There's a man out there doing the gardening. I rub my eyes... yes, he's definitely digging the garden. A fairly old man, by the look of it. What on earth? I throw on the nearest clothes and gallop down the stairs. The grandfather clock in the hall at the bottom was stopped yesterday; now it's ticking loudly, and it reads five past twelve. I've slept for over twelve hours!

I've barely taken that in before the delicious aroma of baking bread hits my nostrils. The kitchen door opens just as I reach it and a woman wearing old-fashioned costume says, 'Ah, you're awake at last, lovey,' in a pronounced Welsh accent, beaming all over her plump features (about as plump as mine, I can't help thinking). 'I didn't want to wake you. You must have been very tired. I hope you're hungry now, though. Come on through and get some dinner. I've made you a nice beef casserole.'

I stand there with my mouth open, speechless. Who is this oddly dressed woman, and why is she behaving as though her presence is perfectly normal? I hurry after her into the kitchen. It's warm and cosy, the range is lit, the dust of the past twelve months gone, cooking smells abound, and my new acquaintance is ladling some casserole into a bowl for me.

'There you are,' she says, beaming again and putting a hunk of fresh bread beside my bowl. 'I'm Mrs Emrys,' she adds.

'The man – there's a man in the garden?' I stutter.

She nods. 'That's Mr Linlade. He does the gardening and handyman work.'

'The solicitors never mentioned any staff working here. I'm a bit confused,' I say. I sit down reluctantly and note that the stew smells very tempting.

Mrs Emrys gives a jolly laugh. 'Oh well, that's solicitors for you.' She shakes her head and turns to the range to carry out some arcane cooking tasks while I wonder how many more degrees of bemusement I'm going to experience.

I take a mouthful of stew – it's delicious, and almost against my will I begin to tuck in with enthusiasm. Whatever she's doing here, she can certainly cook.

She places a golden brown apple pie on the table, next to a jug of cream, and finally sits down. 'Well lovey, I hope you're going to be happy here. Miss Gilbertine told us all about you, so we knew you'd be coming along eventually. Such a shame she had to die in hospital, poor dear. She'd have been so much happier staying here till the end.'

'Miss Gilbertine never mentioned that she was going to leave the house to me,' I say, nibbling at my chunk of bread.

'Never was one for saying much, was Della Gilbertine,' Mrs Emrys comments calmly.

'But why didn't the solicitors mention any staff?' I try again. 'I mean, you must need paying, and the income Miss Gilbertine's granted me won't cover it.'

She busies herself cutting the apple pie and places an enormous, steaming slice in front of me. 'Don't you worry yourself about that, lovey. It's all taken care of. You eat up your apple pie. That's the best thing to do right now.'

I watch her bustle back up to put some more logs in the range and then turn my attention back to the apple pie. I shrug inwardly and pour cream over its sugary crust. No point in wasting it. There's certainly some satisfaction in seeing the apples I'd left in the pantry now turned into a state-of the-art pie, which is more than I'd planned to do with them. And how did she manage to make such a delicious casserole out of the odds and ends that were in the pantry and fridge? As for the bread, I didn't bring any yeast or wholemeal flour. She must have supplied them herself.

I frown to myself as I eat, mulling over this completely unexpected aspect of my new abode. It's vaguely feasible that there is a staff, but then how does that explain the unlived-in state of the place just the previous day?

'You weren't here yesterday,' I say casually.

'No lovey, we only come in when there's someone living here.'

'But what do you live on when there's no one here? I mean, do you still get paid?'

Mrs Emrys gives me another of her beatific smiles and says, rather repetitively, 'No need for you to worry about that, lovey. It's all taken care of.'

I sigh and try again. 'So, um, where do you both live? I didn't see any other houses locally. I hope you don't have to come far?'

'Oh no, it's not far at all,' she replies, crashing away at the washing up in the sink.

Her replies seem unduly evasive. Another trip to the solicitors might be in order. Not that *they* were very forthcoming on my previous visit.

When I've finished eating, Mrs Emrys introduces me to Mr Linlade, who is working hard to return the garden to its former splendour. It looks tidier already. Mr Linlade, dressed in stockings and breeches, gives me a number of keen looks as we exchange small talk about gardens – and what do I know about them, really, having lived in London flats for years? I try to ask him about his living arrangements, and his responses are as slippery as his colleague's.

It's when we return to the house and I decide to soothe my spirits by turning on the old wireless in the living room that I discover the electricity is off.

'Oh yes, lovey, that's normal,' Mrs Emrys replies to my anxious query as she dusts the mantelpiece.

'In what way normal? You mean there's a lot of power cuts?' I ask, my voice screeching like Elli's.

'Oh that electricity just doesn't work very well in this old house, that's all.' She pronounces the word electricity as though it's in a foreign language. 'But not to worry – you'll get used to it. Miss Gilbertine was never much of a one for modern comforts you see; didn't mind the electricity being off. And it's not natural, is it? We don't need that washermachine; I can do your washing with my own two hands and the mangle. Don't you fret about it.'

The *mangle*? Surely there's no need to resort to that relic?

'So the house needs rewiring?' I ask anxiously, wondering if my meagre funds will run to an electrician.

'Oh no, nothing wrong with the wires, just the power doesn't work here. Not natural, like I said.'

'But the solicitors told me there were full services here, and the power was on yesterday,' I say, my guts clenching at the prospect of life without electricity. No electric light, no laptop, no fridge… no TV, even, not that there's one in the house to watch in any case.

Mrs Emrys pauses in her dusting to come over and pat me on the shoulder. 'You don't need it lovey; we've got the boiler for hot water, log fires for heating and the range for cooking –'

'And candles for lighting?' I butt in.

'Of course, them and the oil lamps.'

I grit my teeth. No wonder there's so little technology in the house; no wonder candles adorn every available surface; no wonder the people in the town were so peculiar. But just *what* is it that they know and I don't?

I suppress a shudder and try using my mobile to connect back to the real world, but there's no signal. The dial phone still works though, probably because it's about fifty years old and doesn't require electricity. I ring Dessy and give her the same expurgated version of events I gave Elli yesterday. She obviously detects some strain in my voice as she echoes Elli when she says, 'I'm sure you're going to be lonely there. I think it's pretty scary being somewhere so isolated that you can't even get a mobile signal and the water comes from your own stream.'

Thanks, sis, I think grimly. *You really know how to cheer me up.*

I have to get out of the house, try to clear my head. I leave Mrs Emrys busily cleaning in the bathroom and head past Mr Linlade, who is tackling the overgrown wisteria over the arbour, and take the steep path towards the outcrop above the house. The weather's dry and warm, and hawthorns and rhododendrons are in full bloom around me as I stroll up the wooded path. Although it's hard work, a fitness regimen not having been among my London priorities, I begin to relax and listen to the birdsong.

At the top, I find a pool that looks big enough and deep enough to swim in. I teeter at the edge to look down at the house. The whole valley's full of trees and scrub, but it's obvious from this height that I was right. There are no other houses for miles. It's all pretty wild looking, and the nearest large cleared area looks like it belongs to a distant farm. What's more, the only car anywhere near the house is my Metro. The sound of wood being chopped echoes up faintly from below.

I stroll upstream for a while and discover the spot where the water is being drawn off for the house supply. The pipe runs along the path, the way I've come.

I sit down on a rock to enjoy the peace and try my mobile again for a signal, with no luck. I had hoped to text Jex, as he's usually busy with his fencing business, and we often end up communicating by text and e-mail instead of having real conversations. Now I seem to be stuck without access to either. What's more, without my mobile or laptop, my friends in London won't be able to contact me. Actually, that thought doesn't bother me too much. I snap my mobile shut decisively. What do I need with all my London friends saying 'I told you so'? The laptop's another issue though. As a technology geek, I hadn't anticipated quite such a drastic loss.

I return to the house to find another delicious aroma emanating from the kitchen.

'I'm just baking you a Dundee cake,' says Mrs Emrys. 'It'll be ready in time for tea.'

'Oh. Okay.' I murmur helplessly, thinking it very quaint to be having 'tea'.

I head for the study. It's easy to imagine Miss Gilbertine there, poring over her books. Her desk is still strewn with letters and documents. The solicitors dealt with everything, but it seems that they haven't felt the need to tidy up her private papers. That's seemingly been left to me. I keep an eye out for anything that might have been addressed to me or mentions me. Despite our long correspondence, I'm still unsure why my old mentor picked me to inherit her house.

After a couple of hours of shuffling, I'm disappointed to find that the papers consist mostly of old bills and junk mail. There's certainly no sign of any message for me. I feel a bit cheated – I seem to have been dropped right in it with no explanation for anything.

Mrs Emrys calls me to the kitchen at half past five on the dot, and there's the kitchen table out of my Enid Blyton dreams: a pot of tea, slices of bread and ham, hard boiled eggs, green salad in a bowl, and of course the Dundee cake – brown and moist, just waiting to be sliced. Why is it that food never looks so appetising when I scrape up a meal for myself?

As I gape, my beneficent cook is preparing to leave. 'Well, that's everything done for today, lovey. I've left you some soup in the pantry if you get hungry later and want some supper, and the fresh loaf's in the bread bin.'

She gives me a quick rundown on how to keep the range going and how to boil a kettle on it. I'm anxious at the prospect of being alone in the house without electricity, but I'll be glad to have it back to myself for a while.

I say goodbye to her with every sign that I'm about to settle down to my meal, but as soon as the front door closes, I dart into the living room and duck behind the curtain to look out of the window. She meets up with Mr Linlade a few yards down the path and they stroll off together, talking. I run to the front door and open it carefully, edging out just as they pass out of sight around the corner in the direction of the bridge. I curse my unfitness as I try to run quietly towards the trees at the side of the mill pool, looking for a point where I can see the bridge without being spotted. I get to the edge of the mill stream and lurk behind a handy grove of rhododendrons, catching my breath as I peer through the shiny leaves and watch the two of them, still chatting, vanish in mid-stride.

CHAPTER FOUR

After one of the most restless nights of my life, I head downstairs with a yawn the next morning and nip quickly into the living room to phone the solicitors and make an urgent appointment. If the house is haunted, they should have given me advance warning. But, damn it, I've never believed in ghosts. I take a few calming breaths before I enter the kitchen.

Mrs Emrys looks all too real as she presides over the preparation of a very full English breakfast, her face flushed and perspiring in the heat of the range. Do ghosts *sweat*? Despite my irritable and anxious state, I smile as she places a heaped plate before me. There won't be room for my usual chocolate quotient if she keeps on feeding me up like this.

She hands me a rather long shopping list before I set off for Tref-ddirgel. Her writing and spelling are very poor. Even the least able kids at my school could have done better than that. Maybe she's dyslexic? I long to ask, but by now I've got the message that personal questions of any kind are unwelcome.

Mr Linlade is pruning the roses over the front door as I exit, and his cheery whistle fades behind me as the car noses across the bridge.

Close to the town I pull into a lay-by to try my mobile and have a satisfactory sense of slotting back into normality when I get a signal. I check my texts and find several, mainly from

London friends wondering how things are going, but also two from Jex, impatient for news. I spend a happy half hour texting everyone back, but I don't phone anyone, even Jex. The encounter at the solicitors is looming, and I need to see where that will lead before reaching any conclusions.

Tref-ddirgel looks as pretty as ever in the morning sunlight, and I almost forget the strangeness of two days ago until I stroll over to Jones, Jones and Wynne-Jones, and the sense of being under scrutiny returns. I glance around. An old woman with a small dog exits the supermarket, her gaze firmly upon me, her mouth set. She seems to assess me and then pass with a single curt nod. A young couple are studying the postcard racks: reassuringly normal. The checkout girl from hell is staring at me through the plate glass. I shake myself, straighten my shoulders and stride determinedly into the solicitors office.

The receptionist picks up her phone as I enter. 'Miss Galbraith to see you,' she says, not taking her eyes off me. She puts down the phone with a sigh. 'Okay, you can go in.' She gestures towards the door opposite.

The older Mr Jones is sitting on his own this time and looks up rather resignedly as I enter.

'This is a pleasure, Miss Galbraith,' he lies. 'And what can I do for you this morning?'

I plump myself on the seat in front of his desk with no idea what to say. I feel like a popped balloon.

'Well, now that I've been at the house for a day or so, I have to tell you that some things about it are… um… not quite what I expected,' I begin feebly.

Mr Jones just raises his eyebrows and looks expectant.

'The electricity, for instance, doesn't seem to work most of the time. And then there's the matter of the staff.' I make full eye contact with him as I speak, and there's no doubt he both reacts and at the same time isn't surprised.

'Staff,' he says in a non-committal tone.

'Yes, Mrs Emrys and Mr Linlade. I assume you know about them?'

He seems to be taken by a coughing fit. Just as I'm wondering whether to call the receptionist he recovers, and, putting a hanky to his lips says, 'I'm aware of them, yes. Is there a problem?'

'Well, I mean, who pays them, where do they come from, and what if I don't want them? And what about the electricity? Why doesn't it work?'

He gives me a direct look. 'Miss Galbraith, all I can say to you is that you must accept the house as it is, staff and electricity problems and all, or else refuse the legacy. Is that your wish?'

I shake my head. 'No, that's not what I'm saying. All I want is some answers.'

'Well, I'm aware that the electricity is idiosyncratic at the house, and I'm aware of the two staff you mentioned. You won't need to worry about paying them, I can assure you.'

'I saw them disappear into thin air!' I blurt out.

He smiles and then sighs heavily. 'I believe you.'

'You've seen them, then; you've met them?' I ask, wanting reassurance of their corporeality.

'I haven't met them, but they've been there a very long time.'

'They worked for Miss Gilbertine?'

'Oh yes, and the two previous incumbents,' he says.

'But Mrs Emrys can't be more than fifty,' I protest, 'Although Mr Linlade seems to be in his seventies.'

'Yes indeed. And they've never altered,' he states mildly.

'Never? But...' I trail off. 'They *can't* be ghosts. I mean ghosts don't cook and clean and do the gardening, do they?'

He gives a short laugh. 'Who knows what ghosts do? *I* prefer not to believe in them, but your staff are a long-standing mystery in Tref-ddirgel. They're only present when the house is occupied, and when they're in attendance, the electricity is always off.'

I frown and bite my lip. 'So you're saying they make the electricity go off? But it didn't come on when they left yesterday. It was on when I arrived, though.'

'According to the previous incumbents, it takes a few hours to come back on. If, for instance, you were to leave the house for more than a day, the electricity would be on upon your return, but the staff would be back the following morning, and the power would go off.'

'You say incumbents almost as if it's a job.'

'Well, there aren't many who wish to live there in these circumstances. As I said, you are free to refuse the legacy.'

'What would happen to the house if I did? I mean, surely you couldn't sell it?'

He sighs and looks at his cluttered desk for a moment before seeming to come to a decision. 'No, we wouldn't sell it. You were Miss Gilbertine's first choice, but if you decline the legacy, we will have to go to her second.'

'First choice?'

'The house can't be sold. It must be inherited, and it's a serious matter in Tref-ddirgel as to who inherits it.'

A small shudder runs down my spine. 'Is that why everyone seems to be taking so much interest in me?'

He shrugs. 'It's believed in Tref-ddirgel that the house should be occupied in order to... well, soothe any restless spirits.'

'So they definitely think Mrs Emrys and Mr Linlade are ghosts?'

He nods. 'It's a mystery unsolved for more than a hundred years.'

'Why would ghosts want to be cooks and gardeners?' I murmur repetitively. 'I mean, wouldn't they be doing their haunting in a more... well, ghostly manner?'

He laughs softly and lifts his hands, palms up. 'As I said, Miss Galbraith, I don't believe in ghosts. However, I can't deny that there is something odd about Felin Gyfriniaeth.'

I leave the solicitors with mixed feelings. I'm one part relieved, one part intrigued and one part apprehensive. After all the talk in London of my running away, I seem to have dashed straight into some very thorny bushes.

I still have Mrs Emrys' shopping list to fulfil, which means I have to face the supermarket again. I take a deep breath before pushing through the door. Luckily the checkout girl is busy chatting to a middle-aged man. I concentrate on filling my basket, but as I approach the counter, I can't help overhearing the conversation.

'…Making a few new friends, and she seems to like the staff there,' the girl is saying.

'Well I'm glad to hear she's doing so much better,' the man says, with a trace of an Irish accent, just as I reach the till.

'Hello again, Miss Galbraith,' the girl says rather coldly when I put down my basket, and the man turns to look at me with a smile.

'*You're* Fallady Galbraith?' he asks.

I nod silently, and he grins. 'Takes a bit of getting used to, I suppose, coming from London.'

'Um…'

He laughs. 'Being recognised, I mean. But I admit I'm as intrigued as anyone else in Tref-ddirgel about the new owner of Felin Gyfriniaeth.'

'It wasn't what I expected,' I say, eyeing the girl as she takes her time putting my stuff through the till.

'I should introduce myself,' he says, and runs a hand through his greying brown hair. 'I'm John Kelly, one of the local GPs. Listen, if you're not in a hurry, why don't you come and meet my wife, Alyson? Our house is just a few doors away.'

'Er, well,' I temporise, taken by surprise at such a jovial and laid-back doctor. All the ones I encountered in London were very brisk and detached. The girl has finally finished with my shopping, and I hand over some cash. Dr Kelly is still looking at me expectantly, his homely face open and friendly. 'Okay,' I say.

As we're heading down the road, he says, 'I knew Della Gilbertine quite well. Her health wasn't too good in the final couple of years, so I had to visit the house on a regular basis.'

I nod. Her most recent letters contained vague hints about ill health but no details. 'So you must have met Mrs Emrys and Mr Linlade?'

'Oh yes, they were always around,' he says, shrugging. 'They obviously haven't put you off, though?' Before I can reply, he grins again and adds, 'Sorry, nosiness keeps getting the better of me. One of my worst failings. Don't answer if you don't want to.'

'No, it's okay. I'm just trying to take it all in.'

'What do you think of the view that they're unquiet spirits in need of a home?'

I laugh dryly. 'I've never believed in spirits or ghosts, and even though I've seen them vanish into thin air, I can't say that's what I think they are.'

'Well, you might find that they don't know what they are either. Della had all the same questions as you do, but they were never answered. Either they can't or they won't say. And in the end, maybe it doesn't matter, as long as you're happy.'

'I'm not sure that I *am* happy without electricity.'

'Ah, well, I'm not sure I would be either,' he says, stopping outside a large house painted pale pink. 'Here we are.'

I follow him in to a haphazard and untidy home full of dogs and cats, where, as promised, he introduces me to his wife. I can tell straight away that I'm going to get on with Alyson Kelly. Tall and slim and in her late forties, her shoulder-length blonde hair is in no particular style, and her jeans and T-shirt look worn and faded. She greets me cheerfully and says, 'I might have known John wouldn't waste any time in making your acquaintance.'

'It's nice to know someone wants to,' I say. 'Everyone seems a bit weird around here.'

'Well, it's all too supernatural for some people,' John says, pushing one of his dogs out of the way as he settles into an armchair.

'So how are you finding it?' Alyson asks, as a tabby cat tries to curl up on my lap.

'The house is great, but I'm tying myself up in knots over all the mysteries,' I say, and I tell them all about my visit to Jones & Jones.

'It's a big change from London,' John comments. 'What made you accept the legacy in the first place?'

I decide not to mention the lack of carpers. 'I suppose it sounded romantic and exciting, and I was bored with my job and sick of my flat. My family keep talking about how lonely it is, but I thought I'd like lonely after London. Of course, it's not as lonely as I expected with Mrs Emrys and Mr Linlade there.'

'And you're not scared of them?' Alyson asks.

I think for a minute. 'No, they're not scary, just evasive. But I'm none too keen on the electricity being off. What I don't get is why there's a washing machine and fridge and kettle there at all if you can't use them. I mean, what's the point? And how did people ever manage without fridges? I could get food poisoning.'

John chuckles. 'I *can* reassure you that Della never came down with anything of that sort. I think Mrs Emrys' food hygiene's pretty good, for a ghost.'

'I suppose the good news is the electricity bills won't be high,' I say with a small grin.

'So, what can we tell you about Tref-ddirgel?' John says thoughtfully.

'I'm sure you can think of plenty, being the biggest gossip in town,' Alyson says with an affectionate grin.

'Nonsense. As a doctor, I'm the soul of discretion,' John replies. 'Mind you, I did hear just this morning that Mrs Parry has a new man in her life, and Sioned in the shop was just telling me how her auntie's getting on in the care home…'

I relax and forget about my anxieties for a while, as John and Alyson regale me with a variety of information and gossip, some useful, most not. An hour later I leave the pink house with an invitation to dinner the following week and a sense of relief that I'm not a total pariah in the town.

CHAPTER FIVE

'It's driving me mad!' I say to John and Alyson, stabbing my fork into a conveniently placed piece of meat with some force.

Two weeks have passed in which I've failed to penetrate the mystery by even one millimetre. My mysterious staff have continued to behave in a marginally deferential yet subtly devious manner. No matter how many times or how cleverly I try to winkle information out of them, they never bite; they just brush it all away with a 'never you mind about that, lovey' from Mrs Emrys, or an 'oh now, I wouldn't know anything about that' from Mr Linlade. To my immense frustration, I know no more about them now than I did on the first day.

John grins at me across the dining table at Felin Gyfriniaeth, the candles in the candelabra flickering between us. 'What's driving you mad, as if we need to ask?'

'I need some answers.'

He exchanges glances with Alyson and then says slowly, 'Well, I suppose there's always the ruins.'

'Ruins?' I say, my voice rising with excitement. 'What ruins?'

'As far as we can gather, this watermill was once part of a village. We didn't like to mention it before in case it scared you. Now that we know you better, we reckon you can cope.'

I sit back in my chair and stare at him, the forkful of beef dropping back on to my plate. 'Part of a village? I wondered why there was a mill in such an out of the way spot. But what happened to it? I mean, why is it in ruins now?'

John shrugs. 'That I don't know.'

'I've seen no sign of any ruins. How can I find out where they are?'

Alyson laughs dryly and says, 'Ask Mrs Emrys?'

I shake my head firmly. I'm tired of asking anything of Mrs Emrys.

'You could try the library in Oswestry,' John says. 'I think they have a good local history section. You could ask around in Tref-ddirgel, I suppose, but you know how it is. I get the feeling no one wants to come near this place.'

'They think the whole area's haunted?'

He shrugs. 'Probably. We've only been here for two years ourselves, so anything we know is pretty sketchy.'

I'm living on the edge of a haunted village? Everything always seems so peaceful around the house, and besides, I _definitely_ don't believe in ghosts. Why didn't Miss Gilbertine leave me any explanation, damn it? I've cleared up all the stuff in her study now, and it's obvious I've been left in the dark in more ways than one. I _have_ to get to the bottom of it all.

'The village of Llanycoed, a little over five miles from Tref-ddirgel, was demolished in a localized earthquake in 1799. Only the watermill remained standing, due, it is thought, to its being on higher ground. The ruins are still considered to be dangerously unstable,' I read. Localized earthquake? In _Shropshire_? I know there are occasional earthquakes in Britain, but none of them so severe that a whole village could be destroyed.

After hours spent trawling through local history books full of pictures of border towns, showing people standing proudly outside old-fashioned shops and virtually car-free streets of black and white houses, this is the single nugget of information I can find.

I drive back to the house through a sultry afternoon full of dark-edged cauliflower clouds that promise a storm before too long. I'm hoping the rain will hold off, because my curiosity *has* to be satisfied.

I start my search by standing on what I now think of as the 'disappearing zone'. Right in front of me, the road to Tref-ddirgel crosses the bridge over the stream. Directly on my left, the ground slopes away downwards into dense woods and nasty-looking scrub. I've never thought to go down there because it looks so rough. It surely has to be the place to look.

I struggle my way through the wild rhododendrons and prickly hawthorns at the side of the track, and then I'm descending a steep slope overgrown with brambles and nettles. It's impossible to imagine that there was ever any kind of a track or path leading down, and it strikes me that if you wanted to hide the ruins and keep people out, brambles and nettles would make a very effective barrier.

By the time I reach the bottom of the slope, I'm drenched in sweat, and my hands and arms and even my face are sporting a collection of scratches and stings. I wish I'd thought to bring some shears with me. Luckily the brambles start to dwindle, and there are only large patches of nettles to contend with. I pause to cool down and catch my breath, leaning against a tree trunk. Ahead of me are more trees and nettles, but among them some surprising oddities. A laburnum is leaning at an unusual angle, its drooping yellow flowers just fading to cream; roses trail about on the strangely uneven ground; an apple tree jostles for space among the hawthorns, oaks and beeches.

I'm already in the ruins, and I hadn't even realized it.

I reach into my bag to take out a bottle of water, and my fingers catch the house keys. They're hot. 'Weird,' I say out loud, and my voice fades away into the still greenery. I sip my water slowly, starting to cool off, but the sudden sound of hoof beats up close makes me jump and almost drop the bottle. I pivot around rapidly, expecting to see someone on horseback, but there's nothing, no one. I slip the bottle back inside my bag and wipe my sweaty and bloody hands on my jeans. *I must have imagined it.*

I move further into the ruins, teetering over buried foundations to the accompaniment of distant rumbles of thunder. I eventually find a house that has visible remnants of walls, some of them even delineating rooms. They're full of grass, nettles and valerian, but they're still recognisably rooms. I wander around, trying to imagine what it must have been like to live here. I listen to the rumbles growing closer, all the while fighting a growing sense of unease and the peculiar sense that I'm not alone.

Out of nowhere, there are voices: a child's laughter and the deeper tones of a man. I swivel around, seeing only the dog roses clambering over the low walls, a pear tree laden with tiny early fruit, and motionless trees and shrubs crowding what was obviously once a garden. There's no one here, but the voices don't stop. I head away from the house, trying to work out where they're coming from, but instead of getting closer, they fade. In my distraction I trip over a large, mossy stone and only just manage to catch myself on another, more upright one. I gasp as I realize it's a headstone, and there are faint words etched into it. 'Jennifer... wife of... departed this life... 1776', I read aloud. I seem to have found the churchyard. I ignore the increasing volume of the rumbles of thunder as I explore the graves, most now horizontal and illegible.

I'm crouching down trying to read one when there's the sound of wheels and hooves behind me. A coach and horses! I turn in panic, my heart hammering, and I'm almost certain there's a shimmer in the air, the toss of a chestnut mane, but then the sound just stops, and silence descends again. An unnatural silence, I realize, shivering despite the heat. Even the birds are quiet, or maybe absent.

Darker clouds are beginning to fill the sky. I don't feel in danger, but I'm beginning to have an idea why people don't want to come here. It's time to get back. For some reason, though, I can't resist returning to the one house with walls, and once I'm back there I hear the voices again: a child's piping and the man's response. I shudder in spite of myself and call out, 'Is there anyone there?' The voices carry on as though I hadn't spoken at all. I try to catch what they're saying, but they're muted and carry an echo, as though they're coming down a very long, deep pipe. I call again, with the same result, and then turn on my heel and head back towards Felin Gyfriniaeth, trying all the while to convince myself that there's nothing odd or paranormal going on. *Nothing at all.*

When I emerge from the bushes on to the road, covered in even more scrapes and stings, it's to the sight of my staff just heading down to the disappearing zone. They stop and gaze at me as I come towards them, and I feel like a naughty child caught out eating the sweets. They have mutual expressions of disapproval and dismay on their faces. I almost want to reach up and wipe off the telltale chocolate.

'It's a bit dangerous to go walking down there, lovey,' Mrs Emrys says in her usual tone, through an unusual frown.

'I was looking for the old village,' I say. 'I read that there was an earthquake and only Felin Gyfriniaeth survived.'

Mr Linlade is actually chewing at his lip. I've never seen either of them so discomposed. 'That's true, Miss, but those old ruins are unsafe. You could have an accident down there, and no one would know.'

'I shouldn't go down there again, lovey,' Mrs Emrys emphasises. 'It's all just dusty old bricks, anyway.'

'But there is one house where you can still see the bottoms of the walls, and there's a churchyard. I found the graves.'

'Oh, those old things aren't worth looking at,' she says. 'You should get back to the house and clean up those cuts and grazes. I've left you a nice big spread for your tea.'

I nod, but then add, 'It's a strange thing, though, but I heard voices down by the churchyard. I couldn't work out where they were coming from.'

Bullseye! They both react even more profoundly to that and have difficulty reverting to their usual benign expressions.

'Oh, lovey, it's just the way sound carries down at the bottom of the valley. It was probably people out for a walk in the woods.'

'You know all about it though,' I persist. 'About the earthquake and everything? About Llanycoed being there?'

'Yes, of course, but it's not worth bothering about,' she reiterates, looking up at the sky, which is even darker now. There's a bright flicker of lightning followed all too quickly by a loud crack of thunder. 'It looks like rain. You should get along in.'

'Yes, and you'll both be wanting to get home,' I say mischievously. I carry on to the house and don't even bother to wait and watch them disappear; I've grown tired of that trick.

I eat my meal without even tasting it, listening to the thunderstorm that seems to have settled right over the house. The rain's plummeting down.

Do Mrs Emrys and Mr Linlade live in the ruins of Llanycoed? Haunt the ruins and just come to Felin Gyfriniaeth because it's familiar? Why was my mention of the voices so disturbing to them? I don't think they were expecting that. No, the more I think about their reaction the more puzzling it is. They were shocked, and they didn't believe it was people walking nearby any more than I did. They know no one goes there. And why does no one go there? Have they heard the voices? Is that why they think it's haunted?

I sigh and return to the candlelit study in which I've been spending so much of my time. It's odd how quickly I've adjusted to the lack of electricity, although it wouldn't have been so easy without the staff. I've been so taken up with riddles that I've stopped even thinking about it. My mobile battery has run down, and I've barely spoken to anyone on the phone. Come to think of it, they must all be wondering what's going on. I feel guilty and make phone calls to Elli and Dessy on the landline. They both sound a bit worried and have obviously been talking about me among themselves. Elli in particular sounds very anxious.

'Maybe we could come and see you now you're settled in,' she says. 'Simon's got a holiday coming up next week. What do you think?'

It would be nice to see them, but how can I explain Mrs Emrys and Mr Linlade? How do I explain the electricity – or lack of?

'Well, um, of course, if you really want to,' I say. 'But it's probably pretty dull around here for you two. It's only a little place; there's not much to do.'

'Oh rubbish, Fally; you know we'd love to see it. Anyone would think you don't want us to come. Don't forget all we've seen so far is a blur. And you've already told us there's lots of nice scenery around. We could do with the break.'

What can I say? I know Elli, and she'll just turn up anyway if she thinks something's wrong, probably with Dessy and Jex in tow for force of numbers. I tell her I'll be glad to have her, and we set the date for next Saturday. My mind refuses to contemplate how she and Simon will react to what they find.

I put the phone down feeling completely wrung out. The storm has died down, and it's just raining gently outside. I head for bed – at least the mattress is comfy, despite the rudimentary furnishings.

When I encounter Mrs Emrys in the kitchen the next day, after a night spent dreaming of falling into a white void, she gives me another warning about going to Llanycoed. It does seem sometimes as though the staff are my keepers, but I have a feeling the relationship is deeper than that. I remember what Mr Jones said about them only being present in the house when there's an occupant. They need me, and they don't want anything to happen to me. For some reason they also don't want me to learn the truth about them, or apparently about Llanycoed.

I change the subject by telling her about my sister's impending visit. She reacts with characteristic equanimity. 'Oh, that *will* be nice, lovey. I'm sure you'll be glad of the company, and I'll be happy to cook for them. Now here's your breakfast – some nice bacon and eggs.'

And that's it. Preparations get underway, the second bedroom's given an overhaul and I'm glad to have someone else to talk to when I go to the Kellys for dinner the night before my visitors are expected.

'So what do you think the sounds and voices were?' Alyson asks once I've regaled them with the whole story of my Llanycoed experience.

'I've been puzzling over that all week,' I reply, 'but I'm no closer to working it out.'

'Maybe you shouldn't be quite so determined to dismiss the ghost hypothesis,' John puts in.

'Do *you* believe in ghosts?' I counter.

He shrugs. 'There are things we don't understand: things beyond any rational explanation.'

Alyson grins and nudges him playfully while giving me a meaningful look. 'It's the Catholic upbringing.'

This launches them into a jovial argument about the merits of religion. It's obviously one they've had many times before.

'Anyway,' says John when they finally stop sparring, 'you have at least found out something. You know the staff don't like the idea of your going to Llanycoed. Which I for one think favours the ghost argument. Plus, this business with the electricity's just the sort of thing that's connected with the paranormal. How many more pointers do you need?'

'A lot more than that,' I scoff. 'Anyway, any suggestions on how I'm going to explain these "ghosts" to my sister and her husband?'

'Not much point in trying, really,' Alyson says. 'Why don't you just say they came with the house?'

'And the old-fashioned costume?'

'Just part of their eccentric charm.'

'And the electricity?'

'Temporary power failure. The house is so isolated anyway.'

I sigh. 'It all sounds so simple when you put it like that.'

'It *is* simple,' John says. 'You need to stop worrying so much. I don't want to see you in the surgery asking for tranquillisers.'

I laugh. 'It's not that bad. I just want answers.'

'But not the answers that are staring you in the face,' he says, his expression serious for once.

CHAPTER SIX

I wake up the next morning with a feeling that something's out of kilter, but I can't put my finger on it. As per my new routine, I trot downstairs and open the kitchen door expecting to see Mrs Emrys smiling merrily as she prepares a hearty breakfast, but instead find a bare table and an echoingly empty room. No range lit, no delicious aromas, no Mrs Emrys. I dash outside, but Mr Linlade's cheery whistle isn't audible, and there's no sign of him among the now neat beds or in the garden shed. I check the utility outbuilding, but neither of them is there either. They're never late – they've always been working busily by the time I'm up, which isn't all that early at the best of times.

I return to the kitchen and look around with a sense of panic. What does it mean?

An odd background hum slowly impinges on my consciousness: a buzzing sound and peculiar squelching noises. I search around anxiously, thinking it might be something supernatural, until with a bit of a shaky laugh I finally track it down to the fridge. It's on! With a surge of excitement I try the light switch. The light clicks on, just like that. I've got so unused to electricity at home that I just stare at the radiant bulb for a minute, entranced. I feel like the cave man discovering fire.

I sit down at the scrubbed table with my chin in my hands, seeing blobs on my retinas. So I'm back on my own. Is it deliberate, despite Mrs Emrys' apparently looking forward to Elli and Simon's stay? Either way, she's removed one problem and created another. Now *I* have to cook the meals.

The phone goes, and it's Alyson, checking to see how I'm coping. 'They've gone? Well at least that's a load off your mind.'

'Yeees, but… what do you know about cooking on an old-fashioned range?'

I'm sure Alyson's laughing all the way, but at least she does come over.

In an orgy of gadget-mania, I thrust any clothes Mrs Emrys hasn't yet washed into the shiny washing machine, load up the fridge with all the items that had had to sit in the 'cool but not cool enough' pantry, like dairy and salad items (how I wish they sold smaller quantities) break out the laptop and charge it up, gazing lovingly at those familiar icons, even managing to connect – agonisingly slowly – to my old dial-up through the modem and picking up my e-mails. I turn on the antique radio and tune in to the 'BBC Home Service', now Radio 4 long wave. It's amazing how ordinary everything starts to feel, and how my isolation seems to diminish with the connection to the outside world that the radio and the Internet bring.

By the time Elli and Simon are due, the house is full of sound and cooking aromas, and I'm wearing a floury pinny and look like I'm turning into a domestic goddess. Ah, illusions.

Their posh Audi looks completely out of place, purring its way across the bridge to park next to my rackety old Metro, but I'm so pleased to see them that I'm almost ready to give Elli an involuntary hug. I did say *almost*.

Even so, I can't escape Elli's embrace, and when she lets go, she joins Simon in appraising the house.

'It looks really nice,' she says in a surprised tone, as though she'd been expecting a derelict ruin.

'Hmmm,' Simon agrees with a wry smile. 'We were wondering why you'd been so cagey about it all.'

'Cagey, me?' I say, laughing. 'Come on and see the inside,' I trill. 'It's a bit old-fashioned, like I mentioned, but it's still homely.'

During the tour Elli screeches a lot over the ancient items and the surfeit of candles I'd forgotten all about – 'I get quite a few power cuts,' I explain truthfully – but loves the kitchen range while exclaiming about it being a wood burner.

'How do you get enough wood for it?' she asks.

'Oh, there was a woodpile here when I arrived,' I reply blithely, and realize I have no idea what Mr Linlade does to keep me well stocked in wood. If he doesn't return, I'm going to be in trouble.

By the time I get them installed in the dining room and do my best imitation of someone who can actually cook, doling out the steak and kidney pie and veg, I can tell they're quite impressed. I am too. The pie's not bad, considering I made the pastry myself. Not quite up to Mrs Emrys' standards, of course.

'So you're happy here then, Fally?' Simon asks.

'Yeah,' I say. 'Beats being in London any day.'

'And you don't want to get a job or something?' Elli puts in.

I bite my lip. I've been trying not to think about getting a job. 'I don't know, really. I've just been adjusting to being here. Maybe later, but I don't think there's much call for sys admins around these parts.'

'I just thought you might be on your own too often. Doesn't seem healthy to me.'

Elli doesn't get introverts, although I reckon Simon's at least a marginal one. She can't imagine someone being happy in her own company. Rather than try to explain it, I tell her about the Kellys and how they've invited us all to dinner during their stay. This mollifies my sociable sister, who decides that at least I'm making friends. It's men friends she really wants me to make, though. Single ones. She seems to have the idea that there must be lots of lonely sheep farmers living in this area, and I should be seeking them out. If only she knew!

Every now and again I catch Simon giving me a considering look, and the next day he finally tells me what's on his mind. Elli's doing kitchen duty – she's much more of a domestic goddess than I am and has fallen in love with the ancient range – and we're taking a walk in the garden. Mr Linlade has even created a kitchen garden area replete with herbs, potatoes, several types of bean, peas and various root vegetables. My brother-in-law stares at all this and then turns to me curiously.

'And you did all this work yourself, Fally? I never took you for much of a gardener, but this is immaculate.'

Lies are such hard work, and I'm hopeless at them. It's easier to tell the truth with omissions. 'A gardener comes in every now and again. Apparently he's supplied with the house, and I don't have to worry about it. The solicitors sort everything out.'

'Elli would be glad if he was appropriately hunky and single.'

I chuckle. 'Neither I'm afraid. Looks about seventy and very married.' As I say that, I realize it's true. Mr Linlade doesn't seem single, but Mrs Emrys, in spite of the title, does. Odd.

'Fally, are you sure everything's okay? You don't seem to be quite with us half the time, as though there's something on your mind. I can't help noticing this place is incredibly isolated. If it's not working, you know you can come and live with us until you get sorted out again.'

I'm shocked that he thinks things are so bad. 'No, it's nothing like that. I love it here. I just have a couple of things to sort out, that's all.'

'Things you're not telling us about.'

'Well, yes, but you don't need to worry. It's nothing dire.'

'Okay, but don't keep it all to yourself if you're in trouble. You know we're always available to help.'

'It's nothing like that, Sime, but thanks anyway,' I say, touched.

Simon doesn't mention this conversation to Elli, and she seems satisfied that I'm contented enough, especially after our meal with the Kellys, during which my new friends are completely discreet about Llanycoed and the staff. It's a very convivial evening and ends the week on a high. Apart from worrying that Mrs Emrys and Mr Linlade might come back at any moment, I've enjoyed the visit. We've been out for trips to various local places of interest and even taken a swim in the pool above the house. I've avoided Llanycoed completely, and because the scrub looks so thick in that direction, no one even considered taking a walk there.

Two days after Elli and Simon have headed back to Hemel Hempstead, the house is still strangely empty. I ought to be glad – electricity back on, everything just as I expected it to be when I first arrived – but instead all I feel is a deep unease.

I phone Jones, Jones and Wynne-Jones and the elder Mr Jones graciously consents to see me at short notice.

'I trust nothing's amiss at Felin Gyfriniaeth?' he says, looking a bit worried.

'Not exactly, no. It's just that the staff, or ghosts, or whatever they are, have been gone for over a week. Has that ever happened before?'

He clears his throat. 'Well, as I mentioned last time, they're usually only absent when the incumbent leaves. You haven't been away?'

'No. On the contrary, I've had my sister and her husband to stay. Do they usually disappear if someone else is staying?'

'No, no, they tend to behave as though it's all perfectly normal. This is an unusual event, I have to say.'

'What do you know about the village of Llanycoed?' I ask abruptly.

He looks at me steadily for a moment. 'Well, I know that there are ruins near Felin Gyfriniaeth. Is that what you mean?'

'Do people think it's haunted too? I mean, is that what this is really all about? They think my staff are ghosts from Llanycoed, and that it's all haunted?'

He sighs. 'Yes, that does seem to be the general consensus in Tref-ddirgel. As we discussed before, you are free to refuse the legacy if you're finding it difficult.'

I shake my head vigorously. 'It's not that. I just want to solve the mystery. I want to know what's going on.'

He steeples his fingers. 'Miss Galbraith, after a hundred years it seems likely that the mystery can't be solved. It might be best to let it be.'

I glare at him. 'You sound like Dr Kelly.'

He takes off his glasses and puts them on his desk. 'A sensible man, Dr Kelly. And you have to remember that Della Gilbertine didn't find the answers either.'

'But did she even look for them? I've been hoping to find something from her, a letter to me, but I've had no luck.'

'I think she just accepted things as they were. You'd probably be better off doing the same, you know.'

It's my turn to sigh. 'Well, maybe you're right, but I don't know how good I am at just accepting things.'

I come out of there feeling pretty deflated, and lonely too, for the lack of anyone who shares my need for answers. I never have been able to understand how people can just believe things without proof. That's why religion never penetrated, despite my being force-fed it from my first arrival at Summerdale. I suppose Miss Gilbertine must have had faith because when I look back, religion was always there in the background. But she *knew* I was a rebel and an atheist, and she still left Felin Gyfriniaeth to me.

As I drive back, my anger mounts at just about everyone. I check that Mrs Emrys and Mr Linlade haven't returned and then stomp down the scrubby slope to Llanycoed, flaying away at the brambles and nettles with a pair of shears.

Once I'm in the ruins, I'm not quite sure what I mean to do. The sun is filtering through the trees on to the overgrown garden plants and shrubs from long ago, and I make a sort of game of it, trying to spot the cultivated plants. The best survivors are the roses, but I discover more apple and pear trees, along with plums and cherries. Red valerian is clinging tenaciously to some of the gravestones, and a gnarled, ancient yew has managed to retain its traditional spot among them. An unexpected lump forms in my throat as I try to imagine these poignant remains as church, houses and gardens. All the while, I'm listening for voices and sounds, but this time the whole place is silent, and the peculiar sensation I had in the house with walls is entirely absent. I end up walking up a slight slope that takes me further from the watermill, trying to work off my bad mood in exercise.

When I'm on the rise I pause to look back. I can't see Felin Gyfriniaeth at all from this spot; it's on the other side of the valley. The village is cupped into its bottom and I can detect vague shapes of houses through the trees, and even the outline of the church – a massive pile of oddly compact sandstone rubble that I didn't even try to explore. Surely a lot of people must have been killed in the earthquake? Why was the library record so brief? It's as if Llanycoed has been erased from history.

As I head back down the hill, I want to shout with frustration. What did I hope to find, in any case – a ghostly Mrs Emrys floating about? I'm so engrossed in my thoughts that I forget to watch my step, and trip on something jutting out of the grass. I tumble to the ground, rubbing my leg. I push my hands through the long grass and leaf mould to reveal the culprit: a piece of buried wood. As I try to free it, digging down slightly, it breaks off in my hand. It's old and splintered, but there's a faint outline of letters carved into it. 'Lla y fon 4 m es,' I mouth silently. The tiny village of Llanyrafon *is* about four miles away.

I get up and brush myself off, and I've walked no more than two paces down the slope when there's a sudden sensation that gravity has increased. I struggle to move, thinking I've inexplicably walked into a bog, but I'm frozen in place and sinking helplessly into the ground. I try to grab hold of a tussock of grass, but my desperately flailing hands fail to make contact with anything. The earth seems to fold around me and spit me out again, and then instead of sinking, I'm falling.

I still have my arms out, braced for a knock, but what I get is a cold, wet dousing as I thud, in a most ungainly fashion, into something icy, wet and white. Stunned, confused and gasping at the sudden chill, I'm trying to excavate my way out of it when a male voice utters from close by, 'What devilry is this?'

I manage to extricate my head, pushing damp tendrils of hair away from my face. I stare incredulously at a pair of black boots topped by stockings and breeches, and above them a waistcoat and black frock coat. A grave-looking man wearing what I can only conclude is fancy dress is viewing me with a very disapproving expression. His eyebrows are almost disappearing into his greyish wig. 'Madam,' he says coldly, 'you appear to have fallen out of the sky.'

CHAPTER SEVEN

I stagger to my feet, spluttering and trying to dust off the powdery snow. The man is prompted into even more astonishment as he stares, open-mouthed, at my T-shirt and jeans. 'What kind of garments are these?'

I shiver and look around. I'm standing close to a signpost on a snowy country crossroads, and it's freezing! I rub my bare arms to try and warm them up, and this seems to awaken his chivalry because he starts, takes off his coat and offers it to me, saying, 'Well, whatever manner of person you might be, you will catch cold in those clothes. You had better come to my house. We have a fire lit in the parlour.'

'Um, th-thank you,' I stutter, and put the coat around my shoulders. 'Can you tell me where I am?'

He gives me another of those looks. 'You are in the parish of Llanycoed. May I enquire where else you suppose yourself to be?'

'I do think I'm in Llanycoed,' I say.

I cough; the air is white with my breath. It's so *cold*! How could I have gone from high summer to deepest winter in one second? And if my new acquaintance isn't wearing fancy dress, as I'm beginning to think unlikely, then he's definitely from a different time, which means… I don't even want to think about what that means.

We turn a corner on the road, and I spot buildings ahead. A church, a cluster of houses, and just visible in the far distance, Felin Gyfriniaeth.

'I am Mr Edgemond, the parson,' he tells me.

'Er, Fallady Galbraith.'

'An unusual name,' he murmurs and then lapses into silence. Probably trying to decide what kind of witch I am. Dare I ask him what year it is? I take a sidelong look at his forbidding profile and decide against it.

I'm shivering compulsively by the time we reach a half-timbered house set in its own grounds. It all looks very quaint, but I'm too cold to care.

The parson ushers me indoors, and I'm hit by a strong smell of cooking meat. The house doesn't feel a great deal warmer than the icy outside world, but it's very cosy and well furnished, considering this seems to be the olden days. There's even a carpet on the polished wood floor of the room he shows me into, and several comfy-looking, high-backed armchairs, along with a sofa.

A young maid runs to fetch a blanket for me, and I huddle in one of the armchairs by the fire while my rescuer looks on from the sofa, pursing his lips thoughtfully every now and again. No one would call him handsome, but he's not that bad looking, in a kind of dour and serious way. He looks to be in his mid forties, is dark, average height, and the lips he keeps pursing are full and sensitive. Shame about the wig, though. Oh, and the slight paunch just visible under his waistcoat. Not that I can talk.

An older maid brings tea, and I'm transfixed by her costume. It's almost identical to what Mrs Emrys wears. The parson's clothing is also similar to Mr Linlade's, although far more elegant-looking. I start to tremble as the significance of this discovery sinks in. Is this where my staff come from, and if so, are they here now? And either way, how do I get back? They just stroll in and out of my time as far as I can tell, not fall.

I take the risk. 'Do you know a Mrs Emrys, or a Mr Linlade?' I ask the parson.

His eyes widen. 'They are both servants to the squire, Mr Greenleaf. You are related to one of them? You do not speak like a member of the servant class.'

'Ah no, I'm not... ah... a member of... well, that is... but I have... eh... heard of them.' I say lamely.

Fortunately for me, any reply he might have made is averted by the abrupt entry into the room of a dark-haired, slender girl aged about ten, clutching a wooden doll.

'Papa,' the girl says, joining the parson on the sofa and gazing at me shyly.

To my surprise, the parson's whole face changes when the girl comes in. It loses its serious lines and softens. He even smiles a little. 'Anna, this is Mrs Galbraith,' he tells her. 'Mrs Galbraith, this is my daughter, Anna.'

'Pleased to meet you, Anna,' I say, smiling at her, forgetting for a minute that I'm not at all keen on children, 'but it's Miss Galbraith. I'm not married.'

'Well, Miss Galbraith, am I correct in assuming that you have nowhere to stay?'

'Ah, yes, that is, er, I don't. I'm stranded just now,' I stammer.

'Indeed,' says the parson, and I swear his lips twitch. Perhaps there is hope, after all. Maybe he doesn't think I'm a witch or a devil. 'It is not particularly seemly, but it seems best that you remain here. You certainly can't be seen again in that attire. Perhaps some of my wife's dresses would fit.'

'Your wife?' I say. 'She's not here?'

Anna moves closer to her father, and he puts his arm around her shoulders as he shakes his head slowly. 'My dear wife died three years ago, of the small pox.'

My cup clangs back into its saucer. Smallpox! I'm in a time when there's still smallpox! And if there's smallpox, what other deadly viruses and bacteria are hanging around? How clean is the water? Dare I even drink the tea or eat any food? My thoughts chase one another around in panic, but it eventually sinks in that I can either have a fit of the vapours or I can get on with it. I force myself to take deep breaths and decide on the latter.

'You are pale, Miss Galbraith. Pray drink your tea; it will warm you.' Mr Edgemond says, his manner now far more kindly, and I can hardly refuse when he's my only lifeline, so I gulp it down, glad it's only green tea with no milk, as I have a strong suspicion that pasteurisation won't have been invented yet. How I wish I'd been more interested in history instead of all that science and technology.

'Perhaps you could tell me what date this is?' I say, mentally crossing my fingers.

'It is the twenty-sixth day of February, in the year of our Lord seventeen hundred and seventy-nine.'

I crash my cup into the saucer again. 1779! 1779! Two hundred and twenty-nine years ago. I rack my brain trying to think of anything I know about the 18th century, but nothing rises to the surface. Wait, what about 'The Madness of King George'? Wasn't that set in the same sort of time? But what did that film tell me? That there was no mental health care system. That doctors were mostly quacks. That kings used chamber pots. That they wore nightgowns. That everyone wore wigs. Yes, they all wore wigs, pretty similar in appearance to the one Mr Edgemond's wearing, except his looks fairly plain compared with some of the ones on the film. I sigh. None of it's particularly helpful to me right now.

'It's cold for the end of February,' I say, noticing my voice is trembling and hoping the parson hasn't.

'Indeed,' Mr Edgemond replies mildly. 'Last night it was so cold that the chamber pots were frozen.'

I swallow. So, chamber pots. Frozen chamber pots! Don't they have toilets? I mean, even I know they didn't have flush toilets in Georgian times, but, well, what do they do then? As soon as I think of this, I start wanting to go. I decide not to drink too much tea, just in case. And I thought having no electricity was hard!

The cooking aromas are increasing in level, and there's a lot of bustling and movement from the adjacent room. It seems likely that a meal is imminent.

When I put down my teacup, the parson calls the younger maid. 'Nerys, please show Miss Galbraith to the large guest chamber, provide her with some warm water for washing and find her some suitable garments from my late wife's trunk,' he orders, adding to me, 'We shall be dining at three o'clock and expect the squire and his wife as guests. I hope you will feel able to join us.'

I'm getting up to follow the maid but I turn to look at him in horror. 'Ah... I... er... don't know that I...'

'I'm sure you will be hungry after your ordeal. I shall of course explain to Mr and Mrs Greenleaf about your unfortunate experience. You need not exert yourself unduly in conversation, feeling, as I am certain you must, a little... delicate.'

I narrow my eyes to take him in properly. He isn't at all the person he seemed at first. I'm actually beginning to like him. 'Yes, very delicate,' I respond gratefully and turn to trail the maid up the stairs.

The room I'm shown into is very cold and sports an *unlit* fireplace. It has floral wallpaper, a four-poster bed with a pretty patchwork quilt, a wash stand, a polished wood floor partly covered by a faded carpet, and two large windows curtained in heavy blue fabric.

I dab over my face, hands and arms with the lukewarm water the maid brought, and then look on incredulously as she shows me several voluminous dresses once worn by the parson's wife. I want to laugh out loud at the additional padding of the 'bottom' area with a lump of cork. The former occupant of the dresses was of a similar size to myself and must also have had a rather large behind to begin with. I'm forced to give up on modesty and allow Nerys to help me into the various parts of the costume. As she tightens the stays she exclaims about my underwear. I gather that knickers are not even thought of yet, but I refuse to take them off, telling her they help against the cold. Once I'm dressed, she hands me some low-heeled pointy shoes that are a bit too big for me and then tries to put my disarranged curls into some sort of shape, giving up and just tying my hair back with a ribbon when she hears horses drawing up outside.

I'm torn between regarding my blue-clad, tight-waisted, enormous-bottomed self in the mirror and the childlike urge to run to the window and view the novelty of a horse-drawn carriage. Only when Nerys has excused herself and rushed downstairs do I stagger across the room, nearly falling over the too-long hem of my gigantic skirts, and gape out at the well-dressed couple in their thirties being handed out of a coach. This, then, must be the Greenleafs.

I watch as the horses stamp in the snow and drop piles of steaming dung until a servant leads them around and drives them off out of my view. It occurs to me that I'm observing the scene as if it's a film, whereas everything is actually all too real. My stays pinch, and the dress reveals far too much of my ample cleavage. It's also, to my sanitised, 21st-century nostrils, a bit smelly, although mostly of mothballs and lavender. I pull a woollen shawl around my shoulders in the hope that I might stop shivering, to little effect.

When I eventually get up the courage to totter down the stairs, the parlour seems very full, with the squire and his wife laughing and joking with my host. He's actually looking quite genial, perhaps partly explained by the large glass of wine in his hand. He sobers a bit at the sight of me, and I assume he remembers seeing his late wife in the dress I'm wearing. It can't be because I look like the belle of the ball. Even in my own opinion, I look completely hideous.

'Miss Galbraith,' he says, recovering his composure, 'Allow me to introduce you to Mr and Mrs Greenleaf. I have explained to them the difficulties you are having which require you to reside here for at least a few days.'

'Ah, yes. I… I'm pleased to meet you,' I murmur, wondering how you're supposed to greet people in this time. Bow?

Curtsey? A handshake doesn't seem quite right for a woman…
or is it? Kiss hands maybe? No, that's kings and queens, isn't it?

'Likewise, likewise,' says the squire jovially, and Mrs
Greenleaf comes over and takes my hand in hers.

'Such a shame, my dear, to lose all your belongings like that.
To be sure, Mr Edgemond is such a kind soul. You are most
fortunate to have fallen into his hands.'

I have to bite my lips to prevent myself from laughing, and
kind-soul Mr Edgemond also has a glint of amusement in his
eyes, even though his expression remains bland.

'Yes, indeed. I am indebted to him,' I say and give myself
a mental pat on the back for sounding pretty authentic to my
own ears.

Martha, the Mrs Emrys look-alike maid, steps in then and
says, 'Dinner is served,' just like in Upstairs Downstairs.

To my surprise, Mr Edgemond comes over and takes my
arm, and with Anna holding his other hand we stroll behind
the squire and his lady into the next room where, thankfully,
another fire is blazing, ensuring a temperature of a few degrees
above freezing.

I'm seated next to the parson, who's at the head of the
table, and beside Anna, which prevents me from getting into
too much close conversation with the Greenleafs, although I
receive several further condolences from them on my adversity.

It's a very leisurely meal, consisting of several courses. I'm
already full by the time I've ploughed through the fish course of
tasty salmon, but that's followed by two meat courses of pork
and veal that I just pick at to show willing. Somehow I manage
to do a bit more justice to the final course of blackcurrant tarts.

A strange thing happens throughout this dinner. Whenever
I get confused about which knives and forks to use, or how the
meal's conducted, I only have to glance the parson's way to see
he's noticed. By means of unobtrusive gestures, or picking up
the appropriate instrument himself, he manages to keep me
from making any stupid mistakes. It seems odd to me that he
and I are already in such sympathy.

I keep my head down as much as possible and just listen to the fairly parochial conversation, primarily about the Greenleafs' children, their household and local events. I jump to full attention when Mrs Greenleaf says, 'Oh, and of course Branwen Emrys is back from her father's funeral. It's been quite a struggle in the house without her, has it not, my dear? Poor Clara could barely cope.'

Mrs Emrys just back? I clench my hands on my knife and fork, but the parson doesn't mention my being acquainted with her, sparing me the necessity of making up any stories.

The wine and spirits may as well be on tap, with all but Anna and myself indulging very freely. Even Mr Edgemond regards me oddly when I only have a few sips of wine. The wine is actually excellent, but I'm afraid I'll let something slip if I get merry. Besides, I'm quite shocked to see a parson guzzling back the alcohol like this. I'm even more taken aback when the meal's finally over and a game of cards is proposed, with cash involved. This isn't how I imagined things would be in the past. It seems out of character for a vicar to be drinking and gambling, especially to this extent.

I opt to watch, since the only card game I can remember is rummy, and that's not what they're playing. I've no idea what it is they are actually playing and I'm surprised they have either, given the three empty wine bottles and the almost empty bottle of cognac. I try to talk to Anna, who's also sitting out the game. She looks the picture of a demure little lady as she sits aside with her embroidery. I've always wondered how anyone can enjoy sewing, as I detest it. I ask her what she's making.

'It is a sampler. I am making it for Papa,' she says quietly.

I don't know what a sampler is, but it looks pretty, so I attempt encouragement and tell her so, with some success, as I receive a slight, shy smile.

To my horror, when they tire of cards (and the parson has lost a shilling), they decide to have a singsong. I watch in amazement as first the squire sings a fairly lusty ballad, and then Anna is persuaded into playing the harpsichord and singing.

She does so quite sweetly and has a good voice for a ten year old. I'm also impressed by how well she plays and get a roiling in my guts as I realize that they probably learn to play at their mother's or father's knee here, while I've only ever plonked about on a piano, and that with no skill at all.

Mr and Mrs Greenleaf sing a duet, after which the parson, now very rosy of face, sings a rollicking sea shanty that I recall vaguely from my schooldays. They then turn to me expectantly, and I see I can expect no support from Mr Edgemond now, he being, as I think they used to say, 'well in his cups'.

'Come along, Miss Galbraith,' he slurs, 'perhaps you know a Scottish song with which to entertain us?'

I wonder for a minute what on earth he means, but it's a good job he does think I'm Scottish, because I can actually remember a few old songs of the Scottish persuasion.

'Very well,' I say, and look at Anna, still sitting at the harpsichord. 'Do you know "Speed Bonny Boat"?'

She nods and launches into the first few chords. I stand by the parlour fire with my arms covered in goose pimples and pour my all into my first-ever solo rendition of 'The Skye Boat Song', courtesy of schools radio. Who'd have thought it would ever come in handy?

I've never been known as much of a singer, but the others greet my performance with kind enthusiasm, although I'm a bit puzzled when the squire asks me if I'm sympathetic to the Jacobite cause. I automatically say no and wonder if I've made some awful mistake but my luck's in: horses are drawing up outside, and the Greenleafs prepare to leave. When they've gone, after much hand pressing and good wishes, I sink into a chair by the fire, feeling totally shattered. Anna watches me sympathetically. Mr Edgemond pours himself a glass of brandy. I wonder how far advanced his cirrhosis must be.

'A glass for you, Miss Galbraith?' he enquires.

'No, thank you,' I reply politely. 'I'm not much of a drinker, I'm afraid.'

He nods and sits down on the other side of the fire. 'Indeed. Most unusual. And your timepiece, also most unusual,' he adds, gesturing at my wrist. I gasp as I realize that the shawl has fallen away from my arm and revealed my watch. It never occurred to me to take it off. I mean, who even thinks about their watch? It's as normal to wear one as it is to breathe. 'It appears to be faulty,' he continues, lifting his own fob watch out of a pocket in his waistcoat, 'since it is now eight o'clock.'

Luckily, geek or not I've never been a one for digital watches, and mine is set out in Roman numerals, but still, it's hardly what every 18th-century wench is wearing. The time reads eleven thirty. I recall with a wrench that only seven hours ago I was roving around the ruins of Llanycoed in bright June sunlight. I turn the hands to 8.00pm and quickly try and change the subject by saying, 'Um, I need to um… go to… um', which confused sentence apparently makes sense to the parson despite his inebriated state.

'You need to visit the necessary house? Of course. Nerys will show you – unless you would prefer to use the chamber pot in your bedchamber?'

I refuse the generous offer of the chamber pot and trail after the maid into the dark, snowy and slippery yard and out to a kind of shed where she kindly leaves me to it with a single candle for lighting. I realize too late that even a chamber pot might have been better, and in any case how on earth am I meant to manoeuvre myself on to the rude planking over a smelly pit wearing these ample skirts? It's not my finest hour. As I slide and shiver back to the house, I wonder how soon I can return to the snowdrift and escape to the 21st century, with its lovely flush toilets and water spouting miraculously out of the taps.

I find the parson alone in the parlour. He's reading a book but puts it down when I come in, telling me that Anna has gone to bed and he's dismissed the servants for the evening.

'You acquitted yourself well this afternoon, Miss Galbraith, for a woman who dropped from the sky. Are you now able to explain how this singular event came to take place? It is clear that you are out of your element.'

'Well, yes, I'm not too sure of the customs,' I say carefully, unsure that I can even attempt to explain the situation.

'But you are clearly of some breeding. You speak well, and I assume you can read and write.'

'Yes, of course,' I say, bemused at being described as 'of some breeding,' when as an orphan, I grew up feeling like the lowest of the low.

'You have already informed me that you are not a member of the servant class. Perhaps you have been a governess? That is an honourable occupation for a genteel lady of limited means.'

'Er no, I haven't been a governess,' I stammer, and wonder where this conversation is going.

Mr Edgemond strokes his pursed lips thoughtfully. 'No, you do not belong here at all, do you? Your garments, your manner, even your turn of phrase, all demonstrate amply that you are from elsewhere.'

'My manner and turn of phrase? But I am trying, I mean, to get it right, only history was never one of my... er... oh... I mean...' I trail off, blushing and perspiring.

The parson sits bolt upright in his chair. 'History was never one of your what?' He asks sternly, with his rather attractive brown eyes locked on me. He shows no sign of his former inebriation.

'Never one of my subjects,' I respond lamely.

He nods slowly, his eyes still fixed on me. 'You did not study history,' he states.

'Well, I mean a bit, but not much.'

'And how is this relevant? You are suggesting that to you this is history – that you have by some means dropped into the past?'

I nod helplessly. I'm quickly losing any control over my situation. If the parson decides I'm a witch or a candidate for Bedlam, I'll be doomed.

'From what date?'

'From the 21st century.'

He gasps and sits back in his chair, stroking his lips and gazing into the fire. It's several minutes before he speaks again.

'I cannot but believe you came from somewhere Other, having seen it with my own eyes, but you are fortunate, Miss Galbraith, that it was me and no one else who did see it. Dressed as you were, appearing out of the air, you were a disquieting sight.' He pauses and then adds, 'As an enthusiast of science, I can appreciate possibilities that some do not, but it would be most unwise to mention this to anyone else.'

'But you're a parson,' I blurt out. 'I didn't think parsons in the 18th century were interested in science.'

He smiles, and once again I feel a jolt at the change in his appearance. 'As you have already informed me that your knowledge of this century is scanty, Miss Galbraith, I do not doubt that there is much about parsons of which you are unaware.'

I grin back, taking his comment as more of a jest than a rebuke. 'Well that's true, but in any case you might not have to put up with me for much longer. If I can return to the snowdrift, perhaps I can get back to where I belong.'

'And that is your dearest wish? You do not desire to remain here and gain knowledge of some of the history you lack?' he says.

'Well that's very tempting, but I feel quite out of my depth.'

'You may find it is not so simple as you imagine. I don't quite comprehend how you are to return to the sky. You have yet to explain by what agency you arrived.'

I frown and bite my lip. 'I don't know. I was there one minute and here the next. It was like there was a hole in the ground, and I was sucked into it. I suppose the ground must be higher there. It's the same place though, still Llanycoed.' I cut myself off as I realize that *my* Llanycoed was destroyed in the earthquake and that the earthquake had occurred in the 18th century. Not yet though, not quite – the book said 1799. Twenty years from now. I shake my head. What does it all mean? Am I going to find those elusive answers here?

The parson watches me keenly. 'I should like to know what manner of world you are from, Miss Galbraith. How have we progressed in three hundred years?'

'It's two hundred and... twenty-nine years,' I say distractedly, my mind taken up with fears of being stranded. 'I'm from 2008.'

'And so. I conclude that there are many differences. And in more than manner of dress and in watches,' he says.

'Well yes, there are many,' I say, 'the most noticeable thing is plumbing.'

'Plumbing?'

'Water piped into the house and indoor... um... necessaries.'

He raises his eyebrows. 'I have heard that they are piping water into some London homes. Also I believe that there are some among the aristocracy who have what they call water closets.'

I'm surprised. 'Yes, water closets, but everyone has them. And hot and cold water out of the taps.'

'But then how is it heated?'

'Um, that's hard to explain, really.' Obviously this isn't impressive enough. 'We don't use horses and carriages any more,' I try. 'We have other, much faster vehicles, and planes, um, that fly in the sky.'

Yes, that hits the spot! I try to describe it all to him, but it's hard going, because he wants to know how everything works. He wasn't joking about being interested in science. It's not that I don't know the answers but that he lacks the basic framework for me to lay them out on. It's like describing magic.

He's both an interested and an interesting person to spend time with. When I talk, he gives me his full attention, and his eyes are alight with enthusiasm. The dour man I first saw has receded, and in his place is someone I'd like to get to know.

My voice is hoarse and the candles are down to stubs when we finally wind down and head for our beds. To my surprise I'm actually sorry to part with him on the landing.

Back in my icy bedchamber with the solitary candle smoking and guttering in the chilly draught coming through the distinctly single-glazed window, it dawns on me that, as the servants were dismissed early, I have to somehow get myself out of the layers of garments into which I was thrust hours earlier.

After about half an hour of tugging, dragging and shivering, I'm finally free of the tight, chafing stays and glad to don the thick nightgown that's been kindly placed on the bed, presumably by Nerys. A nightcap has also been provided, but I decide to give that a miss. As I climb between the chilly sheets, I wonder if I'll be able to get any sleep in such a cold room.

CHAPTER EIGHT

When I wake up, it's quite a shock. Not only have I slept soundly in a room temperature of just above freezing, but also I'm still in the 18th century. Damn, it wasn't all a dream!

There's a tentative knock at the door, and Nerys enters. 'It's ten o'clock, Miss, and Mr Edgemond wanted me to see if you needed anything. He's below stairs now, having his breakfast.'

She has a jug of water with her, which she places by the washstand. 'Will you be needing any help dressing, Miss? Only the parson said you were to wear any of Mrs Edgemond's clothes you like.'

I jump out of bed and realize I'm in dire need of the 'necessary house'. I groan aloud and Nerys turns to me, puzzled.

'Er, yes, I shall need help, Nerys, but could you come back in a few minutes? I plan to go for a walk outside later. Perhaps you'll know what would be the best thing to wear.'

She looks at me with wide eyes but leaves me alone. I groan again and reach under the bed. Chamber pots! But even that has to be better than manoeuvring my voluminous skirts in the outside shed.

That duty over, I gasp my way through a cursory wash with the icy water in the jug. Yesterday's lukewarm water must have been a special treat.

Nerys helps me into a less dressy but no less uncomfortable and unbecoming gown, and fusses yet again over my hair, putting it up and leaving some natural curls around my face. Finally I trip downstairs, my heart banging just a little bit harder than usual at the prospect of seeing the parson again.

He's seated at the dining table, alone, which leads me to wonder where Anna is. He smiles at the sight of me and puts down the newspaper he's reading to stand up and bow slightly in an old-fashioned gesture of courtesy. 'Good morning, Miss Galbraith,' he says and pulls out a chair. 'I hope you have an appetite.'

It's a good job I do, because laid out on the sideboard are dishes containing bacon, eggs, oatmeal and bread rolls. I tuck in, and the parson watches me intently for a while, remarking casually that the weather is fine although still cold and frosty, and that the temperature within doors is forty-eight degrees *with* a fire. I'm not at all surprised as I'm shivering yet again, despite the shawl covering my arms and bosom.

Eventually he says, 'Our talk last night was most interesting, Miss Galbraith. When I awoke this morning I did at first wonder if I had dreamt it, as I took rather a lot of wine and spirits. However, I apprehend that you still desire to find the snowdrift into which you fell, and that you propose to attempt a return to this incredible century in which you can travel the world in hours.'

I nod and chew on the bacon, which tastes a lot better than any I'm used to. Weren't there some pigs grunting outside last night when I went to the necessary house? I look down at the rasher on my plate and shrug inwardly. In this world, everything's much closer to home. Besides, I won't be here long. I hope.

'You have not, then, changed your mind?' he asks.

'I have to at least try,' I say, almost apologetically.

He nods slowly, pursing his lips. 'I cannot help but wonder why there might be such a link between our times.'

'I can't help wondering that as well. I just fell through the ground.'

'There was no one else present?'

'No. No. It was... the village was very quiet.' How can I tell him about the state it's in?

When I've finished eating, we prepare to set off out. There's obviously no question that he will accompany me. Nerys kindly provides me with a cloak that I can only say enhances my revolting appearance, as my backside looks colossal in it.

As we slip down the rough, icy lane, Mr Edgemond says, 'You look well in my late wife's garments, Miss Galbraith. You are a fine figure of a woman.'

I come to an incredulous halt and he turns back to look at me in surprise. 'Is something amiss?'

I shake my head and catch up with him, confining my reply to a small, 'Thank you.' Somehow I don't think he'll understand my amazement. Thin doesn't seem to be a priority in the 18th century.

The view is impressive now that I'm in a position to appreciate it: classic Christmas card snow and pretty, half-timbered houses. There are even a few geese roaming around, as well as some mangy-looking dogs. In addition, there's the occasional horse and cart passing by. I want to record it all to take home, and I remember that my digital camera is in my bag. I'm just wondering whether to risk using such a magical item when the parson says, 'I shall be sorry to see you go. Your brief stay has been greatly diverting.'

I feel a pinprick of regret at leaving so hurriedly. After all, I haven't even seen Felin Gyfriniaeth close to, or taken any photos, or encountered Mrs Emrys, or had the chance to get to know Mr Edgemond better. On the plus side, hopefully I won't be getting smallpox, typhoid, rabies or any of the other horrifying diseases that are rife, and I'll never take flush toilets for granted again.

When we arrive at the crossroads the bulk of the snowdrift is still there, looking as innocent as a snowdrift can look. My optimism starts to fade as I walk around it, lifting my arms to feel for something to get hold of. I'm a novice time-traveller after all; I have no idea what to do. The parson watches silently, his lips twitching a little at my futile actions. It's lucky that we're in a country lane and have left the houses behind, but I'm still conscious of how ridiculous I must appear.

Crabwise, I clamber up the snowdrift, which has fortunately hardened into ice overnight, and kneel on the top – hard to do in that garb, I can tell you – asking Mr Edgemond if he can remember from where I fell. When he says he thinks I'm in the exact spot, I wave my hands about desperately and come up with precisely nothing. In desperation I try to stand on the drift and jump up, which results in my slithering down into a familiar ungainly heap and causing a mini avalanche. Mr Edgemond comes to my aid and helps me up, suggesting that I'll catch cold if I persist, but I'm starting to panic. In desperation I try all of these strategies twice more, until the snowdrift has collapsed completely. He stands watching me with his arms folded and a distinct gleam in his eye.

'I think perhaps you will be staying with us for a little longer, Miss Galbraith,' he says, his amusement barely suppressed.

Hands on hips, I glare first at him and then at the demolished snowdrift. Now what? Surely I'm not going to be stranded here for the rest of my days? If so, I suspect those days are going to be seriously numbered. Life in the sanitary and cocooned 21st century is a poor preparation for this disease-filled era.

'But what am I going to do here?' I say in a small voice. 'I can't impose on you for long, no matter how much of a kind soul Mrs Greenleaf says you are.'

He smiles and pats my arm. 'I shall not object to your staying with me indefinitely, and I can educate you in the ways of *this* century, if required. Come, it is cold and we have tarried here long enough. I must make a visit to the church, and then we can return to the parsonage.'

I trail along beside him, feeling lost and dejected. Out of the corner of my eye I notice him taking surreptitious glances at me, but he says no more.

As we enter the lych gate and walk to the church door I rummage in my bag for the camera. The parson turns to look as I take it out. It's one of the miniature ones, but it's still ten megapixels with lots of functions, just the way we geeks like them. I'm not sure exactly when the camera was invented, but suspect it was long after the 18th century.

'What is that silver box?' he asks, opening the church door with a flourish.

'It's er, it's a small machine that takes er... well, takes pictures,' I say, my voice echoing into the deserted wooden pews.

'Takes pictures? I am afraid I do not apprehend your meaning.'

'It, er, captures the likeness,' I try, and congratulate myself once again on sounding authentic. 'The best way to show you would be to demonstrate,' I add, and point it at him as he stands in the aisle. In the dim interior of the church the flash goes off, startling him so much that he nearly falls backwards and has to grab hold of a nearby pew.

'What was that light?' he gasps.

'It's the machine; it makes light to illuminate the scene,' I say and click quickly to display mode to view the picture. Not one of his better moments, given the startled expression. I hand the camera to him anyway.

He stares at the picture in silence and finally sits down in the pew as though his legs won't hold him up. His hand is shaking. 'I could not have imagined such a device,' he murmurs. I decide not to show him my mobile in case it throws him into a premature cardiac arrest.

He hands back the camera reluctantly and totters down the aisle, pointing out various aspects of his church that he thinks are of interest. I take a couple more photos, but don't get too carried away in view of the absence of electricity or batteries here. I'd better save the camera for special shots – always assuming there's going to be a point at which I'll be back home to look at them.

'I must pray for a time,' he tells me, and with complete lack of self-consciousness settles down in a pew to do just that, while I sit nearby and try to adjust to my new circumstances. Natural ebullience is coming to my aid. I fell in; surely I'll fall back out eventually? In the meantime, getting to know the parson better won't be at all onerous, and maybe I'll find my answers here. I try very hard not to dwell on chamber pots and nasty smells and germs.

When he gets up, the parson informs me that tomorrow's Sunday, and he'll be preaching at the church. 'I hope you will be able to come,' he adds.

'Well,' I hesitate, remembering all those compulsory Sunday morning church visits when I was at Summerdale and how dreary I used to find them. 'Of course I shall,' I say brightly. 'What's your sermon going to be about?'

'I believe I shall be changing it,' he says obliquely.

We chat quite companionably as we stroll back to the parsonage, and he returns to the topic of the future, while also repeating that he'll need to educate me if I'm to stay, adding, 'I can't deny that I am glad you are to remain here, Miss Galbraith.' It sounds formal, but he says it so warmly that I'm moved. He's obviously lonely, and once I get past the wig and the funny costume, he's growing on me.

Back at the house we find Anna and a thin lady in the parlour with books open on their laps.

'This is Miss Roberts, who comes in to tutor Anna thrice a sennight,' he tells me, leaving me momentarily baffled as I translate the word 'sennight' into 'week', never having heard it before.

Miss Roberts is in her late fifties and is dressed in black. The costumes of the times were really made for her figure. Why they wanted to emphasise backsides is beyond me. Obviously the phrase least likely to be uttered by an 18th-century woman is, 'Does my bum look big in this?'

The parson looks a little harassed as he glances from me to Miss Roberts, but he says finally, 'I do hope you will excuse me, Miss Galbraith, but I must rewrite my sermon. There are books, should you wish to read them,' and he points to a small bookcase by the window.

'Of course,' I say automatically, but with a sinking feeling as he hastens away.

Luckily Miss Roberts is very conscientious and returns to her teaching, leaving me to pretend to read the first book that came into my hand while really listening to what Anna's learning. I'm quite impressed. I have no idea how highly a parson stands in this society, but obviously parsons' daughters are normally educated. Weren't the Brontë sisters a parson's daughters? Was this their era? I drift off on a flight of fancy and imagine myself coming across literary heroines like the Brontë sisters or Jane Austen. Then I remember that no one wears wigs in Jane Austen's books – and neither did Heathcliff or Mr Rochester. Damn. I try to visualize Colin Firth's Mr Darcy in a wig like the parson's and almost laugh out loud. Well, Mr Edgemond's no Colin Firth, that's for sure.

Cooking aromas are issuing through the house again by the time the parson returns, looking quite pleased with himself. With an apologetic smile in my direction, he turns to Anna and Miss Roberts and quizzes them about today's lessons. I carry on pretending to read, but the book's pretty impenetrable, the language very flowery.

Miss Roberts joins us for dinner, which I'm glad to say isn't as huge as yesterday's but still consists of great dollops of roast pork, along with pease pudding, which is actually quite tasty, and apple tarts to follow. I had wondered how I'd manage it after the huge breakfast, and it's a struggle, but everyone else eats with enthusiasm, and Miss Roberts isn't averse to a few vats of alcohol either.

Despite seeming to drink enough to put himself under the table, the parson doesn't appear drunk when the meal's over. When we've bid Miss Roberts good evening, he suggests that we engage in a game of cards. He forestalls my protests by saying that he and Anna will teach me. He seems to have no problem with Anna playing card games, although I note that he doesn't propose to gamble this time.

It's a companionable and pleasant couple of hours, and Anna shows signs of coming out of her shell with me as she points out the numerous deficiencies in my card-playing ability. The parson seems relaxed, and he's held off on the booze since our meal.

When Anna's gone to bed, he asks to look at my camera again, and spends several minutes gazing at the pictures I took at the church. I take another one of him, and persuade him to take one of me, and then decide it's time to commence my 'education'.

'I need to know a few basic things,' I say. 'Like who's the king, and what's "the Jacobite cause"?'

He actually laughs out loud then, the first time I've heard him do so.

'Your knowledge of history must indeed be scanty, Miss Galbraith, if you don't know your kings and queens. Very well. Our king is His Majesty King George the Third,' he says, and I can hear those capital letters, 'and the Jacobites are those who believe that the Stuarts, rather than the Hanoverians, are the true successors to the throne.'

'The Stuarts – oh, Mary Queen of Scots, King James, King Charles,' I say, dredging them all up from some forgotten well of memory.

'Indeed. And, of course, "Bonnie Prince Charlie", about whom you sang so well last night. As a Scot, I imagined that you would know about whom you were singing, but you do not have a Scottish accent, despite the name.'

'No, it was my father who was Scottish,' I explain, basking in his praise of my indifferent singing. 'I've always lived in England.'

'And now you are here, almost in Wales. If you are a local, as was my mother, you are likely to be adamant that it is still Wales. However, I do not believe you are a local. You are perhaps from the south of England?'

'I moved here just a few weeks ago, to live at Felin Gyfriniaeth,' I tell him.

His ever-mobile eyebrows lift again. 'You are living at the watermill?'

I nod. 'But it's not a watermill anymore; it's just a house. It would be interesting to pay it a visit and see what it's like now.'

'Then we shall do so. By the by, I cannot help but notice that you are considerably averse to liquor. Is it frowned upon in the 21st century?'

I cough. 'Er, no, not exactly. It's not that I'm averse; it's just that... um... well... you seem to drink a lot of it. I'm not used to... um... seeing parsons drink so much. They're quite abstemious, as a rule. And we've learned that too much alcohol – er liquor – can be dangerous and cause many illnesses.'

He frowns. 'I assure you that I don't drink to excess, Miss Galbraith; on the contrary. Dr Benbow advises that plenty of port wine is good for the health – he recommends a maximum of two pints a day, and I have not become ill by it.'

I have trouble keeping a straight face. I can't imagine what counts as excess if the parson's drinking is merely moderate. 'It takes years to progress,' I say, 'and... well, our medical knowledge has increased quite a lot in two hundred years.'

He looks at me as though seeing me for the first time and shakes his head. 'It seems you have scientific understanding that I lack. It is inconceivable to me that a woman might have such an education.'

'Women's roles have changed,' I say slowly, feeling my way over touchy ground. 'We have the same schooling as men, and we do the same jobs.'

'That is most interesting, but surely a woman's priority is to be a wife and mother?'

I almost glare at him but restrain myself and say merely, 'Anna seems to be receiving a good education. What do you want for her when she grows up?'

'Why that she should be happy and marry well,' he replies.

'Just marry and have children? Not more? Not succeed in another area?'

He frowns, and I worry that I'm pushing it. After all, he's a parson, which according to my prejudices indicates that he's likely to be traditional in his views.

'In what area do you mean? Once she is married, her husband will support her. Am I to deduce that this is not the case in your century?'

'A married couple often both work,' I reply. 'But if there are children then the man usually works while the woman cares for them.'

His eyebrows rise so high he's almost knocking his wig off. 'The man *usually* works?' he repeats. 'Then there are occasions when the woman works and the man cares for the children?'

I nod slowly, my eyes locked on his.

He sighs, suddenly and explosively, and then inexplicably begins to laugh and carries on laughing for some time.

When he finally sobers, he says, 'Miss Galbraith, I must thank you for falling into my hands, as it were. You have brought me much amusement and interest. I can scarce imagine what other horrors you have to tell me, but I shall surely enjoy hearing them.'

I stare at him with my mouth open. 'But it's true. I mean, that's how it is.'

'I am sure it is,' he replies, 'but you must consider what an incredible world you describe. You will tell me next that women can become parsons!'

I bite my lip, and his eyebrows disappear under the wig before he starts to chuckle again. 'No, it is unimaginable,' he gurgles, until I give up.

'Very well,' I say, and put on a prim, schoolmarmish tone, 'If you can only imagine women as subordinate to men, so be it, but I can assure you I'm not the subordinate type.'

'I have little doubt that you are not. You are unlike any woman I have yet encountered.'

'And is that good or bad?' I ask, grinning.

'It is assuredly good, although profoundly disconcerting,' he replies.

CHAPTER NINE

I have his repository of advice in mind when we cross the road to the church after breakfast the following morning. Luckily there's been a thaw overnight and much of the snow has melted, although some dirty piles are still lying at the roadside. The thaw also means that we have to dodge the horse-muck on the road – for road, read rutted dirt track – but at least it's warmer.

Mr Edgemond is wearing his cassock and looks disconcertingly vicarly, and I feel very self-conscious as I trip along beside him and Anna in my too-long skirts. People greet him respectfully and file into the church in reasonable numbers, dressed in their Sunday best. Beside the dream-like nature of the experience, I'm also extremely nervous at my first outing among so many people.

The parson leaves us in what he calls 'his seat', which is a special, enclosed pew in the chancel with a good view of the pulpit and the standard pews in the nave. Mr and Mrs Greenleaf nod and smile pleasantly at us from their pew opposite. I grip my prayer book tightly. I try to convince myself it's just the tension, but when Mr Edgemond reappears wearing his vestments, my heart starts thumping again.

A lot of the service is familiar enough for me to feel that I'm back at Summerdale. The prayers and responses are easy to remember from those times, but there are no actual hymns, or even an organ. Instead, the singers, a mere five of them, sitting in the choir stalls in front of me, break into psalms every now and again.

I spend most of the time observing Mr Edgemond, wondering how religious he really is and why he became a parson, especially when he reads, rather ringingly, from the epistle, 'For this is the will of God, even your sanctification, that ye should abstain from fornication; that every one of you should know how to possess his vessel in sanctification and honour; not in the lust of concupiscence...'

Hmmm. Well he's good at reading the lessons anyway. Yet at no time since I met him has he seemed one of those overtly devout people who get on your nerves because they can barely utter a sentence without bringing God into it.

As he steps up into the pulpit for his sermon, I really *am* almost on the edge of my seat. To my surprise, he glances my way before he starts, and when he does begin, he doesn't read from notes.

There's no blood and thunder and talk of hellfire and brimstone, which I was expecting in this era. Instead, he talks about how the unexpected can come up, both good and bad, refers to the deaths of loved ones, like his own wife, and the happy events like Christenings – he mentions a specific local birth of twins in which both have survived despite being early – and how God provides us with these unforeseen events that can change our lives and make us see things differently. He has no artifice at all, and I find it endearing when he turns and looks right at me on the 'change our lives' part, in full view of his entire congregation.

After the service, just like vicars I recall, he stands at the church door and chats with everyone as they leave. Anna and I, standing nearby, are subject to a lot of attention, especially me. I'm obliged to engage in small talk with what seems like half the population of the village and surrounding area, most of them commiserating with me on my misfortune and adding what a kind soul Mr Edgemond is, and how melancholy he's been since his wife died, and even how 'little Anna' would love to have a new mother! Poor Anna's standing quietly by my side. I wonder how much she would really like to have a new mother. I'm not much of an expert on father-daughter dynamics, but she and the parson seem quite close.

The Greenleafs come over, having just chatted to the parson, and tell me that we're both invited to dinner at the Hall in two days' time. I put on a smile of thanks, but my heart sinks. What etiquette will be required for that? On the other hand, it might give me a chance to lay eyes on Mrs Emrys and Mr Linlade. I'm assuming Mrs Emrys is a cook maid and will be serving the food, so I'm bound to see her.

It's as the three of us are walking back through the lych gate that one little piece of the puzzle drops into its slot. Now that the snow's melted, it's easier to get my bearings between this Llanycoed and mine, and when the parsonage and all its outbuildings come into view I recognise it as the house with walls still standing. I stop in the lane with my hand clamped over my mouth, and my companions turn back in alarm.

'Miss Galbraith, are you feeling unwell?' the parson asks, coming back to my side.

Truth to tell, I am actually feeling faint. It hits me that the voices I heard must surely have been those of Anna and Mr Edgemond. 'I… um… I do feel a little strange,' I manage to get out, and I put up no protest whatsoever when he puts his arm about my shoulders to help me into the house.

Once I'm ensconced in a chair and starting to feel better again, I'm embarrassed to see the anxious look on his face.

'I'm all right, really,' I say weakly. There's no way I can tell him what's wrong, or that his house is going to be utterly wrecked in twenty years' time, and so I add, 'It's just hard to get used to at times, that's all.'

Gratifyingly, this results in him taking my hand, and he's not all that quick to relinquish it when we proceed to the small parlour for dinner.

Although there are only the three of us, the spread is still enormous, but I enjoy the roast beef and roast potatoes followed by plum pudding. Oddly, the parson isn't throwing back the jugs of wine as per his usual habit. He's only opened one bottle. He notices me looking at it and smiles wryly. Anna looks from him to me with an air of mild puzzlement but says nothing.

Not long after the meal, he has to leave to say prayers with a dying man, so I ask Anna to teach me to play the harpsichord. She thinks it's great fun having to show an adult woman, and we get easy enough with each other for her to ask me, 'Do you like my papa?'

'Yes, I like him,' I reply solemnly.

'He likes you. He's happy with you here.'

'Was he very unhappy before?'

'He was different. More serious. Except when he had guests.'

'What about you? Are you happy?'

'I believe so,' she says, sounding just like her father. 'I'm looking forward to going away to school.'

'I'm sure your papa will miss you when you're away,' I say, surprised to learn that boarding schools for girls exist.

She nods. 'Yes, I think he will. He does not like to be alone, but he says my education will suffer if I remain at home. Miss Roberts has taught me all she can, and Papa knows little about female accomplishment.'

'There's more to life than embroidery, harpsichord playing and singing.'

'They also teach French, reading and drawing.'

'Do you like to learn? Do you like to know how the world works like your papa does?'

She gazes at me. 'Miss Roberts says it is not a woman's place to study such things.'

'If you're interested in them, it's anyone's place,' I say firmly.

Nerys comes in to take Anna off to bed, preventing me from making any more such seditious comments. Left alone in the parlour, I hunch in front of the fire and dwell on all my new problems.

Luckily, the object of most of my thoughts returns before I collapse under their weight, and despite the sad nature of his mission, he's in good spirits. He tells me he administered the holy sacrament and the man seemed happier and easier afterwards.

Once he's settled down in the chair on the other side of the fireplace with a glass of brandy in his hand, I ask him about something that's really been getting on my nerves.

'Do we have to keep on calling each other by our formal names? I don't really like being called Miss Galbraith. I'd prefer it if you called me Fallady.'

He purses his lips thoughtfully. 'It is not customary to be so familiar on such a brief acquaintance, but I am willing to make an exception in your case, Mi – Fallady. My Christian name is Walter.'

Not exactly a dashing name, but it does seem to suit him.

'Anna told me about going away to school,' I say.

'Indeed. She is very keen to go.'

I nod. 'But she worries that you'll miss her.'

'I would keep her here, were it not likely that it would damage her future prospects.'

'Her future prospects of marrying someone who values her ability to sew and draw and look pretty?' I say, mentally daring him to rise to this bait.

He glares at me narrowly, but his lips form a wry smile as he says, 'Do I take it then, Mi – Fallady, that you cannot sew or draw? Are 21st-century females totally deficient in the feminine arts?'

'That depends on the female,' I say. 'There are those who like drawing and sewing, but those who don't like them have the option to choose alternatives.'

'There cannot surely be many women who would wish to be doctors or parsons. I have thought much upon your revelation of yesterday, but no matter how hard I try to envisage it, a female parson is inconceivable.'

'Why did you become a parson?' I ask. 'Did you have a vocation?'

'A vocation? Not, I think, in the sense that you mean it. It was rather a matter of expediency. My father was a parson, and as an able student I achieved a scholarship to Oxford, where it seemed natural to follow in his footsteps. It is a good living and enables me to spend considerable time on my scientific interests.'

This isn't what I expected at all. 'So you're not devout? I mean, not really, really religious?'

'I hope I am as devout and religious as a parson needs to be. I am not sure I apprehend your meaning, but I gather from various remarks that clergymen in your time differ somewhat. It seems,' he says teasingly, 'that they are veritable saints who barely touch a drop of wine or spirits and devote all their time to prayer and religious pursuits.'

I chuckle. 'Well, something like that. I enjoyed your sermon, by the way.'

He smiles slightly. 'Thank you. I note that the liturgy can't have altered a great deal in two centuries, since you seemed well acquainted with the prayers and responses.'

'Well, yes,' I reply, surprised that he noticed. 'I used to attend church a lot as a child. But we sing hymns now; that's about the only difference.'

He nods. 'Hymns are the province of the dissenters, but it has seemed likely for a few years that they would eventually encroach into Anglican services.'

I have no idea what he's talking about, so just nod as if I do.

'Tell me,' he says, eyeing me intently, 'what was really wrong with you this morning?'

I groan. 'You mean you weren't fooled? You seemed most sympathetic at the time.'

'I *was* most sympathetic, but you do not strike me as someone who would be momentarily overcome without real cause. What was it that affected you so suddenly?'

'It was the parsonage,' I say. 'I recognised it from *my* Llanycoed, where it's just a ruin.'

He nods but doesn't seem surprised. 'I suppose that buildings don't last forever, although it seems regrettable. Then it was merely the shock of recognition?' he says, with a sceptical lift of his eyebrows.

I shrug. 'All right, I'll tell you. Walter, you need to leave this house before 1799, because on October the twenty-fourth the village will be struck by an earthquake that will leave only Felin Gyfriniaeth standing.'

There, I've said it. Now I'll start disappearing from all the photos.

He sits back in his chair and stares at me for so long I wonder what he can be thinking. Finally he intones, 'O the depth of the riches both of the wisdom and knowledge of God! His ways are unfathomable indeed.'

My eyes are wide with surprise. It's the first time he's said anything so... well... vicarly!

'How do you mean?' I ask.

'Your presence here, my dear. It is God's will.'

'You think God made a hole between times for me to fall through?' I can't hide the disbelief in my voice.

He regards me stolidly. 'As you are aware, I have a considerable interest in the sciences, yet in the circumstances you describe I cannot but believe it is the Lord's doing.'

'There must be a scientific explanation,' I insist. 'We just don't know what it is.' I can't believe the same old conflict is cropping up here.

'I conclude then that all your machinery and running taps and indoor necessaries have led to a less religious time than this, despite your abstemious and pious parsons? I suspect you may be an unbeliever, Fallady.'

'Would it matter to you if I am?' I ask, and hold my breath for his reply.

He considers, pursing his lips. 'Perhaps not,' he says finally. 'But if so, why did you come to church this morning?'

'For your sake, because I knew you wished it,' I reply. I can't resist it, I add: 'I thought you looked most fetching in your vestments. You're a fine figure of a man.'

His burst of laughter fills the room. 'Most fetching,' he repeats between guffaws. 'A fine figure of a man!'

I sit back and watch him in satisfaction. I knew instinctively that he'd laugh. It's a peculiar thing to find someone on the same wavelength in so many ways and yet totally alien in others.

I lean towards him. 'There's just one thing I'd like to know.'

'And what is that?' he asks, still chuckling.

'What do you look like without the wig?'

This only prompts further merriment, but when he's recovered and wiped his eyes, he says, 'My dear, you are quite a tonic. As to how I look sans wig, I do not believe I shall appear half as fetching.'

'Why do you wear one? I mean, I noticed that not all the men at church were wearing them. There were a few of them without.'

'Yes, that is true. There are some who are wearing their own hair, but not many, certainly none among the clergy or the gentry. I suppose one becomes accustomed to it. Am I to conclude that wigs are no longer worn in the 21st century?'

'You conclude correctly. They haven't been worn for around two hundred years.'

He purses his lips. 'It is possible that I might stop wearing it,' he says uncertainly.

'You could just take it off now,' I suggest with a cheeky grin.

Ignoring this, he reaches to take my hand. 'My dear, do you still anticipate a return to the 21st century? From my observations it does not seem likely.'

I shrug. 'I'm trying not to think about it. I suppose I'm just expecting something to happen, but I don't know what or when.'

'And should the Lord desire you to remain?' he says, and I glare at him, knowing he's being deliberately provocative.

'I don't know. I don't belong here. As I said before, what can I do? Obviously I can't be a parson or a doctor, or any one of a huge number of other interesting things.'

'An atheist parson would be a contradiction,' he teases. 'But there are other roles. Parson's wife, for instance.'

My own eyebrows almost reach my hairline. 'Are you asking me to marry you?'

'I am suggesting a possible place for you, should your hopes of returning home fail.'

I'm momentarily speechless. 'B-but you hardly know me,' I finally manage to stutter. 'It's only been three days!'

He presses my hand, still held in his. 'I consider that we would do well together. I also trust in God, albeit that you do not. What I am saying, my dear, is that you need not despair, should you remain stranded here. I should be glad if you were to stay, but I shall not try to prevent your departure, should God see fit to return you home.'

I feel a bit overwhelmed, so I try to lighten the atmosphere. 'I seem to recall your mentioning "devilry" when I dropped in.'

He laughs. 'That was before I had made your acquaintance.'

'Suppose we did marry and *then* I returned home? It seems to me that we'd both get hurt, and given what everyone's told me about how lonely you've been since your wife died, it doesn't seem right for you to be hurt again.'

'Those are admirable sentiments, Fallady, but I am five and forty years old and unlikely to find another that I care to make my wife. Should we have only one day or should we have years, I consider it to be worth the risk.'

It's a long time before I get to sleep that night. Our conversation has left me anxious and confused, and I lie in bed and listen to the wind whistling through the window panes, watching my candle flickering and wondering how it would be to stay here for the rest of my life.

I'd certainly lose my independence, because no matter what Walter says, it's clear that a woman in this time lacks the kind of freedom I take for granted. I haven't even told him about diseases yet and how much more prone to them I'm likely to be. I can't imagine the difficulties of life in an age that's pre-railway, let alone pre-car. I can't even ride a horse. But it's not as if I have a choice. I'm stuck here with no sign of a way out. Even if I wanted to try the same spot again, the snowdrift's melted.

CHAPTER TEN

It's lucky there's no culture of early rising, because having been awake half the night, I sleep through until ten, when Nerys finally taps on the door to make sure I'm all right.

I'm yawning when I finally go downstairs. I eat a small, solitary breakfast, and then Nerys directs me to the parson's study. He's alone, working at his desk amid a small pile of rocks. Classifying them, I assume.

He smiles as I enter and puts down his magnifying glass. 'Good morning, my dear. You slept in late. I trust you are feeling well?'

I have to admit that every time he says 'my dear', it gives me a warm, rosy feeling, but after my disturbed night it's not enough to lift my mood. I plump myself down in the chair in front of his desk and sigh. 'Yes, I'm feeling well,' I reply, realizing that it's true. So far I haven't succumbed to food poisoning, at least. As far as all the other diseases go, there's that little thing called the incubation period, so who knows.

'You seem out of spirits. Perhaps you would benefit by a walk to Felin Gyfriniaeth?'

I cheer up at that, and in no time we're strolling through the village on a typically British grey day. The weather's done a complete turnabout, and it's quite warm for the first of March. I've stopped shivering at last.

'I do hope your low spirits are not consequent upon my proposal,' the parson says earnestly as we dodge the piles of horse-muck on the road. 'I would not wish to make you uneasy.'

'Well I'm not expecting to get married any time soon,' I say. 'Something's bound to turn up to get me home. I can't accept that I've left that life behind for good.'

He nods sympathetically. 'But there is no other – no other beau – there for you?'

I give a wry laugh. 'No, nothing like that.'

A posh-looking carriage lurches past, and the well-dressed couple within nod to the parson, who touches his peculiar tricorn hat and bows slightly in a deferential manner.

'Do you regret never marrying? Never having children?' he asks.

I shake my head. 'No. I never really wanted children, and marriage just seems like a trap.' I lift my dragging skirts to avoid a splatter of fresh dung. 'You see, you might regret ever making that proposal if I were to accept it. We have a saying, "not the marrying kind", and I think I'm one of those.'

He chuckles. 'We have that saying too, my dear, but I am not sure there is anything so fixed as that. If your husband was in accord with you, I hope you would not feel trapped.'

'In this time when women are expected to obey their husbands, and where their main duties seem to consist of having babies, housekeeping, sewing and such, how could I begin to fit in?'

Despite our being out in public, he takes my hand and squeezes it. 'Do you think you would be able to keep house?' he asks innocently, and the glint of mischief is back in his eye.

'Not likely, no,' I say huffily.

'And darn my socks? And cook my tarts?' he continues teasing, his mirth barely suppressed.

We've reached the stream, and I stare at the water as it slides over grey pebbles before turning back to him. 'All right then, so how would I fill my days?'

'How did you fill them in the 21st century?'

'I worked five days a week when I lived in London.'

'What was the work you were used to do?' he asks with interest.

I try to describe my old systems administrator job at Solstice Clothing, but he just looks confused.

'You looked after machines? Like the Spinning Jenny?' he asks.

'It's difficult to explain,' I say. 'We have machines for everything. You do realize I barely know one end of a horse from the other?'

'Fallady, I don't care that you know nothing about horses; I can teach you to ride, if you wish. I would not expect you to obey me in all things. If you wished to manage the housekeeping, then that would be most pleasing, as I have had difficulties since Jenny passed away, but in any case you would not need to do the hard work. Fortunately I am able to afford servants, albeit only the four, but it is enough.'

I smile sadly. 'You're a hopeless romantic. You think love will solve everything. I'm not so sure.'

'Are you then admitting to some feelings for me?'

'How can I tell after only four days? I like you a lot. You're not like any man I've met before, and being with you feels… well… it feels as if… it feels *right*, but there are a lot of other considerations.'

'My feelings echo yours, my dear. I do not withdraw my proposal.'

We're getting close to Felin Gyfriniaeth, but we're just out of view of the other village houses, and surrounded by trees.

'All right then,' I say, 'I have an important question to ask you, and I want you to answer it openly and honestly.'

'Very well,' he replies, looking soberly expectant.

'Are parsons allowed to kiss their female friends?'

He bursts out laughing and draws me closer. 'Fallady, my dear, you are most forward, but I assure you that parsons are *allowed* to do whatever they wish. Am I to conclude that you desire me to kiss you?'

I put my arms around him most forwardly. 'Yes, Walter, I want you to kiss me, long and lovingly,' I say, and any more nonsense I might have added is fortunately cut off by the firm application of his sensuous lips.

Well! I can't believe I *was* that forward, but it was worth it. He carries out my 'desire' to the letter, and my libido splutters into unaccustomed life as I kiss him back with a passion that amazes me.

When we finally pull apart, we just stare at each other, both of us breathing heavily.

'Well, that was… um… very nice,' I say, recovering first.

He gives a grunt of laughter and pulls himself together slowly. 'It has been some time since I experienced such a kiss,' he says.

'I've never experienced such a kiss,' I say.

We resume our walk, but we're both unusually quiet. However, Felin Gyfriniaeth is now ahead, and I'm distracted from any naughty thoughts by the novelty of seeing the watermill in action.

Felin Gyfriniaeth in its working lifetime is a very different place. There isn't even any living space; it's just a mill. The owner lives in a separate, less substantial-looking cottage nearby, which has obviously not survived until my time. Walter introduces me to him and says I'm interested in watermills and would like to see its operation, so we get the full tour, with the proud miller telling me that it's been operating for two hundred and fifty years, and showing me the resultant wholemeal flour that it's producing.

As we walk back beside the stream, I sneak out the camera and take a few shots, only just managing to slip it out of sight as a horse and cart jolts up the hill and into view on the rutted road to Tref-ddirgel. It's hard to envisage this road as the mass of nettles and brambles it is in 2008.

I look aside at Walter and wonder whether he was referring to his wife when he mentioned his previous kissing experience.

'You must miss your late wife very much,' I say.

'Indeed,' he replies, his eyes on the giant puddle he's just negotiating. 'It was not a love match but we got along tolerably well, and we developed a fondness over time.'

'Not a love match?' I ask, surprised.

'It was a marriage born of practicality. I needed a wife, and Jenny had been widowed and was lonely. She was ten years my senior, and perhaps that was why she was so afflicted with the small pox.'

'Were you married for many years?'

'Twelve years.' He stops and turns to me. 'My dear, something is puzzling me. Why did you ask about Branwen Emrys and Percival Linlade? If you know nothing of this time, how do you know of them?'

My buckled shoe has just squelched into an unexpected cowpat, and I pull it out and scrape it on the grass verge before replying.

'They were in my time. That's what really led me here. They were there, and I wanted to know why, so I went to the ruins of Llanycoed hoping to find answers. Now I seem to have even more questions but still no answers.'

He shakes his head. 'It is most peculiar. You will likely see Mrs Emrys when we attend for dinner at the hall tomorrow. Speaking of which, I must give you a grounding on what to expect.'

The next morning I enter the small parlour for breakfast after a whole night spent dreaming about etiquette. If I don't know which knives and forks to use after all yesterday's instruction, I never will. Not only did Walter and Anna try to improve my harpsichord playing and my card playing, but they also drummed a few songs into me so that I'll be able to hold my own in the singsong that will likely take place. I was advised most sincerely not to mention my views on alcohol and to try not to be too abstemious, as apparently Dr Benbow, he of the two healthy pints of port a day, will be among the diners. Walter even frowned over his late wife's gowns, picked one and told Nerys to turn up the hem, as he'd noticed that they're all too long for me.

He's also concocted a story to explain my presence, which combines seemliness and respectability. Apparently I've recently lost everything to a rogue male relative, who abandoned me in the snowy lane with only the clothes I stood up in and nowhere to go. I find this story hard to swallow, but he assures me it's quite credible in this time, and it seems so, since even the Greenleafs have accepted it.

Anna is visiting a young friend's house for the day, he tells me as I fill my plate with eggs and bacon. He shakes his head and frowns. 'She has so few friends. That is another reason why I have sought her a place at a good school. I fear she is becoming lonely here, with only her old papa for company.'

'She seems keen to go,' I say, 'but does this school *really* only teach "the feminine arts"? Aren't there any schools that teach science or other more interesting things to women?'

He chuckles slightly and then exhales heavily. 'You do not give up on this matter, my dear.'

'No, because it's important. Women should be able to learn the same things as men.'

'And if they will never be able to use what they learn? Whatever you may think of sewing, drawing, singing and harpsichord playing, they are skills women are expected to have, whereas the ability to dissect a frog or to carry out chemical experiments is considered to be most unfeminine. It would be an unusual man who would seek out such a woman.'

I glare at him until he realizes what he's said and laughs. 'Very well, I am perhaps an unusual man, but I can't be certain that there would be another such for Anna. And furthermore,' he adds firmly as I'm about to open my mouth and interject, 'she has up to now shown no interest in or aptitude for science. She has helped me with my collecting and categorising at times, but I suspect that was out of a desire to spend time with her papa. It is possible that she has a more feminine turn of mind than yourself, Fallady. I have learned that you can't mould a child into what you wish. They are as they are.'

I sigh. He could be right. Maybe Anna really loves embroidery and all those girly things I've always hated. Her reading seemed so advanced when I heard her with Miss Roberts that I've probably projected all my own hopes and ambitions on to her. Plus, of course, it's none of my business – unless I really *am* going to marry him.

He sees my mild dejection and says, 'I shall ask her whether she has any doubts about the school. In the meantime, we have a little time in which to further improve your own education before this afternoon.'

By the time his manservant, Thomas, brings out the parson's horse-drawn vehicle, my mind's whirling with songs and card games and archaic names for things and the correct ways to address people. I'm glad of the excitement of stepping into the chaise to take my mind off my nervousness. Now I'm really starting to feel like a Jane Austen heroine, getting into my carriage and setting off for the squire's house. Except that I'm not dressed in the attractive garb of Austen's heroines but in one of the bum-emphasising gowns favoured by the late Mrs Edgemond, the parson's modest wooden chaise isn't a carriage but rather a cart, there's only Thomas wearing some small approximation of livery, Walter isn't Colin Firth, my stays are killing me, and I'm not wearing any knickers.

The weather's still mild, and if it weren't for all the aforementioned details, I'd be able to pretend I was just a tourist taking a quaint horse and cart ride. As it is, the veil of unreality flutters before my eyes, and Walter and I are unable to exchange anything but small talk due to Thomas's presence. I've seen Thomas around the place quite a lot, carrying out errands for the parson, but not to speak to. He and Walter seem to get along amicably enough, but I puzzle about relationships with servants. I find it disconcerting that they're around all the time and even wonder whether they're listening at keyholes during our evening discussions.

It's not a long journey, but it takes us beyond the bounds of Llanycoed and out into the countryside. I try to work out where we are in relation to Felin Gyfriniaeth, and when Laburnum Hall comes into view, I'm surprised that a building of its size isn't still standing in my time. Was the hall also destroyed in the earthquake?

Mr and Mrs Greenleaf greet us very kindly, and I'm introduced to the other dinner guests: Dr Benbow, a portly man in his mid-thirties; his wife, a timid and very thin woman, slightly younger; another clergyman, Mr Jenkins, a curate for a neighbouring parish; and the Hywels, an older couple with matching expressions of disdain.

The booze is already flowing. I can't take Walter's advice and glug it back the way they're all doing, so I just pretend to do so and hope they don't notice it's the same glass and I'm only taking the tiniest sips. Once he's got a few crates of wine down him, the parson's geniality is back to the fore, and the whole company is laughing and joking when we parade to the dining room, Walter taking my arm.

I concentrate on not making a fool of myself. I'm already seated and checking my array of cutlery before I notice the servants bringing in the food. There are a few more servants than at the parson's, and they're bustling about quite officiously. I'm actually looking right at Mrs Emrys before I realize it's her, and then it's the sound of her voice I recognise and not her appearance, mainly because *this* Mrs Emrys is slim and in her late twenties. She looks my way with no recognition whatever, just the deferential glance of a cook maid. I've almost stopped breathing, and Walter, sitting at my side, murmurs, 'Are you all right, my dear? You are looking very pale.'

I have to force myself to get a grip, and with disappointment surging through my thoughts, I down the whole glass of wine in front of me and whisper back, 'I'll be fine.'

The meal begins to blur as I cope with undue wine and vast quantities of food. I can't adjust to the idea that two different kinds of fish and two choices of meat is a pretty standard dinner, at least when there are guests. And that's before the dessert courses.

With a great effort I manage to join in with the jollity through the card playing and singsong and even sing a couple of the seemly songs Walter and Anna have taught me. I listen rather than join in with the conversation, and I watch the parson to see how well he really fits in with all this. I also take a jaundiced interest in the other relationships on display. The Greenleafs seem just as before, a couple content in each other's company and with little demonstration of male domination from the squire. The haughty Hywels seem united in their assumption of superiority. I have to choke back laughter at some of their mannerisms, but there's no doubt about the hierarchy in that marriage: Mr Hywel is in charge. The third couple are the worst example to my increasingly jaded eye. Dr Benbow is, at least with his standard drink ration and more inside him, loud, jovial and dominant. His nervous wife seems in awe of him and is very much in his shadow.

I'm tired and dispirited on the return cart journey in the late twilight. Walter, seemingly jolly and still under the influence, says nothing until we're back at the parsonage and ensconced in front of the parlour fire.

'I don't think anyone else noticed, but you were in low spirits all afternoon,' he says.

I sigh. 'I hope you're right and they didn't notice. I did try, but it was a struggle.'

'I observed that you did not greet Mrs Emrys.'

'She wasn't my Mrs Emrys. Your Mrs Emrys is twenty years younger. I won't get any answers from her. Whatever brings her to my time happens twenty years from now.' I pause and put my hand to my mouth with a gasp as I realize what's coming in twenty years.

Walter has also caught on, and nods. 'The earthquake.'

'The hall isn't standing in my time. Would they still be working there in twenty years?'

He frowns. 'It is not likely, but it is of course possible. Servants tend to change positions quite frequently unless they are very happy in their place.'

My mind is jumping ahead now, and I begin to cheer up because after all, it's a partial answer. The earthquake *must* be at the centre of all this. Somehow that event has made time travel possible. The effect's localized to Llanycoed, so it would make sense that if Mrs Emrys and Mr Linlade were able to get to my time they would gravitate to the only remaining building.

Walter watches me with his lips twitching in a suppressed smile. 'You have perhaps reached some conclusions?'

We run through the possibilities together and apart from his dogged belief in God's will, he can understand my thinking. I start to relax again and enjoy his company, leaving behind the bad taste in my mouth that dinner at the Greenleafs had given me.

'I think the Hywels put on too many airs,' he says when we've moved on to discuss the afternoon.

'Do you know them well? I assumed you were well acquainted with them all.'

'I have known them for many years, but they are not frequent visitors to the parsonage, or even to church. I don't think you liked them at all.'

'Well, you can't deny that apart from the Greenleafs, the other wives were distinctly under their husbands' thumbs. I'd like to know what you have to say about that.'

He chuckles. 'I cannot deny that most men expect to be master over their wives, but my dear, there are always exceptions.' He slaps his hands on his thighs and gets up, coming over to me and holding out a hand. 'I have a hankering to carry out a small experiment, if you will allow it?'

I give him a puzzled look but put my hand in his, and before I have a chance to react he's pulled me up and into his arms, which isn't at all an unpleasant place to be. Our second kiss is just as intense as the first, but this time we're not in a public place, and things are starting to get quite heated by the time we pull apart.

'That was most stimulating, my dear,' he says with a laugh in his voice. 'But I think perhaps —'

He breaks off because I'm kissing him again.

'Fallady,' he protests with mock dismay when we emerge, 'are all ladies this forward in the 21st century?'

CHAPTER ELEVEN

Fornication at the parsonage? Not a chance. Apart from the religious aspect, we have to consider our reputations and respectability. Whatever he might say, he's still a man of his time.

He tells me over breakfast the next morning that he has to carry out a marriage, and what's more it's no joyful occasion but a forced one because the woman's pregnant. A sort of 18th-century version of the shotgun wedding, but in this case the man can either marry or go to prison, apparently. It's a very alien world at times.

At last two old ladies from the village have come in to do the washing, which is a relief to me, as I might get my knickers back. When the parson's gone to officiate at the wedding, I take a look at what the women are doing. I'm horrified at the great labour of it all. Steaming tubs and kettles and lots of bashing with paddles and scrubbing using hard soap. I never could understand why women wore long skirts touching the ground in a time when washing was so hard. Now it makes even less sense.

I'm feeling pretty grubby myself, because the opportunity for a real wash is never available. There's no bath in the house, and the small amount of water I get every morning isn't even enough for a thorough stand-up scrub. Although I feel at ease with the parson on many levels, I don't like to bring up my dissatisfaction with these aspects of his time, as it seems ungrateful and self-indulgent. I have the feeling that although he's by no means poor, he's not rich either. If he were very well off, I assume there would be fires in the bedchambers, one or two more servants and suchlike. As it is he has Nerys, the upstairs maid, Martha, the cook maid, Thomas, a sort of footman and general manservant, and Dafydd, who does his farming, but what farming exactly, I'm not quite sure.

Anna takes me on a tour around the parsonage grounds and I discover that it consists of large gardens, stables, pig pens, cow byres and a hen house, but I don't think that's the kind of farming Dafydd usually does. All that seems to be taken care of by Thomas and the maids. Even the butter is made on the premises. I've been eating home-laid eggs and drinking milk and eating butter straight from the cow. I try to avoid thinking about all those germs.

By the afternoon it looks as if frost might be on the forecast for the next day, if of course there were weather forecasts. Anna's tied up with her lessons and Walter's still out, but I'm getting stir crazy so I head out of the house, feeling quite brave going alone.

As I wander down the lane in mid-afternoon, it's sunny and clear, a good time to take surreptitious photos. I feel quite dislocated, thinking I'm still in my own time until the discomfort and awkwardness of my clothing hits me, or I see another person walking, or a chaise or curricle passes.

I reach the crossroads where I dropped in and spend some time looking around in the hope that I'll somehow drop back out. Once I've exhausted that avenue, I keep on walking without a destination and follow a path that passes through thinning woods to cultivated fields. Just like Lizzie Bennett, I am, walking for miles and muddying my dress. Unlike Lizzie Bennett, however, I don't come across Mr Bingham's great mansion and discover Colin Firth comfortably ensconced within it. Instead, I walk into a walled kitchen garden and find Mr Linlade in it.

Just like Mrs Emrys, his gaze passes over me without any recognition. However, in contrast with Mrs Emrys, Mr Linlade at fifty is much the same.

'Can I help you, Miss?' he asks.

'Er, yes, I seem to have got a little lost.'

'Was you wanting to visit the squire?'

'No, no, I was just out walking, but it's starting to get a bit dark. Can you tell me the quickest way back to Llanycoed?'

He directs me away from the winding field path I've been on and back on to the rough track of a road. I stride back to the village pretty quickly, despite my skirts. I don't know whether there are any real dangers to worry about in the dark, but I don't fancy being caught out in the full black of night without any streetlights.

It's around six when I get back and well past dusk. Walter's there as soon as I enter the house. 'I was most concerned. You did not tell Nerys where you were going,' he says, helping me off with my cloak.

'I didn't think I needed to,' I say.

'Come into my study,' he says, and I realize why when I hear Anna's sweet singing voice issuing out of the parlour.

'You have guests?' I ask, reaching out to warm my hands in front of his study fire.

'Dr Benbow is here with his daughters. They were hoping to meet you.'

I sigh explosively. 'His daughters? How many?'

'Two, aged eighteen and one and twenty. I believe they have called especially to see you. Will you join us? We shall take tea.'

How can I say no? It's my chance to meet the flower of 18th-century girlhood, and believe me, it's about as much fun as meeting the flower of 21st-century girlhood. They're giggly and silly and keep giving me arch looks and then looking pointedly at Walter. I begin to doubt the seemliness of my presence in his house.

Dr Benbow is a little improved in this context, obviously doting on his daughters and quite jolly with Walter. They share a chat about science and medicine, and I try to listen in, because it's far more interesting than what the girls are telling me about where they bought their gowns and how stylish their bonnets are. They claim to be greatly scandalised by my desertion in the lane and ask me lots of questions about it that tax my imagination. Once or twice during this recitation I catch Walter's eye and know he's having an inner laugh at my expense, even as he and Dr Benbow discuss the merits of bleeding for just about any illness they can think of.

When they finally leave two hours later, Nerys takes Anna off to bed. No sooner are we alone in the parlour than Walter starts chuckling. I stare at him with my hands on my hips, and he just laughs all the more.

'Well I'm glad you think it's funny,' I say, which only prompts even greater guffaws.

'Fallady my dear,' he says between gurgles, 'your face was a veritable picture. When the Misses Benbow were demonstrating the quality of their most costly hats and anticipating your envy, you said, "Hmm yes, they are quite nice I suppose, but I really don't like hats at all."'

I start to giggle then, realising that I've probably put my foot in it with the Benbow girls. Still, maybe it'll keep them from making any more tedious visits.

'I was far more interested in what you and Dr Benbow were discussing,' I say. 'Do you think he would have been scandalised if I'd told him that bleeding has no curative powers whatsoever and is actually bad for you?'

That gets his attention, and he sits up in his armchair, his expression sobering. 'You are serious? It is a common technique and used for many disorders.'

'And useless for them all. It just weakens you. So,' I grin, 'how do you think he would have reacted if I'd told him?'

Walter gives a gusty sigh. 'I fear he would have dismissed your comments out of hand, believing them to be the fancy of a member of the weaker sex.'

'Huh!' I splutter, deflated but hardly surprised. 'And is that what you think, Parson Edgemond?'

'It *is* hard to believe, but I suppose I must, just as I have taken your word about liquor.'

I frown then as I remember the subtext of the Benbows' visit. 'I think perhaps my presence is giving rise to gossip about you – and me. Are you aware of it?'

'Indeed,' he says, coming over to join me standing in front of the fire. 'At first it was accepted because you were a lady in distress, but the longer you remain here, the greater the talk will be, particularly as Anna leaves for boarding school in a sennight. Were we to become affianced, it would be different.'

I laugh shortly. 'But hey, no pressure, eh?'

'I do not quite apprehend your meaning, but no matter. Have you thought any more upon my proposal?'

I just look at him, not knowing how to answer.

'This is troubling you a great deal.'

I shrug. 'I wish I could have the best of both worlds.'

'And would marrying me be the best of this world?'

I study him, taking in his sensuous lips, his ordinary, deceptively serious features and his ridiculous wig and amaze myself by saying with complete sincerity, 'Perhaps it would.'

'But you don't yet feel able to accept my proposal?'

I shake my head. 'I need more time. I don't know what I ought to do. I don't think I've ever felt so confused in my life.'

'Then I shall wait.'

The next morning I finally feel relaxed enough with him to bring up a couple of matters that are troubling me.

'Umm,' I say as I dissect a tasty kipper, 'you remember I told you about indoor necessaries and tap water and so on?'

He smiles. 'How could I forget?'

'Well the thing is, I'm used to washing a lot more regularly. I mean, we all have indoor bathtubs and suchlike and most people have a bath or something like it every day, and I've been here for almost a week – er sennight – now and um… well…

'I'm finding it hard not having a proper wash or being able to wash my hair.'

It's eyebrows-in-wigline time again. It's pretty easy to amaze the parson sometimes. He might laugh at my comical little quirks, but at least I get my own back this way.

'A bath every day? Wash your hair? My dear, I don't even possess a bathtub.'

I giggle. 'I had noticed.'

'As for washing your hair, why, it is normal to wash it only every few months, if then. Many wash theirs only once a year. Surely it is not healthy to wet your head so frequently? You could catch cold –' He stops because I'm laughing, and his own lips start to twitch.

'Once a year, eh?' I say eventually. 'And what about you? How often do you wash yours? Is there any hair under that wig? You still haven't taken it off for me.'

For a moment he looks completely serious, and I wonder if I've gone too far, but then I see mirth in his eyes, and he leans towards me. 'You are correct, Fallady. I don't need to wash my hair because it is more comfortable to wear a shaven head under a wig. I do, however, make a solemn promise to grow my hair and discard my wig should you agree to marry me. But as to washing it weekly, why it beggars belief!'

'Many people wash theirs daily,' I add impishly, and watch his reaction with a grin.

'In any case,' he says, 'I do not apprehend how I am to fulfil your desire to immerse yourself daily. The amount of hot water required would be enormous, and without a bathtub –'

I put a hand on his arm. 'I understand. I just wondered if you could think of anything. I didn't mean daily. Once a week would be a help.'

'I shall think on it, my dear,' he says kindly. 'In the meantime, perhaps you would like to accompany Anna and myself in the chaise to Tref-ddirgel? I must make some purchases, and I won't be free tomorrow – I must bury Robin Griffiths, who died on Sunday. You might like to look at some hats while we are there,' he adds innocently. 'I should like to buy you a gift.'

We're both laughing when Anna comes into the room, impatient for her trip and dressed for going out. 'Papa,' she says in frustration, 'it *is* almost ten o'clock.'

Just as I predicted, the sun's blazing out of a clear blue sky, but it's pretty chilly and frosty. A chaise isn't really a good means of travel in the cold, but since no one else complains, I keep my mouth shut and try to enjoy the trip, especially as we go right past Felin Gyfriniaeth and down my usual road to Tref-ddirgel, so I get to see it from a different angle.

I hardly recognise Tref-ddirgel. Most of the houses are smaller and far more rustic than the ones I'm accustomed to seeing, and John and Alyson Kelly's pink house is a long time off from being built. The oddest thing about it is that there are actually more shops, and while the parson makes his purchases for Anna's new school I look around at the old-fashioned goods and note the personalised service.

It's a bit frustrating for me, feeling so powerless. I still have my purse with me, full of worthless cash and credit cards, which means I'm dependent on Walter for every whim. And this is the norm, surely, if a woman has no money of her own.

Despite his joke about hats, Walter clearly does have a plan, since he takes us to a tiny jewellers – believe me, there are no jewellers in 21st-century Tref-ddirgel – where he picks up a small packet, but then says he'd like me to choose a piece of jewellery as his gift to me. 'A necklace or a brooch, perhaps?'

To my amazement, he chats to the jeweller in Welsh while I browse the small selection, determined to choose the smallest and cheapest item I like. As it turns out, there's a pretty necklace of garnet flowers that takes my eye, and in the 21st century at least, garnets are pretty cheap. The jeweller tells me it will suit my colouring and Anna agrees that it's pretty, so it's wrapped up and added to Walter's bill.

He's very cheery as we rattle back to the parsonage, but I'm uneasy and I can't even think why. Maybe it's because I've so rarely had a gift from a man, or indeed wanted or expected one. It seems to symbolise an attachment I've always tried to avoid.

By the time we get back to Llanycoed, the sky's clouding over, and I'm wondering if we're in for some more snow, as it's still fairly chilly.

I wear my new necklace during dinner, and Walter quizzes Anna on her opinion of his choice of school. She confirms, yet again, that her heart's desire is to study needlework and drawing to degree level and assures him earnestly that she has no interest in science and thinks becoming anything other than a wife and mother would be total lunacy. Walter kindly avoids giving me any 'I told you so' looks.

Afterwards, we repair to the parlour, and he hands Anna the little packet he picked up. It turns out to be a locket into which he has put a small piece of her mother's hair and also some of his own (how did he manage that?). She's delighted with it, and it seems a welcome present for a child going away from home for the first time.

That night in my chilly bedchamber, by the light of a single candle, I stare at myself in the mirror with my hair up, my bosom bursting out above the tight stays, my gigantic backside in the late Mrs Edgemond's gown and my necklace of garnet flowers. I wonder if this is really the same me who had full control of the computer system at Solstice Clothing Co. Ltd. It seems worlds away. It *is* worlds away. Am I really going to end up a wife and stepmother in the 18th century? What's more, at forty-two, I'm still capable of childbearing. There's no convenient pill for birth control here, and as far as I know, no condoms either. I gather the Greenleafs have six children and another on the way. Dr Benbow is lucky to have got off with two daughters and two sons – or rather, his wife is.

I sit on the bed and listen to the wind whistling outside. I've spent another pleasant evening talking and laughing with Walter, and when I'm with him that's where I want to stay. His marriage proposal is becoming more attractive with every day that I'm stuck here.

The next morning Nerys brings me in several jugs of steaming water and washcloths and soap. She tells me the parson ordered it, but her face reveals her disapproval at such profligate waste on mere washing. Once she's gone I make the most of this unaccustomed luxury and don't even care that I still have to shiver my way through a stand-up wash. It's better than nothing! When I head below stairs with my hair still wet, the sky has the leaden yellow look that indicates incipient snow.

While Walter's off doing his duty at the funeral, Anna tells me more about the boarding school and shows me some of her drawings, which take me aback because they're very good. Some of them are of her papa, and one in particular takes my eye because of the way she's captured the humour that has obviously always lurked somewhere inside his dour-looking exterior.

She notices the way I'm looking at it and says, 'Would you like it? I have many, and I can draw more.'

I accept it with a grateful smile and tuck it away in my bedchamber before Walter returns, by which time the weather's taken a turn for the worse, and the threatening snow has begun to fall.

He looks slightly despondent when we sit down to dinner because he's had bad news from the squire. Mrs Greenleaf has started very early labour and he anticipates being called to the hall to name the child at any moment.

By the time we've eaten, the snow is descending in great clumps, and the road outside is disappearing under the deluge, but this doesn't stop the squire's manservant from arriving with stamping hooves, asking for the parson to come to the hall as quickly as possible. Walter orders Thomas to bring out his mare, and within minutes he's galloping off after the servant, telling us he'll be back as soon as he can.

It's a quiet evening for Anna and me. I spend the time telling her all about how women can be much more than housekeepers, wives and mothers and how one day they will be doctors and parsons and even politicians. I don't know how much is getting through, but she listens politely and even asks a few questions of her own. Outside, the wind's getting up, and a full-blown blizzard is coming on. When it gets dark and Walter hasn't returned, I take my lead from Anna and the servants who say he's sure to have stayed at the hall for the night due to the severe weather.

CHAPTER TWELVE

I'd like to say that I have some kind of telepathic warning that something's wrong, but I don't. I wake from a deep sleep in my fridge of a room to sounds of alarm downstairs. All the servants seem to be in an uproar, and Martha's normally calm voice is pitched high with fear.

Nerys bursts into my bedchamber just as I'm getting out of bed to investigate.

'Oh, Miss,' she says breathlessly, 'Jonas says Parson left the hall last night, but Bess has come home without him. And the snow's so deep, Miss. Tom and Jonas have gone to fetch the doctor and the squire.'

I sit back on the bed as my strength drains away. I can feel all the blood leaving my face, and my body becomes icy cold. 'What... when... ' I gulp down my fear. 'When did he leave the hall?'

'About seven o'clock, Jonas says.'

'Twelve hours,' I say grimly, quickly assembling some clothing. 'Does Anna know yet?'

'I'm just going to wake her now, Miss.'

I take a deep, shuddering breath, and blink hard as I feel tears trying to form. 'Well, tell her gently. He could still be all right.'

I dress in a hurry, all the while blinking and biting my lip to keep tears at bay. When I look out of the window at the cold, grey day and see the depth of snow the blizzard has left behind, a tear escapes and falls on to the windowsill. How could he survive that?

The sound of Anna crying rouses me. I've never been at all maternal, but it looks like I'm all she's got right now. I have to at least try.

'He was certain he would be safe,' the squire tells me when he and Dr Benbow arrive with a few other men. 'There was still a little light, and he is an accomplished horseman.'

I put an arm around Anna's shoulders, feeling awkward. The men are polite, but I'm sidelined, as I have no status. My being a woman in a man's world is all too apparent. It seems that the best I can do is comfort Anna, but what I really want to do is join the search party. Of course, they're going to be on horseback, and I don't know how to ride, so I stand by like a spare part and swallow down my instinct to act.

We cluster in front of the parsonage and watch them set out: about twenty men including Thomas, Dafydd and the squire's manservant, Jonas. My stomach is tight with fear. Surely they don't have all that much ground to search? After all, the hall's only a couple of miles away. Only… I swallow on the thought… he could be buried, couldn't he? There's about three feet of snow out there, with some drifts far higher. I've never seen so much snow in my life. I clench my fists and feel the tears well up again.

With the men gone, Anna and I huddle on the sofa together, staring into the blazing fire but saying little. Martha and Nerys try to persuade us to eat, but neither of us is hungry, so they just supply us with tea. We start at every little sound, gazing out of the window, looking for signs. The longer we wait, the more Anna leans against me, her slight body trembling. An unexpected feeling of tenderness comes over me as I look down at her pale, tear-stained face. Maybe I do have some maternal instincts, after all.

It's half past ten when we hear muffled hoofbeats and run outside to find a mournful procession coming our way. By the time they reach us, I've almost stopped breathing. Walter is being carried in a makeshift stretcher, and he's white, ashen. The two servants carrying him shake their heads, and Thomas says, 'I'm sorry, Miss. We were too late.'

Dr Benbow, following behind on his horse, adds sombrely, 'Dead of cold. Been out there all night, but not long passed on. There was a flicker of a pulse when we first found him, but nothing now.'

Between the rush of horror and the sinking feeling of loss and Anna's screech of grief from beside me, there's something else tickling at the back of my mind. It stays there for a while as they bring Walter's body in and take it up to his bedchamber.

Anna is crying great gasping sobs, and Nerys and Martha try to comfort her. I stare at Walter's body numbly while Dr Benbow turns to me and says, 'He'll need laying out.'

I nod, and the procession of men seems to drift away while the tickling memory becomes more insistent. 'Flicker of a pulse'. Cold. Hypothermia. Come on, Fallady, you've seen enough *ER* and *Casualty* over the years; you studied human biology and physiology. Hypothermia. If a person's not been dead for long of hypothermia, they can still be revived.

I turn to Martha and Nerys. 'There might be something we can do. Quickly. We need to get his wet clothes off, and then bring all the blankets you can.'

They look at me as though I've lost my mind. 'But Miss, Dr Benbow says he's gone. We can't –' Martha breaks off because I've started to drag off Walter's icy riding coat.

'Come on!' I say through gritted teeth. 'We don't have much time. Nerys, go and get the blankets. Hurry!'

Anna's gone quiet behind me, and Martha has obviously decided to humour me, because she helps me undress Walter, and by then Nerys has come back with blankets. Once I have him cocooned, I start CPR. I defy anyone who watches hospital dramas in the 21st century not to know how to do

CPR. We've seen it so many times it's ingrained into our very brain cells. I keep on alternating between heart massage and artificial respiration on my own for several minutes while my companions, now joined by Thomas and Dafydd at the door, stare at me as though I'm a madwoman. When I spot Thomas I call him over. 'You've seen how I'm doing this,' I say, still doing heart massage. 'Do you think you could carry on?'

He shrugs and takes over while I persist with the breathing. Breathe, Walter, *please* breathe!

'Martha, light a fire in here. It's too cold,' I order between gulps of air.

I don't know how much longer it goes on for, but Martha has the fire lit before I hear a tiny groan from Walter, and at last, a breath, then a cough.

'The Lord be praised,' says Martha, and she falls on her knees with her hands clasped in prayer.

'You can stop now, Thomas,' I say and feel for Walter's pulse. It's weak, but it's there. Let's just hope there's no brain damage.

'Anna, come over here,' I urge gently, holding out my hand. Her eyes are wide with shock, but she comes over to the bed. 'Your papa's alive, but he's still very ill. We need to warm him up slowly and the best way to do that is to lie beside him so that our bodies warm his. Do you understand?'

She nods and climbs up on to the bed beside her father, putting her arms around him. I tuck the extra blankets over and around them and then get on the other side of him. Without prompting, Nerys covers me too. By this time I'm feeling completely exhausted, and I just manage to get out, 'Don't let the fire die down,' before I either fall asleep or lose consciousness or both.

It's a rumbling sound that wakes me from that exhausted sleep, and I raise my head to see Walter smiling at me. Anna's sitting up on the other side of the bed, and when I drag myself to a sitting position, I realize the room is full of people. Not only Martha, Nerys, Thomas and Dafydd but the squire, Dr

Benbow and a couple of other people I've never even met are all staring at us from the end of the bed.

'Walter?' I say anxiously, turning back to look at him. 'How are you feeling?'

He smiles and takes my hand, albeit feebly. 'As I was just telling all our guests, I am somewhat fatigued, but glad to be alive. I gather I have you to thank, cariad. I believe I have mentioned before that the ways of the Lord are unfathomable.'

His eyes are closing even as he stops speaking, and I get off the bed and cover him again. I take his pulse, and it's strong. Anna comes over to me. 'Is Papa going to be all right now?'

I put my arm around her. 'Yes he is. Yes he is,' I say, and burst into tears in front of everyone. Anna buries her head against me and joins in, and all the men shuffle their feet awkwardly and look anywhere but at us.

'We've prepared some food, Miss,' Martha says to me in a slightly awed tone. 'It's laid out in the parlour. Thomas can stay with Parson.'

I nod and try to compose myself, and keeping an arm around Anna, lead the way downstairs. Everyone's very quiet, even the squire. To my surprise it's dark again. I've slept for six hours, and I still feel shattered.

In the parlour I sip at some tea and nibble a sandwich and try to cope with the peculiar sensation that the world's tilted off its axis.

The unexpected guests set to the food and drink, still eerily subdued. I can tell by the way everyone's giving me surreptitious and curious looks that I have to prepare myself for an explanation. In the end it's Dr Benbow who voices what they're all wondering. 'I have never heard of anyone being brought back from the dead that way, Miss Galbraith. How did you come by this knowledge?'

What a time to have to do some quick thinking! 'My late father was a doctor,' I lie, 'and he taught me a lot. He shared some of his ideas with me, and when you mentioned that there had been a flicker of a pulse when you found Mr Edgemond, it led me to remember what he had told me.'

The doctor nods and harrumphs a bit and seems to accept it. No doubt he's afraid his own reputation's dented, but despite my jaundiced view of 18th-century medicine, I've tried to preserve his dignity for him.

'Well, we are all most obliged to your father and to yourself, Miss Galbraith,' says the squire in his usual jolly way. 'I only wish this had not happened at my behest, but then who could guess his horse would take fright and throw him?'

'Is that what happened?' I ask.

He nods. 'Apparently the horse started at something, threw him and galloped off. He was stunned and confused, became lost in the blizzard and eventually succumbed to the cold.'

Later, when the visitors have left and Anna's gone to bed, I hunch in front of the parlour fire and try to dispel that awful image of Walter lying there alone while the snowflakes cover him in their soft but deadly blanket. There's a tap on the door, and Martha looks in. 'I've made Parson some broth, Miss. Why don't you take it up to him? Thomas says he's awake.'

I take the tray upstairs with a strange twinge of anticipation in my stomach and find Walter sitting up in bed, smiling and looking much more like his normal self. I don't know a lot about recovery from hypothermia – they don't tend to show that on *ER* – so I'm assuming it's normal to recover fairly quickly, although he hasn't had the benefit of the various technologies, pharmaceuticals and IVs that are usually thrown at patients in medical dramas.

'I gather Dr Benbow was a little shocked by events,' he says mildly and sips at his broth.

'Yes, considering he'd declared you dead,' I say. 'I told him my father was a doctor and I learned these things from him.'

'But from where *did* you learn them, Fallady? Is it truly common knowledge in your century?'

'Well, yes, pretty much. A lot of people know how to do what I did.' How can I explain about *ER*?

'Thomas said they thought you were mad with grief. He suggested that you hold me in considerable esteem.'

'Oh did he?' I say with a grin. 'Well I don't think that's a surprise to you.'

'Perhaps not a surprise, but most gratifying, all the same,' he replies.

'You called me cariad in front of everyone,' I say, fighting the urge to touch him, caress him in some way.

He smiles. 'Indeed. Am I to conclude that you know what it means?'

I fold my arms. 'Some Welsh words pop up every now and again, even in London.'

'You are my sweetheart, Fallady. I think you know that.'

'And now the whole of Llanycoed will know it.'

His smile becomes warmer. 'My dear, had they not heard it from my lips, then your own actions were confirmation enough.'

I sigh. 'I suppose so. How very unseemly of us! Anyway, I've finally got my wish.'

He looks puzzled. 'Your wish?'

'At long last I've got to see you with your wig off!'

He reaches up ruefully to run a hand over his shaven head. 'And do you think I look just as fetching, my dear?'

CHAPTER THIRTEEN

'It was God's doing,' Walter insists for the umpteenth time, as he sits at his study desk, surrounded by densely written sheaves of paper.

I sigh. Ever since he woke up on Sunday the main thing on his mind has been his near-death experience, which has magnified his belief that my presence is an act of God. He's been forced to stay at home and rest and is fretting because Dr Benbow advised him not to preach. He had to ask someone else to stand in for him at short notice – fortunately not a great problem in this age when clergymen are thick on the ground. Now it's Monday, and besides writing sermons, he's been showing me some of his notes, journals, records and collections of rocks and fossils.

'Well, whatever it was, it's certainly been an inspiration to you,' I say, indicating the heaps of paper.

'Indeed,' he nods happily.

There's a knock on the study door, and Martha pokes her head through. I tense up, hoping she's not about to announce yet another visitor. We've had a constant stream of those over the past couple of days, all wanting to see the miracle that is the recovering parson, and also, I'm sorry to say, keen to make my acquaintance as the one who saved him from the Very Jaws of Death.

'Miss Anna is home from Mrs Wynne's, and I'm about to serve tea in the parlour,' she says.

Walter puts his quill pen back in its stand. 'Shall we, my dear?' he says, and standing up, he puts out his arm to me. Martha turns to leave the room with a pleased little smile. All the parson's servants are suddenly a lot more respectful towards me. I hadn't even noticed their previous attitude, because I had nothing to compare it with, but I have observed the change. Martha in particular is very much more accommodating.

Anna is already seated in the parlour, occupied as demurely as ever in embroidering her sampler. She seems to have recovered well from the shock of two days ago and has spent a lot of time drawing.

Martha bustles in with the tea and cake, and Walter asks Anna how she enjoyed her afternoon at her friend's house. As I sip my tea and listen, I realize that I'm actually starting to feel at home in this alien domestic environment. What's happened to me? I can barely look at Walter without enormous tenderness gripping my heaving bosom, and my feelings for Anna are very protective and motherly. What about my life in the 21st century? I've been gone for eleven days – are the police even now crawling all over Felin Gyfriniaeth looking for me? Walter's preoccupation with his brush with mortality has meant that he hasn't mentioned his proposal for a couple of days, but I'm still no closer to making a decision.

'I told Kezia that women would be able to do many more things in the future, but she did not believe it,' Anna says. 'Men would not tolerate it, Kezia says. A woman must be ladylike and accomplished.' She frowns as if she's trying to resolve a great mystery, and Walter and I exchange glances.

Anna's attitude has changed since I saved her papa, and she's besieged me with questions. It never was possible to conceal my true origins from her, and being so young, she's accepted it with far more ease than an adult would. The trauma seems to have galvanised her into considerable reconsideration of beliefs.

'When I told her that women would not need to be accomplished as they would have the same knowledge as men, she called me a silly goose.'

'Do not tax yourself so with it, my dear,' Walter says. 'Kezia does not know what you know.'

Anna bites her lip. 'I *so* wished I could tell her, but I did not.'

Thank goodness for that. I'm already the object of enough attention in Llanycoed.

It's snowing again outside, and it's beginning to seem as though that's all the weather ever does in the 18th century. It's a week into March. Shouldn't there be some signs of spring by now?

I watch the snowflakes plummet past as I stand by the window of my bedchamber later. It's now or never, I tell myself firmly. Surely this much snow is not likely to fall again any time soon? It might be my last chance. I *have* to know. I have to choose, but what a choice. *Tomorrow*, I think as I slip between the perpetually chilly sheets. ('We do not warm our beds as do so many', Walter has told me proudly, obviously convinced that only wimps use warming pans.) *Tomorrow*, I think again, sleepily.

I'm on edge as I join Walter for breakfast the next morning. The snow's stopped, but there was a hard frost during the night, and it looks very deep and very nippy outside.

'Are you well, my dear?' Walter asks, looking into my face with concern.

I grip my knife and fork tightly, my appetite for the eggs on my plate dissipating by the second. 'Um. I have to talk to you about… It's just that I think I – I need to see if I can get home. I mean, there might be another snowdrift. I need to try while there's a chance,' I say, my voice husky with suppressed emotion.

He's silent for a moment but then nods very slowly and thoughtfully. 'I suspected you were becoming uneasy. You were quieter than usual yesterday evening.'

I just look at him dumbly, and feel as though my insides are being wrenched in two.

'I am afraid you will be thwarted, however,' he continues mildly. 'The wind was in a different direction. There is unlikely to be a snowdrift in the same spot.'

'Walter, I –'

He reaches a hand out to me, and I grasp it gratefully. 'I know, my dear.'

He purses his lips, looking out of the window. 'The snow is very deep, but let us go and look.'

Anna's busy in the parlour with Miss Roberts, who's giving her last lesson. Misery grips me as I realize I might never say goodbye to her.

Neither of us says much as we make our way to the crossroads. There aren't many people about, which is no wonder because walking is quite a struggle, and my feet and calves are wet through in no time. The sky is grey and low, which suits the bleakness of my mood.

I feel as though I'm being ripped to pieces as we round the corner. I'm clenching and unclenching my fists spasmodically, and I dare not even look at Walter, silent at my side. We come to a standstill simultaneously as we survey the scene.

He was right; there's no snowdrift. Or actually there are snowdrifts galore, adorning the fences and halfway up the rustic road sign, but none where I need them to be. It's beginning to look like this really was a one-way trip. Tears well up in my eyes, and I don't know if they're of disappointment or relief or, inexplicably, both.

Walter's voice comes from far away. 'Fallady, cariad, are you all right?'

I swallow and wipe my eyes as I turn away from the snowy wreckage of my hopes. He puts a hand on my arm, and I look at him, remembering how he seemed the first time I saw him at this very location. 'What did you really think,' I say, my voice a bit on the tremulous side, 'when you saw me drop out of the sky?'

He chuckles. 'I thought you looked exceedingly menacing, particularly the way you flailed about to escape the snow, with your hair in rats' tails and that particularly fetching garment which, wet with snow, revealed your full bosom.'

I gape at him. 'I see. So you noticed my *bosom* on our first meeting.'

'It was difficult to ignore.'

'And you a parson, too.' I say with mock-severity.

He takes me into his arms. 'I may be a parson, but I am also a man.'

Without thinking about it, I lay my head against his chest and hug him, my allergy forgotten. Whatever else is wrong, being in his arms feels *right*.

He holds my cold hand in his as we walk back, maintaining the contact no matter how unseemly.

'Do you mind if we stop at the church, my dear?' he asks. 'I shall not be long.'

I nod in acquiescence, guessing that he wants to get some praying in. It's the first time he's been out since Saturday, after all.

The church feels colder than the outside world, as though the rough red sandstone walls are emitting their own chill. While Walter prays, I shiver and try to work out what I'm feeling. I suppose I've been a fool to think I could somehow 'return to the sky', in any case. If there are pockets of time instability, who knows where they might appear? Something else could still turn up. Only… do I really want it to?

Walter eyes me keenly when he gets up from the pew. 'I am sorry, cariad. This has been a considerable disappointment to you, has it not? And now you are shivering with cold.'

'I'm all right,' I lie. 'What about you? You haven't said much, but you can't have wanted me to disappear back into the sky.'

He takes my hand again as we exit the church. 'I did not, but I could not stand in your way, if it was truly your wish.'

I sigh. 'I don't know what my wish is any more.'

'Could it perhaps include matrimony?' he says, and his lips twitch upwards.

'Perhaps. I'm still, um, thinking about it.'

By the time we sit down to dinner that afternoon, a light rain has started to fall.

'It seems that our excursion to Chester may take place after all,' Walter says to Anna. The journey to the school had been in doubt with so much snow on the ground. I've already begged off from going along, because I have a feeling they'd rather be alone, and I feel the need for a bit of privacy myself, to think about my limited options.

'Are you certain you will be all right?' Walter asks a little anxiously four days later. 'I do not like to think of you left alone for two nights.'

Melting snow had caused floods that delayed the trip to the school, but now the roads are clear, and they're about to leave.

'Sharing the house with four servants can hardly be described as "alone",' I point out with a wry grin.

Anna hands me a parting gift before she steps into the chaise. I open the roll of paper to discover a drawing she's made of me; somehow, she's managed to make me look less hideous in my 18th-century gown than I appear in the mirror. I amaze myself by giving her a hug. I'm a bit worried about her. Boarding school isn't the same as a children's home, but my first year or two at Summerdale were hard, and she doesn't even have the benefit of a brother and sisters.

'Take care of yourself, my dear,' Walter says to me. 'I shall return as quickly as possible.'

As I wave them off, I recall that I could be in Chester in about forty-five minutes in my car, but it will take Walter and Anna hours by coach, over rutted and potholed roads and in chilly conditions.

I spend the morning alternately pacing around the parlour, pacing around Walter's study and pacing around the garden before finally giving up and taking a brisk walk up to the hall.

I return to eat a small dinner, much to Martha's disapproval. Apparently it's a dreadful sin not to eat great haunches of meat at every meal. Still, since Walter's near-death, the servants couldn't have been more obliging, and I factor this into my meditations on potential wedlock. Can I really live in a house full of servants for the rest of my days? Walter doesn't think it's many servants, but I find the whole concept hard to take, and we're never alone, at least not in the house.

The next morning I drag myself downstairs, exhausted after a night spent dreaming of worst-case scenarios. I get smallpox and end up horribly scarred; I have a baby but get puerperal fever; I have a child, but it dies in infancy of one of the millions of appalling diseases that are just waiting to strike; Walter dies of one of them, and I'm left a widow, and so on. How I wish I'd been on the pill and had a supply in my bag, but there was never any need after Andy and I broke it off. As it is, the only medication I have to hand is a couple of packets of paracetamol: handy, but not much use at preventing conception.

I upset Martha again by eating little, and then head out on another long walk, this time to the village of Llanyrafon. The weather has improved slightly, and as the sun shines over the greening fields and verges, it seems that spring is close at last.

After a further restless night, Martha tuts as I ask for only a small breakfast. 'You'll make yourself ill, Miss,' she says and heads out of the dining room after giving my obviously wan features a careful appraisal. Martha's idea of a small meal clearly coincides with that of Mrs Emrys, but in order to avoid any more tuts, I try to eat the mounds of scrambled eggs and mushrooms. My thoughts are still stuck in a downward spiral.

After breakfast I go to Walter's study – without all the usual 21st-century gadgets to hand, the parlour seems a pretty dull place to spend time alone, especially as I find the flowery novels hard going and my harpsichord playing still leaves a lot to be desired. At least the study is cosy, and boasts shelves full of reference books. I peruse learned tomes and Bibles in Latin and what could be Greek, as well as books on theology, science and natural history, before turning to the display cabinets containing Walter's geological specimens and fossils. I don't like to pry into his journals in his absence, but I take a closer look at the items on the walls, which are either portraits of members of his family or his own university certificates.

One frame houses his Bachelor of Divinity scroll. It's made out to The Reverend Walter James Edgemond. Oddly, I'd never thought of him as a reverend. Without the familiar dog collar, it's easy to forget he's a vicar a lot of the time, and his life doesn't revolve around religion, per se. I have an impression from books and TV that 21st-century vicars are rather different, with a lot more religious duties to perform and often more than one church to take care of.

My nosiness exhausted, I spy Walter's medical books and curl up in the chair by the fire with *Domestic Medicine* on my lap. I'm still chuckling over it when I hear horse's hooves, and his welcome voice issues into the house. Martha goes to meet him, and there's a murmured conversation before he strides into the study and gives me a keen look.

'You're back early,' I say with a smile, fighting an unexpected urge to run into his arms. 'Did it all go well?'

'Yes, although the roads were somewhat muddy,' he says, warming his hands in front of the fire and not taking his eyes off me. 'Anna seemed happy to stay there, and the teachers were very pleasant. Martha tells me you have been out of spirits. Were you lonely?'

'Not exactly, but it's good to see you again, Reverend.'

He gives me a perplexed look. 'Why am I being referred to as "Reverend"?'

I point at the scroll. 'I just never thought of you as a reverend before. By the way, I see you went to Trinity College. I was at Corpus Christi.'

He plumps down in the other chair so sharply it's as if his strings have been cut. 'Corpus Christi? You attended Oxford University?'

'What, surprised?' I chortle. It's good fun watching Walter's eyebrows in action. I'm feeling better already. 'I certainly did attend Oxford University. All universities are open to men *and* women in the 21st century.'

'I thought you had lived in London?'

'Not always. I was at an, um… orphanage in Hertfordshire for most of my childhood, but when I was twenty, I went to Oxford to study for my degree.'

'I should not be shocked,' he says with a wry smile, 'and clearly this amuses you greatly, but what did you study at Oxford?'

'It's called PPP – Psychology, Philosophy and Physiology. Back then, I thought I might be a scientist or a psychologist, but once I'd got my degree, computers – the machines I told you about – were coming to the fore, and I got interested in them instead and took other courses in my spare time so that I could work with them.'

He shakes his head, sighing. 'I begin to see how you have come by such medical knowledge. You must forgive me for failing to realize this, but you did not mention it.'

'Well, it isn't a medical degree. I'm no doctor, but I do know a bit about biology, even though I've never really used it for anything.'

'It is hard for me to envisage any Oxford college with women as scholars,' he comments. 'It seemed a particularly masculine environment.'

'Not any more,' I say.

'How was it that an orphan was able to attend Oxford University? Did you receive a scholarship?'

'Times have changed that way as well. Tuition was free then.' I sigh, remembering. 'I nearly didn't make it though. I left the orphanage when I was only fifteen, and I couldn't cope with the huge change in my life. If it hadn't been for Miss Gilbertine, I don't know how things would have turned out. She encouraged me to work for my exams and apply to Oxford because she'd been a student there herself. She's the one who left Felin Gyfriniaeth to me.'

'She was a mentor to you?'

'Yes. She ran the orphanage and I... well, clung to her a bit I suppose. I'm not completely alone in life, though. I still have my brother and two sisters.'

'You must miss them,' he says, reaching forwards to take my hand.

I nod sadly. 'I worry that they're missing me: wondering what's happened to me.'

Martha comes in to announce that dinner is served, and her gaze falls on our linked hands. She gives Walter a speaking look I interpret as, *See, she's all right again now you're back*. Unfortunately that's only partly true, but I am at least able to do justice to the roast neck of mutton she's provided.

It's difficult to have a private discussion over dinner, with Thomas and Martha serving us at the table, so I wait until we're ensconced by the parlour fire before I ask, 'So you're sure the school's all right?'

'It is a very genteel establishment, my dear. I suspect that Anna will do very well there. Are you able to tell me what is wrong? Martha informed me that you barely ate while I was away and that you were gone for most of the day yesterday.'

I shrug. 'I just went for a walk. I needed to get out.'

'I apprehend that this is about your inability to return?'

I get up and start pacing around restlessly. 'I don't know what to do. Marriage is such a serious contract, and I don't want children.'

'As a parson I can hardly argue that marriage is anything other than a serious contract. Is having a child really so distressing a prospect?'

'We have methods of contraception, ways to prevent pregnancy,' I say, flinging my arms about in my agitation, 'and I never imagined being in a position where they wouldn't be available.'

'There are means to prevent you from getting with child?'

I nod silently, and wonder how far I'm pushing his religious boundaries. He's not Catholic, but still, surely in this time they think such matters are God's will?

He sighs. 'There are some such methods employed in this

time, my dear, but they are far from certain. All too frequently young maids become with child after taking a herbal potion that they believed would prevent it.'

'I'm not surprised, but our methods are certain, or at least so close to certain that we don't worry about it.'

'Do many choose to employ these methods?'

'Oh yes. Most women don't want more than two children, and some, like me, don't want any.'

He looks at me quizzically. 'Does not this lead to much wanton behaviour? Is marriage any longer even necessary?'

I smile slightly at his use of the word 'wanton'. 'Yes and no. There's no shame in… well… having relations out of wedlock, or even living "in sin" as I suppose you'd call it and having babies, but the tradition still holds. A majority of people marry, especially if they want children. It's just that it's a choice rather than an expectation.'

'But you have never married. Have you, then, lived "in sin"?'

I stop pacing and sit on the sofa beside him. 'No, and I've only been with one man.'

He raises his eyebrows. 'You did not wish to marry him?'

'No. He asked, but it frightened me, and now I know why. I never loved him.'

He puts his hand over mine. 'And how do you know this?'

'I suspect you know the answer to that.' I prevaricate.

'Still, I should like to hear it,' he says, leaning back and watching me intently.

I find it so hard to express my feelings. 'I know it because you're the only man I've ever loved.' I say at last.

A slow smile lifts his lips. 'And do you then consent to become my wife, Fallady?'

'You still want me even though you know I'm not a virgin? And what about me being an orphan? And if it comes to that, what about me being an atheist?'

'Your being an orphan does not concern me. As to the other matters, you are a constant challenge to my beliefs, but your behaviour since our meeting has been consistently respectable *and* Christian. I cannot judge you by the expectations of this century.'

'Respectable eh? I hope not. What about those brazen kisses?'

'As to those, since it was me whom you were kissing, how could I possibly object? I believe you are bringing up these trifles to avoid the question. Will you marry me, Fallady?'

His hand is gripping mine tensely, and I twine my fingers into his with a small sigh. What else can I do? 'Very well, Reverend, just as long as it's clear that I'm not darning any socks or sewing any frocks,' I say romantically, and the sombre parson's face lights up in a grin of delight.

'I believe this warrants a kiss, my dear,' he says.

When we part, a little shaken by the heat of our ardour, I say, 'What about Anna? How will she feel?'

'She became aware remarkably quickly that we were fond of each other. I believe she will be pleased that we are to marry.'

'And if... somehow... I go back to the 21st century?'

'Fallady, cariad, I love you, and you bring laughter and diversion into my life, which I confess had become more than a little lacklustre after Jenny's death. I don't want to lose you, but if it is God's will, then I shall accept it.'

So, when all these men step through time portals, they get to be heroes, but *I'm* destined to become an 18th-century parson's wife. This never happened to Captain Kirk.

CHAPTER FOURTEEN

Next morning I rise late to find that Walter has taken a sudden trip into Tref-ddirgel. I'm not surprised, as I know he means to arrange a marriage licence, find a fellow parson to marry us and, more than likely, buy me an engagement ring. It's hard to eat much breakfast with such thoughts running through my mind. I hardly seem to be fitting into the category of happy bride-to-be.

I pace around the garden, my mind on what kind of life I can really expect. The reverend will surely hope I'll be willing to take over the wretched housekeeping, in which I have no interest whatsoever. All the same, given what a kind soul he's been, it seems inconsiderate not to help him out with that, at least. I can see it all now; I'll be like the old woman who lived in the shoe with a load of kids hanging around my voluminous skirts while I spend my time sewing and supervising servants. What else is there for a woman to do in this age?

I try to conceal my jitters when my fiancé returns and tells me that he's engaged his friend Mr Jenkins to carry out the wedding ceremony, which will take place at Llanycoed church after Easter, just over three weeks away. Apparently it wouldn't do for a parson to marry during Lent. Not that I'd even realized it *was* Lent, of course. He's set things in motion regarding the licence, and he would like me to 'accept this token, to represent our engagement'.

I open the small box, swallowing, and find a silver ring with hands entwined around a heart, but no alarmingly expensive diamond that I was afraid he couldn't afford. It's a sentimental ring, rather than a grandiose one.

'Thank you, Reverend,' I say, using the teasing tone to conceal my emotions, 'it is most pleasing.'

He laughs as I'd hoped, and the intensity of the moment is eased while I slip the ring on, and thankfully it fits.

I broach the subject of dress for the wedding, but I'm assured that no particular garment is required. 'Although we might take a trip into Shrewsbury to order some new gowns for you, if you would like it.'

'Really? I hope this wedding isn't going to be a huge expense for you. I'm not used to having to depend on a man for clothing. It's very frustrating for me to have to allow you to pay for everything.'

'You need not worry about the expense. I am sure it is archaic of me, but I rather enjoy paying for everything.'

I favour him with a glare. 'Most archaic. And on that note I trust you have not forgotten your promise to me regarding that antiquated wig of yours?'

He shakes his head severely, but his lips twitch. 'I cannot comprehend your objection to my wig. It is most dignified.'

'I hope you don't propose to be married in it?' I insist, guessing that he does.

'It would not be at all seemly to marry you with a shaven head. I most certainly must wear my wig until my hair grows,' he says, with a satisfying amount of alarm.

'Very well, Reverend. I await the day of de-wigging with great suspense,' I say cheekily.

'Day of de-wigging indeed!' Walter chokes. 'And am I to be referred to as "Reverend" indefinitely, madam?'

'I find it an amusing title,' I say.

'It is a most serious title and a solemn charge placed upon me,' he says in his most affected, pious manner.

'So what do I do about being given away? I assume that's still the same in the 18th century?'

'Still the same? Is it not the other way around? Nevertheless, you are correct. Perhaps we could ask the squire or Dr Benbow to carry out this duty?'

'Not Dr Benbow,' I say with a shudder.

'Really my dear, you do him a disservice. He is not so bad a doctor as you suppose. His bone-setting skills are considerable. However, let us ask Mr Greenleaf. I suspect he will be happy to oblige us. I met him on my journey back from Tref-ddirgel, and he mentioned that he will call on us this evening.'

Sure enough, the squire turns up for tea, and Walter wastes no time filling him in on the exciting news. The usual congratulations ensue, and Mr Greenleaf expresses his dismay that none of my family will be present (for the obvious reason that my only relative supposedly dumped me) and accepts the charge of giving me away.

'It is indeed unfortunate that you will have no family to see you wed,' he reiterates. 'However, you can be sure that many in the village will wish to see the parson marry.'

I give Walter a speaking glance. It's bad enough to be getting married, but under the gaze of a crowd of village onlookers, almost all of them strangers to me? My stomach churns at the thought.

As we relax in the parlour later that evening, I ask whether there's such a thing as a honeymoon in this age.

'I am not sure to what you refer, my dear,' he says.

'In the 21st century, most people go away together, to be completely alone – as long as they can afford it. I don't think it'll be much of a honeymoon here with a house full of servants.'

'You desire to be *completely* alone with me?' he says with an amused expression.

'And what's wrong with that?'

'We would then be obliged to cook for ourselves.'

'Well, I can cook, a bit. Of course, cooking methods are a bit different here. How much do *you* know about cooking, Reverend?'

'I can contrive a little,' he replies, and adds, 'Now you will tell me that all men cook in the 21st century.'

'You're getting to know me too well. Although it's not all men, but a lot of them. Even so, we're not that enlightened – women still do the larger part of the household chores.'

'And that is wrong?'

'It is when both the man and the woman go to work,' I say trenchantly.

Walter smiles. 'I still can't conceive of this world that you paint for me, my dear.'

'You'd find it even less conceivable if I could explain it properly,' I reply. 'There are some things I can't even describe. Walter, I'm curious. Was Jenny the only woman you ever slept with?'

His eyebrows are up again, and he shakes his head. 'You are so bold, Fallady. I never know what you will speak of next.'

'I told you I'd only been with Andy,' I point out.

'Well, you are correct,' he says heavily. 'There was a sweetheart in my Oxford days, but it came to naught, and it was not proper for us to have relations. Does this satisfy your curiosity?'

'It came to naught? Did you propose?'

'I did not. I have only ever made two proposals. This Andy whom you mention, how did you meet him?'

'It was when I first went to live in London. We both worked for the same firm. It lasted for nearly a year, but it didn't work. After that I decided to stay alone.'

'Because you were hurt?'

'Not really. He was hurt because I'd turned him down, but I was just disillusioned with it all. I thought I should steer clear of getting serious with men for a while, only it turned into four years.'

Walter has the frown of concentration on his face that I've come to associate with him trying to translate my modern phraseology into something comprehensible. Finally he says, 'What does "getting serious" mean?'

I laugh wryly. 'I think it means what we've been doing.' I pause thoughtfully. 'I suppose I've always been terrified of it. I had other men friends but nothing that went as far as what you call "relations". Nothing like love, either.'

He looks at me very seriously. 'Then we must both make up for lost time, cariad.'

As anticipated, Walter announces our engagement from the pulpit and recites the whole story of his near-death experience as part of his sermon, which I have to say holds the entire congregation, including me, enthralled. After the service, we're both besieged by parishioners offering their congratulations.

My fiancé looks highly contented as we take an afternoon stroll about the village.

'That was an interesting sermon,' I say as we reach the crossroads. 'Very moving, in fact. I could almost get religion,' I tease.

He looks sideways at me. 'Would that you were serious! You are most irreverent, Fallady.'

I turn to face him. 'Are you sure you can cope with that? Sometimes I forget you're a vicar. I might unintentionally offend you one of these days.'

He puts his arms around me. 'I suspect not, but I am willing to take the risk.'

I reach up and kiss him, surprising myself. I've never been given to spontaneous acts of affection. What's happening to me? Naturally he responds very favourably to my kiss, and it's a couple of minutes before we resume our walk.

'What *am* I going to do here, once we're married?' I say. 'You know I'm not the domestic type. I need some purpose in my life, and it's not to be a wife and mother. You have a role and a part to play as the parson, but I don't want to be just Mrs Edgemond, whose existence revolves around the house and who depends on her *husband* for everything. Women fought for decades to get away from all that, you know.'

He looks at me with a mixture of suppressed amusement and bemusement. 'You do me an injustice, my dear, if you imagine that I expect you to turn into a traditional housewife. In point of fact, I can't envision many things less likely. I do not yet know what can be achieved to make you easier about our marriage, but I am thinking upon it. As to women fighting for decades, how did they carry out this struggle, might I enquire?'

I eye him to check for sarcasm, but he meets my gaze innocently enough. 'Even getting the vote was a gargantuan struggle for us women,' I say. 'Some died for the cause, and plenty suffered. They were sent to prison and went on hunger strike and were brutally force fed.'

He looks confused. 'Hunger strike? They refused to eat?'

'That's right. So they were fed by force with tubes pushed down their noses and throats.'

'They endured all this to obtain the vote?'

I nod.

'You are telling me that in your time, voting is open to everyone?'

'Of course, everyone over the age of eighteen who's not in prison and suchlike.'

'My dear, I am one of only a handful of men in Llanycoed who is eligible to vote. And in honesty, I might well prefer it otherwise, since my vote is more than a little coerced at times.'

'How do you mean, coerced? They can't make you vote for someone you don't want to, can they? Whoever "they" are.'

'"They" are Lord and Lady Montgomery, who own a great deal of land, including the living I have been so generously granted here. Elections don't occur too often, but when they do, I am expected to select whomever Lord Montgomery favours.'

I gasp. 'Walter, that's so corrupt. How can you do it?'

He regards me seriously. 'It is easier. And in truth it hardly matters who is elected. Life changes but little.'

We stop by a farm gate, and I watch a man off in the distance tilling a field with a horse-drawn plough. Walter raises a hand, and the man reciprocates. 'It is Dafydd. He ought not to be working on the Sabbath, but the unseasonable weather has made it necessary,' he says. 'This is glebe land.'

I obviously look totally blank.

'It is land that I am permitted to farm as part of my living,' he explains.

'Ah.'

'Do not your parsons do the same?'

'Er... no. Things are really very different. Not that I've had a lot to do with vicars, but they certainly don't farm the land any more.'

'Why have you had so little to do with "vicars", if, as you tell me, you attended church as a child?'

'So I did, but I didn't ever speak to the vicar. I do remember that he used to invite us poor orphans to tea parties in his garden some Sunday afternoons.'

'A right and proper act for a parson,' Walter says approvingly.

'There was a curate who ran the youth club I went to for a while when I was about fifteen, just after I left the orphanage. My foster parents made me go. I told him I was an atheist, and he didn't take offence or anything.'

'And what precisely is a "youth club"?'

'It's a place where young people meet, to socialise and play games and so on – but some are affiliated to the church, or were then.'

'And these clubs are run by parsons? A fascinating idea. I can't imagine doing so. What other peculiar activities do your parsons engage in?'

'Well, there's the parish magazine and Bible study groups and being school governors, things like that.'

'Parish magazine?'

I nod. 'It's a booklet printed just for the parish, telling everyone all the church news, when services are held and so on. The vicar writes a piece for it: probably more than one.'

Walter holds his forehead in his palm and laughs quietly.

'What?' I ask innocently.

'I should be delighted to write pieces for the "parish magazine", were it likely that I should have many readers! However, but a few of *my* parishioners are able to read. Further, I do not believe there is a great deal of "church news" to report in any event, with but one service a sennight, apart from special days.'

I nod slowly and lean on the gate watching Dafydd as he toils in the distance. Sometimes the realities of the 18th century come up and smack you in the face. 'Well all I can say is thank goodness times have changed. Everyone can read in the 21st century – almost everyone. I can't imagine not being able to read, and so much would be closed to you without it.'

'I agree with you, my dear. I have paid for servants to receive lessons over the years, with mixed results.'

'I wonder what you would really make of my time. There are so many more differences even than I've mentioned.'

'I believe I should like to see it. I am not certain that I would like to stay, however.'

'I'm certain you wouldn't!' I assure him vehemently, trying and failing to see him there in any guise whatsoever.

CHAPTER FIFTEEN

I lean out of the chaise, agog, as we pass over a bridge and under a great gatehouse with a tower into the metropolis of Shrewsbury, Walter's birthplace and a town I've never visited in any time. Once through the gateway, we're among a mass of higgledy-piggledy houses overset with church spires. In so many ways I could be in the 21st century – those churches must still be there, and the castle, and quite a few of the houses. Of course the illusion can't hold because of the horse traffic and the quaint costumes, but I feel energised by a place that has a somewhat familiar feel to it.

I expect Thomas to pull up outside an inn, but he detours around the town walls and comes to a halt beside a long terrace of sandstone houses. Walter has an unexpected, secretive smirk on his face as he gets down and holds out his hand for me to dismount.

'What's going on?' I ask him suspiciously.

'We shall be staying with my sister for two nights.'

'Your sister! You didn't even mention having any sisters!'

He laughs. 'I have but the one.'

I climb down just as the front door opens and a woman in her late thirties emerges. She doesn't run down the steps to greet her brother but rather glides; *her* cork rump doesn't bounce about gigantically on her ample buttocks but instead emphasises the small swelling of her backside to best advantage; *her* dress doesn't seem full of unnecessary frills and flounces but emphasizes her slender curves in the right places, and *her* bosom, pushed up by the ever-present stays, doesn't bounce about like twin mounds of jelly but sits firm and porcelain pale above her bodice.

'Walter, it is so pleasing to see you,' she says in a melodious voice and hugs him decorously.

'It is good to see you also, my dear,' he says, while she turns to look at me with a disdainful expression. 'Allow me to introduce my fiancée, Fallady Galbraith. Fallady, this is my sister, Jessica Holney.'

I've learned by now that women make small curtseys on greeting, and so I just about manage to do that, feeling a complete idiot. Jessica curtseys back elegantly and greets me with cold but genteel politeness. I'm wondering how this icy paragon of femininity can possibly be Walter's sister.

Jessica's house is as immaculate and well furnished as her person, but it's also full of children, who greet 'Uncle Walter' with obvious familiarity and stare at me with unabashed interest. Jessica keeps up a constant flow of pleasantries: the practised hostess. I look from her to Walter, trying to spot the resemblance, but there really aren't any. He's told me that he resembles his mother, who was dark like himself, and from whom he learned to speak fluent Welsh. Jessica, who's the same height, is far more the typical Englishwoman with her light brown hair and pale complexion. She's also, obviously, far more affluent than her brother. Her husband Edmund, she tells me proudly, is a successful wool merchant.

We dine together when he returns home, a jolly, plump man and quite a contrast to his wife. Although not quite like being at the hall, this house is opulent by the standard of the parsonage and is also inhabited by quite a bevy of servants. As I eat my mutton, I hope Walter realizes that this isn't the kind of encouragement I need to persuade me of the joys of matrimony. The children, eight of them aged from mid-teens to five, are very well behaved at the table, and he seems at ease in talking to them, but it's an alien world to me.

Later, the children have been taken off to bed, and the four of us sit in their elegant parlour, sipping brandy – very slowly in my case – and Jessica says, with poorly disguised insincerity, 'Walter wrote and told me all about you. I was so sorry to hear about your misfortune.'

Hmm, so he's only told her the abandonment story. Does she think I'm taking advantage of his kindly nature? I'm trying to decide how to respond when he intervenes.

'Fallady was most distressed at the time, but all is well now,' he says.

'Are you truly alone in the world?' Jessica asks me pointedly.

'Um, well, yeah… um yes, I suppose I am now,' I reply, startled into forgetting my Georgian-speak.

'You have no dowry – no money or possessions at all?' she says, disapproval evident in both her tone and expression.

'D-dowry?' I stammer.

Walter takes my hand in his. 'I have no need of any dowry,' he says firmly, staring his sister down in an unusual display of displeasure. 'And Fallady is no longer alone in the world. She has me, and Anna too.'

I press his hand back and wonder if he expected this attitude from his sister. Is this why he never mentioned her before?

'Yes indeed, congratulations to you both on your forthcoming wedding,' Edmund says, breaking a moment of awkward silence by raising his glass.

'Speaking of which,' Walter says, 'Fallady would appreciate your assistance in purchasing some new gowns and other garments, Jessica. Your style cannot be faulted, and I should like to see my bride wed in a becoming gown.'

'Of course,' she replies, slightly mollified. 'I should be delighted.'

Despite her haughty ways, this comes as quite a relief to me. Having to rely on Walter alone to help choose never boded too well, given that he thinks I look good in his late wife's fusty old dresses.

We set out on our shopping trip the next morning, and it soon becomes clear that Jessica is fully acquainted with every dress shop and drapers in town. We let her take charge as she sails through each one, looking at styles worn by models, mantua designs in books, and bolts of material in the drapers. It hadn't even crossed my mind that everything is made to measure, and of course it all has to be hand sewn – luckily not by me. Walter doesn't seem particularly concerned about the expense during this excursion, although I can't help feeling uneasy as I watch it mount up.

At the end of an exhausting morning, there are two pairs of shoes, four new gowns and various undergarments on order, and Jessica also suggests I might want to purchase at least one repulsive item of headgear. When I tell her I dislike hats, I gather from her astonished reaction that such an attitude is as likely in this age as disliking tea. She wears her hair fashionably large and powdered and has a gigantic hat set on top of it. It's the one thing about her appearance that looks ridiculous in my eyes.

Walter wants to show me his and Jessica's birthplace, so we walk across the crumbling Welsh Bridge with its impressive tower to a small and modest black and white house down a little side road. 'Our father was but a curate at that time,' he says.

Afterwards we stroll at leisure through the picturesque streets, constantly coming across people who know Walter or Jessica and to whom I have to be introduced. My curtsey muscles get very tired. I have my camera secreted in one of the tie-on pockets that are part of the female undergarments – actually quite a handy one since they're large pockets – and I long to sneak it out and get a few shots, but I can hardly do that with Jessica at my side.

We return to her house for dinner with the houseful of children, but after the nursemaid has taken the children off to bed, the four of us play cards. I have at least learned the rules of a couple of them and can acquit myself well enough to pass. Walter and I even win a sixpence at Quadrille.

I'm relieved when we leave Jessica behind the next morning, looking just as elegant as ever. To my considerable relief, she and Edmund won't be able to attend the wedding but have promised to send my dresses along as soon as they're ready.

'I do not believe you greatly enjoyed our excursion,' Walter says, as he plays with a glass of brandy.

I'm hunched over the blazing parlour fire, trying to dispel the last few shivers brought on by the chaise journey home in pouring rain. I try not to dwell on the steaming bath I'd have had if this were 2008. To think I used to take baths and showers for granted. This is another of those days when the 21st century seems like some far-off palace of wonders, which is probably just the way Walter sees it. He seems to be none the worse for the ordeal, and has already replaced his sopping wet wig with a spare one.

'You never told me you had such an elegant and genteel sister,' I say, rubbing my arms.

He smiles from his position on the sofa. 'I was not sure how you would take to her, or she to you, but you managed somehow to suppress your more inflammatory opinions.'

I put my hands on my hips. 'Is that so? Well I just hope you realize the shock I experienced at the sight of all those offspring. I can only hope I prove to be barren!'

He ignores this with a dignified look and says, 'Despite the differences, you tolerated each other fairly well.'

'Yes, she was very helpful with the gowns, but I'm glad you're not that rich – it would be too many servants and too much keeping up appearances for me to cope with. And as for all those children… "Uncle Walter" indeed! I hope you don't have any more surprises like that up your sleeve.'

'Up my sleeve? You need not be uneasy, my dear. There are no more.'

'She's not much like you.'

'We were ever opposites. We are not close, but she is my only sister, and I find my nephews and nieces pleasantly entertaining upon my visits.'

'I hope you're not seeking a houseful of entertaining children out of me, Reverend!'

He comes over and takes my hands. 'Just three or four would suffice, my dear,' he says, maintaining a poker face.

I eye him narrowly until he gives in and laughs. 'I like children, Fallady, but if we have none, I shall still be content.'

'Hmmm, well, I certainly shall as well.'

'By the by, I have considered the matter of a "honeymoon", and if it is truly your desire that we spend some time by ourselves, there is a small cottage in which we could stay, for perhaps a sennight.'

'Wow. Where is this cottage?' I ask, pleased.

'It is but a few miles distant, but it lies alone. We are unlikely to encounter anyone in such a lonely spot.'

'Sounds good to me. And definitely no servants?' I persist.

'If that is truly your wish.'

'You don't sound as though it's yours. Have you lived any of your life without them – except maybe when you were at Oxford?'

He purses his lips. 'Even there I had a man servant.'

I fling myself down into a chair. 'A whole life lived under the gaze of servants. I can't even imagine it.'

He watches me with an expression of faint amusement. 'Very well, I shall tell the Widow Evans that we should like to spend a sennight in her cottage. It will be a most interesting experience.'

The next two weeks fly by, with congratulatory visits from most of the local gentry and clergy, long walks with Walter as the weather improves, and an enormous attack of nerves on my part.

With one day to go, Walter takes me pillion on Bess for a couple of miles across the fields, and then we walk up a steep hill to a spot with a view of Llanycoed.

'Are you feeling any better, my dear?' he asks solicitously as we admire the scene. 'You are still looking most pale. It is not like you to have no appetite.'

I shiver slightly, and he puts his arm around me. 'You are cold?'

'No, just scared.'

His arm tightens around me, but he purses his lips thoughtfully and then says quietly, with some effort, 'It is possible to cancel the wedding, if you cannot countenance it.'

I turn to him in surprise. 'Is that what you're thinking, that I've changed my mind?'

He regards me keenly. 'You have been very withdrawn and unlike yourself for the past four days.'

I lean against his chest. 'I suppose I have,' I say, my voice muffled in his coat. 'But it's just… well, six weeks ago I hadn't even met you! What if it's some terrible mistake? We're from such different worlds. What if we end up hating each other?'

'Perhaps we should not dwell too much on what if, cariad. I admit that I had never anticipated such a hasty wedding. It seems to me however, that we should take whatever time we have. The Lord may still have plans for you.'

I pull away to look at him curiously. 'You still think I might get back to 2008?'

'It seems possible, perhaps even probable,' he replies, looking even more sombre than usual.

I reach up to brush his cheek. 'Well don't worry; I don't want to cancel the wedding. Just think how unseemly that would be.'

He smiles slightly. 'Indeed, most unseemly.'

We sit down on the grass and pick out the parsonage and the church in the distance. I try not to remember how it looks in 2008.

'Do you think you might be able to find some measure of contentment here, Fallady?' Walter asks, obviously still anxious.

'I'd feel more free if I could ride, I think.'

'I shall teach you if that is what you wish. And you can always use the chaise.'

'That's not free, not with a servant on hand at all times.'

He chuckles. 'Even I often ride with a servant.'

'Well you're accustomed to it. I need to be alone sometimes, and I couldn't bear being completely dependent. It would be hard to live with no freedom, although you do make up for a lot of things.'

'Even lack of plumbing and hot water?'

'Well, Reverend,' I say, lying back on the grass, 'I think you might just win out over hot baths.'

'I'm delighted to hear it,' he murmurs, looking down at me.

'I'm sure you'll think me most brazen, but I could really do with another kiss,' I hint, squinting at him against the glaring blue sky.

He sighs. 'It is becoming increasingly difficult to stop at kisses. I am glad we have but a few hours to wait.'

The next morning Nerys helps me to dress in my new gown, delivered earlier in the week by one of Jessica's servants. It's made of light blue satin and is free of the frills and bows that the late Mrs Edgemond must have preferred. It doesn't sport a cork rump and is a little more decorous over the bosom, so that my cleavage doesn't bulge out quite so dramatically. My bum still looks enormous, but at least it's actual flesh! I wear Walter's gift necklace of garnets, even though it doesn't really go with the blue, and Nerys tuts over arranging my hair and complains that I ought to have it dressed properly like any other lady. When she's finished I look at myself in the mirror and decide I don't look too bad. To my surprise, I'm looking thinner.

When I descend the stairs to Walter, I'm pleased to see the look of appreciation in his eyes.

'I have never seen you look more beautiful, cariad,' he says.

Did he really just call *me* beautiful? I take a closer look at him, wearing his best of everything: waistcoat, breeches, frock coat, shiny buckled shoes and even his wig. 'You look very fetching yourself, Reverend,' I murmur, 'but it's a shame about that wig!'

He pretends to be offended. 'I can't imagine what you mean. It is my best wig, made in London and reserved for only the most dignified of occasions.'

I laugh. 'Well I'm sure your parishioners will appreciate it, even if I don't. But thank you for calling me beautiful.' Even at the height of his ardour, Andy never called me that.

Given the large congregation that's expected, Walter and I can't just slip to the front of the church, say the words and escape, which is what *I* would have preferred. No, I have to wait outside with just Nerys for company while Walter goes in and assumes the bridegroom's place. Mr and Mrs Greenleaf arrive just as Walter leaves me, and Mrs Greenleaf, having given my arm a squeeze and told me what an attractive gown I'm wearing, hurries into the church. I'm trembling with nerves, and I'm afraid the squire will be able to tell, but he says nothing as he takes my arm and, with Nerys behind us as a de facto bridesmaid, we take the slow walk up the aisle.

The church is full, and everyone's staring at me, although it's surely Walter who ought to be the real object of interest. Luckily I don't do anything embarrassing like trip on my hem while under the gaze of so many curious eyes, and when Mr Greenleaf lets go of my arm and I'm standing beside my bewigged spouse-to-be, I relax a bit, because all that's in front of me is Mr Jenkins.

I glance aside at Walter, and he smiles reassuringly. I try not to think too much about the irrevocable nature of what I'm doing while Mr Jenkins intones the standard words, most of which are pretty familiar, even if they are the ones from the old Book of Common Prayer. It seems as though I'm watching myself from afar as I say the words I never expected to say: 'I, Fallady, take thee, Walter, to my wedded husband.'

What seems like the entire parish gravitates to the tiny local pub, the Horseshoes, where some food's been laid on to complement the vast quantities of ale everyone's glugging back. I barely drink one tankard, but I note that Walter gives up his recent conversion to temperance, particularly as Dr Benbow is there, rosy faced and noisy under the influence. The carousing lasts all afternoon, and my face muscles are tired from smiling by the time we escape to the chaise that's loaded up ready for our honeymoon. Mrs Greenleaf throws a couple of handfuls of grain as we trot off, and I heave a huge sigh of relief and lay my head on Walter's shoulder, at long last completely free to do so in public. In the same spirit, he puts his arm around me, and, you could say, we depart into the sunset, the Reverend and Mrs Edgemond. Horrifying!

CHAPTER SIXTEEN

Luckily for me, the twenty tankards of beer I was sure Walter had thrown back in the pub were a mere trifle and not twenty at all, or so he assures me when we arrive at the cottage, which is only five miles to the south of Llanycoed, but is suitably isolated and adjacent to a fast-flowing stretch of river.

Once inside, we just look at each other across the candlelit living room, as though there's some spell that we don't want to break. After all the suppressed passion and frustration of the past few weeks, neither of us seems to know what to do or say. Finally we both start into movement at the same time and come together laughing.

'I have a surprise for you,' Walter says when we emerge from a lengthy kiss.

'Oh yes?' I say, and wonder if he's suddenly getting into innuendo, especially when he takes my hand and leads me up the stairs. He pushes open the door of a small bedchamber and lifts up his candle. I peer across the room and there beside the single bed my stunned gaze falls upon a wooden bathtub.

I turn to look at him. 'You arranged this?'

'I have purchased it for you, my dear,' he says proudly. 'We shall take it back to the parsonage with us – although I trust that you won't wish to take daily baths, as heating such an amount of water is so costly.'

I hug him and lay my head on his chest.

'I had an inkling you would appreciate this wedding gift more than any jewellery or clothing I might purchase,' he says, pleased.

'You're right about that!' I agree. 'But I wasn't expecting a wedding gift, and I can't buy you one.'

'You don't need to buy me one. You have married me, after all, and I apprehend how difficult this has been for you.'

'Kiss me again, Walter,' I command, putting my arms around his neck. He obliges, very gently, and then shows me to the other bedchamber, which is far larger and decked out very prettily.

'Our nuptial bed, my dear,' he says with a very naughty grin.

'Very nice too,' I say, and waste no time unbuttoning and removing his waistcoat, which sends his eyebrows shooting into his wig.

'Fallady, should we not –'

I lie back on the bed and drag him down, my hands reaching to pull off his shirt.

He groans and gives up, his lips on mine. 'Most brazen,' he murmurs between kisses.

It's a peculiar sensation to wake up with Walter beside me, and what's more a de-wigged Walter, as he's managed to cast it off at some point. I push myself up to look at him, still asleep. His hair has started to grow, and it's almost black, with a few grey streaks here and there. I caress his hairy chest and he opens one eye enquiringly. 'Fallady, cariad,' he rumbles sleepily, and puts out his arm to bring me closer. I lean my head on his chest and think about my situation. Married! Me! This isn't what I anticipated when I moved to Felin Gyfriniaeth. Then again I'm not sure anymore what I was looking for, other than escape. It wasn't romance – I'd given up any such expectations long ago. I wonder how things would have gone if this hadn't happened? Would I have got bored? Would I have looked for a job?

A part of me still wants to return home, but my last attempt proved how difficult it would be to leave the reverend behind. Even so, I miss my family, and I miss being the real me, the free me.

Walter strokes my back. 'Are you all right, my dear? You seem to be sighing into my chest a great deal. I hope you are not regretting matters already?'

I turn my head to look at him. 'No, it's not that. I was thinking about my brother and sisters and wondering if anyone's worrying about me.'

'I am sorry. I tend to forget that you have left this life behind.'

I decide it's better not to dwell on it. 'Well, at least I have my bathtub to enjoy,' I say and get out of bed.

He laughs and sits up. 'And since you insisted on no servants, I daresay you and I will have to fill it with water.'

'Out of the well?' I ask, thinking that dragging buckets of water up from wells looks like very hard work.

He nods, puts his feet to the floor and automatically reaches for his wig, stopping self-consciously when he sees me watching. 'Do I take it, my dear, that you intend to hold me to my promise during our honeymoon?'

'Well, I think your own hair is far more attractive.' I sigh. 'You really don't want to be de-wigged at all, do you?'

He favours me with a wry smile. 'It was perhaps a rash promise. I did not realize that I would have such difficulty in keeping it. However, I shall do so, since it means so much to you.'

'It won't be so bad with only the two of us. Speaking of which, I fancy wearing my 21st-century clothes while we're alone here.'

His eyebrows climb, but he just watches me as I put them on, shaking his head in a slightly reproving fashion. Finally he can contain himself no longer and says, 'I fail to see how such garments can be considered becoming. They resemble sailors' costume more than anything else.'

I giggle. 'They're called jeans, and both men and women wear them. I think you'd look very sexy in a pair of jeans.'

'Very *sexy*?'

'Mind you, those breeches are quite sexy. I mean, they don't leave a lot to the imagination –'

'Fallady, if we are to fill your bathtub, I think we had better avoid this talk of what is *sexy*.'

'Oh?' I say innocently. 'I thought you might be tired out after last night.'

He chuckles and takes my arm. 'We shall both be tired out after a morning hauling and heating water. Not to mention cooking our own food.'

'Well as to that, you asked Martha to provide enough pies and tarts to last us a fortnight, rather than a sennight.'

'I am afraid I don't have a great deal of faith in our combined cooking skills,' he replies.

We head out to the well where Walter hauls up the buckets of water and I help to carry them into the house and pour them into a cauldron over the ancient-style fireplace range. The water seems to take all morning to boil, and then we have to lug the buckets of hot water up the stairs. It's quite an eye-opener on how difficult life was before plumbing. It's no wonder washing isn't high on anyone's agenda.

When my bath is finally full, I sprinkle in some sprigs of dried lavender that had been left for me, apparently, by the lady who's letting us use the cottage, and immerse myself for the first time in what seems like years. The reverend, likely exhausted by his unaccustomed labours, sits on the bed watching me with his arms crossed and an expression of mixed horror and amusement on his face, particularly when I start plastering my head with the awful soap they use.

'Now you're growing your hair, I think it's definitely going to need washing at least once a week,' I say cheekily. 'I think you should use this bathtub too, so that we get good use out of it.'

He shakes his head and purses his lips, but I know he's trying to keep a straight face.

'Haven't they invented the phrase "Cleanliness is next to Godliness" yet?' I persist, as I scrub myself thoroughly.

'They have not!' he says firmly.

'Well, it's a common phrase in my time. Sounds like it was someone religious who said it, don't you think, Reverend?'

'I wash every day, my dear, as you are well aware, and I am not entirely convinced that immersion in such a quantity of water is beneficial.'

Some of his archaic ideas will obviously take some shifting.

'So, are you ready to sample my culinary skills?' I say, changing the subject. 'I have in mind some nice egg and chips.'

'Egg and chips?' he repeats, looking puzzled. 'What are *chips*?'

'Martha did send along those potatoes I requested, I hope? Chips are fried potatoes. Yum yum. I can't believe I'm living in a time before fish and chip shops. How can this even be Britain? At least roast beef is already on the menu, or I should feel even more lost.'

Walter shakes with laughter but tries to maintain a mock severe expression. 'Yum yum? Fish and chip shops?'

I'm forced to explain these key matters at length, babbling away far more than usual.

'You are even more outrageous without any servants present, Fallady,' Walter says. 'I had not realized that you felt so constrained.'

'I have to say it's lovely without them.' I sit forward in the bath and give him a close look. 'When you say outrageous, is that good or bad?'

'*I* find you most entertaining, my dear, but I fear you will find certain aspects of our life somewhat disagreeable.'

'I'm trying not to think about all those aspects,' I say, and sink down under the cooling water. 'I'm concentrating on the now.'

'I am gratified to hear that you anticipate so many disagreeable aspects.'

I gurgle with laughter. 'Well, *you* are most agreeable, and that's what really counts,' I say, trying to swill the sticky soap out of my hair.

When I clamber out of the bath Walter says, 'I believe you have lost weight.'

'I know. I suppose it's because there's no chocolate here, and we've been going on all those long walks.'

'Chocolate? It is a pleasant drink, but very dear.'

'Well, we have it in the form of bars as well. Many, many different kinds of chocolate bar.' My mouth waters as a parade of Mars bars, Cadbury's crème eggs, Aeros and more passes through my mind. I shake my head decisively: best not to think about it. I look down at myself. 'Nice to have lost a bit of weight, I suppose. Does it really not matter to you that I'm fat?'

He raises his eyebrows. 'Fat? You are pleasantly plump. I have told you on many occasions that you are –'

'A fine figure of a woman?'

He laughs. 'Indeed. And if you do not cover yourself we shall be eating very late. I feel obliged to point out that it is midday and we have not yet eaten breakfast!'

I throw on my clothes quickly. 'Very well, Reverend. Egg and chips for breakfast!'

As we jolt back to the parsonage a week later, I reflect with satisfaction on our time alone. We got to know one another better in more ways than one, ate all the pies and tarts, and made many poor attempts at our own cooking. I even stopped being constantly on the alert for diseases. It was the first time since arriving in the 18th century that I could let my guard down and be myself. Luckily for me, Walter seemed to find that side of me very amusing, but he reciprocated for the wig by persuading me not to wear my 'sailors' costume' as much as I'd have liked.

I'm trussed up in my stays again and wondering how life is going to be as Mrs Edgemond. The week away has at least given me the peace to come to terms with it all, and my feelings for Walter have grown. He seems very happy with his lot, particularly as he has his wig back on.

The servants are all in attendance to greet us on our arrival at the parsonage, and the change in my status is immediately apparent.

'Dinner will be served at three,' Martha says, looking from me to Walter and then back at me. 'We've a nice big pike that Dafydd caught yesterday.'

Walter is silent, so I gather I'm expected to make some appropriate comment. 'That sounds excellent, Martha,' I say, feeling like a total fraud. I don't know if it's excellent or not – I've never eaten pike in my life.

Since the servants obviously propose to defer to me on many matters that were previously Walter's responsibility such as, I'm sorry to say, cooking, cleaning and other domestic arrangements, I suspect that that part of my new life will figure highly among the 'disagreeable aspects' that the reverend and I discussed on our honeymoon.

'Mr and Mrs Greenleaf will be dining with us on Wednesday sennight,' I say to Martha. 'Perhaps we can have roast beef with roast potatoes and the Yorkshire puddings I showed you how to make.'

'Of course, ma'am.'

I watch Martha leave the parlour with a sense of relief. I think I actually sounded as though I knew what I was talking about. In the two weeks since the honeymoon, I've been forcing myself to take an interest in the housekeeping and other activities around the house and the little smallholding behind it. I've learned how to use the ancient range and watched (note the key word 'watched') as Martha or Thomas milked the cows, made butter, gathered eggs and fed the pigs.

There's been quite a lot of adjusting to do. One thing that became apparent pretty quickly was my new position in the local hierarchy. Invitations have flooded in, and Walter feels obliged to attend the various dinners and events, principally with clergy and other such worthies in nearby villages or in Tref-ddirgel. 'It will not last, my dear,' he says whenever I protest that we've barely had any time to ourselves. I catch him sometimes, watching me anxiously, as though he suspects I might tire of it all. Not that there's any means of escape if I do.

As promised, he's been teaching me to ride, although to my annoyance I'm expected to ride side-saddle, which is awkward and uncomfortable. To Walter, the idea of my riding astride simply would not be seemly.

It hasn't been too terrible being Mrs Edgemond, and it's good that Walter is around a lot of the time. Instead of the standard hunting, hare coursing and fishing that the squire and other clergy seem to enjoy, he prefers gardening and his study of rocks and plants.

I head over to the harpsichord to get some practice. I've got quite into it with such a shortage of other entertainment, but my talent leaves a lot to be desired.

Walter comes in as I fluff yet another chord. 'Your playing improves daily,' he says kindly.

'How's Mr Fletcher?' I ask, closing the lid.

'I do not think he will last long. Dr Benbow believes he will go tonight.'

'He's married, isn't he?'

'Indeed,' he says, frowning. 'Mrs Fletcher is not too well herself.' He looks pensively into the fire for a moment. 'It occurs to me that you could undertake some visiting in the parish, if you wished to do so. It is quite customary for the parson's wife to visit the sick, elderly and needy, and it might provide you with the additional interest that you seek.'

Visiting the sick! A huge part of me would welcome the chance to do something, particularly as my medical knowledge, modest though it is in the 21st century, might actually be of some use here. On the other hand, we're talking *diseases*. So far, no smallpox, but there are a lot of other nasty things about.

I'm silent for so long that Walter crosses the room and looks at me quizzically over the top of the harpsichord. 'You are unusually quiet. The prospect does not appeal to you?'

'I'm not sure. I'm just thinking about it,' I temporise. 'When you say "customary" does that mean people expect it of me? You never mentioned it before.'

'I had not thought about it. It is not something that appealed to Jenny, although she would make visits very occasionally. It is not *expected*, but I believe it would be welcomed. I tend to make visits myself if I hear that someone is sick, but I believe a feminine presence is often more comforting.'

I bite my lip. 'Would I be able to actually help people though? I mean, make a difference?'

'Sometimes merely being there makes a difference.'

'As the parson, yes, but they want you for religious things –' I break off as Walter splutters into laughter.

'Religious things?' he repeats, shaking his head, but then sobers again. 'Indeed, the sick or dying often desire my presence for prayers and the holy sacrament, but that is not all. Sometimes it is simply enough to listen or to send food or to give money when the parishioner is needy.'

'Hard for me to give money when I don't have any,' I can't help jibing.

He sighs. 'I anticipated that remark. I believe it would be appropriate to give you an allowance to spend as you wish.'

I fold my arms. 'Allowance, eh?' I feel anger rise as the powerlessness of my position hits me afresh. I have to be kept. I'm *allowed* some money. I can't do anything without Walter's approval. It's only his expression of surprised dismay that cools my ire. I shake my head at him. 'Sometimes you have no idea what it's like to be me in this alien world, Reverend.'

He looks at me solemnly. 'So you do not desire an allowance, my dear?'

'I don't want to be in a position where I desire an allowance, but since I *am* in that position, it's obviously the best I can hope for,' I say ungratefully.

He purses his lips. 'You are missing your 21st-century freedoms?'

'I don't like being dependent on you for just about everything.'

He's thoughtfully silent for a moment but then says, 'There are some matters in which I am dependent on you.'

'Which matters?'

'The great amusement and diversion you provide me, cariad. The pleasure I take in your company exceeds any value.'

'No husband could say nicer things,' I admit, getting up and taking his hands. 'As to the visiting, perhaps I could go with you to start with and see what happens? I don't feel very confident among other people yet.'

'Of course.'

I study him in his ever-present wig. 'By the way, surely the day of de-wigging must be getting close? Your hair's grown to an acceptable length, I think.'

'I believe it is not yet quite long enough,' he says firmly.

'I suspect it will never be long enough,' I say and watch his face for the reaction.

'I apprehend that there is only one way to put a stop to this nonsense,' he murmurs.

'And what way might that be?'

Wordlessly, he plants his lips firmly on mine.

CHAPTER SEVENTEEN

'I hope you don't desire to spend too much time riding alone, my dear,' Walter says as we plod along on his mare. He's taking me pillion to a farm halfway to Tref-ddirgel to see about a horse of my own. I'm as excited about it as I would be at home about getting a new car. The horse has become a symbol of freedom to me.

'How much is too much?' I ask, grinning.

He regards me over his shoulder. 'Any is really too much, since few women would do it and it is –'

'Not seemly!' I finish for him.

'It is also not necessarily safe. There are at times highwaymen abroad on the roads.'

'Highwaymen, eh? Well, I don't have much in the way of valuables for them to rob me of. How many highwaymen have accosted you recently, Reverend?'

He gives me a severe look. 'That is not the point. As a woman riding alone without protection, you would be easy prey.'

'So if there was a highwayman lying in wait behind that tree just ahead of us, you'd be able to protect me how?' I ask.

He sighs volubly. 'I would at least be with you.'

'So we'd both be robbed – if we had anything worth stealing. Walter, if you're that worried about it, why are you buying me a horse at all?'

He pulls on the reins and draws the mare to a halt before turning to me. 'I wish to see you happy,' he says simply.

'You're not going to worry about me every time I go out alone, are you?' I ask, touched.

'Will there be so many times? Do you really desire so much to be alone?'

'Just some of the time, that's all. Anyway, tell me the truth, have you ever been held up by a highwayman?'

He's pursing his lips so noticeably that I know the answer before he gives it. 'No, I have not. That does not, however, preclude the possibility.'

'I'm not quite the wilting violet, you know. I shouldn't be as helpless as you imagine. I took a course in self-defence a couple of years ago and I reckon I still remember all the moves.'

He laughs. 'Course in self-defence? Moves?'

'Living in London can make you feel easy prey, as you put it, so I was taught how to defend myself.'

'You could defend yourself against a highwayman?' he asks, in amused disbelief.

'Well, there aren't any highwaymen around in my time, but I could at least try. I can give you a demonstration of my self-defence skills, if you really don't believe me,' I say mischievously. 'But then I might unman you, and that wouldn't be at all satisfactory.'

He bursts into a loud guffaw. 'Unman me indeed. I should certainly not like to be unmanned. You are full of surprises, Fallady.'

He's quite surprising himself, at times. My eyes have been opened on a number of fronts now that I've accompanied him on some pastoral visits. I've seen the other side of the 18th century: the poverty, dirt and untreatable disease. I've also seen a very different aspect to my husband. People are usually pleased to see us and treat us with a mild deference that I find embarrassing, although he naturally accepts it as perfectly in order. He will, however, go to the smallest hovel as willingly as to the hall, and he demonstrates the same interest in all his parishioners as he showed in me, listening to them carefully and offering advice or religious comfort accordingly. I cringe a bit when he says prayers with them (as his spouse, I'm forced to join in for the sake of seemliness), but then it *is* his job, after all. I get the impression, from little comments here and there, that he isn't entirely the norm for a parson in this time.

He's also kept his word and begun doling out what I think of privately as my 'pocket money'. I'm granted £1 per month, but as I've never bought anything on my own, the value of the 18th-century pound eludes me, particularly as I was too young to have been brought up with pounds, shillings and pence, being only three when the changeover to decimal took place. He's had to educate me in that as well, and I've explained to him at length just how much more logical the decimal system seems to be.

When we arrive at the farm, we're taken to see the horse that's for sale. She's a chestnut with a white blaze, and despite my former ignorance of the equine, she looks pretty sweet to me. Walter examines her with the thoroughness of the expert horseman and declares her to be a fine beast for the price. 'What do you think of her?' he asks me.

'I think she'd do very nicely,' I say, stroking her nose.

'Then we shall purchase her, my dear,' he says, and moves off to discuss payment with the farmer. I stroke the mare's nose again and fight back the lost feeling that comes over me at such moments of disenfranchisement. It's not Walter's fault; it's the way things are, and after all, many women are willing even in my time to have a man take charge of things. Many *want* a man to take charge of things. But I've never been that kind of woman. At least he did say 'we shall purchase her', I remind myself: a small improvement.

I cheer up when the mare's saddled and bridled and I get to ride her back alongside my husband, who asks me a lot of questions about London and my life there. That whole lifestyle of work, unavoidable socialising (none of my flats were the kind you wanted to spend a lot of time in) and the loneliness that you get from being the wrong person in the wrong place is becoming a dim landscape in my memory. Given a choice between the two, I would opt for parson's wife, despite its many annoyances.

'I believe you might be the better person to talk to Abigail Davies,' Walter says at the dinner table two days later. 'She appears to have rejected Christ. I had hoped I might eventually prevail, but thus far I have failed.'

I raise my eyebrows. 'Am I the right person for someone who's rejected Christ?'

He laughs softly and humourlessly. 'This is a particular instance, my dear. She has for some time behaved with considerable impertinence towards me.'

I nearly choke on my roast chicken. 'Impertinence? Towards the parson?'

He nods. 'Indeed.' He smiles slightly, catches my eye and adds, 'It is rare, but it does occur.'

'So what's caused it?'

'I am uncertain. Her parents are regular churchgoers, and are what you describe as "very religious". She had always seemed such a good, dutiful girl, but of late she has entered a state of rebellion against them and against their beliefs. She has recently attended church with only the most sullen reluctance.'

'Let me guess, she's a teenager?'

'You are correct. She is fourteen. It is not so simple, however. Mr and Mrs Davies are very poor and desire her to go into service. They have, with my assistance, secured her a position at the hall. She now insists that she will not take it, and has even hinted that she might run away to London. It is causing them considerable distress and anxiety.'

'Isn't there anything else she can do?'

He gives me one of his looks. 'There are few choices available. A position at the hall is considered an excellent start.'

'To a career as a servant,' I say.

He grins. 'I knew I should engage your sympathies, my dear. I trust then that you agree to this visit?'

'But what do you want me to achieve? I can't tell her God's going to solve all her problems and she should accept her lot in life and get to work scrubbing the squire's floors, or whatever it is you have in mind for her.'

He raises his eyebrows innocently. 'Can you not? I was certain that that was exactly what you would tell her.'

I eye him narrowly and he laughs. 'I leave it entirely to you. Her reasons elude me, and her sauciness towards me renders me somewhat speechless.'

I giggle, trying to imagine Walter rendered speechless. 'I assume I'm likely to get that attitude as well, especially being your wife.'

He nods. 'I fear so, but I do believe you might better understand her reasoning.'

Next morning I decide not to waste any time and walk the half a mile down the road to the cottage in which Abigail lives with her parents and eleven brothers and sisters. The cottage is one of the kind I'm used to seeing on calendars, with roses around the door and blossom-covered trees in the garden, but it's a very small house for fourteen people.

A worn down woman wearing a worn down dress and apron opens the door, curtseys and ushers me in as if I'm some kind of royalty, having recognised me at once from church. The house is full of children, just like Jessica's, but Mrs Davies chases them all out of her tiny parlour except for Abigail, who leans against the door jamb and stares at me rudely, her coppery hair lank and straggly around her pale, freckled face and her clothing rough and homespun. I hate the sense I have at that moment, that I'm some rich Lady Bountiful come to tell her what to do. Me of all people: little orphan Fally. At least Walter always has his religion as his reason for what he does. I have no real excuse except some confused need to be useful.

'Mr Edgemond was here to talk to Abigail yesterday,' Mrs Davies says, looking a little flustered.

'Yes, he told me. He thought it might be a good idea if I called as well.'

'It's very good of you, Mrs Edgemond,' Mrs Davies says, twisting her apron between her hands. 'I fear for her mortal soul, I do indeed. The Lord knows we've brought her up to be a good Christian girl, and this is how she repays us. We're at our wits' end, no mistake about it. Our wits' end.'

I look at Abigail, and she has an expression of scorn on her face. She meets my gaze boldly and doesn't look away. I feel a giggle trying to rise as I imagine the reverend faced with such an attitude from a mere slip of a girl.

'Could I speak to Abigail on her own, Mrs Davies?' I ask.

'Oh, well, yes, of course. Of course. I have a pie baking in the kitchen. Now mind your manners, Miss,' she says to Abigail, who doesn't respond.

When we're alone, Abigail flops down on to one of the chairs and flicks a hand through her hair. 'I suppose you're going to tell me all about my sins,' she says.

'I'd have thought you didn't believe in sins any longer, if you've lost your faith in God,' I answer, to be rewarded with a look of surprise.

She folds her arms and glares at me. 'I thought you'd be here to talk about God, being Parson's wife.'

'I'm not here to talk about God, unless you want to. I gather you don't want to take the position at the hall?'

She flicks her hair again, but instead of answering just stares sullenly out of the window.

'Is there anything else you could do?'

She looks me up and down, and I'm conscious of my fairly new gown, which is decidedly elegant compared with the drab brown dress she's wearing.

'What would you rather do?' I persist in the face of silence. She tightens her lips.

'Can you read, Abigail?' I ask, prompted by sudden interest. 'I know my letters,' she mumbles.

'Enough to read?'

'Enough to write my name.'

'Would you like to be able to read?'

The shrug I was expecting doesn't come. Instead I get an intense stare. 'It's not my place,' she says bitterly.

'Who says that?'

'My parents, everyone. God made us poor, and we should be content.'

'So you're not content to work at the hall?'

She laughs hollowly. 'Skivvy to the squire, like my mother and her mother before her. The best a poor girl can expect.'

'So who are you angry with?'

She opens her mouth to reply and then stops and resumes her affectation of sullenness.

'It couldn't be God, could it?' I say softly.

Her eyes flash. 'God is for rich people, like you.'

I nod in understanding, while my mind whirls about trying to find some purchase. 'Do you believe you shouldn't learn to read?'

She looks at me properly then. 'No.'

'Because if you want to learn, I could teach you.' What *am* I saying?

She stares at me with her eyes wide, and I add, 'There's nothing wrong with learning, and learning is for everyone. Even if you have to work at the hall for a while, if you have some learning, it shouldn't be forever.'

'I'm but a girl – why would you bother with me?'

'I believe in learning.'

'It won't change my mind about God. And my parents might not allow it. They believe I should be content; they've no time for book learning.'

'I suspect they'll allow it if you take the position at the hall. Besides, once you can read, you can study the Bible for yourself and then decide whether God is only for rich people.'

There's a tiny spark of hope in her eyes that stays with me as I walk back to the parsonage a while later. I have no idea what prompted me to make the offer, but I'm now committed to teaching a flouncing fourteen year old to read. Her parents, as I'd thought, gave in. I'm afraid some of their objections were overridden by their sense that I was their 'better', which was just one of the cringe-making aspects of this morning's work. What's Walter going to think?

I find him in the garden, happily watering seedlings.

'You look somewhat fatigued, my dear. The visit did not go well?'

I sink down on to one of the wooden benches he has dotted about. 'That depends on your point of view.'

'Have you persuaded Abigail back to God?' he asks, with a decidedly mischievous expression.

'I have not, and you knew full well I wouldn't.'

'And have you persuaded her to take up the position at the hall?'

'Indeed I have, Reverend, but at a price.'

He raises his eyebrows. 'And what is the price?'

'That I teach her to read.'

He puts down his watering can and joins me on the bench. 'She asked this of you?'

I shake my head. 'I volunteered. She's crying out for it. She wants to be more than a maid – wants to know more than she's being allowed to know. I couldn't stand by and do nothing.'

'Have her parents agreed to this arrangement?'

I nod wearily. 'They're not too keen, but they agreed.'

A slow smile begins to form on his lips. 'Well, my dear, it is an interesting solution, albeit a surprising one.'

'There's more. Did she tell you why she stopped believing?'

'As she would barely speak to me other than in monosyllables or saucy remarks, the answer to that is distinctly not.'

'She thinks God is only for the rich. Her parents have told her it's their place to be poor and that it's God's will. That's not what you preach though, is it? Not at any of the sermons I've heard anyway.'

He purses his lips. 'It is a difficult matter. It is a common belief among both clergy and laity, but it is not what I believe, and it is certainly not what I preach.'

'Well you'll be pleased to know I told her when she can read, she'll be able to find out for herself by reading the Bible.'

He splutters into laughter. 'Did you indeed? Well, cariad, it seems that you have made a success of your first visit. Am I to assume that Abigail will be coming to the parsonage for her lessons?'

'That's the idea, but I didn't know how you'd feel about it.'

He's silent for a moment. 'Perhaps the small parlour would be best. The servants might object, were we to entertain another servant in the great parlour. Likely I shall hear some grumbles in any event, but no matter.'

'I hadn't thought of that. Can Martha and Nerys read? Or even Thomas and Dafydd?'

'Thomas can read comparatively well, but I believe the other three have only their basic letters. Are you proposing to teach them also?'

I shrug. 'I don't know… this could get complicated!'

CHAPTER EIGHTEEN

In mid-May, history is made at the parsonage when the reverend can bear my jibes no longer and with the greatest reluctance discards the wig for good.

I watch with amusement as he teases his hair this way and that, trying to give it the rather effeminate appearance easily achieved with a wig. His expression is one of considerable distaste as he observes his appearance in the mirror.

'You look very sexy,' I say encouragingly, glad it's still too short for him to primp or curl too much.

He gives a brief grunt of laughter but says, 'I do not know that my parishioners will think the same, my dear.'

'I certainly hope not, but I'm sure they'll think you're just as dignified and imposing a parson as you always were.'

He turns to look at me, humour returning to his sombre features. 'Dignified and imposing – is that how you see me, Fallady?'

I grin. 'I see you as many things, Reverend. Speaking of which, there's something I need to talk to you about.'

'Something serious?' he asks, sitting on the bed beside me.

I bite my lip. 'Perhaps. You might have noticed I haven't bled yet this month.'

His eyes virtually blaze with delight. 'You believe you may be with child?'

'Possibly. Of course, there's no pregnancy tests here so we'll just have to wait and see. I didn't realize you were quite that keen, but you know how I feel about it. I thought I'd be less fertile than this, being in my forties, but it's just my bad luck, I suppose.'

'Pregnancy tests? No matter.' He takes my hand. 'Of course I should like more children, but I do not wish you to suffer. Can you not reconcile yourself to it?'

I sigh gustily. 'I don't really have much choice. It could be a false alarm, though, so I wouldn't get your hopes up too much.'

He squeezes my hand. 'When you speak so much in 21st-century colloquialisms, I know you are distracted with anxiety.'

I laugh. 'We're getting far too familiar with each other's peculiar little ways. Still, at least I've taken your mind off your wig.'

Walter's de-wigging is far more of an event than I could have imagined. A few days later, over dinner at the parsonage, Mr Greenleaf, Dr Benbow and Mr Jenkins *all* express their astonishment. I squirm inwardly and feel horribly guilty, wondering if they've guessed that I'm at the root of it, but it doesn't seem to have crossed their minds. Walter certainly doesn't let on as he defends what he himself finds pretty indefensible.

'It is costly to maintain so many wigs,' he says stoutly, 'And there are a number of others wearing their own hair nowadays.'

'But none among the clergy,' Dr Benbow splutters, tipping back his glass of red wine, his own wig far larger and more elaborate than Walter's ever was.

'And few among the gentry,' the squire adds.

'It is a vanity,' Walter says firmly in his most vicarly tone, 'that I am offering up to God.'

I lift startled eyes to behold my husband, who carefully avoids my gaze but has effectively quieted his critics.

Someone else has noticed my startlement though – across the table, Laura Martin, invited because she's Mr Jenkins' intended, catches my eye and grins before returning demurely to her plate. Miss Martin is a bit of an unknown quantity, having moved to the village only a few weeks before to live with her maiden aunt. Mr Jenkins seems to have fallen for her with almost as much haste as Walter and I fell for each other, and they plan to marry in a few weeks, by banns, and with Walter officiating.

Laura Martin is a beautiful woman, but she seems at pains to try to conceal it. Unfortunately for her, it isn't working. Her blonde hair is dressed fairly simply, but still cascades over her shoulders in glorious curls and frames a well-proportioned face with a peaches and cream complexion. Given her beauty, I can't help wondering how she's reached the age of thirty and remained unmarried. Not that being single is at all uncommon in this time, but with her looks, she must have had a fair few proposals by now. That in itself interests me, and now, in that glance of sisterhood, she's captured my attention even more.

She and I are partners when we play cards after dinner, and she manages to slip into the conversation that she'd like to help with my 'school'. There's a small silence at this, since Dr Benbow is one of those who disapproves most heartily of the project. Luckily though, Mr Jenkins holds the opposite view.

'An excellent proposal,' he says, gazing at her fondly. 'What do you say, Mrs Edgemond?'

'Of course,' I reply with a smile. 'Any assistance would be most welcome.'

The school has turned out to be a lot more successful than I could have imagined. Initially, Nerys admitted she too would like to learn to read, and I began teaching both her and Abigail. Once word spread around the village, I gained several other pupils as well, most of them children, but all of them already employed either as servants or farm workers. There have been mutterings among some in Llanycoed, but luckily for me the squire is on my side, and with Walter preaching about it from the pulpit, the grumbles have eased off to an underlying murmur.

On cue, Dr Benbow winds into a monologue about the dangers of educating the poor and how it will result in turmoil throughout the land, but we've all heard it before in one form or another, and no one takes a great deal of notice, not even his wisp of a wife.

Later, when everyone's left, Walter and I sit on the window seat in the parlour. It's a balmy May evening, and the garden looks very colourful through the panes. 'So, offering it up to God, eh?' I say, running a hand through his hair.

'It seemed most appropriate,' he says, a glint of amusement in his eyes as he catches my hand.

'I feel so guilty. I didn't realize it would cause such a stir as all that.'

'Your school has also caused a stir, it seems.'

'Are you *still* glad you married me? I'm bringing so much turbulence into your ordered world.'

His familiar guffaw bursts out, and he puts his arm around me. 'I am quite content with a little turbulence, cariad, although at times it is more like a whirlwind.'

I lean against him and sigh. 'You know, if it really pains you so much, I won't hold you to the de-wigging promise.'

He holds me closer. 'It is too late, my dear. The Lord shall have my offering and gladly given, particularly as you tell me how *sexy* I look without it.'

After a moment he adds, 'I am glad you will have some help in teaching. The number of pupils has become far larger than I anticipated.'

'I know, and I don't see how I can turn people away. I had no idea there would be such a demand.'

He purses his lips. 'I do not think it is solely the fact of learning that has brought so many to the parsonage. I believe there is also the matter of... your approach.'

'My approach?' I extricate myself from his arms and stare at him.

'It is apparent that you have no concept of hierarchy. You treat everyone in the same manner, from the squire to the servants. The subtle nuances of behaviour that I learned from childhood elude you.'

'So everyone can tell I don't belong?' I ask worriedly.

'No, it is merely that you have a refreshing openness of manner that strikes everyone, particularly the poor of this parish. They come to you because you treat them equally. Were you a different type of person, this school would have but one or two pupils.'

'Do you think the squire's noticed?'

He laughs. 'He would not be so impolite as to mention it, but I suspect that he has indeed.'

I sigh. 'Does it matter? I don't think there's much I could do to change it.'

'I should certainly hope you will not try, my dear. It is a part of your charm.'

'Part of my charm, eh?' I muse. 'Well, I just hope I don't get you into any more trouble.'

'I envy you, Fallady,' Laura says.

I turn to Miss England 1779 in some surprise. 'In what way?'

She looks up from her sewing – like Anna, Laura actually enjoys sewing and carts pieces of embroidery around with her wherever she goes. 'You are so… so much yourself.'

I frown. 'I'm not sure I know what you mean.'

'You do not seem to care what anyone might think of you.'

'Oh, you mean I don't care about seemliness?'

She giggles. 'In part, but it is more than that. You ride out alone, even though you know Mr Edgemond disapproves, you forget to curtsey a considerable amount of the time, you do not dress your hair at all, and I am not sure you even notice that you behave in just the same way towards men as towards women. I should not dare to behave as you do, but I often wish that I could.'

'Mr Edgemond might well prefer me to be more decorous,' I say, 'but he's willing to put up with me as I am.'

'No, he loves you as you are. According to my aunt, he is a different person since he met you. You must know, however, that your riding out causes considerable talk in Llanycoed.'

I shrug. 'I need the time alone, and I enjoy it.'

'Are you not frightened?'

'No. No, I'm not. Perhaps I should be – Walter keeps reminding me about highwaymen.'

'My aunt tells quite a story of being held up near London when she was a girl. She claims that there were three robbers.'

'Well, let's hope there aren't any hanging around these parts. How is your dress coming along?'

Laura is happy to launch into a discussion about her wedding dress, which she's decided to sew herself, and I'm glad to get off the subject of highwaymen.

It's good to have a real female friend, and over the past month she and I have settled into a companionable routine with the teaching. She often stays to dinner, and also keeps me company sometimes when Walter has to carry out a vicarly duty. This evening he's out naming a child.

'I do not know how you have avoided learning to sew,' she says now.

'My father was happy for me to study sciences when he saw that my talents lay in that direction,' I say glibly. I'm beginning to believe the lie myself.

She sighs in sympathy. 'It must have been dreadful to lose him and find yourself with no fortune, left to the mercies of that odious cousin.'

I nod and wish I didn't have to persist in that part of the deception. In any case, Laura's own story is surprisingly similar. Her parents died in quick succession only two years ago, and she found herself being farmed around to her aunts, trying to make herself useful to them. Her Aunt Esther took her in only grudgingly, being used to a solitary life, and she was anticipating another move until Mr Jenkins proposed.

'Do you think you might come to love Mr Jenkins?' I ask.

She gives the question serious consideration. 'I do not know. I am fond of him, but it is not the way you feel about Mr Edgemond.'

'He loves you, though.'

'He is a kind man, but it is not *me* he sees or loves. It never is.'

'So that's it – the reason why you don't emphasize your attributes, not that they need any emphasis.'

'I do not like to be an ornament. I turned down many proposals because I could not find what I sought: what *you* have, Fallady,' she gazes at me earnestly, 'but my position dependent upon my aunts' whims led me to reconsider.' She drops her hands into her lap. 'Perhaps, with time, he will come to care for what is beneath the golden hair and pretty face.'

I reach out a hand to her, and she takes it gratefully. 'I have still much to thank God for,' she says briskly. 'A home of my own, at last. I am sure I shall be as content as anyone.'

Walter is delighted when I tell him my pregnancy's certain. 'It's due in January,' I say and add with some trepidation, 'what do women do about being with child in this time? I mean, I can guess there's no ante-natal care, but I *trust,* Reverend, that I'm not expected to endure any attentions from Dr Benbow.'

My husband gives me one of his looks of bemusement. 'Ante-natal care? I think not, my dear, if I understand my Latin correctly. However, for the time of birth there are midwives, of course. Mrs Greenleaf favours Dr Robbins, a very successful man midwife.'

'Does she?' I say, having a strong desire to start biting my knuckles already.

'But there are also female midwives. You need not deal with Dr Benbow if you would rather not.'

Further enquiry reveals that man midwives have no qualifications at all and just call themselves doctors anyway, whereas female midwives don't call themselves doctors or have as high a status as male midwives, even though they had been delivering babies for centuries before men got in on the act. I decide that a female midwife sounds like the best of a bad lot, and I'd better be sure to find one who can be persuaded to adopt antiseptic techniques – or the closest approximation to them that I can organise. I'm glad January's still seven months away. I'd never expected to have a baby at all, never mind having one outside the safety net of the NHS.

I sigh with pleasure as Cherry trots along one of the now-familiar rutted roads spattered with horse muck. Despite what everyone in Llanycoed seems to think about my solitary rides, I keep them to a minimum for Walter's sake. Now that I'm pregnant, he worries even more. Even so, there are times when I just *have* to get out of the house on my own, and this is one of those times. He's gone to a meeting of clergy in Oswestry; there's no school today, and what's more the sun is shining in a blue sky that is completely free of clouds or vapour trails.

It's difficult to explain to Walter how bizarre I find his hushed world. I'm forever expecting to hear the hum of traffic off in the distance somewhere or the roar of a plane cleaving the sky. Without them, all the smaller sounds seem amplified. As Cherry trots southwards at a gentle pace, I breathe the unpolluted air and watch the birds and insects. Every now and then we encounter other road traffic, usually a chaise or a pair of riders. By now I'm used to the odd looks I receive, and I tend to avoid eye contact with anyone.

I spot a small stream in a little glade a short way off the road and dismount to eat my picnic lunch. With Walter out, dinner won't be until late. The sun filters through acid-green leaves and warms the grass. I revel in the chirrups of crickets and grasshoppers and the drone of bees as they meander in and out of the wild flowers that border the burbling stream. The 18th century certainly does have its good points. It's hard to find this kind of solitary serenity in England in the 21st century.

I remount and urge Cherry back to a trot. The landscape changes from green fields and copses to gorse-covered moorland. I'm feeling relaxed and almost at home in my adopted time when an unpleasant smell wafts my way just as the road curves around to a crossroads. I cry out involuntarily as, right in front of me, an unrecognisable corpse swings sluggishly on a crude wooden gibbet. All my peaceful thoughts are shattered, and I fumble desperately to turn Cherry aside and urge her in any other direction, so that I won't be able to see or smell the corpse. Even so, it's too late to hold down my lunch. I dismount hurriedly and give way to the urge to vomit, while fighting back the unexpected tears that threaten at the shock of another 18th-century smack in the face.

As I sit back on the grass to recover, I realize I have company. A thin, patrician-looking older man sits on his horse watching me. I look him over quickly but don't see any sign of a pistol, so I assume he's not a highwayman. He looks fairly well off, as far as I can tell, with elaborate wig and elegant riding clothes, and he isn't smiling.

'Are you lost, madam?' he says.

I'm feeling cranky, as my idyll was wrecked so effectively, and I don't like his tone. 'Er, no. I'm just out riding,' I say coldly. 'Why should I be lost?'

His lips tighten as he makes a point of looking all around. 'You appear to be alone.'

'That's right,' I say. 'I am.' He's beginning to annoy me. 'But being alone doesn't indicate lost, after all.'

'Does it not, madam? I am led to question what kind of woman would take a solitary ride on the highway.'

I stand up and put my hands on my hips. 'What kind of woman? Perhaps the kind of woman who likes solitary rides,' I say, wondering who this snooty git might be.

His eyes widen with displeasure. 'I do not believe I have made your acquaintance,' he says, peering down his nose. 'I am Lord Montgomery. Perhaps you have heard of me?'

So, it's Walter's rich landowner. Damn. Well, I'm not going to start bowing and scraping, that's for sure.

'I have indeed heard of you,' I reply even more frostily. 'I am Mrs Edgemond.'

'The rector's wife? He permits you to ride alone?'

'Permits me?' I explode. 'I am my own person, Lord Montgomery. I do not need to ask my husband's permission for every itch and scratch. I am not a pet or a plaything or a possession of my *husband's*,' I spit. Temper seems to have sharpened up my Georgian-speak.

Lord Montgomery regards me in amazement. I stare back at him implacably, my hands still on my hips and distinctly reckless rage coursing through me. 18th century be damned: gibbets, supercilious gits and all.

'You are aware, Mrs Edgemond, that your husband's living is in my gift?' he says icily.

I glare at him. 'Are you insinuating that I should genuflect to you because of that? I'm not my husband. He is not responsible for *my* actions, nor I for his.'

'It is clear indeed that you are not your husband, madam. He would mind his manners before his betters.' He sniffs and adds, 'I have heard of you and your school for servants.'

'Do you object to it?' I ask combatively.

Lord Montgomery gives a toss of his bewigged head and doesn't reply. 'I assume you have recovered from your fit of sickness. I note that for all your bold words, you were overcome by the sight of such a commonplace as a corpse on a gibbet.'

'I may have some sensibilities, Lord Montgomery, but I do not have any inclination to judge people my inferiors.' Oh Walter, if you were here you'd probably be wishing the ground would swallow you up by now!

'I have no need to *judge* people my inferiors, Mrs Edgemond, when it is all too apparent that they *are* my inferiors.'

I can't help it; I know it's all a total disaster, but I can't help it. It starts with a giggle, then turns into a chortle, and finally becomes a guffaw. I'm not quite rolling on the ground with my legs in the air, but I'm afraid I put Walter to shame in my paroxysms. Lord Montgomery is so blatantly abominable. Surely he can't be real?

He watches me impassively, and I eventually sober up and wonder if I've lost Walter his living and everything he holds dear.

'Kindly accompany me to the manor, Mrs Edgemond,' Lord Montgomery orders as I take Cherry's reins and prepare to mount up.

'T-to the manor? What manor? I mean, for what purpose?'

He regards me haughtily. 'I desire you to accompany me, and I suggest most strongly that you do *not* disoblige me in this matter.'

I shrug. What *have* I done?

He sets quite a pace across the moors and fields, and I struggle to keep up, not being confident to do more than canter yet. Eventually a gigantic mansion comes into view – one that could swallow Laburnum Hall about six times.

A groom takes Cherry in hand, and I trail along in Lord Montgomery's wake. For a man of around sixty, he seems very fit and active. He still hasn't told me what he has in mind, and I'm not going to lower myself to ask. What's more, if he thinks I'm going to be overawed by the palatial house and bevy of bewigged and liveried servants, he has another think coming.

As soon as we enter the house, he's pounced upon by a pack of greyhounds, which then start sniffing around me. He shoos them off and gestures peremptorily to me to follow as he heads for the stairs, which go up on either side of one of those gigantic halls we've all seen in countless films and TV dramas. There are portraits of various aristocratic figures along the walls on both sides.

He stops so abruptly outside a door that I almost cannon into him, and in a manner completely at odds with his former behaviour, he raps gently and opens it tentatively. The room beyond is dim, but again he gestures me in. There's a small, slight figure lying in the big four-poster bed. A woman, maybe ten years my senior, moves fretfully as we approach.

'How are you feeling this afternoon, my dear?' Lord Montgomery says to her.

'But a little better,' says the woman in the bed, her voice weak and her face pinched and pale under her nightcap. She looks pointedly at me and then back at him, questioningly.

'This is Mrs Edgemond, wife of the parson of Llanycoed. She is the most impudent and disrespectful woman it has been my misfortune to meet, but it occurred to me that you might find her entertaining. Mrs Edgemond, this is my wife, Lady Lavinia. I shall leave you alone together for a time. Kindly ensure that you speak to me before you leave.'

When he's gone, Lady Lavinia gives a soft laugh. 'What did you do to him?' she asks.

'Um… argued, mostly. He didn't think I ought to be out riding alone.'

She peers at me. 'You argued with him? That was very bold. Few *men* would dare to argue with my husband.'

'Well, I didn't know who he was at first, but by the time I did know it was too late. I was too angry to stop.'

She laughs but closes her eyes as though it hurts. 'Please come and sit down, Mrs Edgemond, and tell me the whole story.'

I have no idea what Lord Montgomery thinks my presence can achieve, but his wife seems quite ill. And it's no wonder, if Dr Benbow is an example of the best medical practitioners available. Trying to please, I do as she asks, to be rewarded by her soft laugh at various points in the tale.

'I am surprised that your husband does not object to your riding alone,' she comments.

'He would certainly rather I didn't,' I confess.

'But he gives you your head.' She moves restlessly in the bed. 'I have met him, of course, Reverend Edgemond. He has always seemed a most dutiful rector: more so than many.'

'Yes, he's happy in his living, I think.'

'You need not worry. My husband mentioned the living merely to test your mettle.'

'Test my mettle? You mean –'

'He is unaccustomed to opposition. Indeed, Mrs Edgemond, you are likely the first person to oppose him in many a year – and a woman at that. It is inconceivable that anyone would laugh at him when he had given one of his best put-downs. Would that I had seen such an historic moment,' she murmurs.

'Are you in a lot of pain?'

She sighs. 'I am plagued by fatigue, headache and melancholy. If I take laudanum I do little but sleep, and I do not like its effects. My husband seeks ways to distract me, and indeed you are a refreshing change. Perhaps you could return, in a day or so.'

'Of course,' I say, watching as she closes her eyes wearily, then easing slowly out of the room to find a maid waiting, charged with taking me to Lord Montgomery.

'Well, Mrs Edgemond, what did you make of my wife?' he says, reclining on a chaise longue, surrounded by lolling greyhounds.

'She seems quite unwell,' I say carefully.

'Did you manage to amuse her?'

'I think I probably did. She suggested I come back in a couple of days.'

'Then I trust that you will do so,' he says in a tone that suggests I have no other option in the matter. 'You may come with your husband, if you choose.'

'I'd be happy to come back, but is there nothing that can be done to help her?'

He pats one of his greyhounds and doesn't look up at me as he replies. 'It seems not. The physicians have bled her and blistered her and drenched her in their potions, and not a one of them has improved matters.'

As the maid leads me out of the door, Lord Montgomery adds, 'Mrs Edgemond, you would do well to recollect that it is customary to curtsey, particularly to one's betters.'

I turn to look at him, but his expression is as solemn as ever. 'I shall try to remember that, Lord Montgomery,' I say, but still fail to curtsey, as that would be admitting he's my better.

CHAPTER NINETEEN

Walter returns that evening and finds me sitting in his study, sorting out my little heap of paracetamol. He looks at the packets with interest. 'What are those, my dear?'

'Painkiller tablets,' I say.

'You are in pain?' he asks, concerned.

'No, nothing like that. I… um… I met Lord Montgomery today.'

The reverend looks aghast and sits down rather quickly. 'Indeed? When you were out riding?'

'Yes. It was an… interesting experience.'

'Fallady, are you attempting to tell me that you have offended Lord Montgomery?'

'That's one way of putting it.'

Walter is a little pale. 'Is there another way of putting it?'

'Well, he thinks I'm the most impudent and disrespectful woman it's ever been his misfortune to meet.'

There's a moment's silence. 'What did you say to him?' he asks heavily.

'Quite a lot. I didn't know who he was at the time.' I pause while Walter regards me in dismay. 'We had a… discussion about behaviour towards betters. He assured me that *you* would have minded your manners if you'd been present.'

'Whereas you did not?' My spouse is looking decidedly sombre.

'He was rude and annoying. I told him you weren't responsible for *my* behaviour.'

'No doubt that improved his mood inordinately,' he says dryly, in spite of himself.

'Well yes, it certainly did,' I say, letting through a tiny giveaway smile. 'He insisted on my going to the manor with him and introduced me to his wife. That's why I got out the painkillers – she suffers from headaches, and she doesn't want to take laudanum.'

Walter puts his head in his hand and starts to shake with laughter. Eventually he says, 'My dear, only you could manage it. Pray tell me *exactly* what transpired in order that I may reassure myself I am not about to lose my living.'

I relate the whole story, and he's suitably horrified and amused by turns. I suggest that he might like to accompany me to the manor in two days' time.

'I believe I had better, although I have no inkling as to how I might explain your behaviour, if asked.'

'You don't need to. I *am* the only one who's responsible for it.'

'That is not how most would view the matter.'

'Don't worry, but don't expect me to curtsey to him. It's a battle of wills now.'

He shakes his head disapprovingly, but then says, 'I should, I confess, have liked to see his expression when you were so impertinent as to laugh at him.'

'Do you know what's supposed to be wrong with his wife?'

He purses his lips. 'I believe she has been an invalid for some time.'

'An invalid!' I repeat. I hadn't realized it was that bad. 'What did Lord Montgomery mean when he said the physicians had blistered her?' Even as I say it, an unpleasant image from my source work, *The Madness of King George*, comes into my mind.

'It is a technique used to rid the body of ill humours. Blisters are caused on the back in order that the damaging matter is released.'

I bite my lips. 'I see. Walter, promise me you won't ever let any doctor bleed you or blister you.'

'Blistering is also ineffective?'

'It is indeed. It's unnecessary torture. That poor woman. Who knows, maybe if the doctors were kept away, she might recover.'

We ride over to the manor two days later and find Lord Montgomery in the drawing room, once again keeping company with his pack of greyhounds. He puts down his newspaper as we're announced, and of course Walter bows – more deeply, I note with interest, than he usually does. Lord Montgomery stares at me and raises his eyebrows, but I can't bring myself to curtsey, even for Walter's sake.

'So, Mrs Edgemond, you persist in your impertinence, even in your husband's presence,' he says.

I dare not look at Walter when I say, 'My husband knows what type of woman he married, Lord Montgomery.'

'Indeed. And have you had occasion to regret it, Mr Edgemond?' he asks.

Walter doesn't hesitate. 'I have not yet had that occasion, sir,' he replies.

Lord Montgomery looks slightly surprised but gestures to us to sit down. A maid comes in with a tray of tea and begins pouring it out.

'How is Lady Lavinia?' I ask.

He frowns. 'She is suffering from a surfeit of doctoring this morning. I have heard that you have some skill at the art yourself.'

I'm a bit taken aback. 'I know a little about it,' I say.

He sips delicately at his tea. 'Enough, in fact, to bring Mr Edgemond back from the dead.'

'Well, yes. It was… er, knowledge I gained from my father.'

'So I was informed. Perhaps when we have taken tea you would oblige me by attending upon my wife for an hour or two. In the meantime, you might care to come a coursing with me, Mr Edgemond. My greyhounds are in need of some exercise.'

Walter looks quite pleased by this offer and accepts at once, despite telling me he'd lost interest in hunting and hare coursing.

I find Lady Lavinia looking worse than ever.

'Lord Montgomery said you'd seen a doctor?' I say to the wan figure in the bed.

'I have seen many doctors in these past months.'

'Do you mind if I ask what they say is wrong with you?'

'It varies from one to another. I have had to keep to my bed these six months. I am perpetually tired yet cannot sleep without laudanum, and have little appetite for anything. My husband tells me that you have some knowledge of medicine?'

'A little. I do know that bleeding and blistering are not going to help, whatever it is that's wrong,' I tell her, unable to remain silent when I know she's suffering needlessly.

She laughs mirthlessly. 'Those are the only matters on which they are united. I have been bled, blistered and purged so many times that I fear I have no fluids left.'

'Well, all of those will weaken you and make you feel worse. I've brought something that will ease your headache and won't make you sleepy. My father prepared it, and I find it helpful at times. Would you like to try it?'

'I have nothing to lose,' she says, lifting herself up in the bed with some difficulty.

I've ground up a whole pack of paracetamol and put the resulting powder into little sachets consisting of two tablets each. She wastes no time and takes the first packet of powder without hesitation, barely grimacing at the bitter taste.

'Your father must have been a remarkable man, Mrs Edgemond. Tell me, what other theories did he have?'

Under the handy guise of my maverick-doctor father, I manage to propound all my own views about the worst aspects of 18th-century medicine. By the time I've related the whole story of Walter's revival from death, I'm convinced she's looking and sounding easier. We move on to talk about my school, and we're still talking some time later when a maid brings some broth for her mistress. 'Lord Montgomery and Mr Edgemond have returned,' she tells me. 'His lordship requests your presence in the drawing room.'

Walter and Lord Montgomery are both looking rosy from their exercise, and the greyhounds are lying in unusually quiescent heaps at their feet.

'How did you find my wife today, Mrs Edgemond?'

'I believe she may be a little better now,' I say. 'I gave her some powders made by my father. They seem to have helped.'

'Indeed? It is to be hoped that your father's potions are more efficacious than those of the quacks we have had attending her recently.'

I restrain my giggles with some effort and say, 'I hope so too.'

I'm still trying to work him out. He seems such a serious person, but his wife is not, for all her claims to melancholy. Why did he bring me to the manor when I'd been so obviously offensive in any 18th-century aristocrat's eyes? He obviously does care a great deal about his wife. I suppose, given that he doesn't need to put up any pretence, that his reason was the one he gave me.

As Walter and I are riding back I turn to look at him. 'So, hare coursing, eh?'

He smiles. 'As ever, my dear, you have missed the subtleties of the situation. It is hardly commonplace for a baron such as Lord Montgomery to hobnob with a mere parson. I could certainly not refuse such an honour.'

'Ah,' I say. 'You're right, I didn't think of that.'

'Lord Montgomery expressed considerable interest in you,' he says.

'Oh yes? I'm not sure if that's good or bad.'

'You do seem to attract a great deal of notice.'

'Are you wishing you'd married a compliant and passive woman now, Reverend?'

He laughs. 'I am not. Such difficulty as you do place me in is amply compensated.'

'Even if I'd lost you your living?'

He regards me gravely. 'I do not think either of us would have been greatly happy with that outcome.'

On my next visit, a few days later, I'm pleased to find Lady Lavinia up and sitting in a chair.

'I do not know if it was your powder or refusing any more of the doctors' attentions, but I feel a little better. Even the melancholy has lifted somewhat,' she tells me.

'I'm glad to hear that, whatever the cause.'

'My husband would have been pleased to see you today, but he has had to go down to London. He will be gone for at least a fortnight.'

'Does he still think I'm impudent and disrespectful?'

She laughs. 'I believe he will always think that.'

To my surprise, she takes a lot of interest in my school and tells me she's long held the belief that servants should be better educated.

'I should like to visit and see what you are doing, once I'm well,' she says.

'Well of course, but… '

'But?' she says with a small smile.

'We're very humble at the parsonage.'

'*You* do not know how to be humble, as my husband has observed.'

'Well, what I mean is –'

'I know what you mean, but I should like to see a little more of life.'

I shrug. 'As long as you're sure.'

Walter greets this proposal with a smidgeon of alarm. 'She is coming to the parsonage?'

'That's the idea. I'm thinking it's probably a good thing, for her.'

'In what sense, my dear?'

'Well she's depressed – I mean melancholy – and seems bored with her life. It's something different for her to think about, at the very least.'

The reverend purses his lips for a moment. 'I confess I had not imagined a baroness finding life tedious. You present me with some interesting insights at times.'

'I did tell you I studied psychology.'

'And does your psychology tell you that this household will be thrown into turmoil at such a visit?' he asks with a lift of his eyebrows.

'It does indeed, but we'll cope.'

A few days later, we're having breakfast when a sudden stab of pain makes me gasp slightly and put down my knife and fork.

Walter looks up from his newspaper. 'Is something amiss, my dear? You seem pale.'

'I'm not sure. I feel a bit um… strange. Maybe it's the heat.'

He frowns. 'It is indeed most oppressive today. I anticipate a tempest before long.'

'Not while you're officiating at the funeral, I hope.' He's due to leave shortly for Tref-ddirgel.

'Indeed, I also hope not.' He puts aside his paper and gets up, regarding me keenly. 'Perhaps you should lie down for a time. Nerys can bring some cold water.'

He puts his arm around me to assist me upstairs. 'It might be advisable to summon Dr Benbow,' he says. 'I'm sure he would be happy to attend.'

'I'd have to be at death's door first,' I say resolutely, but I'm glad of his arm and relieved to be able to lie down.

Nerys brings the water, and Walter dabs my face with a wet cloth. I can see he's in two minds as he's pursing his lips. 'I do not like to leave you in this state, cariad. Least of all with no medical attention.'

I laugh. 'Dr Benbow's attentions can hardly be described as *medical*, Reverend. On the contrary: more like witchcraft, if you ask me.'

My spouse raises his eyebrows and sighs. 'You do not sound too ill, but you are still very pale.'

'I'll be all right. Go to the funeral. You can't leave them in the lurch.'

'I shall be gone for most of the day. You will ensure that you rest?'

'Of course.'

Despite my assurances, my spirits sink as I hear him riding away. I dared not admit it to him, but I'm getting scary cramps that could mean something's going wrong with my pregnancy. It's one of those moments when I long to be back in my own time. How I wish I could just pick up the phone and ring my GP for advice. I couldn't explain to Walter how completely useless Dr Benbow would be, but it's not much fun being on my own either. I lie there wondering if the pain is going to stop and berating myself for telling Walter to go when I had a suspicion of what was coming.

The cramps get steadily worse, and I don't want to tell Nerys or Martha, because they'll just send for Dr Benbow, so I haul myself up and stagger downstairs to the necessary house. I'm losing blood, but the cramps are still going on, and I begin to panic as I realize that it really does look as though I'm going to lose the baby. Amazing as it seems, I'm probably the most medically qualified person around, but I know almost nothing about obstetrics.

As the cramps worsen, I get so desperate that I even seriously consider Dr Benbow, or maybe one of those man midwives Mrs Greenleaf favours, but then I imagine all the things they could do that would make things worse. I'll just have to wait it out, but seeing this much blood is frightening, and it's making me light headed. I lurk in the necessary house for so long that Nerys comes looking for me, and I have to fib and tell her I'm suffering from a bout of diarrhoea. I don't even know how many hours I sit there, but eventually there's a contraction that makes me cry out loud followed by a huge rush, and I know it's over. I've had a miscarriage.

I'm feeling scared, lost and lonely and have a desperate need to be away from anyone. I don't want to talk to the servants, and I long for 2008 and all its safety and security and certainty. My legs are decidedly wobbly from loss of blood, and I'm not really thinking straight as I leave the house without a word and make for the pool above Felin Gyfriniaeth. It's quite a struggle, and halfway there I wonder whether I should turn back, but I can't bear to. I plough on, feeling weak and tired and very sorry for myself.

As I arrive exhausted at the pool, I look down at the mill and try to will myself safely back in the 21st century. Nothing happens.

I rip off my sweaty and confining clothes and sink into the water, remembering that the last time I did so was with Elli and Simon, all those years in the future. The water feels cool and fresh and clean, and it's hard to get those things in a house without running water.

I float there for a long while, not really thinking about anything, losing track of time, my body feeling battered and my mind numb. The sun's evening rays are slanting through the trees, but I still don't want to move, can't bear to face up to anything, just want to drift forever.

I'm startled out of my watery repose by the sound of hoof beats coming up the rise. As far as I'm aware, no one comes up here in any time, but when I notice how red the sky is, I have a pretty good idea who it's going to be. It's too late to get out, so I move to the edge where it's darker, just in case I'm wrong and it's Dick Turpin on a bad day or something.

I'm not immediately in view when Bess, Walter's mare, plunges into the quiet glade, but he pulls her up and looks around, his face pale with anxiety. My stomach wrenches to see him look that worried on my account, and I call out his name and swim out into the centre of the pool so that he can see me.

With a sharp sigh of relief he throws Bess's reins over a branch and steps across the rocks to the water's edge. 'Fallady, what has happened?'

Tears have started streaming down my face, and he gasps with dismay and starts throwing off his own clothes to get into the water with me. I don't know if he thinks I need rescuing or what, but I'm glad of the comfort of his arms around me, skin to skin, and the tears just pour out. I reckon it's mostly hormonal, but he doesn't even know what hormones are, and I'm in no state to explain it all to him.

He holds me until the tears start to ebb, saying little except soothing nothings, until finally I look up at him blurrily and stammer out, 'I lost the baby.'

He looks so shocked and vulnerable at that moment that my stomach lurches again. 'I'm sorry. I just couldn't face anything. I needed to get away.'

He carries me out of the pool and regards me anxiously. 'I looked for you in many places. I began to despair of finding you, but at last it occurred to me that you might be drawn to Felin Gyfriniaeth.' He looks up at the darkening sky. 'It is very late, my dear. Do you feel able to dress?'

I nod mutely, wiping my eyes with the back of my hand.

He retrieves my clothes from the branch I'd thrown them over and helps me on with them before getting dressed himself, his eyes barely leaving me.

'I'm all right. Really,' I say, wanting to see the look of fear leave his face. Fear, I realize belatedly, that I could die. Without antibiotics or blood transfusions available, even a miscarriage could be fatal in this age, and my actions were hardly sensible.

He purses his lips. 'No doubt you will allow me to ask Dr Benbow to confirm that, cariad?' he says, with just a tiny glimmer of humour returning.

'Huh, that I won't, Reverend.' I put my hand on his arm. 'Don't worry. It was early. The bleeding seems to have slowed down. I should be all right.'

He covers my hand with his. 'Come, we must return home. The servants will be most concerned.'

He helps me up onto Bess and sets off at considerable speed. If I wasn't feeling so overwrought I might think it most romantic to be rescued by my knight on a grey charger and galloped back to the parsonage.

That night we're cuddling together in bed when Walter, who's been uncharacteristically quiet since our return, says, 'Fallady, please promise me that you will do nothing so untoward again.'

I sigh. 'Of course I promise. I hardly knew what I was doing at the time. You looked so worried when you arrived at the pool. Were you afraid I'd gone back to the 21st century?'

'I did fear that something unexpected might have occurred.'

'Which it has, in a way. I didn't expect to lose the baby. Everything seemed to be fine. You must be really disappointed.'

He strokes my arm. 'And you are not? I know you did not want a child, but I suspect you had begun to care for it, at least a little. You were most distressed at the pool.'

'I think that was mostly for physical reasons, but you're right, I don't feel too good about it.' I'm surprised to find myself suffering from a powerful sense of loss and still feel very wobbly emotionally.

Walter holds me closer in tacit understanding. After a while, he says, 'I can't help but feel that God still has plans for you, my dear. You have not solved your mystery, after all.'

The mystery hasn't been at the forefront of my mind lately, with so much else going on. 'The answer doesn't seem to be here,' I say. 'I've walked all over Llanycoed and nothing's cropped up.'

He laughs softly. 'It is not difficult to walk all over Llanycoed. It is the matter of but a few minutes.'

'Well, quite. If there is an answer, I don't think it's in this time.'

'Yet your presence here will likely save many lives. That is in itself an answer.'

'Well, as we say in the 21st century, what is the question?'

'God will reveal it to you in time,' he says in the vicarly tone he always uses for such pronouncements.

CHAPTER TWENTY

The Sunday after my miscarriage, Anna's home and comes with us to church. She's changed a bit in the two months she's been at school, is more grown up in her ways and also, to my pleasant surprise, slightly more assertive. Her drawing and painting teachers believe, like me, that she has real talent, and she's spending a lot more time on these activities than she did before. Apart from all that, though, she's still just as good-natured, and to my relief, shows no sign of resentment at my having married her papa.

By now I know many people in the village and surrounding area, and going to church as the parson's wife is quite an entertaining experience. I see all the nuances of relationships and how attendance at church is as much a social as a religious ritual. Walter's aware of it too and doesn't mind all the flirting and gossiping that goes on under his nose. He's so very at home here and obviously well thought of among his parishioners. I don't enjoy all the praying, of course, but I like listening to his sermons, and I still get a kick out of seeing him in his vestments.

The singers have just finished a psalm, and Walter is leading prayers, when there's a sudden rumbling sound. The church shudders, Anna grabs hold of my arm, people are shouting in fear and even the reverend looks up as though he's expecting the roof to fall in, but it's all over in seconds, or should I say, it's all over in seconds for everyone except Walter and myself. As people start to leave their pews to head outside and there's a general flurry of chatter and activity, these words issue through the air: *'But look how the church is so – well – completely demolished. It's as though... it's as though it's sunk!'*

'I believe you may be correct, my dear, but I cannot conjecture as to what that may mean.'

I know he hears the same words that I do, because our eyes lock across the pews and across his parishioners who continue to exit the church with no sign of hearing a thing. Anna, still standing resolute beside me, says, 'Fallady, should we go outside?' and the spell's broken. We follow the rest of the congregation into the churchyard. Walter looks as pale as I feel, and it's not just the earth tremor that's the cause, but hearing our own voices coming out of nowhere, speaking words that we have, as yet, never uttered.

The service being aborted, the congregation starts to calm down and filter away, and we three walk back to the parsonage to find the servants still somewhat shaken up. Martha and Thomas were at the service and only Nerys had been in the house, but all's well there, although she felt the tremor, just as we did. Everyone's talking about it, but no one mentions having heard anything out of the ordinary. It's quite a strain as we have dinner and try to reassure Anna and behave normally when all that's in my mind is *what is Walter doing in the 21st century?*

'I do not apprehend why no one else appeared to hear anything,' Walter says when we're finally in the privacy of our bedchamber and able to talk about it.

I can't resist. I say, 'God moves in a mysterious way, his wonders to perform,' and use Walter's vicarly intonation to boot.

Walter lifts his head from the pillow and shakes it severely at me, biting his lips to retain his solemnity. 'Really, Fallady, that is most – although we were in the house of the Lord. What can it mean?'

'I'd say it's a dead cert that you're going to see the 21st century!'

'A dead cert? I assume you mean it is certain?'

'I don't see what else it could be. We had to be standing on the ruins, and this time displacement thing let our voices pass through to this time. It's just like when I was in the ruins of the parsonage and I heard your voice and Anna's.'

He stares at me intently through the candlelight. 'You did not mention this before.'

'It seems so long ago now. I couldn't catch what you were saying – it wasn't like today.'

'It is all most disconcerting,' he says. 'Are we to anticipate a fall into a snowdrift, perhaps?'

I laugh. 'At least we know we'll be together.'

The prospect of returning home *with* Walter is very tempting. It's only when we finally give up on speculation and I start drifting off to sleep that I realize the implications. He'd have to leave Anna behind, and he'd suffer from severe culture shock. Whatever's going to happen, I don't think it's something we do voluntarily, any more than my falling into the snowdrift was a matter of choice.

I lie on the sofa feeling weak and listless; I knew those 18th-century germs would get me in the end. I've just spent a week in bed with severe stomach pains, vomiting and diarrhoea, convinced I was dying of food poisoning. That's what you get in a world without fridges – all that fly-blown meat just lying around, harbouring who knows what.

It's been a fragile month all round. I've recovered physically from the loss of the baby, but it's shaken me up quite a lot, and I'm terrified of getting pregnant again. On top of that, there's the constant sense that something is going to transport Walter and me back to 2008, and I'm not sure I even *want* to return to the 21st century. The 18th century would be quite fun if it weren't for the non-existent plumbing and the diseases and the lack of proper medical care and the total absence of

technology and no independence and no contraception and…
On the other hand, there are many aspects of it I'd miss. I've
been getting a lot of satisfaction out of the teaching. Abigail
has proved to be a quick learner and is our star pupil. She's
working at the hall with very bad grace, but when she's reading
and writing, I see a different girl emerging.

Lady Lavinia has maintained her interest in the school and,
as promised, she visited the parsonage to see it in action. She's
a different woman now. A grand lady has replaced the sickly
invalid, and she cuts an impressive figure with her elaborate
gown and powdered and dressed hair. It wasn't quite a royal
visit, but it caused stir enough, and I had no alternative but to
curtsey with so many people watching.

When we introduced her to our pupils, she showed far
more delicacy than even I would have given her credit for, and
chatted to them about what they'd been learning in an only
slightly condescending manner. To my amazement, Abigail
behaved perfectly. The pair of them seemed to really hit it
off, and instead of flouncing, she was positively animated as
she explained what learning to read and write meant to her,
and how much pleasure she was starting to get from her first
attempt at reading an actual book. Her ladyship even discussed
her own enjoyment of reading – with a mere servant. What
would Lord Montgomery have thought?

She asked for a private word with me as she prepared to
step into her carriage, liveried coachmen and all.

'Your pupil, Abigail, seems most keen. She says she is
working at Laburnum Hall?'

'Yes, as a kitchen maid, but she's not at all happy about it. I
think I've given her reason to hope for better. I just hope I'm
not misleading her.'

She smiled wryly. 'I do not believe a girl like that will stay
a kitchen maid for long. And by the by, I was most impressed
by your curtsey earlier. I'm sure my husband will be pleased to
hear of it.'

I groaned. 'No doubt he will.'

I was encouraged by Lavinia's interest in Abigail. Fond though I've become of Anna, it's Abigail who's more like me in spirit, and I want to see her succeed. Sometimes I lie awake, worrying about all the changes I might have wrought in our tiny corner of the tapestry of history, but I don't see how I could have acted any differently.

I adjust my blanket and pick up *Tom Jones*, which is quite amusing and not so flowery as many of the other books on Walter's shelves. This period of enforced idleness has at least given me a new appreciation of 18th-century literature. Laura, whose wedding took place only two weeks ago, is looking after the school on her own while I recuperate.

I hear a carriage pull up outside and wonder who can be visiting this morning. To my surprise, Nerys enters in a fluster and announces Lady Lavinia. Her ladyship certainly seems intent on slumming it at the parsonage.

'You look better than I feared,' she says, as she settles herself in one of the well-worn parlour chairs.

'The tables are turned, eh? You visiting me on my sick bed,' I say. 'I'm nearly recovered, just quite weak still. Certainly too weak for any curtseying!'

'Have you *ever* had any respect?' she asks rhetorically.

'Probably not,' I reply cheerfully. 'I'm glad to see you, anyway. You look well.'

She nods. 'I'm not sure why, but I am much improved.'

'Keeping away from all those quacks might have had a lot to do with it.'

'Mr Edgemond is out?' she asks when Nerys has left us with the tea.

'Yes, he's churching a woman, and then I gather he has a baptism.' An unusually busy vicarly day.

We talk about Lord Montgomery, now back from London, and about the school, which really seems to have engaged her interest.

'Does it not cause some difficulty that the school is located within the parsonage?' she asks.

'Well, it's a little awkward at times, but that was the only place it could be, really.'

'And were there to be more suitable premises available?'

I stare at her. 'More suitable? Where?'

She laughs. 'You forget that we own most of the land in the vicinity. I have been considering the matter, and now that my husband has returned, I have proposed that the old granary be repaired and used for the purpose, unless you object.'

I'm silent for a moment. I get the feeling no objections of mine are going to stop the rollercoaster that is the recovered Lady Lavinia, assuming I really have any.

'The function of the school could be enlarged and more pupils accommodated,' she adds.

'True,' I say at last. 'It's an interesting proposal. Lord Montgomery doesn't disapprove?'

'He is all too pleased to see me off my sick bed.'

'Well it sounds like a good idea, if you're really sure,' I say.

'It could even become a proper school for all the children in the village,' she enthuses.

'That might be a bit too much for Mrs Jenkins and me, though,' I say slowly.

'I should like to help with the teaching,' she says, and watches with unaccustomed diffidence for my reaction.

I admit I'm surprised and a bit worried. Given what Walter said about the school succeeding due to 'my approach', won't Lavinia's condescension have the opposite effect? On the other hand, she did manage to get on with Abigail, and I don't see how I can oppose a school for all the children, if it works.

I take a deep breath and hope I'm not making an enormous mistake. 'Well in that case, how can I object?'

A low August moon glimmers yellow among the trees as we approach Llanycoed. It's dusk, and the evening is cooling, and we're both looking forward to getting back to the parsonage after an enjoyable fortnight in Oxford, the one place we both share. It's been a long day of travelling, but although we arrived at Shrewsbury by coach in mid afternoon, we picked up the horse and chaise there and decided to press on home rather than visit Walter's sister, partly due to my far-from-subtle hints to that effect.

We cross the bridge over the stream, and Felin Gyfriniaeth looms up on our left. The track to Llanycoed slopes downwards ahead, and I'm thinking longingly of as warm a bath as I can manage when we get home, when suddenly there's a sucking sensation, like being pulled into or through something, and Walter struggles to bring the horse under control – she's very skittish, tossing her mane and even rearing a little – and he draws us sharply to a halt.

He looks at me, and I look back at him. 'That was most peculiar,' he says, getting down to quiet the mare, who's still stamping in alarm.

I step down and look around, feeling cold. 'It was the same sensation as when I fell into 1779.' I say with a shiver, taking in the quiet wooded scene in the moonlight. 'But this isn't 2008. It hasn't altered.' In fact, it's colder and darker than it was just moments ago, and there's a dank, autumnal scent to the air.

'You believe we may have passed into a different time?' Walter asks, still trying to calm the mare.

I point to the miller's cottage, a few yards down the lane towards Llanycoed. 'There's a light. Why don't we go and ask the miller if all's well? We can just say the mare's spooked.'

We leave the horse settling down and walk to the cottage. Walter knocks on the door, and I start to think we've imagined the whole thing.

There's a flurry of activity and anxious voices from inside, and the door opens to reveal Mrs Emrys – my Mrs Emrys, plump as ever!

'Mrs Emrys!' I cry.

'Fallady!' she says at exactly the same moment, looking me up and down and taking in my 18th-century costume.

A section of the jigsaw falls into place inside my head. 'The disappearing zone,' I say, forgetting that only I know what I'm talking about. 'We just passed through the disappearing zone, but where are we, Mrs Emrys, what *time*?'

'Oh lovey,' she says in a sorrowful tone. 'You'd better come in.'

We follow her into the cottage, which is rather cramped, and there in the parlour, watching us enter with some anxiety, is Mr Linlade.

'Parson! Fallady! How did you get here?' he asks.

'The same way you always do,' I reply. 'But not from 2008, from 1779. What year is this?'

Mrs Emrys shakes her head sadly. 'It's 1799.'

'The year of the earthquake,' Walter says.

'You know about that, sir?' asks Mr Linlade.

'Fallady has told me about it,' Walter explains, and I'm glad he hasn't resorted to formality and called me Mrs Edgemond. That's going to take some explaining.

'Is this where you came every day when I saw you disappear?' I ask.

'Yes, but we didn't know you'd seen us,' Mrs Emrys replies from the kitchen.

'What happened to you?' I ask. 'I knew you weren't ghosts from the start.'

Mr Linlade sighs. 'To all intents and purposes we *are* ghosts,' he says sadly.

'How so?' Walter asks.

'We've been trapped since the earthquake. We were walking towards the mill when it happened. We were knocked off our feet, that's all, but when it was over we found we couldn't get out.'

Mrs Emrys bustles in with tea and cake. 'Except for your time, lovey. It's the only place we can go.'

'But you're not dead. You're flesh and blood,' I insist.

'We never age. A hundred years, and we've never aged.' Mr Linlade says.

'I don't comprehend what you mean when you say there is no way out. You are in your own time. In what way are you trapped?' Walter asks, frowning.

'We can't leave the ruins of Llanycoed. The only place we can go is Felin Gyfriniaeth in the future.'

'What happens when you try to leave?' I ask breathlessly.

'As soon as we get past the mill, or try taking the other road to the hall and Llanyrafon, we get stuck. We just can't move,' says Mrs Emrys.

'A force field!' I gasp excitedly, only to be confronted by three pairs of confused 18th-century eyes.

'What is a force field, my dear?' Walter asks.

'Well, it's um… it's um… never been invented, but theoretically it's um… an electrical field that… well anyway, that's what it sounds like to me!'

'Oh, that electricity, I never did like it,' says Mrs Emrys, and Walter gives me a significant look.

'Was everyone in Llanycoed saved from the earthquake?' I ask.

'Well, the parson – begging your pardon, sir – told everyone he'd dreamt about it,' Mr Linlade says. 'There was a lot of grumbles, but even the squire went away, so all the villagers left for the day, just in case. We were the last out.'

'So Mr Edgemond had gone too?' I ask.

'Oh, he'd gone before that, lovey, to live with his daughter in Tref-ddirgel.' Mrs Emrys looks apologetically at the reverend as she says this. It's hard juggling all these times between us, but it's not lost on me that no wife is mentioned.

'So you live here and just come into 2008 and work at Felin Gyfriniaeth? But why?'

'What else is there for us to do?' says Mrs Emrys.

'I'd rather be doing the garden at the mill, seeing different people, watching the seasons and weather change, than stay here where nothing ever changes,' Mr Linlade elaborates.

Walter is deep in thought, pursing his lips. 'You have a wife, do you not?' he asks.

'That's right, Parson, my Becca,' Mr Linlade says. 'And Branwen has – well, perhaps I shouldn't say so –' he hesitates.

'Mr Willis asked me to marry him, and I had a mind to accept,' Mrs Emrys finishes.

Walter raises his eyebrows. 'Robert Willis who farms at Leabrook?'

Mrs Emrys nods. 'I've been a long time a widow, Parson.'

'Indeed,' Walter agrees thoughtfully. 'Then it is clear that what is needed is to be released from this... force field... in order that you can resume your lives in 1799.'

Mr Linlade laughs mirthlessly. 'That's all, Parson. A hundred years and we haven't been able to do it.'

Walter still looks thoughtful. 'So why did we pass through from 1779?' he says, almost to himself.

'I hope you're not stuck here like we are,' Mrs Emrys adds in an anxious tone.

'But you can get through to 2008,' I say.

'Only when there's someone in the house.'

'And I'm not in the house because I'm here. When was the last time you saw me? I mean, just before I fell into 1779, you'd been gone for ten days, and I had no idea why.'

'The gate's been closed. We thought you'd gone away.'

'Does any time pass here?' I ask, trying to get things straight in my mind.

'It seems like it does for us, but when we wake up in the morning or come back from 2008, it's always the same here. Same food in the pantry, even though we've eaten it, same hole in the roof, even though Percy's fixed it.'

'So it's always the same day here, but time moves in 2008. You always pass through to a different day.'

Mr Linlade nods. 'That's how we normally count the days. Last time we saw you was a couple of days after you'd been to the ruins and heard voices.'

'Yes!' I say. 'And then I went back to the ruins and fell through to 1779.'

'But why are we here now?' Walter repeats, stroking his lips.

'And if we came through from 1779, maybe Mr Linlade and Mrs Emrys could get back there.'

'But we're already there!' Mrs Emrys exclaims. 'It wouldn't be decent.'

'We should see if we can pass back through this gate,' Walter says decisively.

We all troop back up to the disappearing zone. I'm remembering the many times that I tried and failed to pass through it before, but keep that to myself.

'The gate's here,' Mr Linlade says, and steps forwards, but nothing happens – just as on all my attempts, he stays in the same time. 'It's still closed,' he says resignedly.

Mrs Emrys also tries and fails.

Walter and I make an unspoken decision to try it together. I think we're both afraid that the other won't make it, and we'll be separated. We hold hands as we walk forwards, and to my surprise, there's that sucking sensation again, and we emerge on the other side, safe. Not only that, but I start jumping up and down, because there is *my* Felin Gyfriniaeth and my clapped out old Metro, and we're in 2008!

Walter gazes at the car in a bewildered fashion. 'This is 2008?' he asks.

'Yes it is, yes it is,' I almost sing. 'Come on,' I say, and drag him by the hand in my haste to get into the house.

'What is that peculiar carriage?' he asks as we pass the car. 'It is of an unusual hue.'

I laugh. The Metro is kingfisher blue – very bright, and not as popular a colour in 2008 as it was in 1996 when the car was actually produced. 'That is my car, Reverend,' I say, reaching into my bag for the keys to the house. Six months down the line, and they're still where I put them on the day I wandered down to Llanycoed in a bad mood.

CHAPTER TWENTY-ONE

The keys feel hot, just as they did on the day I arrived, but when I open the door the house looks the same as I left it, except for a reassuringly small pile of post on the floor of the hall. Walter looks around him with interest as I point out the living room and study before gravitating to the kitchen.

'There is no fireplace,' he says at once.

'No, but there is a range,' I reply, pointing it out. 'I wonder if the electricity's on.'

The reverend watches keenly as I flick the switch on the wall, and lo, the bulb up on the ceiling bursts into a brilliant white-yellow glow. Walter jumps back in surprise, reminding me of the moment in the church with the camera. I have a glimmer of an idea how he's feeling; I'm shaking myself. Everything looks so clean and bright and… well, shiny. I feel like a stranger in my own house.

Walter recovers from his momentary shock and starts doing a circuit of the room, running his hands over the old Formica countertops that used to seem old to me but now appear the height of modernity, pausing at the incomprehensible white oblong that's the fridge and the equally bizarre squat object which seems to have a porthole set into its front. He stops in front of the stainless steel sink and points at the taps. 'Could this be the plumbing about which I have heard so much and at great length, my dear?' he asks.

I grin. 'Why don't you try turning them on?'

I hide my amusement as he turns on each tap and then tests the water spurting out of them until, eventually, steam begins to rise from the one labelled 'H'. The immersion heater is obviously still on.

'It is a very different matter to see it rather than hear about it,' he says.

I pick up the kettle and fill it. My hand's still shaking as I turn it on. I don't know why I'm boiling the kettle, since we only just had a cup of tea at the cottage, but it seems like an automatic thing to do, plus it's certainly a heck of a wonder to demonstrate to Walter.

'Just think of all that boiling over the fire or the range at the parsonage,' I say to him. 'This kettle will be boiled in about three minutes.'

My spouse demonstrates a satisfactory amount of awe at the kettle spouting steam, the ice in the fridge freezer and the drum turning inside the washing machine. Most of the rest of the house isn't so much of a surprise to him. More pieces of the jigsaw click into place as I see it through his eyes. Of course there aren't wall-to-wall fitted carpets, because you can't usually use a vacuum cleaner, and everything has to be done the labour intensive way, just as in his time. Whoever installed electricity in the house must have had a big disappointment, only discovering its idiosyncratic properties *after* they'd paid out all the money. It seems likely to have been the incumbent before Miss Gilbertine.

I introduce the reverend to the rather ancient toilet and bath with a flourish. 'Here we are,' I say proudly. 'The Indoor Necessary – or toilet, as we call it. And what do you think of *this* bathtub, eh?' The wooden one he bought for me would look tiny beside the claw-footed, white-enamelled monstrosity that graces this bathroom.

'Most impressive,' he says abstractedly, lifting the toilet seat and then looking up at the chain. 'What happens when this lever is pulled?'

'All the water that's in the cistern above rushes in and flushes away the contents,' I reply, and add, 'What am I thinking? I can take off these clothes at long, long last. I can have a bath by just turning on the taps!'

Walter chuckles and watches with interest as I put the plug in and do just that. By the time I'm stark naked, the bath's half full.

'You could get in with me. This is a big bathtub, and the water's going to be nicely hot.'

He regards the steaming bath with some disquiet. 'I am still not convinced of the benefits of... ' he looks back at me and gives in. 'Very well, my dear – if you are set on it.'

While he's undressing, I get into the filling bath and one by one pick up my containers of bath foam and soap and shampoo and just sniff them. Bliss. The reverend observes me as though I've lost my mind, but the sight of his pile of clothing reminds me that we somehow have to get him some contemporary gear. I can't wait to see how he looks in a pair of jeans.

We spend a happy hour together in the bath, or at least I do. I don't know how Walter feels, it being such a shock to his system. Almost five months of marriage and this is his first bath, and certainly his first proper hair wash.

We're just getting out and drying ourselves off and I'm wondering what Walter can wear when there's a knock at the door downstairs.

He looks at me with alarm, and I must admit I'm a bit worried myself. No one comes to Felin Gyfriniaeth.

'I'll go and see who it is,' I say. 'Don't come downstairs yet.'

I throw on a bathrobe and put a towel around my head.

'You are going down dressed like that?' the reverend asks in horror.

'Don't worry, I'll only open the door a crack.'

His eyebrows are virtually in his hairline, but I take no notice and trot down the stairs laughing. I open the door on its chain, but I needn't have worried. It's only John Kelly.

'John,' I say, taking off the chain. 'It's good to see you.' I mean it, too.

He steps into the light and stares at me as though he's never seen me before. 'Are you all right?'

'Yes. Why?' I ask in surprise.

'You look… different.'

I glance down at myself in the bathrobe and then back up at him, puzzled. 'How different?'

He laughs and shakes his head. 'A lot thinner!'

'Oh!' It hadn't crossed my mind it would be that noticeable. 'Come on into the kitchen. I was making some tea about an hour ago. Did you come for a reason? Alyson's all right, isn't she?'

'Yes, she's fine, but we were worried about you. She's tried to ring you several times in the past few days. We were getting ready to phone the police and report you as a missing person or something. I just came down here on the off chance – I've been on a house call at Nantmawr Farm.'

I flick the kettle switch on again, rejoicing inwardly in being able to do such a simple, commonplace thing.

'We thought you might have gone away, but Alyson was sure you'd have mentioned it.'

'I've been away, all right,' I say, getting out the cups and wondering if the milk's going to be off if it's a week that I've been gone. I realize I need three cups and am all too aware of Walter upstairs.

'Health farm, was it?' says John, eyeing me sceptically.

'Only if the 18th century can be described as such,' I say and avoid his look of amazement to go back out into the hall and call up the stairs. 'It's all right, Walter. It's John Kelly. You remember me telling you about him.'

John's expression is still one of comical astonishment. '18th century? Walter?'

I grin and busy myself making the tea while Walter descends the stairs. I'm betting he's put his clothes back on, as nothing would induce him to be seen below stairs in a state of undress, and I'm awaiting John's reaction with considerable inner amusement.

The reverend enters the kitchen in full garb and looks at us enquiringly.

'Walter, this is John Kelly. John, this is Walter Edgemond, my husband,' I say and watch the ripples of incredulity cross John's face.

'I'm pleased to meet you, Walter,' John says, recovering and holding out his hand.

Walter gamely shakes John's hand after only a moment's hesitation.

I'm having great trouble holding back my mirth, but I feel the need to bolster my husband's confidence so I say, 'Walter's a vicar. The Reverend Walter Edgemond, rector of Llanycoed.'

'Of *Llanycoed*?'

'The village is still there in 1779. That's where, or rather when, I've been. I went to the ruins, and while I was looking around I fell into an 18th-century snowdrift.'

And on that bombshell, I pass around the teacups, and we all sit at the kitchen table.

'Fallady tells me that you are a doctor,' Walter says politely.

'Yes, in a practice in Tref-ddirgel,' John says, sipping his tea.

I catch both their eyes and can contain my giggles no longer. 'All right, John,' I gurgle, 'I know you want to hear the whole story, but have you got the time? Do you have any more calls?'

'No, but I ought to ring Alyson and tell her you're okay. Won't be a sec,' he says and flips out his mobile phone. 'No signal – no surprise. Can I use your phone, Fally?'

He goes into the living room, and we hear him talking.

'To whom is he speaking?' Walter asks.

'To his wife, in Tref-ddirgel. Are you all right?'

'It is all most illuminating, my dear, albeit also bewildering. I believe I am coping quite well, although this tea is a little unusual.'

'Ah, I forgot that the tea would be different.' It tastes good to me though, after months of green tea with no sugar or milk.

John's back quickly. 'She's relieved to hear you're okay, anyway. I have no idea how to explain about… everything else,' he says.

'Join the club,' I say, and Walter raises his eyebrows at my incomprehensible slang.

'You mentioned a snowdrift?' John prompts.

Walter and I tell the tale between us, with occasional interruptions from John on matters such as smallpox, my 'miraculous' saving of Walter and my low opinion of Dr Benbow. Finally he joins in our speculation about my staff still trapped in 1799, my theory that the church itself is a focal point and given that the question has become 'how are we to rescue Mrs Emrys and Mr Linlade from 1799?' we're nowhere near an answer.

'There's another question, too,' he says slowly, looking at each of us in turn. 'Which is, what about the two of you? Assuming you can get back to 1779, do you go? Or does Walter stay here?'

We both shake our heads at that.

'I can't leave Anna alone, an orphan,' Walter says.

John's eyes are on me. 'Will *you* go back? It's risky for you; you've already mentioned that yourself.'

'She had not mentioned it to me, however,' Walter says.

'It wasn't going to make much difference. I couldn't get home.'

He nods. 'But now you are home.' He pauses before adding, 'Fallady, according to Mrs Emrys I will be living in Tref-ddirgel in 1799, and you won't be there. Whichever choice you make, it seems we will not be together for long.'

I take a deep breath to control my emotions. 'Please, let's not talk about this now. We don't even know if we can get back. Let's just enjoy being here alone together for a while.'

'Unless of course Mrs Emrys and Mr Linlade reappear,' John says with a wry smile.

'Well that's all right. Mrs Emrys is a great cook, which is more than can be said for me or Walter.'

'I believe I know how to cook egg and chips, my dear,' Walter says gravely, his deadpan expression belying the usual gleam of mischief in his eyes.

As John's getting ready to leave, I mention Walter's lack of 21st-century clothing. 'No problem,' he says, 'I'll bring some tomorrow, along with Alyson, if that's okay.'

'Of course! Come to dinner. I'm sure we can make something a bit better than egg and chips.'

When he's driven off and we're left alone again, we just look at each other for a moment and then embrace. 'I don't want you to go back without me,' I say.

'I cannot say that the prospect appeals to me either, cariad.'

'Oh, let's just go to bed!' I say.

'It certainly has been a long and tiring day,' he says, and I realize with a start it's still the same day we set out from Wolverhampton in the coach, and yet in this time it's only nine at night and not even fully dark yet.

I cuddle up to Walter in bed as though I'm afraid he won't be there in the morning, and even he is unnaturally quiet.

The next day seems surreal. I dress in comfortable jeans and T-shirt, much to Walter's lip-pursing disapproval. He fills the range with logs and gets it going, and I charge up the mobile and the laptop and show him how all the household gadgets work. Afterwards, I fiddle around with the laptop, picking up e-mails and noting a number of increasingly anxious ones from my siblings, which prompts me to try and phone them all, without success.

Walter amuses himself in playing with the radio. And I mean *playing*. He flicks from medium wave to long wave to short wave, listening with complete fascination to the jumble of sounds and asking me a lot of questions that fortunately I *can* answer, being a geek. He finds 21st-century pop and rock 'hardly harmonious', loves the fact that he can just turn the dial and listen to classical, but above all is enthralled by Radio 4: all that talking, and most of it incomprehensible.

'There is a great deal of political discussion,' he says after shaking his head through the whole half-hour of 'The World at One'.

'There certainly is. What did you make of it?'

'I apprehend that there is a crisis over the price of fuel, but I do not know to which fuel they refer.'

I explain all about oil while I plug the camera into the laptop and download the pictures I took in 1779.

'Come and look at this.'

'More marvels, my dear?' he says with a wry smile, but he comes and stands at my shoulder while I play through the sequence in a slideshow. It's a peculiar sensation seeing some of those shots again: Walter looking stunned in the church; Llanycoed in the snow; Felin Gyfriniaeth; Walter and me in his parlour; the hall; some country scenes; Tref-ddirgel; interior and exterior shots of the parsonage; a couple of Walter posing in the pulpit wearing his vestments (my personal favourites); Llanycoed in summer; Walter, Anna and me during the week after my miscarriage; Shrewsbury when we went back in July; Oxford.

I look up at him and he's smiling. 'How well I recall the moment that you used the flash in the church,' he says. 'You were distressed because you had not been able to return, and I was both concerned on your behalf and relieved on my own because I did not want to see you go, even then.'

'After one day?'

'One day which contained more diversion than I had enjoyed in many a year.'

I grin and reach up to caress his stubble. 'Well, you're pretty diverting yourself, despite your serious exterior.'

We take a walk into Llanycoed, as the reverend wants to see the ruins for himself. One of the first things he notices as we walk down the road is a plane going over. He's already mentioned hearing them a couple of times, and they even sound strange to my ears after all the months of silent skies. This time the plane's visible in a clear blue sky, and he watches as it arrows upwards until its vapour trail enlarges and dissipates. 'Incredible!' he murmurs, staring for so long that I eventually have to drag him off.

Nothing happens when we pass through the disappearing zone. I'm both relieved and anxious. Shouldn't Mrs Emrys and Mr Linlade have come across today, if all's well? Why do the goalposts keep moving with this time displacement situation?

It's quite affecting to Walter to see his parish in scrub-covered ruins, and he's very quiet, particularly when we reach the parsonage. I follow him as he wanders from room to room, and now of course I too know which room is which and have memories of us all in them. I take his arm as we walk across to the rubble of the church, and can tell that it hurts him just as much to see the place in which he's preached many times in this condition. Now I have to put myself into the story too. It *is* the church I got married in that's lying beneath our feet, not to mention the church in which I've ogled him on many a Sunday.

We wander around the debris and talk about its state, and without even realising it, I say: 'But look how the church is so – well – completely demolished. It's as though… it's as though it's sunk!'

And Walter replies, 'I believe you may be correct my dear, but I cannot conjecture as to what that may mean.'

Even as we say those almost forgotten words, heard after the tremor two months ago, we stare at each other, realizing that we've fulfilled the prophecy, so to speak.

'Well,' I say shakily. 'That's that then.'

Walter puts his arm around me. 'And I still cannot conjecture as to what it may mean.'

I laugh. 'God moves in a mysterious way, Reverend,' I say.

He looks down at me hopefully. 'Are you certain you are not beginning to believe, Fallady?'

CHAPTER TWENTY-TWO

We return to Felin Gyfriniaeth feeling a bit subdued, but as we emerge from the scrub onto the road, I come to a sudden standstill. Three cars are lined up next to mine. There's nothing I can do to forewarn Walter as Elli runs headlong towards me, leaving Simon, Dessy and Jex to follow in her wake.

'Fally! Thank God you're all right!' my sister screeches. 'Where've you been? We've been worried sick!' She halts as she takes in Walter's appearance and just stares.

'I've been trying to phone you all half the day,' I say. 'I wondered where you were.'

'It's been a whole week that we haven't been able to get hold of you, Fally,' Jex says reproachfully. He looks meaningfully at the reverend, standing at my side. 'What's been going on?'

I look at Walter, who smiles back encouragingly but says nothing. 'Well, um, this is Walter. Walter, these are my brother and sisters, and that's Simon, Elli's husband.'

'I am delighted to meet you,' Walter says and does his little bow, which leaves them all gaping.

'Let's go into the house, shall we?' I say, and grab Walter's hand, which makes them gape all the more.

'It looks as though you've been having interesting times, Fally,' Simon says mildly as we walk to the door.

'You could say that,' I agree.

'Where *have* you been? Dessy asks.

I open the door. 'In the 18ᵗʰ century,' I reply, and Walter presses my hand reassuringly as the exclamations rain down.

By the time they've stopped exclaiming, we're in the living room, and Elli's looking at my left hand. 'Fally! You're wearing a wedding ring!'

I shrug. 'Walter and I were married on the 7ᵗʰ of April 1779.'

The whole lot of them plump down on the sofas and stare at us.

'I have heard a great deal about you,' Walter says into the stunned silence. 'Fallady was most disappointed that none of you were able to be at our wedding.'

Simon is the first to find his voice. 'How did all this happen?'

'Walter's a parson. He rescued me when I fell into his time. I was in 1779 for six months, but only a week seems to have passed here.'

'That explains the weight loss,' Dessy says, looking me over.

'But how – I mean time travel… it's a bit hard to swallow,' Simon says.

'It's a long, long story,' I say, 'And I've just remembered John and Alyson are coming to dinner, and we haven't even started cooking yet. Hey, Elli, how do you feel about doing your domestic goddess act now that there are going to be so many of us?'

'And since Dr Kelly is bringing his wife particularly to hear the story, perhaps we need tell it but once,' Walter adds.

Jex shakes his head as he looks at Walter. 'Fally, you married a vicar?'

'Yeah, have you gone and got religion all of a sudden?' Dessy joins in.

I laugh, and Walter says, 'Would that she had. As it is, she attends most closely to my sermons for all the wrong reasons.'

'Fally goes to *church*?' Elli screeches.

'Only to see Walter in his vestments,' I say, grinning.

'Indeed, my dear, I do hope that at least part of your attention has been devoted to the services themselves,' Walter says semi-seriously.

'You really are from the 18th century aren't you?' Simon says.

'I am afraid so,' Walter agrees.

'But you believed Fally, though, that she'd come from the future? I mean, no offence, but I was under the impression people in the 18th century might be a bit… well… superstitious,' Simon comments.

Walter laughs. 'I had no alternative but to believe her, since she fell from the sky before my eyes.'

The afternoon turns out to be quite a lot of fun. Despite their scepticism, my siblings can hardly ignore the reality that's before them in the form of my loving spouse. He, of course, has no trouble dealing with the onslaught of so much curiosity and is quite happy to chat to everyone as Elli supervises the dinner preparations.

I explain that we only returned yesterday and Walter still isn't at all well acquainted with the 21st century, so they take it in turns to think of marvels with which to impress him, while I tell them about the trials of the necessary house, chamber pots and lack of any plumbing.

'Really my dear, I had no idea you found it all quite so difficult,' the reverend protests.

'And then there's the knickers,' I say. 'There aren't any knickers in the 18th century!'

The others laugh, but Walter turns to me in mild disapproval. 'Is it customary to discuss undergarments in mixed company?'

'Don't worry, Walter,' says Jex. 'Anything goes, these days.'

I can tell Walter is struggling with the informality as well, but it wouldn't do for him to be calling my own family by anything other than their first names; they'd think it decidedly odd.

'It's a real shame you don't have a telly,' Dessy says. 'I'm wondering what Walter would make of that.'

'Yes, why don't you have a TV, Fally?' Simon asks. 'You never explained that when we were here earlier – in fact, there's quite a lot of things you didn't explain.'

'Ah well, that's the other part of the story. I didn't see how I could explain them, and they'd gone missing when you were here.'

'Who's "them"?' Elli asks from her position of authority, in charge of the range.

I tell them all about Mrs Emrys and Mr Linlade while Walter takes an excursion into the cellar and selects a few bottles of wine that look good to him, although the years are all wrong, of course.

We prepare the dining room too, and despite the electricity being on, we light the candles. I never imagined I'd have such a lot of company, but I know the reverend is enjoying it.

By the time John and Alyson arrive, everyone's getting a bit merry. Alyson's agog to see Walter, and he obviously fulfils all her requirements, wearing his only clothes of a linen shirt, waistcoat, breeches and stockings, buckled shoes, frock coat and white neck cloth, and being suitably quaint in his mannered bow of greeting and his elaborate way of speaking.

She looks me over in some shock. 'John told me you'd lost a lot of weight, and he wasn't joking.'

I laugh. 'Six months without chocolate and a dose of salmonella, that's what's done it. Oh, and plenty of long walks and a bit of horse riding.'

Walter pours more wine for everyone, just as he used to back at the parsonage. It's a pleasure to see him acting the host, especially as I'd been afraid he'd be overawed by all the wonders of the 21st century. He seems to be holding up very well so far. I look around the crowded dining table with the lit candelabra and watch the faces of my family and friends and husband all engaged in a variety of animated conversations. Walter amazes me sometimes, the way he can be so effortlessly sociable, even in difficult circumstances like these.

After dinner, the story's a long time in the telling, especially when everyone keeps butting in with questions. Walter finds himself having to explain the whole matter of wigs – you'd think they'd all be more interested in the metaphysical aspects, but no. Wigs and necessary houses and chamber pots and just about every other unsavoury side of the period are what interest our rapt audience. My experience with the gibbet is picked over with macabre glee.

When, eventually, Walter gives his opinion that God has a hand in matters, neither Alyson nor I is surprised to see John nodding his head and taking a similar view. After some minutes of lively discussion on the subject, they look up and realize that the rest of us are sitting with our arms crossed, just watching them.

'Don't tell me you're *all* atheists,' John says with mock exasperation, and my siblings laugh and profess no great interest in religion one way or another, while Simon confesses to being an agnostic.

'Fallady has told me a lot about what she calls "vicars",' Walter says. 'I apprehend that they are above all reproach in this century.'

'You ought to meet Mrs Durham,' says Alyson slyly. 'She's the vicar of Tref-ddirgel church.'

'A woman?' Walter says, his eyebrows rising. 'And a veritable saint, perhaps?' he adds, his expression serious but his eyes full of amusement.

'I didn't know the vicar of Tref-ddirgel was a woman,' I say. 'What's she like?'

Walter looks at me reproachfully. 'I don't understand how you could not know your own parson, my dear.'

'Things are different in the 21st century,' John says. 'Most vicars are only catering to a small part of the population. People like Fally, who don't go to church, hardly get to meet them, even in a small place like Tref-ddirgel.'

'Fallady has told me of her few experiences with clergymen, but I do find it difficult to imagine. I am acquainted with all my parishioners, whether they attend church or not.'

'They don't all go to church then?' John asks.

'Regrettably not,' Walter sighs. 'The congregation is frequently small.'

'Anyway,' I butt in before they go off on any more tangents. 'What about this Mrs Durham? What's she like?'

'Well, I haven't had a *lot* to do with her,' Alyson says. 'She seems pleasant enough, though.'

'She's not your conventional vicar type,' John adds.

'What is the conventional vicar type?' Walter asks. 'Pious and abstemious perhaps?'

John laughs. 'Well I don't know about abstemious, but I suppose the stereotype is the one we see most of on the television, sort of unworldly and gentle and kind and, yes, pious.'

'You could hardly describe the Vicar of Dibley in those terms,' says Dessy.

We all laugh, but the joke's lost on Walter. 'I'll explain it to you later,' I murmur in his ear.

'Frances Durham isn't like the Vicar of Dibley either,' John says. 'She doesn't really fit any stereotype. You'll see what I mean if you meet her.'

'I should like to see Tref-ddirgel church again,' Walter says. 'It was most disagreeable to see my own church in ruins.'

'We can go there tomorrow,' I promise. 'Only... what if there's a grave there for you?'

'I believe I shall cope, my dear.'

I gaze at him and think, *What if there's a grave for me?*

Later, in bed, with my family squashed into the other rooms, I'm restless and can't sleep, going over everything in my mind. Walter's awake as well, which isn't like him.

'You're not asleep, are you?' I say finally, turning to look at him in the dimness.

'You are correct, my dear. I am pondering many matters.'

'Oh yes? What matters?'

'What is a vicar's place in this society? It does not sound as though we are held in very high esteem.'

'What makes you say that?' I ask, peering at him.

'It is an impression I gained from the general conversation. And who is "the Vicar of Dibley"?'

I giggle. 'She's a fictional character in a comedy series. I think I still have my DVD. I'll get it out tomorrow, and you can watch it on the laptop. Highly educational material for you, Reverend. On the other subject, it's true it's not much like it was in Llanycoed, all that hobnobbing with the squire and everyone knowing you. Are you worried about what you'll do here if you don't get to return?'

'I don't see how I can be a parson,' he says, a little sadly.

'Well I'm not so sure that they're overwhelmed with parsons. They might even be short of them. Anyway, don't worry. Vicars are respected – they're just not as important as they used to be.'

'Which is only partly reassuring.'

CHAPTER TWENTY-THREE

The next day's sunny again. A fairly unusual event in British weather, but it is June – still – I suppose. Walter dresses in his 21st-century garments with considerable discomfort. Once he's donned jeans, shirt, jacket and casual shoes, I gaze at him with wide eyes.

'Wow!'

'Is that good or bad?'

'You look most 21st century, Reverend. I can hardly believe it's you.'

He regards himself in the mirror and laughs quietly. 'You are right. I can hardly believe it's me, either. I shall be relieved to be able to shave.' His shaving equipment is still in 1799, along with the rest of our luggage.

'Well, you fit in nicely in the 21st century with your designer stubble,' I say, kissing his prickly cheek.

My siblings leave later that morning with many warnings to keep them informed from now on. Walter watches the cavalcade of cars pass over the bridge and out of sight and then turns to me. 'They are amazing machines. I could not have believed it until I saw them.'

I laugh. 'Well, you're about to ride in one. Are you ready for this? Once we're a few miles from here, the 21st century's going to burst in on you. It'll be noisy and hectic.'

'I am not greatly uneasy,' he says. 'I believe I shall survive it.'

When we get into the car, he takes a great deal of interest in everything I do and is very quiet until we're chuntering down the road. Finally he shakes his head. 'It is marvellous,' he says. 'And this vehicle runs on oil, as we discussed yesterday?'

'That's right,' I say, pulling up at the junction on to the Tref-ddirgel road. 'Have you recognised anything yet?'

'Not particularly,' he says, pausing as a car shoots by. 'Surely that is a dangerous speed?

I laugh. 'You just wait,' I say, and then pull out, picking up speed myself.

He says little during the journey, starts a few times when lorries thunder towards us and breathes a noticeable sigh of relief when I eventually park safely in Tref-ddirgel. I turn to look at him, and he's distinctly paler than usual.

'I did warn you,' I say, patting his arm reassuringly.

'You were correct about noise, my dear. And colour. Everything seems very bright,' he comments as we step out of the car.

I grin. 'Well, now's your chance to see a supermarket.'

'Perhaps you would care to enlighten me as to what a supermarket might be?'

I point to the only supermarket in the town. 'Normally it's a very big shop, but here it's just a shop that sells everything,' I say, remembering my first day and the peculiar behaviour of everyone I encountered. It occurs to me that Walter's presence isn't likely to go unremarked in this town. The sense of being under scrutiny never really goes away. This time though, I grin inwardly. If only they knew!

'Be careful how you speak,' I warn him. 'I'm hardly anonymous here. Nothing you or I say or do will go unnoticed.'

'You make it sound most sinister,' he comments.

'I thought it was when I first arrived. Now I know it's just fear.'

'Fear of ghosts.'

'Yes, and you might well be considered to be one, especially if you talk.'

He laughs. 'Then I shall endeavour to remain silent.'

As we walk to the supermarket, he turns his attention, just as I did in 1779, to the state of Tref-ddirgel. Given the amount of sad head shaking, I conclude that he's disappointed in what he sees. I know from experience how unnerving it can be.

He gives me a small smile as we enter the fluorescent world of the shop. Just my luck, it's Sioned on the checkout. Prior to my drop into 1779, I'd even started going out of my way to the nearby towns of Oswestry and Welshpool just to avoid her. I slip off my wedding ring and put it into my pocket. Walter notices this and raises his eyebrows but makes no comment.

I select a few odd items, feeling incredibly liberated now that I can spend my own money again and am my own free person. I have the impression, though, that Walter's emotions might incline in the opposite direction. He certainly looks pretty bemused by the goods on display. I watch out of the corner of my eye as he picks up a packet of peanuts or a tin of carrots and studies the labels with a frown.

While I have an inner debate over a packet of crisps or six, wondering how I lived without them for all those months, a female customer goes up to the checkout and talks to the girl in low tones, with occasional glances thrown our way. I don't know what they're saying, because they're speaking in Welsh, but Walter stiffens beside me. There aren't that many Welsh speakers here in the borders in the 21st century, but I've noticed them a few times in Tref-ddirgel.

At the checkout, Sioned looks at us both in that intrusive manner of hers and says, 'Haven't seen you in here lately, Miss Galbraith.'

'No, I've been away for a week or so. My friend's come to stay for a little while, to keep me company,' I say brightly.

'Must be lonely at the watermill,' she says in fake sympathy.

'It can be at times,' I reply.

As we exit the shop, Walter says, 'Diolch yn fawr,' and her mouth drops open as if it's on a hinge.

We hurry away down the road, laughing. 'Okay, you obviously understood them. What did you say, and what were they saying?'

'I merely said thank you. As to what they were saying, they were speculating as to who I might be. They were not unkind, but I apprehend why you find their interest intrusive.'

I sigh. 'That's just the way it is here. Sorry about the wedding ring. It occurred to me that it might look a bit odd, as I wasn't wearing one when I arrived. It's a good job you don't wear one, or they might spread rumours that I'm living with a married man.'

'You *are* living with a married man,' he quips.

'Well in any case, you gave her a shock.' I pause and say reluctantly, 'I suppose it had better be the churchyard next.'

He takes my hand. 'Come, cariad. I believe I can find the way to the church, even in *this* Tref-ddirgel.'

He stops just inside the lych gate and takes an appreciative look. 'It has barely altered,' he says in surprise.

For obvious reasons, I've never been an expert on churches, but this is bigger and grander than the one in Llanycoed. We have it to ourselves, and Walter wanders up the aisle and to the pulpit. 'I have preached here several times,' he says. 'It is a pleasure to see it so well preserved.'

'Churches and old buildings are our specialty,' I say, watching him look at the lectern, where a large book lies open.

'This is most interesting,' he breathes, reading it.

'Is it the Bible?' I ask.

'It is the Book of Common Prayer. It contains readings from Bible.'

'The same one you use? The King James Bible?'

'Indeed.' He smiles. 'There is another?'

'Well, we have versions in more modern language now.'

'These are certainly the readings to which I am accustomed.'

It's poignant to see him at home here, in one of the few environments that have remained virtually untouched in the two hundred years.

After a minute leafing through the book, he peers at me through the gloom. 'Are you all right, my dear? Shall we explore the graveyard?'

It doesn't take us long to find Walter's grave. It's in a surprisingly prominent spot next to the gravel path. There's a large headstone, and unlike some of the other, more recent gravestones that have been eroded by acid rain, it's still completely legible; it seems to be made of a different type of rock, and the inscription is barely worn. We read it together.

'In memory of Reverend Walter Edgemond, father of Anna, rector of the parish of Llanycoed, who departed this life 18th October 1805 aged 72 years. God moves in a mysterious way, his wonders to perform.'

I can't bear it. I know it's ridiculous, with him standing beside me, but seeing those final words chokes me up, and Walter turns to me anxiously. 'Do not be uneasy, cariad. I am still here.'

'Who could have put those words on there? Anna?' I say, trying to hold back my emotions. It seems so likely to have been *me*. It's just the sort of thing I might do as a final jest.

He shakes his head. 'Perhaps. We have not seen a grave for Anna,' he says, 'and I must admit to being relieved. I know it is difficult for you.'

'Look at these,' I say, crouching down to pick up a small bunch of flowers. 'Who could have put them there? And there's some here, too.'

A second bunch is lying to the side of his grave, where there's a small block made of similar stone. It's not a gravestone and would have been easy to miss altogether. I push aside the curtain of ivy that's fallen over it and gasp as a surge of icy shock passes through me.

'In memory of Fallady Edgemond, beloved wife of Walter Edgemond, who departed this life August 1779. Love abideth.'

I bury my head in Walter's shoulder, and he too is uncharacteristically quiet, his arm around my waist. After a couple of minutes I manage to get out, 'So you go back alone and leave me a memorial stone?'

'It would seem so,' he replies, subdued.

'Are you still convinced it was a good idea to come to this graveyard?'

He just holds me, and I hug him back, and we stand there together like that until we're wrenched back to reality by a large dog suddenly bounding on to our legs, its owner calling it back hopelessly from the rear. We separate awkwardly and turn to find ourselves facing a slender woman of about fifty. She has short, dark hair sprinkled with grey and rather formidable and determined features.

'I'm so sorry,' she says, dragging the dog off. 'He's only a puppy and not fully trained yet.' She pauses and looks us over for a moment before adding, 'I can't help noticing that you look... well... quite upset. Can I help? Or the church is open if you need some spiritual comfort.'

I give a croaking laugh, and Walter regards me reproachfully. 'That is most kind of you,' he says.

'The rectory's just across the churchyard,' she says. 'I can offer tea and sympathy. I'm Frances Durham, the rector.'

Despite everything, Walter's eyes light up. 'I believe a cup of tea would be most pleasant,' he says, and looks at me almost pleadingly. 'Would it not, my dear?'

I don't have the heart to refuse, so I murmur, 'Yes, perhaps it would,' and we follow Mrs Durham and the giant sheepdog puppy across the churchyard to her house, which is fairly modern for a vicarage.

'I don't think I've seen either of you before,' she says as she shows us into her kitchen, which is gleaming and shiny and full of gadgets like a microwave, a posh modern oven and a sink with mixer tap. I try to indicate these to Walter with my eyes, while Mrs Durham carries on, 'Are you parishioners or just visiting?'

'Um,' I gulp, thinking quickly. 'I suppose I'm one of your parishioners. I live at Felin Gyfriniaeth. Walter's just visiting.'

She turns to look at me with considerable interest. 'Really? So *you're* Fallady Galbraith.'

Walter laughs quietly, and I groan. 'Does everyone in Tref-ddirgel know my name?'

'I'm afraid so,' the vicar says, putting the kettle on and opening a cupboard. 'The watermill's rather notorious around here.'

'Don't I know it,' I say.

'Della Gilbertine was a friend of mine. I had been meaning to pay you a visit when you arrived, but things being so hectic, I haven't had a chance.'

'It's nice to meet someone who knew Miss Gilbertine,' I say. 'I haven't met many local people at all.'

'Well, the legends keep most people away I suppose.' She looks at me keenly. 'But Della seemed to think you'd be happy there.'

'Did she ever say why she left the house to me?'

'I gather she was fond of you. She used to mention your letters.'

'I've searched around for a message from her, but I haven't found one.'

'I don't think you will. Are you unhappy there? Obviously something's wrong. The pair of you looked so anguished.'

Walter and I exchange glances while Mrs Durham puts the cups on the table.

'Do you know a lot about the graves? I mean, anything about the people who are buried here?' I ask suddenly, knowing I'm treading on precarious ground but feeling too wrung out to care.

She finally joins us at the table and regards us seriously. 'Was it any particular grave you were thinking of?'

'Yes, um, Walter Edgemond's,' I say, and my hand reaches for Walter's under the table. I'm relieved when he folds it in his.

'Oh yes, Reverend Edgemond,' says the vicar. 'I don't really know much more than it says on the headstone, I'm afraid. He was the parson at the old village of Llanycoed – the ruins are near Felin Gyfriniaeth. His second wife's memorial was in Llanycoed graveyard, and he had it moved here in 1799, I think. You have a special interest in him?'

'Yes. It's family history,' Walter replies. 'Do you know what happened to his daughter, Anna, or her descendants? It seems possible that they may still live in the locality.'

I squeeze his hand. Bravo. He's beginning to get the hang of this.

Mrs Durham shakes her head slowly. 'I'm not aware of any grave here for her. Perhaps she moved away.'

'Someone had left flowers on the grave,' I put in.

'I don't know of any local descendants, but of course there could well be some. It seems more likely that it was someone who was visiting. Sometimes people will just put flowers on old or neglected graves for sentimental reasons.'

We nod, and she looks from one of us to the other. '*Are* you finding it difficult at the watermill? I assume the electricity's off?' she says, looking at me.

'Do you believe in the ghosts?' I ask.

'I've met them, if that's what you mean. They're not very alarming ghosts, though. It's the ruins of the old village that really frighten people around here.'

Walter pays close attention. 'Why do they frighten them?'

'Well, seemingly it's a hotbed of ghostly activity. But I shouldn't tell you this, Fallady, if that's what's bothering you.'

'It isn't that – it's really nothing like that. People have seen other ghosts there?'

'Seen them, heard them, spotted strange lights, all kinds of things. It's all part of the legend.'

'But as a vicar, what do you believe?'

'I believe, as Della Gilbertine did, that there are more things in God's creation than we can know.'

Walter smiles and gives me a meaningful look, but Mrs Durham has caught the exchange.

'You're an atheist, though, aren't you?' she says to me. 'I seem to remember Della mentioning it.'

'I'm an atheist, but Walter isn't.'

She looks from one to another of us again. 'You're together?' She looks puzzled. 'I didn't realize you had a partner. I thought you'd be living there alone.'

'We've met since I came here,' I tell her.

'Quick work,' she says, looking at Walter. 'Obviously ghosts don't bother *you* then?' she adds.

He regards her in silence for a moment. I don't think he knows quite what to make of her yet. 'No, they do not,' he says, just as the door opens and a tall teenage boy comes stomping in.

'Mum, I can't find my favourite sweatshirt, and I'm going out in half an hour. What've you done with it?' he says petulantly.

'It's in the washing basket, just dried,' she says in the ultra-patient tone of the sorely tested.

'Well where's the –?'

'In the corner.'

The boy goes over and takes his time rummaging through for the sweatshirt. Walter watches with his eyes almost on stalks at this demonstration of filial disrespect, and Mrs Durham gives us an apologetic look.

'What time will you be back?' she asks the teenager.

'Oh, I don't know. Late, I expect,' he mutters and exits without a backward look.

'My son, Danny. Sorry about that,' the vicar says, looking embarrassed. 'So there's nothing I can help you with? I don't think you've mentioned the real problem.'

'It's difficult,' I say and sip my tea.

'I think perhaps the circumstances warrant the telling, my dear,' Walter says.

I look at him closely. It's obvious that he really wants to tell his fellow vicar, woman or not. 'Okay, you go ahead,' I say with a small shrug.

'I *am* the Reverend Walter Edgemond,' my spouse says simply.

Mrs Durham just stares at him for a long minute.

'How could that be?' she asks eventually.

'There are no ghosts at Llanycoed,' Walter says. 'Mrs Emrys and Mr Linlade are my parishioners, stranded in time.'

She sits back in her chair. 'And you?'

'Fallady fell into my time when she explored the ruins of Llanycoed, and we have just passed into 1799 and from then to now. It seems that God has a purpose for us in the 21st century.'

'So you were looking at your own grave,' she muses.

'Indeed. And Fallady's memorial.'

'The memorial to Mrs Edgemond? I don't think I ever looked at it closely or I'm sure I would have recognised the name.'

I nod. 'We married in 1779.'

She teases at her cup thoughtfully. 'This is all hard to believe, to say the least, but on the other hand, there's a certain logic to it. All those years Della had no idea. Even Mrs Emrys herself seemed to believe she was a ghost.'

'I don't think they knew what to make of it,' I say. 'They were afraid of what had happened to them. They got pretty worked up when they realized I'd been to the ruins.'

'It must have been a very interesting experience, finding yourself in 1779,' she says, with a quirky smile.

'Oh yes, it certainly was, marrying the parson included.'

'Now that we have seen Fallady's memorial, we are forced to conclude that we will be separated,' Walter explains.

She nods slowly. 'So that's how it is.'

We tell her all about it, and I begin to warm to her, despite her being nothing like any of the stereotypical vicars in my mind. Walter is of course delighted when she offers to pray with us, and I sit there feeling embarrassed while she asks God to give us courage to face whatever is to come.

As we're leaving the rectory, she says to Walter, 'So I can expect to see you at church on Sunday?'

'I believe we shall be there, Mrs Durham,' Walter agrees, unconsciously speaking for me, as is his wont.

'Please, call me Frances,' she says.

We return to the graves for another look, and then Walter wants to go back to the church, so as is becoming a habit I sit in a pew and watch him pray. When he finally gets up, he's looking a bit more peaceful. 'Did it help?' I ask, trying to keep the scepticism out of my voice.

'Undoubtedly, my dear,' he says. 'Shall we return to Felin Gyfriniaeth?'

'I think that's a good idea,' I say with a sigh.

I wake up curled into a ball with Walter's arms around me, but I sense immediately that he's not asleep. I turn to look at him. 'Hey,' I say, looking into the familiar brown eyes.

The sensuous lips curve into a smile. 'Hey? What does that mean, cariad?'

'You know full well. What do you want me to say, good morrow?'

He pulls me to him. 'I want you to say that you are all right,' he says, seriously. 'You were very quiet throughout yesterday evening.'

'I *am* all right. It's just… being here, in my time, with choices, is more agonising than being in yours, with no choices.'

'Perhaps I was mistaken in wishing to visit the graveyard,' he says heavily.

'No. I don't think so.'

'You were most shocked.'

'I wasn't the only one.'

'I wish you believed in God, my dear. There is some comfort in turning to him at a time of need.'

I sigh. 'It's never going to happen, Reverend.'

'Then at least share your thoughts with me. I gather you have been trying to make a choice.'

I put my arms around his neck. 'I've made the choice. I've decided I won't be separated from you willingly.'

'Very well, my dear. We shall see what comes to pass,' he says gravely, but I can tell he's pleased and relieved.

CHAPTER TWENTY-FOUR

24TH JUNE 2008

It seems apt that I should write about my time with Fallady in the 21st century. We neither know when it will end nor what God's purpose is for us, but we both feel that this period may be fleeting and the last that we will have together.

I have already seen many wonders, and even this simple thing, writing with a metal pen that retains its own ink, instead of a quill that requires constant dipping, is remarkable. My wife suggested that I might like to try 'typing' on her 'laptop', but it seems better to restrict myself to the form of writing with which I am familiar for the present.

I suspect Fallady is a little disappointed in me, as I have failed to express enough enthusiasm for the many 21st-century wonders that she desires me to see. Nevertheless, we arrived yesterday in my birthplace of Shrewsbury for a brief stay at an inn. I endured the journey in considerable unease, which I hope I was able to conceal. Whilst it is an inordinate pleasure to have music playing while travelling, I found it difficult to enjoy the Bach emitting from the radio as I feared for my life each time an enormous vehicle approached at speed in the opposite direction.

These roads upon which we travelled appear to have been built by giants and are of incredible smoothness, and the land itself is studded with great metal constructions that I was informed are electricity pylons, street lights or mobile phone masts. The street lights bear no resemblance to those that I have seen in London. Wooden poles with looping metal strands line many roads, and these, apparently, are for the telephone. My wife seemed surprised at my many observations – I do not believe she is even aware of the intrusion of these constructions in the landscape.

The amount of traffic increased inordinately as we approached Shrewsbury and crossed the Welsh Bridge – a new bridge, and very different in appearance. I endured the clamour and smell – these vehicles emit an unpleasant odour, of which, once again, Fallady is seemingly unaware – as best I could until, the Lord be praised, we reached our destination inn.

This inn is one with which I am familiar, and the exterior is little altered. While my wife wishes to impress me with wonders, I am fully occupied in assimilating a considerable number of smaller shocks. I have of necessity accepted women parsons, yet it is but a symptom of the altered world. Here in the hotel, young, pretty girls dressed in garments that display much of their legs act as receptionists, their manners as confident and assured as those of any man.

I was most embarrassed to stand at Fallady's side as she handed over a small card as a guarantee of payment, but the young woman who served us showed no surprise at all that I would not be paying the bill, and it is clear that to Fallady it is perfectly in order to take the lead. It is only now that I apprehend how truly difficult must she have found life in 1779.

When we took a walk into the town, I was struck afresh by the clothing that is worn. I felt obliged to avert my gaze from the almost naked bodies, both male and female, on display. I have seen female legs only rarely, and whilst the sight of them is most agreeable, I am of the firm opinion that male legs are better concealed. As to the habit of some men of wearing no shirt in the heat, these naked chests are an exceedingly unpleasant sight. Many women wear only the minimum to cover their bosom and bottom and walk in the style I was used to associate with common strumpets, and yet I am assured that they are not. It is apparent that the deplorable T-shirt and jeans favoured by men and women of all ages is one of the more decorous forms of clothing. I do not feel at all comfortable or like myself wearing such attire, but I should feel even less comfortable dressed in what Fallady calls 'shorts'. I can only be grateful that Dr Kelly did not furnish me with any such items.

Despite these surprises, I was able to enjoy our stroll about the town, and Fallady permitted me to choose where we went, although her enthusiasm for this course dimmed somewhat when she discerned my intention to visit a number of churches. My experience in Tref-ddirgel had led me to expect the Shrewsbury churches, with which I was once very familiar, to be in a similar condition of preservation and usage. I was therefore horrified to find St. Chad's a complete ruin and St. Mary's, where I was once a curate, used primarily as an architectural attraction, even housing a tea shop to draw visitors. I could scarce express my dismay at this discovery, although I suspect Fallady had some idea. She waited patiently while I prayed for God's guidance to withstand a world in which a church of such beauty is used but seldom for its true purpose of worship.

We dined within the inn, but there was insufficient steak on my plate to assuage my appetite, although there was a large quantity of chips and fripperies of mushrooms, lettuce and cucumber with which, I assume, were meant to make up for the lack of good, honest meat. During this meal, Fallady asked me what was the most surprising thing I had as yet observed about the 21st century. It was difficult to pick out one among so many, but as it was by this time evening, and the light was fading, I was struck suddenly by the brilliant illumination in the restaurant. Of all things, it seems to me that electric lighting is the greatest revolution. The air within doors is also much improved without the unpleasant taint that permeates the parsonage when many tallow candles must be lit.

Our room comes furnished with several electrical devices, including a television. I do not entirely understand the workings of this apparatus, but it is clearly a significant influence in the 21st century. No longer do people make merry around the harpsichord or play cards together. Instead, it seems, they entertain themselves with their television, radio and computers.

Fallady desired to acquaint me with television and handed me a small box mounted by buttons with which I was to select which entertainment to view. She, in the meantime, sat beside me in bed with her laptop and proceeded to 'surf the 'net', something which, I am informed, it is very difficult to do satisfactorily from the watermill.

The television revealed all too quickly that my series of shocks was far from at an end. If I already believed the world around me was so foreign as to be almost beyond comprehension, the scenes and behaviours to which I was now subjected demonstrated that I was far from fully informed in the matter. A significant number of programmes were spoken in what Fallady described as an American accent. Indeed, seemingly the American colonies now dominate the world! I had great difficulty comprehending the dramas, whether in an English or American accent, but further buttons brought such matters under my gaze as 'My Penis and Me', 'I Hate my Breasts', 'How Clean is Your House?' and 'Sex for Girls'. My wife, who was unable to disguise the great amusement my discomfiture afforded her, eventually relented and by some arcane means obtained a programme that, she averred, I might find more to my liking. This drama was set 'close to my time', and it was at least considerably diverting, albeit that the only parson in it, a Mr Collins, was portrayed as an odious individual, which does not inspire me with any greater hope that clergy are respected in this time. Further, I was informed at some considerable length of the charms of Mr Darcy, and apprised that my wife, in common with many women, finds him most sexy, and that a scene in which he bathes in his undergarments is apparently iconic. Fortunately she informed me that nevertheless I am the only man for her, and she finds me just as fetching as Mr Darcy.

25TH JUNE 2008

I was this morning educated in the workings of the shower. It is, I am advised, the preferred method of washing in the 21st century. I confess I found it pleasantly invigorating and am beginning to enjoy the simplicity and ease of merely turning taps to obtain water.

I have discovered that Shrewsbury School, which I attended, has now become a library. It was most disconcerting to walk the halls and classrooms that I once knew and view them filled with bookshelves.

We spent much of the afternoon in a lengthy stroll along the river, where I discovered that the new Welsh Bridge was built in 1795, and that I shall likely see it again in the same form, and Fallady was greatly taken by a peculiarly greasy odour wafting down a riverside alley and insisted that we partake immediately of the 'traditional British delicacy' of fish and chips. I agreed to this with some reservations, wondering whether my beleaguered constitution could tolerate any more chips, and became considerably less enthusiastic when I observed that these items were thrust willy-nilly into paper and presented to us as a greasy package. Fallady, however, considered this to be a great treat and carried the parcel reverently to the river's edge, where we sat underneath some weeping willows and consumed the squashed contents.

Now, I believe, I am about to be educated in 'surfing the 'net' while we have the 'faster speed' provided by the inn. Fallady responded to my enquiry about the statue of Darwin outside the library with a promise that she will reveal all about him by this means.

26TH JUNE 2008

We have returned to Felin Gyfriniaeth, and I confess that I am somewhat relieved. The many wonders I have encountered are difficult to assimilate, as is indeed *The Origin of Species*, which I have spent considerable time reading since last night. Fallady assures me that the Anglican Church does not generally believe Darwin's work to be at odds with the Bible, but I confess that I find the idea that I am descended from an ape very disconcerting. The 21st century is quite alarming as a whole, and I am concerned that there is no place for me within it. I am also most anxious about Anna. Fallady is certain that little or no time will be passing in 1779, and that therefore Anna will be unaware of our absence. I trust that she is correct.

28TH JUNE 2008

Branwen Emrys and Percival Linlade returned to Felin Gyfriniaeth this morning. I was greatly relieved by the prospect of Mrs Emrys' cooking, and thanks be to God they are no longer completely trapped in 1799, as they have been for more than a fortnight. Regrettably, it is not all good news for Fallady, as she has lost her electricity and can no longer use the machines that she holds dear. I gather that she has the intention of utilizing the car in some fashion to ensure that we can continue to use the laptop. I confess that I now appreciate the infinite information provided by that device.

29TH JUNE 2008

We attended church today, but while on my part it was most interesting, I fear Fallady's thoughts were elsewhere. The liturgy was little altered, apart from the introduction of hymns, and it would not have caused me much difficulty to perform the service. I gather that it is now Queen Elizabeth II for whom I must pray, and apparently the Holy Sacrament is administered every Sunday, rather than solely at Christmas or on Good Friday. We spoke to the rector, Mrs Durham, afterwards, and she mentioned that two of the retired clergy who normally assist her with some services are currently unwell. She suggested that I might like to help her through this crisis. Naturally I was delighted. She assures me that she can instruct me in the ways of the 21st-century Anglican Church. It will be a relief to be of some use, although I do not know that there will be any payment involved. I am all too aware of my dependence on my wife – as she points out with not a little glee, the tables are turned.

30TH JUNE 2008

This morning Fallady drove me to the rectory to commence my education with Mrs Durham, who has now supplied me with several books to study. As I surmised, the 1662 Book of Common Prayer is still used in the parishes for which Mrs Durham is responsible, and I hope, if I am eventually permitted to preach, that I can craft my sermons to reflect the different times. It is the foreign nature of the society to which I would be preaching that I must study to overcome.

2ND JULY 2008

As I had many times admired the planes flying overhead, Fallady has been attempting to persuade me to see them at closer quarters, and at last I succumbed to the temptation, although it meant a lengthy drive to Birmingham. We passed along vast roads full of vehicles of every shape and size at alarming speed, but the airport and the planes are truly the greatest wonder I have ever seen. We watched many take off and land, and I was astonished to learn to which far-off lands some were heading. It was a tiring but worthwhile day, and I know well that my wife took great pleasure in it.

Working with Mrs Durham has proved most illuminating. Despite the liturgy having changed little, I have come to realize that the Anglican Church is indeed greatly altered, and that what Fallady has told me about parsons is more accurate than otherwise. Mrs Durham is a widow, and her income as rector is low by the standards of this time. As far as I can see, she has little choice but to be abstemious, with two teenage children to support. I am humbled by the dedication she shows in her work and by the amount of time she must give to it.

CHAPTER TWENTY-FIVE

I'm heading towards the rectory to meet Walter when a male vicar approaches from the other direction. I assume it's a friend of Frances' and barely glance at him, until he stops and laughs.

'You look somewhat surprised, my dear,' he says mildly.

'You could say that,' I murmur.

'You do not think I look most dignified? Frances suggested that it would be appropriate if I dressed this way, since I am now in a position to assist as her curate. She proposes that I carry out the service at Tref-ddirgel next Sunday.'

'Really?' I say, leaping on to the last part of his news. 'So you'll be wearing your vestments again?'

He regards me reproachfully. 'Am I to assume that you *will* be attending church this weekend, my dear?' he says, hinting at my having given it a miss on the previous Sunday.

'I suspect I might be, Reverend. And you certainly do look very much the reverend dressed like that. I hope you realize how much you now have to live up to. Abstemious and pious, and a veritable saint besides.'

'I shall have to write a sermon,' he says happily. 'It will be most agreeable to preach again.'

I shake my head, surprised at my own reaction. To see him dressed like that shatters all my stereotypical images of vicars and reveals prejudices I didn't even know I had. Vestments are one thing, but the dog collar is another matter altogether.

It's been a strange few weeks, all round. I've been feeling dislocated, missing the school and the things about the 18th century I'd come to like and enjoy, and Walter has been bewildered on many fronts and struggling to cope with profound culture shock. Fortunately, being recruited by Frances has given him a focus, and apart from his studies on the Anglican Church, he's been pumping me for information about contemporary culture and viewing my DVD collection on the laptop.

The service at Tref-ddirgel is an odd experience for me. Walter looks different but distinctly dignified in his more colourful 21st-century vestments. He sticks firmly to the gospel message for his sermon rather than branching out to discuss aspects of contemporary culture he doesn't yet fully understand. Even so, he's confident enough to work, as usual, without notes. He just memorises the gist, and it all comes out in a seemingly effortless manner.

He seems pensive on our journey home, but it doesn't take him long to tell me what's on his mind, in fact no longer than it takes for us to get out of Tref-ddirgel.

'Do you remember asking me if I had become a parson out of a sense of vocation?' he says.

I nod. 'Of course.'

'I replied that it was not vocation but expediency. And that was indeed the case. Now, however, I believe my feelings have altered.'

I raise my eyebrows. 'You think you have a vocation?'

'Indeed. My time here has revealed to me that it is, after all, my calling, and what God wants of me.'

I start a little. 'How do you know what God wants?'

He sighs. 'My dear, I do not think you understand my faith at all.'

'True. But you could try and explain it.'

'I am not entirely certain that theological discussion would benefit our marriage, unless of course you are having a change of heart and desire some biblical instruction.' He says this seriously, but even though I'm concentrating on the road, I know he has that glint of humour in his eye.

'No thanks. I had enough instruction when I was a child. I just wonder what it feels like, that's all.'

'To have faith?'

'To believe in God. What *is* God? No one ever answers that question. When I try to understand it, I feel like I'm clutching a handful of fog.'

He chuckles, and I look aside at him in surprise. 'What?'

'My dear, in my twenty years as a parson, I can honestly state that no one has ever before asked me "what is God?", and prior to encountering you I should likely have viewed anyone asking such a question as being in very poor case indeed.'

'A heathen, eh?'

'Something of that nature. As to what it feels like... when I pray there is a sense of peace, of touching something far greater than myself.'

'Hmmm... well, I suppose that's some kind of answer. Anyway, I'm glad you're happy in your work. I wish I could have the same certainty.'

'About what, my dear?'

'My life. What I would rather be doing. I think I took a wrong turn somewhere. When I took up computers with such enthusiasm I really believed they were what *I* wanted to spend my life working on.'

'And now you do not?'

'I'd already tired of them, or rather of working with them, by the time I left London.'

'And you did not find your vocation as my wife?' he says provocatively.

I laugh. 'I most certainly did not, Reverend. Being a wife is no more of a role in life than being a husband.'

'As I believe you informed Anna at some length.'

'Mmm, and let's hope she took at least a little notice of me. But the teaching... there was something rewarding in it. Like the way Abigail started to realize there's a whole other world in books. It was magical at times.'

'You could not do that here?'

I shrug. 'Maybe. Things are a lot more complicated here though. Anyway, your sermon sounded good to me. I'm sure it went down well with the Tref-ddirgel busybodies.'

He smiles. 'It was a pleasure to have you there watching, cariad.'

I grin. 'You do realize they probably think we're "living in sin"?'

He looks shocked. 'I trust not! A parson would not behave so, even in this time, surely.'

I shrug. 'I must admit I hadn't really thought through how it would look if you got to be known in the town, and you're certainly doing that, at least among the religious fraternity. I know how much you like wearing the old dog collar and so on.'

He gives me a small smile. 'I believe it is called a *clerical* collar, my dear – and I know you don't like it, but I am not sure why.'

'It's the aura of sexless holiness it seems to project,' I say.

'Would that not be more appropriate to Catholic clergy?'

I shake my head. 'I think it's the way vicars are portrayed in the media. Like they don't even know what sex is, and every little thing shocks them. Like they're too holy for anything so base and primitive. I just didn't realize how pervasive it was.'

'I have noticed that I am treated differently now, despite being neither sexless nor holy. You were correct when you informed me that your clergy are esteemed, despite the differences in role.'

'So if you were stuck here, you could cope with being a 21st-century cleric?'

He chuckles. 'I believe I could, although it is considerably harder work.'

'Are you tired of the 21st century yet?'

He purses his lips. 'I can't deny I shall be pleased to return home and to see Anna again, but it is the manner of that return which concerns me.' He smiles suddenly. 'Yet now I should miss the laptop and the DVDs and the indoor necessary and even the bathtub. I am corrupted by luxury!'

Surprisingly, he's taken very much to the joys of surfing the 'net, primarily for information about the various scientific and theological/philosophical matters that have puzzled him all his life, as well as contemporary culture. I have to keep the laptop charged up via a car charger so that he can engage in this new interest, and also to ensure that we can watch my DVD collection and listen to CDs.

We take a walk into Llanycoed that evening under a threatening grey sky that's been almost constant since our arrival back in the 21st century. There's been so much rain that the ground's saturated and slippery with mud, but we don't seem to be able to keep away.

We're surveying the sad wreckage of our former home when I notice that the keys to Felin Gyfriniaeth, which I'd thrust into my jeans pocket, are hot.

'Weird,' I murmur to myself, taking them out gingerly.

'Something is wrong?' Walter says, watching me.

'Do you remember me telling you the keys get hot when there's something going on? Like when we pass through a time, and when I first arrived at the house? So why are they hot now? See any ghosts or time portals or anything?' Up to now, our visits to Llanycoed have been without incident.

'How would I recognise a time portal?' Walter says with a quirky smile, since by now he knows all about them, having been subjected to topical episodes of Star Trek as part of his DVD education. I don't think he knew what to make of them, but he watched gamely enough.

'Hmm… well, apparently in Llanycoed it resembles a bit of ground covered in leaf mould,' I say, 'but I suppose it could equally look like a heap of rubble.'

I'm still holding the keys, very gingerly, by the key ring, and they begin to vibrate just as they did when I arrived at the house back in May. I get the peculiar feeling of being observed that I had before at the parsonage, just as Walter exclaims beside me.

'Look, my dear, where my study used to be.'

I turn and watch as Walter's study appears out of the wreckage, just as I remember it. It's lit by the glow of candles, and sitting at his desk, writing, is Walter himself! Even as the two of us move closer to the ghostly study across what was once the floor of the parlour, the other Walter looks up and stares straight at us, as though he can hear and see us too. This Walter is far older, his face lined, his long hair as grey as his wig used to be, his paunch perhaps a little larger under the waistcoat, but it's still him, and I want to reach out to him across the centuries – despite having the current reverend safely by my side.

'Walter?' I almost whisper. 'Can you see us? Can you hear us?'

The ghostly reverend gets up from his chair without taking his eyes off me. 'Fallady? I see you but dimly – and indeed the fine figure of a man with you.'

I chuckle, then sober and say, 'We were right, weren't we? You went back there alone?'

He nods sadly. 'Indeed, my dear. But it is a joy to see you on this the eighteenth anniversary of our wedding. God has granted me a great gift this day.'

The glowing image starts to fade, and the ghostly Walter says, 'Love abideth, cariad.'

'I love you, Walter!' I cry out, just as the image fades, and the study reverts to its ruined state.

I turn to the real Walter, who looks completely stunned. 'Do you think he heard me?'

He gazes down at me. 'I heard you, cariad, in both times.'

I give him a hug. 'You looked so lonely,' I say, my voice catching on a sob.

'I also looked very old!' he says. 'But I could not have been so unhappy if I was able to jest.'

I sigh. 'Perhaps. Well, now we know for certain how things are going to go – just not when.'

We return to the house, and the keys are still hot when I unlock the door.

'I am curious as to *why* the keys become heated,' Walter says, looking them over. 'They are quite ancient, and I am unsure of what metal they are made.'

'Surely the keys couldn't be the key, could they?' I say, only semi-seriously.

The reverend looks up from his spot on the sofa and merely raises his eyebrows at me. He's starting to demonstrate some distinctly 21st-century ways.

I sit down beside him. 'There is one strange thing about those keys,' I say. 'The solicitors never gave me any clues as to which ones were for which doors, and even now I have no idea what the two smallest ones are for.'

'That is most interesting,' he says thoughtfully, fingering the two keys in question. 'And there is another matter that occurs to me. I don't know why it did not do so before, but then I have been familiar with them since childhood.'

'Been familiar with what?'

'The names, my dear. Felin Gyfriniaeth means "mystery mill", or even "mystic mill", whereas Tref-ddirgel means, effectively, "town of the hidden secret".'

I gape at him. 'Mystic mill! Hidden secret! They've always been called that? I mean, in known history?'

'To the best of my knowledge. This watermill has been in existence since the sixteenth century, I believe, but Tref-ddirgel was established long before that.'

'And Llanycoed, what does that mean?'

He laughs softly. 'Village of the trees, or church of the trees, since it would not be a village without a church.'

'So nothing mystical there then,' I say, 'even though it seems to be at the centre of everything.'

He purses his lips in thought. 'Indeed. There was never any hint of anything untoward in Llanycoed, and yet… '

'Suppose Tref-ddirgel came first, and it was known that there was something odd out here, but then that knowledge got lost as time went on and Llanycoed became a village,' I say.

'Which leaves the watermill,' Walter says. 'Someone knew there was a mystery here, and indeed it is not merely Llanycoed itself that is at the centre of everything. Felin Gyfriniaeth is where the one certain time gate lies; it is to the mill that Mrs Emrys and Mr Linlade are permitted to come, and it is only Felin Gyfriniaeth that still stands out of all the buildings in the village.'

'The library book said that's because it's on higher ground.'

He shakes his head. 'It is on the other side of the time gate.'

'This house has been altered a lot even since your time when it was only a mill, yet the keys are still the originals from when it was built, surely?'

'I imagine so. These two smaller keys must therefore fit something inside the house or grounds.'

'I went around looking when I first moved in but had no luck. I thought maybe they were defunct – the doors they used to open might have been removed when the place was renovated and turned into a house.'

Walter sighs. 'I fear you will find this amusing, my dear, but I do not believe God has guided us this far in order that we shall not find the doors to fit these keys.'

I curl up against him. 'What was it like seeing yourself aged three and sixty?'

He puts his arm around me. 'It was not so disagreeable as you might suppose. I believe I still looked fairly dignified and imposing. Do you not agree?'

I giggle. 'I was most gratified to see you hadn't gone back to the wig! It's just a shame we couldn't talk for long.' I sober before adding, 'The one thing we now know is that everything we're doing, looking for doors and so on, is going to lead to our separation.'

He sighs again. 'Indeed. I know you cannot share this opinion, but I firmly believe it is the Lord's will. Whatever is happening here is a fault, an error, and we must correct it.'

I bite my lip. 'Only *what* is it that's faulty? And will we know how to fix it when we do find it?'

He pulls me closer, and I lean my head on his chest. 'God will help us in this quest, my dear,' he murmurs.

'I hope you're not getting even more religious in the 21st century, Reverend,' I tease. 'It must be all the stuff you have to live up to now you're wearing the dog collar.'

He chuckles. 'Well, cariad, it was you who advised me that I must be pious and abstemious. I note that I have certainly been the latter. I have drunk barely a drop of liquor since my arrival here, and as for gambling, since playing cards is no longer an acceptable social pursuit, I have had no alternative but to abstain.'

'Barely a drop, eh? Well, I suppose it might be considered such, given your previous enormous consumption.'

He looks down at me in mock outrage. 'Enormous consumption indeed! I was barely disguised in liquor in my life. I may perhaps have become considerably merry on occasion during my Oxford days, but never since I became a parson.'

'Hmmm… well, the day I met you, I did notice you got pretty close. You only seemed to sober up when I told you where I really came from.'

'Ah, that was a considerably unusual day. You shook my entire world. I am not sure you realize how profoundly. In any event, I suspect that if I have become more religious it is due to you also.'

'Oh yeah? How'd you make that out?'

'I assume you are speaking English, but I am entirely unsure of what you said. No matter, I can guess. Your arrival, your bringing me back to life and my experiences in the 21st century have all altered my perceptions.'

'Of God?'

'Perhaps, to the extent that he seems closer and more real. What do you suppose caused the vision of myself this evening?'

I sit back and look at him, and I can see the gleam in his eye. 'Okay. I know what *you* think it was because Walter number two told me. *I*, however, assume it was part of the general sequence of time displacement events.'

'It did not seem peculiar to you that it was a particular date?'

'Sheer coincidence,' I say firmly, although I had wondered about that myself.

He chuckles. 'I cannot but believe that the Lord has a hand in these events, and you, my dear, despite your lack of belief, are at the crux of them all.'

I stare at him. 'I hope you're not hinting that I'm God's instrument or something.'

'The ways of the Lord *are* unfathomable,' he says, looking very solemn, and then grins and adds, 'You need not fear that I have changed. I don't envisage wearing a hair shirt or spending countless hours on my knees at my devotions, despite my now being "a vicar". It is that which really concerns you, is it not?'

I shrug. 'I often used to forget you were a vicar in the 18th century, but here... '

'The clerical collar is a constant reminder.' He purses his lips in thought. 'Frances is hardly unworldly, I think, despite having nothing in common with *The Vicar of Dibley*. I do not comprehend how it is that children in this time are permitted to be so disrespectful towards their parents.'

'Danny and Rachel giving her a hard time, are they?'

'*They* certainly demonstrate no consideration for the saintly vicar. They are frequently ill-mannered towards their mother, and even myself, should I happen to be present.'

'That's teenagers for you.'

'I trust Anna will not behave so when she reaches that age.'

'I can't imagine Anna ever being ill-mannered,' I say.

He purses his lips. 'She is perhaps too quiet and reserved. I am in hopes that the school will draw her out.'

I put my hand over his. 'I don't think any time will have passed there. She won't even know you've been away.'

He gives me a small smile. 'I hope that you are correct, but I do have moments of doubt on the matter.'

CHAPTER TWENTY-SIX

I'm waiting for Walter outside the tiny church at Llanyrafon, and looking around the graves to see if I can spot one for Laura or Mr Jenkins or any descendants, when I overhear a couple of older ladies chatting nearby.

'Nice to have a male vicar for a change, eh, Mary?' says one.

'Yes, seems all right. Talks a bit old fashioned though.'

'Well that's vicars for you, I suppose. Bit rarefied aren't they?'

I choke back a laugh. The vicar stereotype is actually helping Walter, it seems.

He appears after the minuscule congregation has filtered away, looking quite happy and extremely vicarly. It's becoming hard to imagine him back in his 18th-century costume, and I've adjusted to the dog collar at last.

'It was somewhat like old times today, my dear,' he says.

I nod. 'You're starting to understand your audience a lot better.'

'Indeed. I have much to learn, but I do feel more at home.'

It's true that there are still many things he doesn't understand – even with the 'net, how can he appreciate germ theory or electricity or computers (despite using one) in seven weeks?

Back at the house, Mrs Emrys is preparing to dish up her usual Sunday roast, and while Walter heads to the study, I go down into the cellar seeking a bottle of wine. We've been making considerable inroads into the stocks, and I have to go to the back of the dingy cave of a room in search of one of the last reds. Just as I'm about to pick one up, the keys in my pocket start jangling. I reach in to pull them out – they're hot and vibrating madly. I scan around, expecting some sort of time displacement event, but no ghostly Walter appears before my eyes this time. Instead, when I hold the keys in the direction of the back wall of the cellar, they jangle even more imperatively.

I lift my torch to study the wall carefully and run my hand over the bricks, hoping to trigger something that reveals a priest hole or an ancient passageway, but instead the keys rattle again, and there's a slight pull downwards. I crouch down to take a look at the floor, shining the torch on the stone flags and scraping away with my hand to remove the layer of dust and grime that must have been accumulating for centuries. My fingers catch a small hollow and at the same moment one of the keys aligns itself in its direction as though being drawn by a powerful magnet. I scratch off the dirt in the indentation, which is immediately adjacent to the wall, and shiver slightly with anticipation. It's as though this moment just had to come, from the moment I put the first huge key into the front door of the house. I shine my torch into the nondescript groove I've revealed. If it hadn't been for the keys I'd never have noticed it, but one thing is certain: it's definitely key-sized. I take a big gulp of air to steady myself and take the over-excited key off the key ring. It's almost too hot to hold, and I slip it quickly into the slot and stand back, awaiting I don't know what. There's an immediate ping from the key and then a click, and I watch in astonished silence as the flagstone pulls back slowly and creakily, revealing a set of stone steps spiralling downwards and a cold, dank smell wafting upwards.

When I've got over the shock, I call Walter, and Mrs Emrys and Mr Linlade follow him down. We cluster around the hole, shining our torches and speculating.

'What can it mean?' Mrs Emrys says, a little fearfully.

'There has to be something down there, something that's causing the time displacements,' I say, feeling icy sweat sheath my whole body.

'It must surely lead to Llanycoed,' Walter says, playing his torch down but revealing no end to the stairway.

'It fits in with what you said, about the mill being… um… key,' I say.

'Indeed. Perhaps we shall find your answers down this stair.'

'It looks dangerous. You could hurt yourselves,' Mrs Emrys says.

'God has granted us the opportunity, and we must avail ourselves of it,' the reverend intones, and for once I don't mind that he's speaking for me as well.

'You are certain that you wish to do this, Fallady?' He asks me later as, along with Mr Linlade, we prepare to make the descent.

I nod firmly. He hasn't tried to dissuade me, but I know it goes against all his chivalrous instincts to lead me into potential danger.

The stairway, although apparently ancient, isn't at all worn. There's no handrail, so we have to tread carefully as we wind deeper and deeper into the cold dampness. The further we descend, the stronger the dank, sandy smell becomes. The steps eventually peter out, and we're in a cavernous tunnel that slopes slightly downwards between smooth rock walls. I run my hand over the shiny surface – it feels like glass.

As we move forwards, there are occasional cracks in the walls: signs that all is not completely intact. Water has penetrated here and there, and there are even one or two small stalactites in places.

The tunnel levels off and widens, and the keys, which I'd thrust back into my jeans pocket, are heating up again, just as our torches light on a massive cave-in ahead. We must be looking at the area of the church.

The blockage is a mess of soil and rock and tree roots, and Walter purses his lips as he studies it carefully. 'We must find a way through. Percival, I believe your oil lamp may be of assistance.'

Mr Linlade hands him the lamp, and he removes the glass chimney to expose the flaming wick, then passes up and down the blockage, watching the flame carefully for any change. I'm holding my breath, hoping we're not going to be thwarted now that we're so close to an answer.

'There,' Walter says at last in satisfaction, and we peer at the flame as it flickers slightly in a tiny breeze passing through the seemingly impenetrable rubble.

It's lucky that Mr Linlade has a more practical turn of mind than Walter or myself. He's come equipped with a shovel for safety purposes, and now breaks it out willingly and starts to dig at the cave-in. Walter looks askance at me as I join him in pulling away what we can with our bare hands, but he refrains from comment. After about an hour of hard work, we're hefting aside large lumps of red sandstone. Walter stares at them sadly as he realizes they're remnants of his church. A white light startles us as it flickers through the remaining rubble.

Without thinking, I cry out, 'Is there anybody there? Can you hear us?'

We stand silent, listening, but there's only a sort of ripping sound. I swallow down my fear. What are we going to find through there?

Walter puts his grimy hand over mine. 'God is with us, cariad.'

I give him a grateful, if tremulous, smile, although I don't believe him, of course.

My hands are bleeding from the constant scraping of the rocks, and my arms and back are aching by the time Mr Linlade reaches the other side of the blockage and jumps down over the last few heaps of debris. We follow behind, and Walter helps me down into a passage just like the one we left behind, except that not far ahead there's an open arch and emanating from it a sort of coruscating glow. I run the back of my hand over my sweaty and grubby forehead and notice that my skin is starting to crawl. Walter's hair is standing slightly on end. Mr Linlade, being almost bald, has no such trouble. The closer we get to the archway, the more static there seems to be. Along with the flickering light there's that unpleasant ripping and spitting sound, like an electrical short. This is beginning to feel dangerous.

We peer through the arch to a scene that's enough like Star Trek to satisfy any geek. In a fairly small chamber hewn cleanly out of the rock stands a bright white central column that looks like it's made of crystal. Electricity plays over the glittering facets, but every couple of seconds energy spurts out at random with the loud electrical spit as an accompaniment. The reason is all too clear. The ceiling above the crystal is badly cracked, and water is dripping down a long, spiny stalactite. The stalactite is itself caught within the electrical field – the spurts of energy cascade around it seemingly at random – but it's the trickle of water that's having the worst effect.

Two more passages meet at this chamber, and we shine our torches down them. One is partially blocked by debris, but the other is clear. It seems obvious that this cavern is the centre of everything.

In front of the column stands a rock platform topped by a large computer-type screen. I brave the spits of energy to take a closer look. The whole plinth is caked in dirt. Is it the dust of aeons or just two hundred years? Walter helps me to scrape it away while Mr Linlade stays rooted to the doorway. I don't blame him. My hair is haloing around my head, and my skin feels like it's on fire.

More than anything, the device resembles a 'hole in the wall' cash dispenser, with metallic buttons alongside a shiny flat screen. To my surprise the screen is intact. At last, something I might understand. Except that the instructions beside the buttons are in arcane-looking symbols. So, I find a computer, but it's all in gobbledegook. Great. Now what?

'I believe the crystal is quartz,' the reverend says.

I nod. 'I wish I could read this language. If I could understand it, I might be able to work out what all this is for. As it is, it's meaningless.'

He peers at the panel with its peculiar symbols and then stiffens in surprise. I watch him curiously as he runs his finger over the buttons, his lips moving unconsciously.

'What is it?' I say. 'Do you recognise it?'

'It appears to be Ancient Greek.'

'Ancient Greek!' I screech. 'And you can read it?'

He nods. 'I studied it at Oxford, and I was uncommonly good at it,' he says modestly.

'Can you translate it?

He looks at it closely, pursing his lips, and says after a moment, 'Whilst I can translate the words, I cannot correctly ascertain the meaning. I assume the context to be outside my experience.'

'Maybe I can understand the context,' I suggest, and then jump as a very loud spit emanates from the column.

While the static plays over us and the bolts of electricity spit out every few seconds, Walter starts giving me the literal translations of the words, and I carry out my own translation into technospeak.

There are three buttons at the side of the screen, and the adjacent script carved into the metal reads:

Status
Information
Contact

I glance at Walter, who just raises his eyebrows as I press the button for *Status* with a shaking hand. The screen lights up immediately, and a list unfurls in its centre in orange script. We decipher it slowly and painstakingly.

Operational.
First cluster: standard.
Second cluster: interrupted.
Third cluster: standard.
Fourth cluster: malfunction.

The list concludes with a flashing message. *Further details?*

I press the button again to indicate yes, and the display changes instantly to:

Severe damage minus three thousand five hundred twenty.
Unit one: non-functional
Unit two: intermittent
Unit three: functional
Unit four: intermittent
Unit five: non-functional
Auto repair attempt failed.
Potential danger: high.
Shutdown mode unavailable.
Damage limitation initiated.
Technical help requested.

'Unit three – I wonder if that's the time gate near the house?' I shout, as some particularly fierce spits emanate from the column. 'And one of the intermittent ones could be what made me fall into 1779. But what damage limitation? And what technical help? Requested of whom? Where?' I say, beginning to feel incredibly tired and tetchy.

'*We* appear to be the technical help, my dear,' Walter says, regarding the crystal warily.

I stare at him. 'We are, aren't we? But we've been a long time getting here.'

Just as he's about to reply, there's an even louder spit from the column, and one of the rogue surges of energy jags across the chamber and hits me on the arm. I sag to the ground with pain prickling through my body. 'Fallady!' Walter cries and scoops me up, carrying me safely beyond the archway and as far as possible from the static.

'I'm okay,' I murmur as he sets me down gently on the ground near the rubble. 'Really. I'm okay. It was just an electric shock. Not enough to kill me.'

'I am relieved to hear it, cariad,' he says, his face white.

Mr Linlade pours me some hot tea from a flask thoughtfully provided by Mrs Emrys. I gulp it down gratefully and flex my arm. It still feels a little odd, but it doesn't seem to be damaged.

'I think it is time we returned home,' Walter says as I struggle to get up and find my legs are still very wobbly. 'Are you certain you have recovered? You are still somewhat pale.'

'I'm all right,' I say, trying to look sprightly but obviously failing, given his sceptical expression.

I'm glad of his chivalrous arm on the return journey, which has suddenly become very hard work. By the time we reach the top of the seemingly endless staircase I'm exhausted, but even Walter and Mr Linlade are not looking too good.

A hot bath and a doze on the bed later, I wake up disorientated in the twilight and head downstairs. There are voices coming from the living room; Walter is expounding on our adventure to a clearly fascinated John Kelly.

'You are looking much better,' Walter says as I enter the room.

John looks me up and down in an appraising fashion, and I just glare at him until he grins in surrender and says, 'What do you make of it all, Fally?'

I sit on the sofa. 'I'm not sure yet. If we're the long-awaited technical help, then what are we meant to do? Contact the makers or somehow shut down the machine?'

Walter regards me steadily. 'Perhaps both, my dear,' he says quietly.

'But *who* are the makers?' John asks.

'Aliens?' I suggest.

John shakes his head. 'You've watched too much Star Trek. Would the aliens really write in Ancient Greek?'

'Well, who knows? On the other hand, I can't see how time travel comes into it.'

'This was a wild and barbarous land at the time of the Ancient Greeks,' Walter puts in.

'This is far beyond anything the Ancient Greeks would have known – it's far in advance of even 21st-century technology,' I say.

'But why leave it behind? I mean, why create something so incredible as that – a time machine or whatever it is – and then leave it under the ground to moulder away over the millennia?' John says.

'Mmm, and what is it really for?' I muse. 'This is something bigger than time travel. Interdimensional. We saw Walter in 1797, but we didn't leave 2008.'

'I find it hard to believe that event was random,' John says.

'Don't tell me you agree with Walter that God was involved,' I say with a grin.

'Well, if not God, then some other hand.'

'But that would suggest there's someone operating the thing, and they can't be because it's falling into ruin.'

'Unless the thing itself is sentient.'

'Sentient quartz? But even if it was… I mean, why would it care if we saw Walter in 1797?'

'We received a message, my dear, just as we did at the time of the tremor in the church.'

'Hmmm, and that was in 1779. There is the possibility that it wasn't mouldering away, I suppose. It is now, but it might not have been before 1799. Maybe it was working properly before that.'

'But working properly at what?' John says.

'That, I think, is the new question,' I say and look at Walter, guessing what he's going to say.

'I believe I did mention that God would reveal it eventually,' he says, bang on cue.

He's very quiet as we cuddle on the sofa after John's gone home.

'What's wrong?'

'I am most uneasy on many aspects of this matter.'

'Me too. It's hard to think everything that's happened to us could just be down to a glitch in some weird ancient computer.'

'I am not certain I believe that, cariad.'

'Well, I wish I didn't. I don't like to think of us being together due to some stalactite interrupting an electrical flow. It's amazing that things are as stable as they are.'

'Indeed. I suggest that it does not seem likely.'

I turn to look at him with a grin. 'All right, I know what you're saying. Tonight I have to admit I wish I could believe in some benevolent deity. It's all pretty scary.'

He tightens his arms around me. 'Perhaps that is a start.'

'Don't go getting any ideas, Reverend.'

He smiles. 'I agree with you that it is "scary". I asked John whether one of those lightning bolts could kill and he suggested it is possible, though unlikely.'

'Well you're not going to get killed; we know you get back to 1779.'

He looks down at me gravely. 'Indeed. But we do not yet know what happens to you, my dear.'

I ignore his implication and say, 'The thing is, if we leave that device alone, what will happen? Will it get worse; will it cause mayhem? And there's still Mr Linlade and Mrs Emrys to think about.'

He sighs. 'I believe we have no choice but to take the path God has given us, but that does not make me any more easy.'

'There's one key left… '

He nods silently, and I know we're both thinking the same thing. It seems likely that the last key will shut the machine down, and shutting it down almost certainly means saying goodbye. A sense of dread is settling around me like a cold, black cloak.

CHAPTER TWENTY-SEVEN

'Okay, so we've got five "insertion units" spread rather vaguely under Llanycoed, a quartz power supply that we don't understand one little bit and lots of dire warnings that the device is dangerously unstable and recommends its own immediate shutdown,' I say, sighing over my wine glass.

'And that is not enough?' Walter asks with a wry smile.

'Not for me. I thought "Information" meant just that. I want answers.'

John chuckles from his position on the sofa. 'Remember where that search has got you so far, Fally.'

'Perhaps some questions are not meant to be answered, my dear,' Walter adds.

'Huh, you two, honestly. Come on Alyson, you must be on my side in this, right?'

Alyson has been pretty quiet over the last few days, while Walter and I, accompanied by John on one occasion, have returned to the cavern and the computer plinth.

'I don't know,' she says. 'To be honest, the whole thing scares me. I had nightmares after you pressed that "Contact" button.'

'Don't remind me. The biggest disappointment of all. An information button that gives out only system information and a contact button that doesn't contact anyone! Useless.'

The others grin and shake their heads at me.

'Seriously, though,' I say, 'it's going to irk me forever if Walter and I have to be separated without really knowing why. If only there were some way that we could save Mrs Emrys and Mr Linlade and then both go back to the 18th century before the machine shuts down.'

'But the key must be inserted manually, my dear, and we do not have control of the time gates.'

I sigh. 'I know. It's just –'

It's just that every day the surges of electricity seem angrier, and the incessant rain means there's definitely more water running down the stalactite. The machine has taken to issuing a warning every time I touch the plinth. *Urgent manual shutdown required,* it flashes imperatively. I've searched in vain through the menus for something meatier than schematics of the underground complex showing the extent of the damage, instructions for manual shutdown, or details of what it calls 'insertion units'. We've even been down the tunnels to look at Units Three and Two, but there were no answers there, either. At the end of each tunnel we found a smaller version of the crystal in the cavern. Unit Two, which is beneath the crossroads, was flickering fairly wildly, but Unit Three just dimmed every now and again. The other 'intermittent' unit, number four, turned out to be beneath the parsonage, but the tunnel to that is blocked.

'It's just that we must make the decision?' Walter says, interrupting my reverie.

I nod. 'I'm afraid of what might happen if we don't do it soon.'

'Indeed. I do not think we can delay any longer.'

One matter of importance that the machine *has* coughed up is that 'all extant insertions will be reversed at the moment of shutdown'. Surprisingly enough, the machine has recorded every full insertion it's ever performed, and there were thousands at the beginning of its existence, tapering off gradually over the next two millennia or so until in the past two hundred years we can calculate that the only full insertions have been those relating to Mrs Emrys, Mr Linlade, Walter and myself. Everything else that's happened has been the result of partial insertions caused by the faulty equipment activating and deactivating itself at random. Even the 1797 Walter at the parsonage was a partial insertion, and we're assuming any other 'ghostly' happenings have had the same origin.

All we have to do is place the final key into its slot on the plinth, and shutdown will occur. We can only hope that this will mean the end of the 1799 time/force field as well. We don't have any excuse to delay. Except...

'I don't think you have much choice,' John says. 'I didn't like the look of that machine when I saw it. And I don't think it would be giving so many warnings unless the alternative to shutdown was pretty dire.'

'That's the point though. How dire? What will happen? A fracture in the space-time continuum? Ancient Greek aliens suddenly beaming down in their thousands?'

John and Alyson laugh. Walter peers into his brandy with an anxious frown. 'I do not know that either of those options sounds greatly appealing,' he says. 'John is right, cariad. We must do what we do not wish to do. It may be that I will not be returned, or even that you will be returned with me.'

I give him a sceptical look, knowing he's trying to make it easier.

'It is my last service at Tref-ddirgel tomorrow. Perhaps we should make the attempt afterwards,' he adds.

I bite my lip, and Alyson gives my arm a comforting squeeze. It's going to be *hard*.

Tref-ddirgel church is two-thirds full, and to my surprise, John and Alyson are sitting in one of the front pews. I can barely hold back the tears as Walter goes through his vicarly rituals. It's the last time I'll see him in his vestments, or preaching, or even saying all the interminable prayers in the ancient text of the Book of Common Prayer. I take note of every little thing, storing it up, and somehow it all seems apposite to our situation.

The gospel reading is the familiar parable of the Good Samaritan, and the reverend reads it with considerable feeling. I know he's based his sermon on it, and I'm curious about the revisions he's been up half the night making.

He leans forwards in the pulpit and looks first at the congregation in general and then, for one brief moment, directly at me.

'I think there are times when we all wish that we could, like the Levite and the priest, pass by on the other side,' he begins. 'It is tempting to ignore the neighbour in need or avoid the task we don't want to undertake. In so doing we're hoping, perhaps expecting, that someone else will render assistance, that the duty will not fall to us. But what of the day when there is no one else? We can none of us know for certain when that day has come, and perhaps it is better to consider that *every* time could be that time.'

I'm already making surreptitious sweeps of my eyes with the back of my hand, and the rest of the sermon doesn't help. He's pulled out all the stops on this one. Finally he says, 'This is my last service at All Saints, but I shall continue to do God's work some distance from here. It has been a pleasure and a privilege to preach among you.'

Then we're into the prayers, and at least I can keep my head down as the tears threaten to flow.

'Hear what comfortable words our Saviour Christ saith unto all that truly turn to him,' the reverend intones. I'm feeling anything but comforted as he continues, 'Come unto me all that travail and are heavy laden, and I will refresh you.'

I wonder what Walter feels as he says those words. Not for the first time, I wish I could understand what anyone gets out of religion. I know it helps him at times like this.

While most of the congregation goes up for Holy Communion, I amuse myself wondering why the church is unusually full.

When we're singing the last hymn and Walter comes down the aisle in his vestments, our eyes meet. I want to run into his arms but somehow manage to hold back and force myself to keep on singing.

I stay in the church as the congregation filters away. John and Alyson come and ask me if I'm all right, and I assure them I'll be out in a minute. It's actually several minutes, because the parishioners are taking their time chatting to Walter, and I realize belatedly that the reason for the unusual numbers is actually down to him. They're sorry to see him go. Somehow he's managed to make an impact, even in the short time he's been helping out.

When I emerge, Walter is talking to John and Alyson.

'An excellent sermon, Reverend,' I say in a deliberately teasing tone. 'Probably the best ever.'

He smiles with pleasure. 'John and Alyson were suggesting that they return to the house with us and bear us company,' he says.

I look at them doubtfully. 'Well… '

He catches on at once. 'Perhaps it is something that we need to do alone.'

I nod silently, feeling my stomach tighten with fear.

'Okay, but I don't like to think of you alone afterwards, Fally,' John says.

'Phone us. You know we'll be waiting to hear,' Alyson adds and gives me a hug.

We're both quiet on the drive back to the house. Mrs Emrys and Mr Linlade are waiting, and there are no Sunday dinner aromas today. They look as pale and anxious as I feel. Their lives are on the line, too. I wonder how they'll feel at being plunged back into the 18th century after over a hundred years of becoming accustomed to the 20th and 21st centuries. I suspect it's going to be difficult for them, but at least they won't be trapped anymore.

Walter changes into his 18th-century clothing, transforming himself from vicar to parson. I've got so used to seeing him in the dog collar over the past month that he looks odd, yet comfortingly familiar. When he's tied back his hair with its black bow, he turns to look at me with a wry smile.

'Do you think I look dignified and imposing, my dear?'

I throw myself into his arms. 'As dignified and imposing as ever,' I say, my voice muffled in his waistcoat.

He holds me tightly, and I can feel the tension in his arms, hear his heart beating faster than usual. I pull away and look at him. 'Shall we go?'

We say goodbye to Mrs Emrys and Mr Linlade, and I feel unaccountably sad. Despite the shaky start, I've become quite fond of them.

The steps and passage seem interminably long, and we can hear the loud spitting long before we get to the blockage and clamber over it. The whole cavern is zipping with energy – the water is no longer trickling down the stalactite but flowing in a constant stream.

'God is with us, cariad,' Walter murmurs as we step into the maelstrom.

It's hard to even think straight amid all the noise and static. I press the *Status* button, and the familiar blinking message forms: *Urgent manual shutdown required.*

I press the button for the shutdown procedure, but as I do so there's a surge of power into my body and mind. Stunned, I fall backwards into Walter's arms. He exclaims in alarm and lifts me up and carries me out, away from the static, just as he did when the lightning bolt struck me. But that was no lightning bolt.

He's looking down at me in concern, taking my pulse, but I'm not hurt.

'I've got them at last,' I say in a shaky voice.

The reverend looks at me as though I've just lost my marbles. 'Got what, my dear?' he asks gently.

'Answers. The machine just gave me some answers. The information sort of shot into my mind. Looks like it took a while for the contact to be returned.'

He gazes at me thoughtfully, his sombre features lit with white flashes from the chamber just feet away. 'And what are the answers?'

I smile wryly and lean against him. 'Well, this isn't really the time for long explanations, but you should know, before you go.'

His arm tightens around me, and I curl into the warmth of him for what I know is the last time.

'They don't say who they are, but millennia ago they wanted a base, a place "from which to investigate and research", so they built this complex at Llanycoed because, as you said, it was a wild and barbarous land and was suitable in other ways, something to do with rock formations and maintaining the power supply.

'There was no written language here then, so they used Ancient Greek and supplied a caretaker who spoke and read that language. He was to live here with his family and pass on the vital information about maintenance to his chosen successor, preferably a family member.

'It worked for three thousand years. After the watermill was built, the caretaker became the miller and passed on the responsibility to whoever in his family seemed best equipped to handle it. By your time, the machine and the complex was almost redundant; its makers didn't need it anymore, whether for time travel or whatever else – they're not exactly forthcoming about that – and it began to fall into disrepair. Over those last few centuries, the caretakers learned their job by rote but were rarely called on for any duties.

'Then there was that slight earth tremor we felt in 1779, which did a bit of damage, followed by the one in 1799. There never was a severe earthquake, but it was enough, with the complex neglected, to cause serious damage. The machine was programmed to shut down automatically when the danger point was reached, but as we know, the shutdown failed and terminal damage was done to Llanycoed. At that point the caretaker was summoned by stimulation of the keys, but apparently the miller never turned up.

'Instead, the machine carried out what precautions it could to prevent partial or accidental insertions, but that meant a sort of quarantine force field around Llanycoed at the moment of the failed shutdown, which trapped Mrs Emrys and Mr Linlade. I don't know whether their reprieve in being able to get out to the watermill in the future was the machine's doing or not.'

'And you became the caretaker after Miss Gilbertine, but even she did not know of what she was caretaker,' Walter muses.

'I assume she didn't. I wonder what happened to the miller in 1799? Could Miss Gilbertine have been one of his descendants?'

'His name was not Gilbertine. However, perhaps I shall learn what becomes of him. And the danger? What would happen were we not to carry out this shutdown?'

I frown, picking through the peculiar new memories. 'They insist that the instability is highly perilous and shutdown is imperative, but they don't say what the alternative might be.'

Walter chuckles slightly. 'You have, then, only partial answers, cariad.'

I sigh. 'I suppose I'll just have to be content with that.'

He helps me up from the rubble we've been sitting on, and we return to the console. This time nothing odd happens when I select the manual shutdown option, but I can almost hear the crystal breathe a sigh of relief. A slot opens in the plinth, and I pull the key out of my pocket. It's virtually shrilling in excitement.

'This is it then,' I say, my voice wavering.

'It is what we must do, my dear. And it is God's will.'

Without any conscious thought, we're in each other's arms. I'm holding him so tightly I can hardly breathe. My throat is choked with grief and fear. Our last kiss is sweet and tender, and then we're pulling apart, staring into each other's eyes, seeing matching resignation there.

'Give my love to Anna, and make sure Abigail stays at the school and that it keeps running, and… ' I choke off.

'I shall do all these things, Fallady. Try not to grieve too greatly for me. We have had but a brief summer, but it has been the best of my life.'

I force myself to turn away and put the key into its slot, my hand trembling so much that I can hardly aim right. As it pings, I put my hands into Walter's, and he grips them tightly. Tears are running down my cheeks as he says, 'Love abideth, cariad.'

'Love abideth, Reverend,' I croak, and he's gone. The energy dies, the noisy spitting ceases, and the crystal darkens to black. I'm standing alone in a cold, dark, silent cavern, and the roof starts to split above my head.

I run back down the tunnel with the sound of debris falling behind me. The rocks are cracking and crumbling, and I stumble and slip and graze my legs and arms as I try to clamber over the earlier cave-in. I'm sobbing and my face is wet with tears and I wonder why I'm running for my life when Walter's gone from it. I reach the passage on the other side of the blockage, but even there, the roof is splitting. Surely the shutdown routine ought not to include the death of the caretaker? Is Felin Gyfriniaeth going to survive this? The run through the passage seems endless, and by the time I reach the stairway I'm covered in bruises and choking on rock dust. I stop, gasping for air, and shine my torch back down the tunnel. The worst seems to be over; there are a few faint cracks and booms and the sound of debris settling. About thirty feet along there's a new blockage, and I doubt that anyone is ever going to get through it. I trail up the stairs, trying and failing to control the wrenching sobs. Once I'm back in the house I run through every room, checking. I have just enough presence of mind left to ring John and Alyson.

'He's gone; they've all gone,' I blurt out to Alyson when she answers.

'Are you okay?' she asks anxiously. 'You don't sound okay. I think we should come round.'

'No, it's all right. I'm just really tired. I'll come there in the morning.'

'Fally –' she says, but I put the phone down. Exhausted, I collapse on the sofa and eventually the gasping sobs ease off and I sleep.

When I open my eyes again, it's very dark and quiet. I move slightly, and my various cuts and bruises pulse and throb. I struggle up and head for the bathroom, wincing as the light clicks on. *It's over.* No more Mrs Emrys. No more Mr Linlade. *No more Walter.* I run a bath numbly and sit on the rim, watching without seeing as the taps gush and steam rises. How am I going to bear it?

I slip into the hot water and groan as it hits my cuts. I feel battered inside and out. What time is it, anyway?

When I emerge from the bath, light is just starting to filter through the trees. I wander outside and take a look at the disappearing zone. It's just as it was. There's no sign of anything that's happened. I walk down the slope to Llanycoed, and it's a different story there. I put my hands to my mouth as I gaze at the wreckage of the parsonage. There are no longer any walls remaining. Just like the church, the parsonage has collapsed beneath the ground.

There are no tears left. I'm like a dry well. The state of the parsonage echoes my state of mind.

The sun starts to rise, red against low cloud, as I drive into Tref-ddirgel. It's only half past six, and the town is hushed, the river rippling slightly in a morning breeze. No one but a paperboy sees me as I run from the car park to the churchyard. The gravel path seems to crunch very loudly in the stillness as I approach Walter's grave.

I read the inscription anxiously, but nothing has changed. I crouch down and lift the ivy from my memorial. No change there either. With a sigh of relief I turn away and head towards the pink house.

It's a strange thing, but all old churches smell the same. It seems to me to be the scent of *age*: beeswax and old wood and ancient stone, tempered with just a hint of flowers.

Frances blinked slightly when she spotted me in the pews two Sundays after the separation. I'd only attended one service of hers before and had no idea why I decided to go. Well okay, that's not true. I was seeking Walter in spirit if not in flesh, and even watching Frances perform the now-familiar prayers and rituals was some small comfort. All the same, without Walter, I can never escape the feeling that I'm a fraud, an interloper in the Christian Club. The tiny measure of comfort I gained from attending was mitigated by this sense of alienation.

So instead of attending services, I've taken to spending quite a bit of time in the quiet dimness of Tref-ddirgel church. I stare at the carved wooden pulpit and try to imagine Walter in it; I wander up and down the aisle and study the various memorials and gravestones; I sit in a pew and observe the way the sun slants through the stained glass windows; I watch a spindly spider waving her legs delicately between the pews, her single strand of web caught in a stray gleam of sunlight.

I breathe in parfum de church and think of Walter and about his god and his religion. Both he and Frances would claim that God was bringing me to church, but when I try to envisage a God – a benevolent presence around me, comforting me – I fail. No matter how much I contemplate Walter's image of God, I end up with the same handful of fog as ever. There's no relief for me in religion, but going to the church makes me feel slightly better.

I'm just coming out of the door on a chilly October afternoon, actually the 203rd anniversary of Walter's death, when I bump into Frances. Her dog, Hector, bounds up, his tongue lolling eagerly, but Frances frowns at the sight of me.

'I thought I saw you go into the church,' she says.

'Don't tell me you disapprove,' I say with a slight smile.

She shakes her head, still unsmiling. 'Not of that, no. Look, Fally, come to the house. I think we should have a talk.'

I shrug and agree, and as Frances bellows for Hector to come to heel, I follow just as meekly, wondering what on earth she means to say.

It's a strange friendship that she and I have formed. Initially it was based around Walter, but since the separation we've talked quite a lot. I haven't seen so much of her in the past three weeks though, as she's been very busy, and I've been busy pretending to be fine.

Once we're ensconced in the living room of the rectory, Frances sits down, her expression still unusually serious.

'Have you looked at yourself lately?' she asks bluntly.

'How do you mean?'

'I mean really *looked,* in a mirror.'

I stare at her. I know what she's saying, but I don't want to hear it. 'You're telling me I've let myself go?' I say, trying to keep it light.

She exhales explosively. 'It's a lot more than that, and you know it. Have you got on the scales? You're beginning to look positively anorexic.'

I swallow. I know she's right, about all of it. The person who once downed a four-hundred-gram chocolate bar in a couple of days has virtually stopped eating. I haven't even looked at the scales. I barely look at myself at all.

Frances leans forward earnestly. 'You need to make a change, Fally. This isn't healthy. I know it helps you, coming to the grave and the church, but it's not good to spend so much time thinking about your loss. You need to do something else.'

'Any suggestions?' I say, slightly flippantly. As ever, I'm trying not to show my emotions. Even in my previous talks with Frances I've managed to maintain a stoic demeanour.

She smiles wryly at last. 'Yes, surprisingly enough. It seems to me you've got too much time on your hands. You need to think about someone besides yourself.'

I raise my eyebrows. 'What did you have in mind?'

'Many years ago, the church set up a scheme called Good Neighbours. It's pretty well outgrown its original remit now, and any church involvement is peripheral. The volunteers visit elderly or housebound people and help them out. You know, getting shopping, chatting to them or driving them to doctor or hospital appointments. What do you think?'

I feel so numb inside that I don't even think about it. 'Okay,' I say.

CHAPTER TWENTY-EIGHT

I've just brought back one of my oldest ladies, Mrs Morgan, who's eighty, from a hospital appointment in Oswestry, and we're chatting in her Llanyrafon cottage when we hear a key in the door.

'That'll be my grandson, Gwilym,' she says. 'He said he'd be arriving today.'

Sure enough, a man appears in the doorway, grinning. 'Hiya Nan,' he says in a pronounced Scottish accent, and he comes over to give her a hug before turning to look at me.

'This is Fallady. She helps out with the church. She took me to my hospital appointment today.'

He doesn't just glance at me but looks at me intently, so much so that I'm sure he's heard of me and all the mystic stuff, but all he says is, 'Hello, Fallady. That's an unusual name you have.'

I freeze for a moment as I remember Walter saying pretty much the same words the first time we met. This keeps happening. The slightest word or phrase will set me off. I have to force myself to speak, but all I say is, 'Hello.'

'Gwilym's come to live in Tref-ddirgel,' Mrs Morgan informs me and pours him a cup of tea while he sits down. 'He's bought a house there. You live there as well, don't you?'

'Yes, at the watermill.'

'That's right. Supposed to be haunted, so they say, but I never did hold with all that nonsense.'

Gwilym smiles merrily in my direction. 'What about you, Fallady? Do you hold with all that nonsense?' he asks, his voice with the long drawn out Scottish 'a' seeming to caress my name.

'No, I don't,' I say firmly. 'There are no ghosts at Felin Gyfriniaeth.'

'That's a shame,' he says, still looking amused.

To my relief he turns to Mrs Morgan and asks her how she got on at the hospital, and I'm able to look at him more closely. He's around my age, is taller than Walter, has brown hair that he wears unfashionably long, green eyes like my own, a face that isn't quite handsome but has an engaging quality about it, with lips curving upwards, and he dresses like a dandy. Not jeans and T-shirt but ruffled white cotton shirt, black drainpipe trousers and pointy black boots! I find myself wondering if he's gay, but something about the way he looks at me suggests otherwise.

I realize I've been staring when he smiles at me and raises his eyebrows. Once again I have to take a deep breath. One of these days little words and gestures won't make me ache.

'Well, I'd better be going,' I say, getting up abruptly.

'I'll see you out,' Gwilym says, unravelling his long legs.

'It was good to meet you, Fallady,' he says at the door. 'I expect I'll see you around Tref-ddirgel.'

'Probably,' I say shortly, and he regards me quizzically but says no more.

As I drive home he seems to stick in my mind, and I try very hard to put him out of it again. Men are the last thing I'm thinking about.

As November drags its way into December, I get more hassle, this time from John. 'Look Fally, our admin and IT person at the surgery's going to be away for a couple of weeks, and we need a temp. How do you feel about doing it?'

'Not too keen.'

'Come on. You're still not getting out enough, and it's only for a couple of weeks. You need to be around people more.'

'So everyone keeps saying, but it doesn't seem to do me any good.'

'Just a couple of weeks,' he insists.

At the start of the second week there, I'm sitting in the little cubbyhole of an office I've been allocated, when Gwilym Morgan pops his head around the door.

'Fallady!' he says, obviously as surprised to see me as I am to see him.

'Gwilym Morgan,' I say repressively.

'So, now we know we've remembered each other's names,' he says with a grin.

'What are you doing here?' I feel forced to ask, trying hard not to laugh.

'Working. Just like you, apparently. I've been dragged in on some pretext along the lines of being short of doctors and me conveniently happening to be around.'

'You're a doctor?'

'Surprised, eh?'

'Well, yes. I had you down as some sort of arty type.'

He sits down in the only other chair in the room. 'Ah. Arty type. And what was the giveaway?'

'Could have been the unusual dress sense,' I murmur. 'But you're looking a lot more conservative today.' I have to admit he looks far more dull in an ordinary suit and tie and with his hair dragged back into a short ponytail.

He laughs. 'Forced back into my box. Patients aren't so keen on flamboyant long-haired doctors. But you're right, I am an arty type; painting's my preference. Fifteen years as a GP in Pitlochry was enough for me. Only considerable grovelling on John Kelly's part has persuaded me to come in and help him out.'

'Same here,' I say. 'Well not so much grovelling as dogged persistence.'

'I heard that,' says John, coming to the open door. He looks from Gwilym to me and says, 'So, you two have met then.'

'We'd met before, at my nan's house. Fallady took her to an appointment.'

'Ah. Well, Fallady's helping out with the IT for the next week, so if you have any computer problems, you know where to come.'

'IT, eh?' Gwilym says. 'I had you down as a churchy type doing lots of good works.'

John bursts out laughing while I glower. 'Churchy type! Well, obviously my intuition functions better than yours.'

'Never call an atheist a churchy type, Gwilym,' John says. 'Come on, I'd better show you around before morning surgery.'

Gwilym has the cheek to wink at me as they leave the room. I'm not sure what to make of him, but I have to admit he does intrigue me.

The surgery closes for forty-five minutes at lunch time, but I'm engrossed in repairing a PC when he turns up in the doorway. 'Not having any lunch then?' he asks.

I look up at the clock and realize it's gone 1.00pm. 'No, I'm not all that hungry.'

'You don't fancy coming for a cup of tea and a snack with me, maybe?'

I put down my screwdriver and lean back in my chair. 'There's only one café in Tref-ddirgel,' I say, temporising.

'Or there's my house, just a couple of hundred yards away,' he says.

I sigh. My back's aching, and I could really do with a break. 'Oh, all right. Why not?'

'Gracefully put, Fallady,' he says sarcastically as I pick up my coat. I flash him a look of dislike, which he ignores.

'So how was morning surgery?' I ask when we're walking towards the river.

'Oh, much the same old stuff but with Welsh accents instead of Scottish ones. You don't have a Welsh accent, though. London or the Home Counties is it?'

'Yes, both really. I've only lived here for... um... seven months. You sound as though you hate being a doctor.'

He smiles. 'No, it's not that bad. It just gets wearing, especially when you're dragged in under the old pals act while you're engrossed in a new painting.'

'Old pals act? John's an old friend of yours?'

'We worked together as junior doctors. Or rather I was the junior – John was a little more elevated.'

We reach a row of terraced Georgian houses backing on to the river. I recognise them from 1779, when they looked pretty new. I follow him in to one of the end terraces and look around with interest.

'The people who owned it before tried to retain all the old features,' he tells me.

'It certainly looks authentic,' I murmur, wishing I could tell him how I know that.

On the walls in the living room, which sports two huge windows, hang two distinctly Scottish landscapes, one of mountains and waterfalls and the other of a lake. 'Are they yours?' I ask, impressed.

'They are. What do you think?'

'They look really good to me. Is that what you like to paint, landscapes?'

'Pretty much. I like the wild and lonely spots. I'm hoping to find some around here, too.'

'Well there are some, but probably not as many as in Scotland.'

In his kitchen he puts the kettle on and looks at me. 'You ought to eat something. You don't look as though you eat enough. What about a slice of toast?'

It still surprises me that anyone thinks *I* don't eat enough. I shrug. 'Okay.'

'So what about you, Fallady?' he says, putting two slices of wholemeal bread under the grill of his shiny cooker. 'If you're not the churchy, charity type, then what are you?'

'I used to be a systems administrator in London. I've been doing the voluntary work because –' I pause. Do I really want to tell him all my business?

'Because?' he prompts.

'Because I… lost my partner four months ago.'

'So that's what it is,' he says. 'I did wonder why you seem so sad.'

'There's no Mrs Morgan then?' I say quickly, trying to change the subject.

He shakes his head. 'No, and never has been.'

He turns to get mugs out of a cupboard. 'Tea or coffee?'

'Tea thanks, no sugar. How's your nan?'

He sighs. 'I came to live here because she hadn't been too well, and unfortunately she's not going to improve.'

'I'm sorry to hear that.'

He nods as he turns the bread over under the grill. 'She's my only living relative. I lost both my parents in pretty close succession back when I was in my twenties.'

'You weren't born in Scotland though? Surely not with a name like Gwilym Morgan?'

'You're right,' he says as he brings over the drinks. 'I was born in Llandudno. And you?'

'Buckingham, but my parents were killed in a car accident when I was five. I've got two sisters and a brother, only they're scattered around the country.'

'So why did you move here?'

I tell him about being left the watermill and about Miss Gilbertine and Summerdale, and by the time I've finished he's putting the toast and butter on the table.

'So you don't really know what you want to do now?'

I shake my head. 'I don't want to go back to London, and I don't want to go back to sys admin. Unlike you, though, I'm not aware of any other great talents.'

He laughs. 'I'm not sure about "great talent". It's just something I'd rather be doing. Whether I can make a living at it remains to be seen.'

I nibble at the toast because he's watching, but I start a bit when I realize he's pursing his lips thoughtfully. I'm so reminded of Walter that tears spring into my eyes. I quickly lower my gaze to my plate, hoping he hasn't noticed. How much longer am I going to spot Walter in all and sundry?

'So why does everyone think the watermill's haunted?' he asks.

I shrug. 'Some old stories about the ruins nearby.' I can hardly tell him the truth. It's become difficult to interact with people now that there's so much I can't say.

'What's in the ruins?'

'It's an old village. There was an earthquake that destroyed it all except the watermill.'

'It does sound pretty spooky,' he says. 'Aren't you lonely there?'

'Not exactly. I love the house.'

'Doesn't stop it being lonely. You are going to eat *all* the toast, aren't you, Fallady?'

'If you insist. I told you I wasn't hungry.'

'And that's because you had a huge breakfast is it?' he says.

'What are you insinuating exactly?' I ask, with a flash of amusement.

'*Did* you have any breakfast?'

'What's it to you?'

'So that means no.'

'My cook's been away for some time,' I say and force down the last mouthfuls of toast while he chuckles.

'Cook, eh? I take it cooking's not among your talents?'

'Hardly. Anyway I'm never hungry these days.'

He nods slowly, sipping his tea. 'For four months?'

'More or less.'

'What if someone cooked you a meal – something more elaborate than a slice of toast. Would you eat it?'

'Don't tell me, you can cook as well as paint?'

'Yes, I enjoy cooking. I suppose I see it as another art form.'

'Wow. Cooking as an art form. Well I'm glad someone enjoys it.'

'You haven't answered the question – if I invite you to dinner on Friday night, will you come, and more importantly, will you eat?'

'I'd have to if you'd cooked it, wouldn't I? But whether to come – I'm not up to much socialising these days.'

'I was thinking of dinner for two – just dinner, Fallady.'

'Well, all right. But I'm not sure I'm very good company.'

'Another graceful acceptance,' he says, and I flick my eyeballs skywards.

To my surprise, the next morning he's in my office with two packages. 'Breakfast and lunch,' he says. 'Be sure to eat them. I've got to run. I'm late, and I'm taking calls. I'll see you this afternoon if I get the chance.'

I look at the packages, touched. Has he done it because he's concerned about my health or because he likes me? Maybe both, I suppose. I open the one labelled 'breakfast' and find a home-made oat and raisin biscuit, a handful of nuts and a small container of orange juice. He's obviously taken my minuscule appetite into consideration. Somehow I end up taking sips of juice and munching the nuts and biscuit as the morning goes by.

At lunchtime I decide to walk to the churchyard, and I pick up the other package to take with me. I sit in the nearest seat to Walter's grave and open the parcel. I look at the delicate salmon salad sandwiches and slices of apple with a smile. It's just small enough for me to bring myself to eat, and I down the lot while I sit in the quiet graveyard thinking about Walter.

I don't see Gwilym that afternoon, as it turns out. It looks like a pretty hectic surgery, and when I leave he's still seeing patients. Even so, the next morning he's back again with two more packages.

'You really don't need to do this,' I protest.

'I know I don't, but you did eat them, didn't you?'

'Of course I did. Very nice too, but I just –'

'That's all right, then.'

He's off in a hurry again before I can reply. I can't help wondering if making these packed meals for me is making him late for work.

John puts his head around the door. 'How's it going? Was that Gwilym I just saw haring down the corridor?'

'Yes, I think he's late for morning surgery.'

'Found the time to pay *you* a visit, I see.'

'I don't know what you mean,' I say innocently and then add, 'He's greatly concerned about my health. Look, he's made me breakfast *and* lunch – this is the second day running.'

'Has he indeed?' John says. 'And you're eating them?'

'Well, he went to a special effort.'

'Hmmm. Very interesting.'

'He said you were colleagues when he was a junior doctor.'

'That's right. What am I missing here?'

I laugh. 'What, *you* miss something? We've just had a couple of chats, that's all.'

'I see. Chats.'

'Shouldn't you be working?' I hint.

'I suppose I should,' he says with reluctance. 'But I still feel like I'm missing something. It's your duty to keep me informed, Fally!'

'I'll bear it in mind,' I say, grinning.

I've long eaten my breakfast snack by the time one o'clock arrives and am actually experiencing slight hunger pangs; the first I've really noticed in months. I take my lunch to the churchyard again. It's a cold and frosty day. Walter's headstone even has a rime of ice on it. I run my hand over the ice and remember our first meeting on that snowy February afternoon. I've drifted off into a reverie when I hear Gwilym's voice behind me.

'Fallady?'

I turn sharply and have no idea why I feel so guilty.

'Sorry,' he says. 'I was just cutting through the graveyard on my way into town and saw you there.'

'Oh. Well, don't let me hold you up,' I say, hoping he doesn't notice the headstone.

He smiles wryly. 'Okay, I get the message. You have eaten your lunch, though?'

'Yes thanks, very good, too. You don't have to keep on doing it, you know.'

'It's not a problem.'

As he hurries off, I turn back to look at Walter's headstone. Did Gwilym read it? I glance at mine. It's so well covered by ivy that hopefully no one would notice it. It's occurred to me that Fallady being a made up name – and as far as I know me being the only one – anyone seeing that memorial is going to wonder. I kick a few leaves over the ivy, just to be on the safe side.

Chapter Twenty-nine

Gwilym keeps up the food parcels until the end of the week but to my relief doesn't mention the grave. John seems to have kept him very busy, and I don't see a lot of him.

I visit Alyson at Friday lunchtime, and she's impressed that Gwilym has gone to so much effort. When I tell her he's cooking dinner for me later, she's even more intrigued.

'Like I told John, he's just trying to get me to eat,' I say.

'Yeah, but it's working as well. You seem better.'

'Better than what? There's nothing going on between us.'

'Better than you were, Fally. There doesn't have to be something going on, but you must like him to be going to dinner. It's been hard enough to get you to come around here all these months.'

I shrug. 'I suppose I do like him. He's different. But he knows I'm "bereaved". I think he just feels sorry for me.'

Alyson thinks for a minute. 'Maybe, but he likes you as well, you can be sure.'

'So I should be worried? I'm not looking for anyone!'

'Why should you be worried? You can still be friends.'

I have all this in mind when I turn up at Gwilym's disconcertingly Georgian house at seven. He's back in a ruffled shirt and tight jeans and looking much better for it. I follow him through to his kitchen, where he's laid the small table. 'We have to eat in here – the house is too small for a dining room, but at least it's cosy.'

'Where do you do your painting?' I ask.

'Ah, that's the beauty of this house,' he says. 'The whole second floor's my studio. I can show you later, if you'd like to see it.'

'I'd love to,' I say. 'And this painting, as well – the one you're engrossed in.'

He laughs wryly. 'Or was, until John dragged me away. Luckily it looks like his colleague's got over her illness, and she'll be back next week.'

'So you'll be free again.'

'And you, too.'

'Yes, I'm glad to say. I don't know why John thought working at the surgery would do me good.'

'He told me he thinks you spend too much time alone.'

I glare at him. 'I hope you haven't been discussing me with him.'

'Only briefly. He mentioned the packed meals.'

'He's so nosy!'

'Don't I know it.'

By this time he's dishing up the meal, which couldn't really contrast more with the haunches of beef and venison we used to consume at the parsonage. He's prepared delicate pieces of sole in almonds and butter, baby potatoes boiled in their skins and an attractive salad.

'I've kept it small, so you should be able to eat it,' he says. 'Don't feel you have to force yourself if you get really full.'

'Thanks. Why did you make those meals for me anyway?'

'You told me your cook was away,' he says with a grin. 'Besides, I enjoyed it – and you did eat them.'

'True,' I say, as I savour the sole. He certainly can cook.

'I hope you're not going to go without again after this.'

I just give him a patient look.

'Who was Walter Edgemond?' he says suddenly, startling me so much that I drop my knife and fork and nearly choke.

'Fallady!' he cries. 'I'm sorry. I just – you've gone pale. I didn't think –'

'I'm all right,' I say between coughs. 'I'm all right, really.' I take a slug of water and try to compose myself.

'I'd never have mentioned it if I'd thought you'd react like this. I just assumed he was some distant ancestor or something.'

I laugh humourlessly. 'No.'

He regards me helplessly. 'Okay, now I've put you off your meal, which is the last thing I want to do.'

'I'll be all right, but can we just talk about a nice neutral subject like painting or Scotland or something?'

'You mean you want *me* to do all the talking? Well all right, if it'll get you to eat.'

'I can't believe you're so concerned about my diet. I used to be fat you know, just a… few months ago.'

'That's hard to imagine, looking at you now.'

'I know. I don't even recognise myself in the mirror. Anyway, tell me about Scotland. You said you were in Pitlochry? My brother Jex lives on the borders.'

He humours me, and I relax and enjoy the meal, but I'm hung up on how to explain about Walter. It's unbearable to imagine being disbelieved. Okay, so I have photographic evidence, but I don't want to have to resort to it. It was all so much more fun when the proof – Walter himself – was undeniably real and present. It's easier to say nothing.

Afterwards he shows me his studio, which is one huge attic room on the second floor. There are finished paintings ranged about the room, and I'm impressed, especially as the subjects appeal to me: rivers, streams, forests and mountains. I admire his current work, which he's doing on a larger canvas. It's of a colourful sunset in a rugged valley.

'I was out on a walk in the mountains when I came across this scene. I was so impressed I knew I had to capture it.' He sounds a lot more enthusiastic when he talks about painting than he does about medicine.

'So it's back to the voluntary work next week?' he says afterwards as we sip coffee in his living room.

'Maybe. Probably.'

'You really are a bit lost aren't you?'

'What do you mean by that?' I bridle, eyeing him narrowly. 'You don't feel sorry for me, do you?'

He watches me and purses his lips. Damn, damn, why does he do that? My whole stomach clenches.

Eventually he says, 'I'm *interested* in you, Fallady. You're an enigma.'

'An enigma?' I exhale sharply. 'Well, maybe you're right. But as to being lost, I suspect I'm no more lost now than I was when I first came here.'

'Maybe what you need to do is find another talent.'

I gaze at him, remembering my teaching in the 18th century. I really was of some use. Suddenly the irony of it all strikes me – I thought I'd have no role there and found one, and now I have none here. I start to laugh, and his baffled expression makes it worse. I'm not sure whether I'm laughing or crying by the time I sober up, but the patient look on his face suggests the latter.

I wipe my eyes and favour him with a glare. 'Stop looking at me like that.'

'I'm trying to puzzle out the enigmatic laughter,' he says with a small smile.

'Yeah well that's exactly what it was. I can't explain. Just something that struck me.'

'About talents?'

'Gwilym, do you think a person should be over a loss after four months? Seriously. I mean four months is nothing, is it? Why does everyone think I should be back to normal and carrying on as though it never happened? It's not even four months yet. A hundred and seventeen days. That's all it is. There's a gaping hole in my life, and I can't fill it up with charity work or temporary IT work or whatever everyone thinks I should be doing. I *can't.*'

He doesn't answer my rather rhetorical rant but just says, 'Do you want to talk about it?'

I shake my head and stare unseeingly at his carpet. 'I can't. Not really. I just miss him beyond belief. All his funny ways and mannerisms and his peculiar sense of humour and his kindness and – I just miss him.'

I wipe my eyes and twist my hands together in anguish, but he puts his hands on mine and stops me. 'Fallady. It's okay to still miss him. And you're right about four months. It's just not really a good idea to set about joining him by not eating and so on.'

I give another humourless laugh. 'That wouldn't work.'

He shakes his head. 'Sometimes I don't understand what you're really saying.'

'That's because I don't want you to.'

He smiles. 'See: enigmatic as ever.'

By the time he sees me off at the door, I've invited him to Felin Gyfriniaeth the following week.

'Should I bring my own food?' he quips.

'What, beans on toast not good enough for you?' I retort. 'Anyway, I'm sure I can manage something vaguely palatable.'

He frowns and then seems to come to a sudden decision. 'Look, I'll give you my phone number, and you can ring me if you want to.'

I open my mouth to protest, but he's writing down the number, and I'm not sure what I ought to be protesting about. I don't expect I'll phone him – it would seem too needy – but it's kind of him to offer.

On the drive back home, I reflect quite a lot on him and what he must be thinking about me. I quite like being an enigma, but it would be good to be able to talk about Walter. Obviously Frances, John and Alyson have been there to listen, but I can't really go on and on every time I see any of them. Eventually there's a point where you've said it all, where you feel that they've heard as much as they can endure, and you're meant to be recovering. My failure to recover has led me to keep quiet about it and feel guilty, and my guilt has increased with my inability to eat. At least having Gwilym agree with me that four months isn't so very long is a small help.

Midweek I have dinner with Alyson and John. They bombard me with questions about my friendship with Gwilym.

'That's all we are,' I say firmly and glare at John. '*Friends.*'

'Okay, but he's not one to spend much time with one woman unless he likes her a lot,' John says. 'Obviously it's been quite a few years,' he adds, 'but I do remember that beneath the jovial exterior is a pretty reserved person. Not much of a one for socialising – not shy, but just not keen on parties or small talk. It doesn't surprise me that he's never married, but it's not as if he never had any girlfriends.'

'Oh yeah? So he had lots?'

'Well like I said, he never seemed to be with anyone for long, but he wasn't ever short of company – if he wanted it, which he often didn't.'

'Have you seen his paintings? He likes wild and lonely spots.'

John shakes his head. 'You have to be privileged to see those, Fally, which you obviously are. You've got to him somehow.'

Gwilym arrives promptly on Saturday evening and observes my cooking preparations with a tolerantly amused expression.

'We're having omelette?'

'*Spanish* omelette,' I say and keep a straight face with difficulty. 'Won't take long to cook, that's for sure.'

'Are you sure you don't want me to cook it?'

'Well, you can if you want to. All the ingredients are ready, and I've made a salad to go with it. I don't know what gives you the impression I'm *incapable* of cooking. I might not be that keen on it, but I do know how to make a few things.'

'Was that a yes?'

'As long as you can do it on the range.'

'I think I can handle it.'

I watch in awe as he produces a degree-level omelette. I've laid the table in the kitchen, as I didn't want to eat in the dining room with all the memories that would invoke. For the first time since Walter, I've been down to the cellar and picked out a dusty bottle of white from the almost empty racks.

We eat companionably, but I start to get a hint that something's wrong. He's both as affable and as sarcastic as usual, but behind all that there's a new reserve, a sort of well of disquiet. It's only intuition on my part, but I tend to trust my judgement on that kind of thing, and I know I'll have to get to the bottom of it before the evening's out. I'm too used to Walter and his completely open nature to be able to bear a mystery.

'That's an impressively old bottle of wine,' he says when we've finished the meal.

'Miss Gilbertine left me a cellar full of them.'

He sits back in his chair and regards me. 'It's good to see you eating normally.'

I flick my eyeballs upwards and get up to clear the table. 'Thanks.'

'Have you been eating all week?'

I put the plates by the sink. 'Yes I have, as a matter of fact. Gwilym, what's wrong?'

'How do you mean?'

'I don't know exactly, but you're not quite your usual self.'

He sighs. 'I don't know how you picked up on that, but you're right, there is something bothering me.'

'Is it about your nan?'

He shakes his head. 'No, it's about you.'

I flick the kettle on. 'Me? Well what? You might as well tell me – I won't be able to stand the suspense.'

'I'm not sure that's a good idea. Last time I brought up a similar subject, you nearly fainted.'

I get a sinking feeling and lean back against the cupboard with my arms folded, watching him. 'This has to do with graves?'

He purses his lips. Damn, he did it again. I blink and swallow and wait for him to get around to it. 'Yes,' he agrees finally. 'I suppose I was just being nosy, but I took another look at that grave that seemed to upset you so much.'

'And?'

'While I was checking it out, I noticed a smaller memorial stone by the side of it.'

My legs wobble. I sit back down at the table. 'So you looked at the memorial?'

He nods. 'How many Falladys can there be? You told me your dad made it up.'

'So you conclude what?'

'I conclude that something odd's going on. But it's not as if you owe me an explanation or anything. I thought it would be better not to bring it up.'

I stare at the tablecloth and then look back up at him. 'Well, there is an explanation, but I was afraid you wouldn't believe it.'

'Does it include your being Mrs Edgemond?'

I nod silently.

'So it *is* Walter Edgemond you're mourning?'

I swallow. 'Yes.'

'And Llanycoed?'

'That's the village here – the one that's in ruins.'

He looks at me sympathetically. 'You don't have to tell me anything if you don't want to.'

I rest my chin on my hands. 'It's just well, time travel… you'll think I'm a nutter.'

He laughs softly. 'Not the way you've been trying to keep it from me. How though? I mean how did it – how *could* it happen?'

Haltingly, I start telling him the story, and as he listens without any apparent signs of scepticism I eventually show him all the photos. As I relate the final sequence of events, it's so painful and raw that I can't help it when the tears come. I try to choke them back, but when I reach the moment that Walter disappeared, I break down completely. Gwilym takes my hand in his until the tears start to abate.

'I won't be an enigma anymore, eh?' I say, wiping my eyes.

'Oh I don't know. There aren't many people around who've spent any time in 1779. It makes you unique.'

'What do you think?' Gwilym asks and indicates a large, yellowed painting he's leaned against a chair in his lounge.

I narrow my eyes to get a better view of it. It looks pretty old, but is clearly of a trio of children.

'Was that at your nan's?' I ask. His nan died back in April, and I've been helping him clear her house for the last few weeks.

'Yes, it was one of the last things I found in the attic yesterday. It's an original, but I can't read the signature. It needs restoring, but it's pretty good. Whoever painted it knew what they were doing.'

'I wonder who the children are. Maybe they're ancestors or something.'

'That's crossed my mind.'

I look at the picture again. The three children, two boys and a girl, are dressed in old-fashioned costume, and it strikes me that they appear rather 18th-century. 'There's nothing written on it? On the back or anything?'

Gwilym shakes his head. 'No, and I don't remember Nan ever mentioning it, either.'

I look at the dusty old boxes that are also adorning the floor. 'So what's in those?'

'Oh, some old books and stuff, I think. I haven't really looked yet, but they were pretty heavy. Why don't you have a look while I go and finish dinner.'

'What's on the menu tonight, Chef Morgan?' I tease. 'Roast pork and pease pudding perhaps?'

'Not quite. Pan-fried sea bass,' he says, and heads off to the kitchen.

I feel a bit intrusive opening Mrs Morgan's old boxes, but there's always some curiosity about what people have been keeping in their attics, possibly for decades. I pull aside the cardboard of the first one with interest, getting my hands filthy from what seems like aeons' worth of dust and cobwebs. I lift out some large envelopes and glance inside. Two of them contain very old letters, and the other two are full of yellowed drawings. With the thought that they might be by the same artist as the one of the children, I pull out some of the drawings to have a closer look.

The top picture is of a handsome man of around thirty, smiling quizzically. I stare at it and am sure I can see Gwilym in that quizzical expression. It's not that though, that gives me pause, but the style. Something about it seems familiar. I start rifling through the pile. There are more of the man, and of the three children at various ages, and one of an attractive woman in her late twenties. My suspicions are confirmed as I take a close look at the woman. My hands shaking, I open the other envelope, and as I pull out the heavy old sheets of paper, one slips on to the floor, face up. Walter's sombre features gaze up at me. He looks a few years older, and he's wearing his cassock. I go through the stack, my breathing rapid and my throat constricting with emotion. There are more of him at various ages, two of me, and several of the parsonage from various aspects. These are all Anna's work! And the children? I stare at the painting again. *Walter's grandchildren.* They must be. And the handsome man has to be Anna's husband.

I open the first of the envelopes of letters and take one out at random. I nearly choke when I see the writing. It's Walter's – a letter he sent to Anna when she was at school. I can't bring myself to read it; it hurts too much. My eyes brim with tears as I delve further into the box. There's a big pile of books, and I take one out and open it at random. '14th June 1778' it says at the top of the page in Walter's neat script. 'Much rain today and only twenty at church' I read, before closing it quickly. With tears running down my face, I open the other box: more diaries, and a bulky envelope on the top. I thrust a shaking hand inside the envelope and find a letter and a small package, both sealed and both addressed 'Fallady' in Walter's handwriting. I clutch them in my hands and stare at them.

Gwilym comes back into the room. 'Anything interesting?' he asks and then stops dead at the sight of me. 'Fallady! What is it?'

'I know who painted it,' I say in a wobbly voice, indicating the painting.

'Who?'

'Anna. Walter's daughter, Anna,' I croak.

'But that would mean –'

'Walter's your ancestor!'

'How do you know?'

I show him the drawings, including the one of me.

'She was good, no doubt about that,' he says with his artist's appreciation.

I point out the handsome man. 'I think he must have been Anna's husband. And he does look a bit like you.'

He crouches down beside me to look more closely at the picture.

'Walter's diaries are in the boxes,' I add, trying to wipe away the tears on my cheeks with the backs of my hands. 'And letters he sent to Anna. And these.' I show him the letter and package.

He stares at them and then looks at me. 'So are you going to open them?'

'I can't believe they're real. All this time sitting in your nan's attic.'

'I wonder how long they had really been there or if she ever looked at them herself? Open them, Fallady. I'll get back to the food before it burns.'

I take a deep, shuddering breath and open the wax seal carefully, as if the very paper is an ancient artefact. I'm barely breathing at all as I unfold the densely-written pages. My vision blurs with tears again, and it's a couple of minutes before I can finally read the words.

26th August 1779

My dear Fallady,

It is but one day since we stood together and shut down the device. One moment we were holding hands, and the next I was back here, in 1779, with my horse and chaise, at exactly the moment in which we left. I can only conclude that the same occurred for Mrs Emrys and Mr Linlade: that they were returned to 1799 and were no longer trapped. As for you, my dear wife, I fear that you are suffering terribly, being now entirely alone, and it is a cause of great distress to me that I cannot help you from such a distance. I wish you could believe in the Lord and turn to Him, but I suspect that to be an impossibility.

It seems that what we saw in the churchyard at Tref-ddirgel will come to pass. As I returned home without you, I was forced to report your death and burial in Oxford and have ordered the memorial for you in exactly the form that we have already seen. I shall have it placed in Llanycoed graveyard. There is much sympathy in the village and great concern at your passing. Tomorrow I shall bring Anna home for a time to be with me. I have not yet told her what has happened, but I shall tell her the truth and ask her to retain this letter unopened after my death. I hope it will reach you, although how I know not.

I have prayed much upon this since my return. We were right to make the machine safe and to release Mrs Emrys and Mr Linlade, and although it is true that we are now suffering, each in our own century, we do at least have the satisfaction of knowing that good has come of our actions. His ways may seem unfathomable to us now, but they will eventually become clear.

I shall keep my diary daily, which I had not done before your coming, and I hope that someday you will read it and know what became of me and of Anna. Do not doubt that I shall never forget you or believe that I shall ever cease to consider you my wife, and in the terminology of the 21st century, my soul mate. I shall think of you every day. I am forever yours, and you mine.

Your loving husband,

Walter.

When Gwilym returns from the kitchen he finds me sitting with the pages clutched to my chest, tears still streaming down my face. I hand him the letter. 'You might as well read it,' I say, my voice hoarse.

He sits beside me and takes it, putting his hand on mine while he reads. When he finally looks up and meets my gaze, I can tell he's pretty affected himself. 'It's something to have had that kind of love,' he says. 'No matter what they say, I don't think many people do.'

I nod speechlessly.

'What about the package?' he asks.

I bite my lip and tear off the old and fragile paper to reveal a small wooden box. My hand trembles as I open it. Inside, wrapped in a scrap of velvet, is a gold locket. I lift it out gently and open the hinge. On one side is a miniature of Walter, surely Anna's work, and on the other a lock of his hair. Still black hair, too, with just a few grey strands, much as it was when I was with him. There's some engraving on the back, and I turn it around to see the words, 'Fallady and Walter, Love Abideth'. I show it to Gwilym and put it around my neck, realizing that the last person to touch it before me was Walter.

Gwilym puts an arm around my shoulders, and it feels comforting but reminds me too much of Walter. 'That's why!' I say suddenly.

'That's why what?'

'Why you often remind me of Walter. I thought it was my imagination: you know, grief bringing him into my mind all the time, but no, you purse your lips just the way he does. Every time you do it, I get choked up.'

'You never told me that,' he says.

'How could I? I thought it was just me.'

'I didn't even know I pursed my lips that much,' he says, and I chuckle in spite of myself.

'Walter's descendant, eh?' I say. 'You don't look much like him. You look a lot more like that other bloke, Anna's husband.'

'And just as handsome, I assume?'

'Well, no, I reckon the handsome genes must've got a bit diluted down the decades,' I tease, to be rewarded by a Walter-like shout of laughter.

Later, when I leave, we load up my car with the boxes.

'Can I hold on to these, though?' Gwilym asks, and indicates the drawings of me.

I shrug. 'I can't imagine why.'

'I don't know, there's just something about them,' he says, unconsciously pursing his lips.

CHAPTER THIRTY

I read Walter's diaries eagerly, hoping to learn everything that happened after our separation. The entries prior to that are sporadic, but once he'd returned on his own, he kept a daily record.

Excerpts from Walter Edgemond's diary, August 1779 – October 1805

26th August 1779

I have returned home to the parsonage with as heavy a heart as I can express, alone and lost without my dear wife. I am bereft.

27th August 1779

I fetched Anna home from school today and told her the story of how Fallady was lost. She was most distressed. It seems she had quite attached herself to her stepmother. I fear that she has taken many of the (seditious!) things Fallady told her to heart.

30th August 1779

My friend Mr Jenkins carried out a memorial service for Fallady at Llanycoed church today. There were many in attendance, although my wife did not live long among them. Both Lord and Lady Montgomery were present, as were Mr and Mrs Greenleaf. Anna and I were both overcome during the service.

7th April 1780

Fallady and I were wed a year ago this day. We had but six months or so together, but they were the sweetest of my life. I took a long walk and went by Felin Gyfriniaeth and up to the pool above. I sat there some time, thinking over past events.

5th July 1780

I fetched Anna home from school today. She has become quite a young lady. She insists that she does not desire to return to the school and would prefer to remain with me. I have told her I shall think upon it, but she is only twelve years old and requires more company and education than I can provide. I am all too aware that it is her papa's loneliness that is behind this suggestion.

14th July 1780

I had a long talk with Anna concerning her future. She has matured a great deal, and we were able to determine that she now longs, above all, to become a painter. I pointed out that there are few women painters, and none that I am aware of in England or Wales who has been greatly successful, but she stated, in strident tones, that 'it is time for women to prove that they are as good as men', and 'if no one tries, then of course they won't be successful.' I confess that I am somewhat alarmed at this change in my little Anna, who was used to be so dutiful. I fear that she has been considerably corrupted! However, I have consented to seek either a better school or a painting tutor. I have agreed that if necessary I shall educate her myself.

20th November 1780

*Received a letter from Anna expressing her satisfaction with her
new school and the extra time and tuition that she is being allowed
for painting. I am still uneasy that she is so far away in North
Wales. When she was at Chester, I knew that she was but a day's
travel distant.*

3rd May 1781

*It appears that in leaving off my wig two years ago, I was at the
forefront of fashion. I read in the papers that men are increasingly
wearing their own hair. I have grown accustomed to it, but there have
been times, particularly when in the company of other clergymen,
that I have wished I were wearing it.*

30th September 1781

*The Widow Appleby paid me another visit today. I am at a loss as
to why she persists in such frequent visiting. She has no particular
reason, it seems to me.*

1st January 1782

*Anna and I sat up to see in the New Year, and we talked much.
She is still of the opinion that once she is fourteen, she should
come home and take charge of the housekeeping. I have explained
that I would have great difficulty in procuring a painting tutor in
Llanycoed, or even Tref-ddirgel, and I am hoping that her art is
more important to her than keeping her papa company. I fear she
would find it very dreary here after these years at school with so
many young friends around her.*

7th April 1782

As has been my habit these two years, I walked to the pool above Felin Gyfriniaeth and thought much upon my dear wife.

23rd June 1782

I dined at the Hall with Mr and Mrs Greenleaf and Mr and Mrs Jenkins. I have not lately dined out a great deal, and it was a very pleasant meal and evening. The squire advised me privately that Mrs Appleby has been paying me so many visits out of interest in me! Apparently it is known throughout the parish. I had been completely blind to her blandishments, and I must now confess that she did indeed demonstrate them rather amply on some occasions. Clearly I must disabuse her of any belief that I return her interest, although I am somewhat uneasy about how to carry out this aim.

25th February 1783

An interesting piece of information came my way today when I was visiting Tref-ddirgel. Mr Ridley, a well-known painter of both portrait and landscape, has moved into the town. I did not hesitate, since Anna's letters complain ever more frequently that she should be at the parsonage, but went immediately to his address. He was not at home, but I left my compliments.

4th March 1783

Mr Ridley paid me a visit today, and we discussed the possibility of his tutoring Anna. He was surprised to hear of such a young woman having a powerful desire to become a successful artist, and I believe this intrigued him. I showed him some of her paintings, and he expressed both criticism and approval. He agreed to see her when she returns home at Easter, and if he is satisfied that she will make a suitable student, he informed me that he would be willing to become her tutor.

26th August 1783

I confess that I am increasingly enlivened by Anna's company and have found these two months since she has been home to be far more agreeable than the four years preceding them. I am usually in very low spirits at this time of year, as it is the anniversary of Fallady's death. It is still greatly on my mind, but Anna does her best to divert me.

24th December 1783

The parsonage has become like a whirlwind at times, with two of Anna's former school friends paying us a visit. I note also that there has been a significant increase in the number of unattached male visitors. My lonely days are over for some time to come, it seems.

13th June 1784

Mr Ridley believes Anna has considerable talent and that she is making great improvement. He also comments on her commitment to her work, which he states is 'the equal of a man's'. High praise from Mr Ridley!

3rd February 1785

Anna's suitors grow in number! I could not have believed that there were so many bachelors living in the vicinity and beyond. Until now she has been indifferent to them, but today, for the first time, she expressed considerable interest in one young man, Gareth Morgan. He has been lately apprenticed to Dr Llewellyn in Tref-ddirgel, as he comes from a poor family and has little aptitude for much else. He is but twenty, yet it seems that he above all others is the only one who can tolerate Anna's newly discovered desire to 'be her own woman'. It does seem sometimes that Fallady is still here, whispering in my daughter's ear.

15th October 1785

Anna sold her first painting today. It was a view of Llanycoed and one of my favourites. She is most gratified and encouraged. Mr Ridley believes there is little more he can teach her.

7th April 1786

It is difficult to believe that seven years have passed since Fallady and I were wed. How would it be were we still together, I wonder? I am now two and fifty, and Fallady would be nine and forty. Those months we had together are like a golden ray of memory. I made my annual pilgrimage to the pool at Felin Gyfriniaeth this evening. Sometimes it feels as though my wife is there; I can hear her voice, almost feel her touch.

17th September 1786

Anna has today showed me a painting of Fallady. I had not known she was working on this, but it seems she wished to surprise me with it. She had made drawings when Fallady was here, and she used these to create the portrait. It is shockingly lifelike. She proposes to have it framed and suggests we hang it in my study. I am most touched. I shall feel closer than ever to my dear wife when I am writing these journals, or working with my rocks and plants, or composing my sermons.

25th November 1787

This day Anna consented to marry Mr Morgan. He has matured considerably in the two years and more since Anna first confessed her interest to me. Dr Llewellyn has expressed satisfaction with his apprentice and believes he may be a suitable successor to his practice. They are to marry by banns in June, and will live in Tref-ddirgel, at The Lilacs.

10th June 1788

Anna today became Mrs Morgan. Mr Jenkins carried out the service at Llanycoed church. It was a most pleasing moment. I wished that both Jenny and Fallady could have seen it. I am content to see my daughter happy in her new life, but I suspect that life at the parsonage will now become considerably quieter.

15th August 1789

My first grandchild, James Ifor Morgan was born today. I travelled to The Lilacs in the chaise to see him, and he looks well and healthy, as does Anna. I believe her painting will be of necessity somewhat neglected for a time. I drank several glasses of wine and spirits. It has been some time since I have drunk so much, and I felt much in liquor on the journey home. Fallady was correct, however; my late abstemious ways do appear to have prevented me from developing the gout, which normally strikes a man long before this age. I thank almighty God for it, and for sending Fallady to me as He did.

20th January 1791

Gwynfor Walter Morgan was born last night. He was not so healthy at first, but he has now rallied and is expected to survive. Anna was also very fatigued, it being a difficult birth, but she is now recovering. I am considerably easier in my mind now than I was this morning.

15th August 1791

I spent the day and dined at The Lilacs on the occasion of James' second birthday. He was very happy and enjoyed his gifts. Gareth is now allowed to call himself Dr Morgan, and has almost taken over the practice, Dr Llewellyn being eight and sixty. He asked me a prodigious number of questions about why I believe I have not had a touch of gout, and why I am so careful in the drinking of liquor. I explained that my dear wife's father, also a doctor, had believed too much liquor and too much meat led to gout. He was most interested in this, but there was little more I could tell him. Anna caught my eye on several occasions during this conversation, in which he also desired to hear the full details of Fallady bringing me back to life. Gareth expressed regret that he had never met my wife's father. I, too, regret that!

18th November 1794

Jenny Sioned Morgan was born this day, in Anna's easiest birth so far. I thank God for it.

17th April 1796

Anna showed me her latest painting today. It is a most pleasing portrait of the children. It is one she has made especially to hang in the parlour of The Lilacs. I am sure it will look well there.

7th April 1797

This was the eighteenth anniversary of my wedding to Fallady, and I had anticipated a gift from God this evening, in which I was not disappointed.

25th September 1797

Gareth departed this life at ten o'clock this morning. We are all most shocked and distressed and cannot comprehend how a strong, healthy young man could be taken so quickly of a fever. Anna and the children are greatly grieved and I shall remain at The Lilacs for a time.

18th December 1798

I have today left the parsonage and moved in with Anna and the
children at The Lilacs. Although I am well for my age of four and
sixty, it seems best to leave Llanycoed before too long, and Anna
herself suggested it. I have engaged a curate to serve my church, but
I fear he need serve only ten more months in any event.

23rd October 1799

I have done my utmost in these past weeks to persuade everyone
in Llanycoed that my vivid dreams of a pending earthquake have
come from God. I have described my visions in dramatic terms to
everyone, including Mr and Mrs Greenleaf and Lady Lavinia. I
have visited every home in the locality and attempted to persuade
the occupants of the danger to come. I cannot say that I have not
met with some resistance and disbelief, even grumblings that I am
perhaps in my dotage, but with the squire's backing and Lady
Lavinia's authority, I pray to God that it will be enough. I spent
many hours on my knees in the church this afternoon, knowing that
it will be the last time I shall ever do so. Some villagers joined me
in my vigil, and as evening arrived I had a full church, including
Mr and Mrs Greenleaf. I said prayers and administered the Holy
Sacrament, as it seemed appropriate to such a terrible occasion.
As we exited the church, I was gratified to see that many were
leaving either on foot or in carts. Perhaps I have persuaded them, or
perhaps it is the squire or Lady Lavinia. I know not, but I have
hope now that all will be saved.

24th October 1799

All of Tref-ddirgel has been full of talk of the earth tremor,
which was felt here at midday. News arrived via a passing coach
this evening of the terrible damage done to Llanycoed, but praise
be to God everyone had evacuated the village and no one was killed.
However, the population of my parish is now made homeless. I

am meeting tomorrow with Mr Greenleaf and others at Llanycoed to assess the true state of the village and render what aid and assistance we can.

25th October 1799

It pains me to describe what I saw today at Llanycoed. Most of the buildings have collapsed, the church is laid to rubble, and the parsonage is rendered a ruin with but the lower walls visible. Even Laburnum Hall, two miles distant, is slightly damaged. Many villagers were there, picking through the rubble and seeking to remove as many of their possessions as possible. I spent much time among them and prayed with them. Most are to stay with relatives in the interim, and the squire is attempting to find work for those whose livelihoods have also been lost.

I ordered Fallady's memorial, which is still intact, to be uplifted and placed in Tref-ddirgel churchyard. Jenny's grave is also whole, but there are many broken, including those of my grandparents on my mother's side. On visiting the hall with Mr Greenleaf, I came across his servants Branwen Emrys and Percival Linlade. They had been travelling past Felin Gyfriniaeth when the earthquake hit, being unfortunately delayed and therefore the last out of the village, and they were thrown to the ground. They believe they saw a white light in the vicinity of the church. Fortunately they were unhurt and were able to return to the hall soon afterwards, to be the first to discover the damage. They made considerable mention of the oddity of Felin Gyfriniaeth being the sole building still standing, along with the small cottage belonging to the miller, although the latter is cracked and part of the roof has collapsed. Sadly, Mr Cook the miller died of a fever but two days before the earthquake, and his family will not return to the house, since there is no village left to serve. The damage is too extensive; Llanycoed is no more.

7th April 1800

It is my wedding anniversary and the first time I have not visited the pool above Felin Gyfriniaeth. My heart was not in it with the ruins still so fresh and the village empty. In addition, I had been asked to preach at All Saints church in Tref-ddirgel, which duty I took on with great pleasure. I have much missed preaching since leaving Llanycoed. There was quite a large congregation, and I took the opportunity to speak of love and loss as part of my sermon, even mentioning my dear wife Fallady, and so our twenty-first anniversary was well marked, and the sermon well received. Many former parishioners from Llanycoed attended.

17th May 1802

Anna's painting comes on apace now that the children are older. She is becoming a popular artist and has sold a number of works.

17th October 1805

It is hard to know this is the last entry I shall make, and that this must be accordingly the last day of my life. It is not given to many to know their ending. I am not ill, although not as robust as I once was, and yet I know I shall be dead before the end of tomorrow. Fallady, my dearest wife, I have written this diary for you over the twenty-six years of our separation. I have had much joy with Anna and my grandchildren, but the best part of my life was those few months we had together. They have been ever at the forefront of my mind and have been a glowing ember with which to warm myself whenever times have been hard, or I have felt lonely. It seems all too apt that I should conclude this diary with the words from Cowper's hymn which you, cariad, quoted oft, perhaps failing to realize that I had at that time never heard them.

God moves in a mysterious way, his wonders to perform.

There's a short addendum written in a different hand:

18th October 1805

My papa died in his bed at six o'clock this morning of a sudden seizure. We are all lost without him.

Chapter Thirty-one

'It's a beautiful afternoon, and I can guess you haven't seen the sun for days,' Gwilym says over the phone. 'Why don't I bring a picnic, and we could go up to that pool you've told me about? I still haven't seen it.'

I sigh. 'All right. I do have a lot of things to tell you,' I say, realising that he's right. I've been stuck indoors, mired in emotion and memory and have barely eaten more than a couple of slices of toast in forty-eight hours.

As we stroll up to the pool I tell him about Mrs Emrys and Mr Linlade being returned properly to 1799 and about the phrase at the end of Walter's diary that was not, after all, my final jest, but his. I had no idea they were the words to a hymn, but thought they were out of the Bible. Anna, seeing them written there so significantly, must have decided to have them inscribed on his headstone.

'Anna married a Gareth Morgan, and he became a doctor. And she became quite a successful painter. The three children in the painting are James, Ifor and Jenny. It would be nice to find out which one you're descended from, James or Ifor, don't you think?' I babble. 'And another strange thing: apparently Anna painted a picture of me especially for Walter, but you don't have it, and it's not in the ruins of the parsonage either.'

'No. But I think I know where it is,' he says.

'Where?'

'In the National Gallery of Wales.'

I stop in my tracks. 'There's a painting of *me* in the National Gallery of Wales?'

He laughs softly. 'There was something familiar about those drawings of you, but I couldn't pin it down. It seemed likely that the signature on the painting of the children was 'Anna Morgan' so I looked her up on the 'net. It seems she became very well known. I had a look online at the three paintings that are in the gallery – there's one of you and two landscapes.'

'That's incredible. The way things were in 1779, she was heading for a life of domesticity, but going by Walter's diaries it looks as though I might have made a difference.'

He nods. 'I'd seen the pictures before, but I was just a kid when my parents took me to the gallery, before we moved to Scotland. I think that's why I recognised the drawings.'

'But that means they must have known Anna Morgan was your ancestor.'

'Yes, but if they told me, I was too young to take a lot of notice, and I don't remember it ever being mentioned when I was older.'

When we get to the pool he lays out an impressive spread under the trees. I sit on a rock and wonder if it's the one Walter used to come and sit on to remember me over all those years. I tell Gwilym about it, thinking it strange that he suggested we come up here today.

'I wish Walter could see us here now and know I've had all his messages. I wish he knew how successful Anna became – and what a fine figure of a man his descendant is, of course.'

He looks up at me from the grass. 'Am I really a fine figure of a man, Fallady?' he asks with that quizzical expression of his.

'I'm sure Walter would think so.'

'I want to know what you think,' he persists.

I sit down on the grass beside him. 'You're an excellent cook,' I say, picking up a chicken wing from the cornucopia of food he's laid out.

'Uh-huh.'

'And a fabulous painter.'

'Uh-*huh*.'

'And a good friend.'

'Mm-hmmm.'

'And you certainly do look most fetching with your long hair and your *unusual* dress style.'

'Mmmm?'

'So all in all, I suppose I would have to say yes, you *are* a fine figure of a man.'

He sighs. 'That's good to know.'

'Why is it so important?' I ask and remember what John and Alyson told me.

He reaches out and touches my face lightly with a fingertip. 'Because, Fallady, I think you're a very fine figure of a woman.'

I gasp. Gwilym's touch arouses me in a way I haven't experienced since Walter, and his expression, before he hides it, is tender and loving. Could he be telling me obliquely that he cares for me?

I don't have a chance to dwell on it for long, because he launches into a spate of questions about Walter's diaries, which keep us both safely engrossed for the duration of our picnic.

While we're clearing up I tell him laughingly how Anna changed from dutiful to strident after being corrupted by me.

'But look where it got her,' he says.

'I wonder, did I really change things, or would she have done it anyway? She was always good at art; I noticed that right away. Did my urgings really spur her on?'

He smiles slightly. 'You know they did. Maybe *I* wouldn't even be here if it weren't for you.'

'She was sure to have met Gareth anyway, I'd have thought.'

'Well, maybe the old, dutiful Anna wouldn't have interested him. Maybe he wouldn't have interested her. He sounds like a bit of a maverick himself.'

I chuckle. 'A doctor ancestor, too, and hopefully a better one than Dr Benbow.'

When we get back to the house, he says, 'Would you like to see the paintings at Cardiff? I'm interested in seeing them again, and we could go together.'

I don't hesitate. 'I'd love to,' I say, and realize that the prospect of a day or two in Gwilym's company isn't at all unappealing.

I drop into John and Alyson's the next day with lots to tell them. They're amazed to hear about the diaries and Gwilym's illustrious lineage.

'I wondered why you'd been so quiet,' Alyson says when I've filled them in on the whole story.

'How does Gwilym feel about it?' John asks.

'I'm not really sure. He's not so quick to say what's on his mind as Walter was.'

'I imagine it's quite a lot to live up to.'

'But he doesn't have to live up to it,' I protest.

'He might think so, though, Fally.'

I deliberately change the subject slightly. 'He and I are going to see Anna's paintings in Cardiff on Thursday.'

'Won't you have to stay overnight?' Alyson asks.

'Yes, but *separate* rooms,' I emphasize.

'Just good friends, eh?' John says.

'Exactly,' I agree, beginning to wonder if that's really all we are.

'Fally,' John starts, and then hesitates before starting again. 'Gwilym – he's not going to get hurt, is he? I mean, I told you before he's not the type to… well, I think he has to be pretty fond of you. More than fond. For him to turn out to be Walter's descendant – well, it's a lot to absorb, and like I said, a lot to live up to.'

I bite my lip. 'You could be right, but I don't compare him with Walter.'

'Are you sure?'

I'm not sure. I've been clinging to the idea that we're just friends, and there's a sort of boundary we wouldn't or couldn't cross, but his gesture of yesterday indicates that he'd like to cross it. And if he does, where does that leave us?

Two days later, Gwilym picks me up in his snazzy Passat. For some reason he didn't fancy going to Cardiff in my old Metro. We pass most of the journey talking about Walter and Anna. He's been reading the diaries and is full of his own observations, as well as starting to acquire a greater appreciation of his most venerable ancestor.

'He had quite a sense of humour,' he says.

I nod. 'It didn't show on the outside, but it used to be very easy to get him laughing.'

'I can't believe you forced him to stop wearing his wig.'

'Forced him!' I protest. 'He promised he'd take it off if I married him. Even then he took a couple of months to get round to it. Just one excuse after another.' I look across to meet Gwilym's eye, sharing a grin with him.

After a minute he says hesitantly, 'Do you think you can imagine a future for yourself now?'

I tense up slightly. 'How do you mean?'

'When I first met you I had the feeling you'd given up on life. I might be wrong, but I don't think you've been spending quite so much time around the church lately. You can talk about Walter a lot more easily now. You've even put in an application for that teaching course at last.'

I nod slowly. 'I suppose I can imagine a future, but I'm still not sure what it's going to be.'

He lapses into silence for a few minutes, until I encourage him to tell me all about his latest painting, which is his first of the area around Tref-ddirgel.

When we arrive in Cardiff, we check into our rooms in the hotel and have a quick lunch before heading to the National Museum, where the art is housed.

I'm nervous as we find our way to Anna's paintings. The idea of seeing myself on a gallery wall is disconcerting, and I haven't given in to the temptation to look at the picture online. Gwilym is in his element, pointing out various other works of note as we pass, but I'm too uneasy to take them in.

The portrait is in an alcove on its own, and as we enter I come to an abrupt halt, hold my hands over my mouth and stare. I'm shown full length in one of the hideous bum-emphasising gowns. Walter's gift garnet necklace is around my neck, and my hair's just tied up in a ribbon, the way I usually wore it. I'm holding a flowery novel in my hands, but instead of looking at the book or right at the artist, as is often the case with portraits, I'm looking off to the side, and my expression is a smiling mixture of teasing and tenderness. Since Anna didn't paint this from life, she's obviously used artistic licence. It seems to me she had the idea that I'm looking at Walter, across the room out of view. I stand there trying to control my emotions and wonder how often Walter looked at it and whether he guessed that he was just off stage but so clearly in the picture in spirit.

Gwilym looks down at me and notices the unshed tears in my eyes. 'Fallady,' he murmurs, 'are you okay?' He always calls me by my full name, just as Walter did, and at that moment it strikes me as odd that they're the only two to do so.

I nod. 'It's just the expression on my face, like I'm looking at Walter.'

'Yes, she's captured it well. It's hard to do stuff like that – one reason why I stick to landscapes.'

Anna's landscapes are in a different section. One is of somewhere around Tref-ddirgel, with the rolling green landscape interrupted by copses and sheep, and the other is of Llanycoed when it was intact; a cluster of houses surrounded by trees with the tiny church standing in the centre. It would look idealised if I didn't know it had been real.

'It's hard to believe Llanycoed once looked like that,' I say sadly.

'She's managed to avoid too much sentimentality of style though,' he pontificates. 'It's easy to fall into that trap with this kind of subject.'

'So you're proud of your famous ancestor?' I say in a slightly teasing tone. My thoughts are still dominated by the painting of me. I had the peculiar sensation that Walter might walk into it at any moment.

'I'm proud of *all* my famous ancestors,' he says, looking at me seriously.

It's too much for my fragile self-control, and I choke back a sob. He puts his arm around me while I recover my composure, and for the first time I'm aware of being this close to Gwilym, rather than being reminded of closeness with Walter.

Afterwards we explore the rest of the gallery and museum. Gwilym expounds at such length on some of the paintings that I wonder if he's destined to be the next TV art critic. Later, we have a meal at a restaurant, and when we've finished our desserts I tease him about his Sister Wendy impression.

He smiles but doesn't answer, just plays with his wine glass.

'What's wrong?'

He tips the glass and the wine almost sloshes out. 'Can we go and talk somewhere more private?' he says, and finally looks up at me.

'One of our rooms?' I say doubtfully, with an idea of what's coming.

He chuckles. 'I promise to control myself, difficult though that is with you looking so particularly fetching tonight.'

'Did you think I looked fetching in the portrait?' I ask with a grin as we walk back to the hotel through the cool June night. Anything to distract myself from the way my heart's thumping.

'Yes I did, as a matter of fact,' he says. 'You look all the better now for having regained some weight. Skinny doesn't suit you.'

I give him a disbelieving look, but he continues to meet my gaze. 'My favourite part of the whole costume was the way it showed your cleavage to best advantage,' he says, and I splutter with laughter.

'My cleavage? What about my bum?'

'Well I have to admit that wasn't shown to best advantage,' he replies in a completely different tone.

At the hotel we head for my room. I perch decorously on the end of the bed. 'So what did you want to talk about?'

He sits down beside me. 'The future I asked you about earlier.'

'What future did you have in mind?' I ask with a small smile.

He regards me quizzically for a moment. 'I had in mind a possible future with me.'

My hands clench on the bedspread. What do I feel? I've been swamped with emotions relating to Walter for so long that there hasn't been room for much else.

He watches me silently as these thoughts chase around in my mind, and for once his emotions are all too apparent. His expression reminds me powerfully of that evening at the pool after my miscarriage. It's the way Walter looked when I told him I'd lost the baby: the same naked vulnerability. It's not an expression Gwilym would normally allow me to see.

'That *is* a future I can imagine for myself,' I hear myself say.

Gwilym relaxes visibly, but says, 'Are you sure about that? Descendant or not, apart from the lip-pursing, I don't think I ever will be much like Walter.'

'You don't need to be. There could only be one Walter. I like you for you.'

'Only like?'

'More than like. But I don't… I don't really know what I feel.'

He nods. 'I know you're still hurting, but it's been on my mind for a while now, and I can't keep quiet any longer. I didn't think I'd ever say this to anyone, but I love you, Fallady.'

I put my hand on his arm. My old difficulty in expressing my feelings is coming to the fore, and I have to force myself to speak because, I realize suddenly, this is too important. 'Gwilym I – I like your sarky ways and your funny dress sense; I like your Scottish accent and the way you say Faaallady like a caress; I like watching you cook and eating the results; I like the way you look and the way you paint; I like talking to you and listening to you and being with you. I like *you*.'

He gazes at me in amused surprise. 'That was quite a speech coming from you,' he says, covering my hand with his.

'I need you to know.'

'My sarky ways?' he says on a breath of a laugh.

'I did say I like them,' I grin.

'Well,' he says, 'I suppose I'll have to be content. Neither of us is much good at saying how we feel, I think.'

I nod slowly. 'I'm not ready for more… I can't… not yet,' I say. 'I mean, it's still too soon.'

'I know,' he says gently. 'But at least I know you *like* me, and in so many different ways, too.'

I laugh and very tentatively allow myself to lean against him. In response, he puts his arm around my shoulders, and I don't protest. It feels good. It feels *right*.

EPILOGUE

It's a cool but sunny September day and I'm sitting on the seat closest to Walter's grave. A nearby horse chestnut tree has begun shedding its ungainly, rust-coloured leaves and I'm watching them fall, thinking about nothing in particular, when a younger woman approaches with two small bunches of flowers in her hands. She gives me an apologetic smile and crouches down in front of the graves, carefully placing one bundle of bright chrysanthemums beside my memorial and another in front of Walter's headstone. I watch her closely, my body rigid with surprise. She lifts the ivy over my memorial and runs her hand gently over the cold stone. Who *is* she? I've never seen her before. Every so often I've come to the graves and found these little bunches of flowers, but I've always assumed Frances was right, that it was just a sentimental act.

The woman gets up after a few moments and gives me another look of apology. She's about thirty, very smartly dressed, hair neatly cut. 'I do this a few times a year,' she says. 'It's like a pilgrimage of sorts.'

I smile encouragingly. 'Were they ancestors of yours?'

She joins me on the bench. 'No, nothing like that. It's something that's been passed down the family. Kind of a Powell legend. The story goes that Fallady Edgemond – that's her memorial, the small one – changed my great-great-great-something-grandmother's life. Abigail, her name was.'

I jump and turn to look at her sharply, but luckily her gaze is still focused on the graves.

'Apparently she was some sort of kitchen skivvy, the lowest of the low, but Mrs Edgemond taught her to read, and then she got a job with the local lady muck at some great manor – demolished now, I gather. She got to be a lady's maid, but eventually the lady gave her the chance to prove herself teaching at the village school. She turned out to be a good teacher; she loved it.

'Then a couple of years later she met Richard Powell. He was a poet and free thinker, and they eventually got married.'

She turns to look at me. 'She was convinced she'd have ended her days a servant if Fallady Edgemond hadn't given her that break. God sent Mrs Edgemond, that's what she claimed.' She exhales and gestures at the flowers. 'So that's why I come. Who knows where we'd have been – who knows if I'd even be here, if it hadn't been for her.'

'She –' My voice is hoarse with emotion. 'She said God sent Mrs Edgemond?'

She nods. 'Oh yes. She was very religious. Never missed a Sunday service unless she was too ill to get to church. Said Mrs Edgemond told her she'd be able to read the Bible for herself, and now she had.'

She gets up. 'Well I suppose I'd better get going. It was nice talking to you.'

I watch her stride confidently across the churchyard, and once she's out of sight I move over to Walter's grave. 'So, Reverend,' I murmur, wiping my eyes, 'it seems I brought Abigail back to God after all!'

I swear I hear Walter's voice issue through the air in its most vicarly intonation: 'God moves in a mysterious way, his wonders to perform.'

THE END

Acknowledgements

With grateful thanks to Rev. Ron McCreary for copious information about various aspects of Christianity, and to Rev. Philip Williams for help on the Church of England and on 'being a vicar'. Thanks also posthumously to James Woodforde for his Diary of a Country Parson, which provided me with a rich source of research material. Any errors on religious matters (I hope there are none!) are my own.

Special thanks to Tori Howell for being the first person to read the manuscript, for telling me which parts she loved and where she cried, for advice and suggestions, for urging me to seek publication, and for constant encouragement throughout that at times disheartening process. Also thanks to Julie Phillips for reading the manuscript and giving me helpful feedback.

Thanks to my mum and sister for their support and for being my third and fourth readers.

Thanks also to the Open University for its creative writing courses, and especially to my tutor on A215, who gave me the first indication that I could succeed with my writing.

Finally, many thanks to everyone at Snowbooks for publishing the book!

About the Author

Jill Rowan once worked in accounts but gave it up to concentrate on her passion for writing. She lives in the Shropshire countryside, where she occasionally drags herself away from her books and laptop to engage in desultory gardening, lazy walks and leisurely cycle rides. Although she obtained her BA degree in 2009, she remains addicted to study with the Open University. She has studied subjects as diverse as astronomy, creative writing, languages, environmental science and religion and sees herself as a perpetual student. She is currently writing her second novel, set in her dream country of New Zealand.